BY MIKE CHEN

BROTHERHOOD

STAR WARS

BROTHERHOOD

MIKE CHEN

NEW YORK

Copyright © 2022 by Lucasfilm Ltd. & ® or ™ where indicated.

Published in the United States by Del Rey, an imprint of Random House, a division of Penguin Random House LLC, New York.

DEL REY and the CIRCLE colophon are registered trademarks of Penguin Random House LLC.

Hardback ISBN 978-0-593-35857-3
International edition ISBN 978-0-593-49915-3
Ebook ISBN 978-0-593-35858-0

Printed in the United States of America on acid-free paper

randomhousebooks.com

2 4 6 8 9 7 5 3 1

First Edition

Book design by Elizabeth A. D. Eno

For Mandy, who, like Anakin, said we'd find a way

THE *STAR WARS* NOVELS TIMELINE

THE HIGH REPUBLIC

Convergence
Light of the Jedi
The Rising Storm
Tempest Runner
The Fallen Star

Dooku: Jedi Lost
Master and Apprentice

I THE PHANTOM MENACE

II ATTACK OF THE CLONES

Brotherhood
The Thrawn Ascendancy Trilogy
Dark Disciple: A Clone Wars Novel

III REVENGE OF THE SITH

Catalyst: A Rogue One Novel
Lords of the Sith
Tarkin

SOLO

Thrawn
A New Dawn: A Rebels Novel
Thrawn: Alliances
Thrawn: Treason

ROGUE ONE

IV A NEW HOPE

Battlefront II: Inferno Squad
Heir to the Jedi
Doctor Aphra
Battlefront: Twilight Company

V THE EMPIRE STRIKES BACK

VI RETURN OF THE JEDI

The Princess and the Scoundrel
The Alphabet Squadron Trilogy
The Aftermath Trilogy
Last Shot

Shadow of the Sith
Bloodline
Phasma
Canto Bight

VII THE FORCE AWAKENS

VIII THE LAST JEDI

Resistance Reborn
Galaxy's Edge: Black Spire

IX THE RISE OF SKYWALKER

A long time ago in a galaxy far, far away. . . .

BROTHERHOOD

The CLONE WARS have erupted. Caught off guard by the quickly expanding conflict, the overwhelmed Jedi Order has rushed the advancement of Padawans to better integrate into the Grand Army of the Republic and assist the war effort.

Newly promoted Jedi Knight Anakin Skywalker is increasingly torn between his growing duties to the Republic and his secret marriage to Senator Padmé Amidala of Naboo. With his Knighting, his mentor Obi-Wan Kenobi has been elevated to the Jedi Council under the rank of Jedi Master.

As dark forces push the Jedi further toward their transformation from guardians to soldiers, Anakin and Obi-Wan find themselves on equal footing yet opposing paths, each pondering the meaning of peace and justice during a time of war . . .

CHAPTER 1

RUUG QUARNOM

CATO NEIMOIDIA WAS A WORLD of mist.

High above that mist, cliffs and branches poked through, carved at all angles into immense mountainous spires. The thick stone of the planet's largest rock arches and peaks loomed, casting shadows in a seemingly infinite stretch before being absorbed into the dense vapor below. Between, over, and on top of these natural wonders hung gilded cities with ornate towers and reflective sidings, structures suspended as bridges between massive colossal ridges.

But Cato Neimoidia did have something beneath all of that, a foundational layer at the base of the thick fog. On normal days, taking the journey from Cato Neimoidia's bridge cities to the surface meant a gradual descent into an ever-thickening blanket of white.

Today, however, was not a normal day.

Because today, something had gone terribly wrong. And the lower the shuttle flew, the more the milky hue of the mist darkened as harsh streams of blackened ash mixed in.

Ruug Quarnom had seen destruction all her life. As an elite commando of the Neimoidian Defense Legion, she'd dealt with explosives and blasterfire, rockets and shrapnel. And death—so much death, most of it by her own doing courtesy of the custom sniper rifle that felt like an extension of her own limbs.

Murder and destruction. That was her life for so many years, doing the will of her government to carve out a better place for Neimoidians in the galaxy. Even now, in her new "assignment" as a royal guard for Cato Neimoidia's capital city of Zarra, her goal remained the same: the protection of her people.

Ruug had taken the assignment in good faith, even though she knew it had been for questioning the judgment of the Trade Federation, a perspective considered dissent by those who held much more sway than a military grunt. Such good faith was being challenged right now, in a time when the galaxy dared to rip itself in two.

"Look at that," said the voice of her young partner next to her. Ketar Nor's mouth opened, holding a thought in limbo as a thick dull gray began to envelop their craft, visibility coming and going from the cockpit of their patrol ship. "It's worse than I imagined."

A steady hand. And open eyes. That was the only way to approach this. Not only for the flight to the surface, but to understand just what had occurred—and why. The call for all available security to go beneath the mist came so fast that Ruug piloted their craft on a direct downward path, leaving the port of a neighboring city and abandoning a scheduled prisoner transfer to plunge through the mist. They hadn't even been informed of *what* they were investigating, just that an emergency so catastrophic had occurred that everyone within a two-hundred-kilometer radius was requested—no, ordered—to drop their tasks and go.

Details filled in over comm chatter. A bomb. No, several bombs. A building collapsed—no, an entire plaza.

No. Despite the speculation on the comms, the reality of the situation became clearer with each passing second.

And it was far beyond what anyone could have ever guessed.

An entire portion of the bridge city, the neighborhood known as Cadesura. Blocks and streets of Neimoidian civilization severed within an instant, the structural supports that fastened the district to the rest of Zarra evaporated in a blink.

All those people. All that *life,* dropped straight downward through the mist of Cato Neimoidia to a sudden violent fate, dirt and rock mashing into alloys and flesh.

But why?

Cato Neimoidia is neutral, Ruug thought. Despite the recent chaos of Geonosis, despite the use of Trade Federation battle droids, the war stayed an arm's length away. Viceroy Nute Gunray led a splinter faction to ally with the Confederacy of Independent Systems; the Trade Federation proper was free from the influence of Count Dooku and his Separatist ideals. Senator Lott Dod made sure of that with his place within the heart of Republic politics.

But here, on the surface, Ruug's eyes told her everything she needed to know. The twisted shrapnel of once-elegant structures now reduced to cracked and broken material, scattered into countless pieces. As their shuttle approached, the devastation amplified with each passing second. What appeared as a lump of rubble gradually formed into the jagged debris of buildings and bridges; closer still, as Ruug maneuvered the craft for a flat place to land, details came to life.

Not just the destruction of structures. But within the fallen wreckage, bodies. So many bodies, of so many ages, from so many walks of life. Bodies bent into impossible positions, thrown into places they shouldn't have been due to the chaos of gravity pulling an entire district to the surface.

And through it all, so much smoke, the massive plume of gray from above breaking down into individual currents of black the farther down they went, streams feeding a river of death. Ruug stepped out, flecks of ash landing on her dark-green skin, and even amid the cool air of the planet's base, heat poked through in every direction from the endless fires entwining in and through and over what used to be mighty structures.

"Who . . ." Ketar started, swiveling his view all around. He blinked as he took in the horrific possibilities, his mouth open. "How . . ."

Ruug had seen Ketar driven by emotions on the job before, sometimes anger and sometimes fear—fear that he *tried* to hide, but she knew better. It came with an innocence, the type that only shattered after killing someone. For better or worse, such actions callused over fear, layers thickening with each successive murder. Yet the frozen expression on his face right now displayed his mix of emotions clearly, a grief stemming from a deeper well than he'd ever let on.

"Steady, Ketar," she said, moving next to him. From a mound of rubble above, arms waved, along with a cry that someone had been found alive. "They need our help."

"The *Republic*," Ketar growled, his long fingers bending into a single shaking grip. "The Republic did this. They're blaming us for Nute Gunray."

"We don't know that. And right now, it doesn't matter." Which was wrong, of course. The culprit behind this *did* matter, and whoever they were, they needed to be brought to justice. But there was a time and place for retribution. "Focus. They called us here to help people. That's what we need to do."

Though Ketar faced the team screaming for help from the top of the rubble, their pleas seemed invisible to him. Instead, he stared blankly ahead, like everything was a hologram glitching in and out.

But it wasn't. This was real, any doubt erased by the harsh burning odors entering her smell glands beneath her eyes. "Ketar," Ruug said quietly.

"You're right," he said, suddenly nodding. His demeanor shifted, his catatonia abruptly swapped for movement with a very swift and direct purpose. The young guard grabbed his bag of medical supplies and ran off, as if a single person with a small case of bacta and synthflesh might make a difference.

Ketar's youth carried an expected naïveté, an earnest desire to do right by his people. Ruug knew better; an individual had limitations, no matter how dedicated they were. She pulled out a small metallic circle, then clicked a button to generate a holographic map of the region. Around her, other transports landed: medical personnel, security officers, government officials, and people who simply wanted to help. So many of Ruug's fellow Neimoidians zigged and zagged—some lifting up debris, some screaming into comms for help, and some pacing, head buried in hands. Droids of all sizes soared, a mix of small surveillance units flying in between larger rescue droids that dropped extinguishing chemicals, fire by fire.

No matter which direction she turned, her vision filled with devastation, all on a far greater scale than she could ever remember. She understood Ketar's urge to dash off with bacta, the feeling that one person might be able to somehow fix all of this.

In a way, Ketar was right. They had to start somewhere.

Because even though Cato Neimoidia was neutral, it had been gravely wounded. And someone had to pay.

But who?

CHAPTER 2

ANAKIN SKYWALKER

ANAKIN SKYWALKER STOOD AS HE always did, feet planted slightly wider than his hips in a balanced stance, arms behind him with his hands clasped at the small of his back.

Hand, actually. One of his limbs remained his organic arm, part of the flesh and blood born of Shmi Skywalker and raised under the unflinching desert suns of Tatooine.

The other hand was metal and wire and sensors, a synthetic extension that moved nearly-but-not-quite the way he intended. Not perfect yet, but he was getting better at it. And though the textures of the mechanical replacement were so *unnatural* that he covered it with a glove, his wife never treated its touch as anything but his own, at least in the short time they were able to be together following his duel with Count Dooku.

His *wife*. Where was she right now? Senator Padmé Amidala, always meeting with people or talking with people or talking *about* people. She'd returned to Coruscant and was likely heading to the Senate District, a single beacon of hope dashing somewhere through this massive structure of a planet.

Anakin closed his eyes while Jedi Master Mace Windu continued to talk to the assembled, the latest group of recently promoted Jedi Knights. For a thousand generations, the Jedi had their traditions of trials and ceremony, of ascending rank and recognizing achievement.

But that was before Geonosis. Before the Clone Wars started, before an oath to be peacekeepers somehow evolved overnight into roles as soldiers and commanders—an overlap the clones themselves couldn't quite comprehend, leading to the informal title of "general" on the battlefield. Anakin had always imagined his Knighting to be a significant life milestone, a sea change in his heart and mind. Enough time had passed since the official transition that his once-short hair had started to grow out, and now this ceremony felt more like a procedural step, a footnote to go along with the bigger issues facing the galaxy. This gathering, filled with ceremony in the shadow of the Jedi Temple training courtyard, seemed simply unimportant, so much so that an urge tugged at Anakin to go, to fast-forward the cadence of the galaxy itself so he could finally reunite with his wife tonight.

He had, after all, a keepsake to deliver within the small pouch buckled to his belt.

Master Windu walked the perimeter of the courtyard under the shadow of the Great Tree, Anakin standing with the rest of the new Jedi Knights while behind them, current Padawans observed. To his left, D'urban Wen-Hurd, the Tholothian notable throughout training for her twin shoto lightsabers. To his right, Keer Stenwyt, Olana Chion, and several others. Across the courtyard stood their mentors, at least the ones available: Moragg Bomo, a Kel Dor with black tunic and blue-tinted goggles, Siri Tachi, Ma-Dok Risto, and more.

And of course, Obi-Wan Kenobi, the newest member of the Jedi Council. Sort of. After the loss of Coleman Trebor at Geonosis, various Jedi rotated into his Council position. No one would say if this method was permanent or if the rotations were simply temporary assignments, something born out of necessity given the push and pull of the war. Either way, the Council had recently picked Obi-Wan for a rotation. In turn, Obi-Wan approached every task with his usual seriousness, even treating this glorified speech like a war decision. Anakin didn't need the Force to feel the weight of his former Master's stare. Behind his back, Anakin's fingers balled into fists, the synth-net neural interface of the mechno-arm reacting the same way as his real hand did. And yet, it didn't. Just as with his organic hand, the mechanical fingers pressed in frustration, but no emotion came from the gesture on that side, no tiny ripple through the Force to yet again give away his feelings to Obi-Wan.

It was merely a limb. Functional, even stronger than flesh and bone, but not a true part of him.

"You are Jedi Knights." Master Windu's voice boomed out as he paced back and forth, as if to call any waning attention back to his intimidating form. "Responsibility. Peace. Discipline. You are the examples the galaxy looks to. Your successes will carry through the Republic and beyond. As will your mistakes. Your choices will matter, helping the Jedi maintain order during a time of discord." The Master paused, his lips pursed in thought. Anakin figured Mace had given a form of this speech several times now since Geonosis, but perhaps this time he tried his hand at improvisation. "The younglings look up to you. Your choices matter to them. And some of you will receive Padawans of your own. Your choices"—Mace enunciated each word with heightened diction—"will matter to them as well."

The thought caused Anakin's lip to curl up ever so slightly. A Padawan? For him? That sounded like the worst thing in the galaxy. And as if on cue, his eyes caught Obi-Wan looking directly at him.

Of course Obi-Wan saw his smirk.

Anakin forced his expression back to neutral, then adjusted his posture, pushing his chest out and chin up to uphold Jedi formality; if he had been speaking, his voice would have reverted to the formal monotone he always used around elder Jedi.

"We are at war. This is unprecedented within our lifetimes," Mace continued. "And you are among the first to reach Knighthood during this time of war. Remember that war is like a fire across the galaxy. It spreads and it consumes. We must never waver in the face of that fire. We are keepers of the peace. We are Jedi. The Republic needs us more than ever, which means our faith in the Force, our connection to the Force must never waver." Though Mace's face remained stoic and cold,

Anakin detected the most unexpected shift coming from him, a single drop in the ocean of the Force. But it rippled outward, and while most probably didn't notice it, Anakin had always found his senses tuned in to emotions at a far deeper level than others.

Maybe because he actually let himself feel emotions. He reached into the Force for a further understanding of this strange deviation.

Was that . . . concern? From Mace Windu?

But the ripple passed, evaporating as would happen with any Jedi and their emotions. Anakin wanted to shake his head, figuring the moment was nothing more than an extension of Mace's constant disdain for his being there, his very existence. From the moment Qui-Gon Jinn presented Anakin to the debriefing after Geonosis, Master Windu always seemed irked by his presence, like he should not have even been there. One time, Anakin caught his look when fellow Padawans mentioned the Chosen One prophecy—in jest, of course—and the power of his instant glare felt more deadly than his renowned fighting technique.

Anakin rubbed him the wrong way. He always had, and this was probably just another example. Anakin reminded *himself* to be bigger than that petty moment and push it aside. He took in a breath, and though his eyes tracked Mace during the rest of the speech, his mind wandered to his childhood. The ceremony played out as the opposite of those Tatooine nights when the desert chill would work its way through the cracks of their worn-down home. Rather than the cold grand speech amid the Jedi Temple's exquisite designs, he thought of his mother retelling a story for the umpteenth time in their small hovel, the warmth of her hand enough to reassure his whole body and mind. "The sun-dragon lives inside a star, guarding everything it loves and treasures," she would say, as she had done so many times throughout his childhood. Generations of Tatooine dwellers heard the same story told with their own family variations, but his mother's version carried the most feeling—appropriate for a myth about heart. "It guarded them through the fire and flame, always keeping them safe. It could persevere through anything, even life within a star itself. Because the sun-dragon has the biggest heart in the galaxy, a furnace of flames powerful enough to protect everything and everyone it loves. The strongest heart—stronger than the heart of a star." She told

Anakin this story dozens, possibly hundreds of times when he was growing up, usually after he'd gotten into an argument with Kitster or Watto
was unnecessarily cruel or one of his inventions exploded in his face.

He could see her expression now, the way her smile brought lines to
frame her mouth, the way her eyes never judged, the way stray hairs fell
across her forehead after a long day. Those were the moments she'd always squeeze his hand and look him straight in the eye. "You are the
sun-dragon. You have the strongest heart. Always believe in it."

Suddenly the loving face of Shmi Skywalker disappeared from Anakin's mind's eye, replaced with the blistering cool of night, the flicker of
flame, the cries of Sand People.

The smell of blood.

All through these thoughts, he stood stoic alongside his fellow Jedi
Knights, fighting to keep his feelings at bay. Another memory arrived
with a surprise, one that draped calm over the open wounds of Tatooine. It echoed, a feeling as real as the moment it first happened:

The strong hands of Qui-Gon Jinn on his shoulders, his soothing
words whispering in his ears.

It wasn't the first time he'd felt the presence of the fallen Jedi. Whether
a flash of deep memory or one of the Force's great tricks in his favor, the
presence always recentered him, in a way that Obi-Wan's lectures never
did.

"It is your time to serve the galaxy and the Republic," Mace said.
"May the Force be with you." The group began clapping as Mace walked
off without hesitation to take his place next to Master Yoda. Obi-Wan
looked around the courtyard, then back at the other Masters. They all
exchanged glances, and Anakin caught a rare moment of confusion
from his old teacher.

Obi-Wan, able to negotiate and improvise his way out of anything
with grace and tact, now stood flustered because of an apparent sched-
uling problem. *This is Obi-Wan Kenobi,* Anakin thought with an amused
sigh, *frustrated by protocol and formalities in a time of war.* He watched
as Obi-Wan ran his fingers through his hair, thick locks flowing to his
shoulders, having grown even longer since Geonosis. "Well, it appears
that our guests are a little late," he said, stepping in front of the group. By
"guests," he referred to Chancellor Palpatine, various senators, and a

few of the clone commanders who happened to be onplanet, a mixture of ceremony and duty for each of them. "I'm certain they will be here soon. In the meantime—"

An electronic chirp rang through the space, something urgent enough for Yoda to wave his hand at the control panel for holocommunications at the far wall. Palpatine did appear, but as a hologram floating in the middle of the courtyard rather than in person. And instead of a two-minute cursory speech about duty, the chancellor addressed Yoda and Mace specifically, not the gathered invitees. "Master Yoda. Master Windu. We have urgent news that is sure to impact the war effort. Cato Neimoidia has been bombed."

Yoda and Mace looked at each other, only their eyes moving. Obi-Wan had a slightly more animated response, at least for a seasoned Jedi—a small inhale, then a hand up to his beard. The others reacted within the range of those extremes, though the air itself shifted. Yoda tapped his stick. "Padawans and younglings, this discussion they do not need. To further study, they should go."

Obi-Wan moved over to gather, then direct them out, and Anakin took a reflexive step forward until he felt a hand on his shoulder. Obi-Wan spoke, his voice gentler than his usual redirections of Anakin's instincts. "Not you. You are a Jedi Knight now, remember?" He looked over to the Padawans, who had started to leave. "We are equals," he said with a slight and forced smile beneath his beard.

Anakin wondered if the gesture's awkward nature was because of the dire circumstance about Cato Neimoidia or if his old Master simply hadn't gotten used to seeing Anakin as something other than an apprentice. "Do I still have to call you Master?" he asked, more bite to his question than it should have had. A flush came to Anakin's cheeks, betraying the muscle memory that wanted to argue with Obi-Wan about rules and fairness no matter what the situation.

"Only if you know your place," Obi-Wan replied, but this time his smile gave off a genuine glow, almost amusement at their old push-and-pull relationship. The courtyard cleared of Padawans, the Jedi now gathered in front of the holographic figure of the most powerful man in the Republic.

"Bombed?" Mace asked Palpatine. "How bad? By whom?"

"Intelligence is still coming in. But early reports indicate the scope is a larger catastrophe than Cato Neimoidia has seen in recorded history. It is—"

A clone commander faded into view. "I'm sorry to interrupt, Chancellor. But we have further details." Palpatine nodded, and the clone continued. "It appears an entire segment of the capital city of Zarra has been severed from the foundational struts. It has completely collapsed."

CHAPTER 3

OBI-WAN KENOBI

OBI-WAN STOOD SIDE BY SIDE with his former Padawan, just as they'd done many times over the past decade, and yet this was different. This *felt* different. Together, they watched the holos of Palpatine and the clone commander flicker, alongside intercepted security recordings from Cato Neimoidia that lacked enough clarity to fully define the scope of the devastation. But for several seconds, Obi-Wan ignored galactic catastrophes and instead thought of Anakin, who stood quiet with arms behind his back, his usual commanding stance with intense eyes taking in the unfolding conflict.

A powerful Jedi, an intense heart, an uncontrollable impulse—all of those things were central to Anakin's being. And now, an equal, his Padawan braid severed. But more than the symbolism of his braid, Anakin's emotional transition to Jedi Knight was proving rougher than Obi-Wan expected. Rather than a simple flick of a mental switch, Anakin seemed to take several steps forward toward confident decision making before skirting back into deference.

Anakin Skywalker seemed unsure of where his place was. Which was quite unlike him, given all of the arguing they'd done for years, all those times Anakin insisted he was right.

Perhaps the war muddied those waters. He thought back to his own early days, his ascension into Jedi Knighthood counterbalanced by the loss of Qui-Gon Jinn, and while his peers seemed to take their promotions in stride, his own circumstances created so many stumbling blocks. How long did it take for him to feel like he'd earned the title? And now that he was given an opportunity to sit on the Jedi Council, how could his input possibly carry the same insight and weight as that of more experienced Jedi Masters?

A memory fluttered through Obi-Wan's mind, an exchange with his former Master he hadn't thought of in nearly a decade. "Don't center on your anxieties." Obi-Wan exhaled and felt the ground beneath his feet, returning to the here and now.

"Early estimates put the death toll at four thousand, based on daily traffic of the Cadesura district," the clone said. "The bridge held important political targets including the Trade Federation licensing office. But it also housed an arts district with numerous commercial buildings. I'm afraid the civilian casualty toll is high."

Palpatine's holographic visage flickered as the chancellor frowned. "Understood. Thank you for the report, Commander."

Yoda stepped forward. "Neutral, Cato Neimoidia is. No reason for military targeting. Work with all sides, the Trade Federation does."

Obi-Wan considered the recent tactical report he'd seen on the splinter faction led by Nute Gunray, one that Lott Dod claimed was completely disconnected from the Trade Federation. "Has Senator Dod been informed?"

Palpatine nodded. "He is just outside of communication range, but as I understand it, he is aware of the situation."

Yoda's stick tapped on the floor. "Insight, our new Jedi Knights have?" Obi-Wan caught Anakin's eyes dropping, as well as the short inhale that he quickly swallowed.

"Could loyalists from the Republic have guerrilla fighters who went rogue?" Keer Stenwyt said, and though her voice projected confidence, she glanced at her mentor Ma-Dok Risto, who offered a subtle nod in return.

"Bounty hunters?" D'urban Wen-Hurd offered. "War always drives their economics. It could be a coordinated effort to create demand for their services."

"Perhaps," Yoda said. "Perhaps a true accident, this is."

"A Separatist trick," Anakin finally interjected, the gravity of seriousness in his voice. "A ploy to gain sympathies. The Neimoidians are unscrupulous cowards." The judgment in his voice caught Obi-Wan's attention, though given his long, volatile history with them, it wasn't that surprising.

"That seems counterproductive. Even for Nute Gunray. He would not sacrifice a civilian population of his own people," Mace said, his glare strong enough for Obi-Wan to feel from several meters away.

Anakin inhaled to retort but then caught eyes with Obi-Wan again, and that mere thread of connection seemed to be enough to halt the young Jedi's impulses. Yoda shook his head, his ears trembling with the movement. "Possibilities, war has created," the old Jedi Master said, a rare disgust in his words. "Points of view, distorted. The scope of the Clone Wars, beyond the peacekeeping tradition of the Jedi."

Anakin straightened, turning back to the hologram of Palpatine, who looked off to the side before nodding and continuing. "Count Dooku appears to be making a statement right now."

And with that, the fallen Jedi appeared alone, his regal maroon cape draped over his shoulders as he stood in what was apparently a small office in his Serenno home. The feed caught him mid-sentence, though his tone and words quickly filled in the blanks. ". . . act of terrorism. As the primary representative of the Confederacy of Independent Systems, I assure the Trade Federation and the citizens of Cato Neimoidia that we have no involvement in such senseless violence. We condemn such things, and our relationship with the Trade Federation is, as it has always been, merely transactional in nature.

"However, we make no secret that Viceroy Nute Gunray and his associates are key officials of our movement." Emotion surged from Anakin, a tangible wave at the mention of the Trade Federation viceroy. Obi-Wan observed his former apprentice, from the way his shoulders locked to the tightening of his jaw, a tension that came and went quickly—but not as quick as most Jedi. "I think the evidence is clear.

The Republic targeted Nute Gunray, who was visiting the Cadesura district a mere hour before the bombing. Had the viceroy stopped to enjoy the cuisine of his people, or to take in the local museum to immerse himself in the culture he dearly misses, he would have been killed."

Dooku straightened, his unblinking eyes looking straight into the cam, piercing the distance from Serenno to Coruscant. "But despite this mountain of evidence against the Republic, I am nothing if not honorable. I invite the Republic to explain this action. I will stay away to avoid any perception of conflict. After all, the Trade Federation is a neutral entity and should be allowed to pass judgment using their own system of justice. For the Republic to truly be open to discussion of such a catastrophic event, it seems only right that Chancellor Palpatine himself go to Cato Neimoidia." The mere suggestion caused a ripple through the space, from Anakin's suddenly tensed fist to Mace's furrowed brow. Next to Dooku's hologram, Palpatine's translucent image flickered, though the shock on his face broadcast clearly to all watching. "Such an action would be a remarkable gesture," Dooku said with a smile, "in the name of transparency."

Yoda turned as Dooku's feed broke apart, the count of Serenno's image quickly disappearing. "Discuss this further, we will. Facts must be gathered. The Senate, we need."

"No," Palpatine said, his mouth weary. "There is no time for Senate deliberation. I will go. I must leave as soon as possible. Every second counts. Without my presence, Dooku may sway the Trade Federation's allegiances to the Separatists. They are far too important a galactic power to let that happen."

"I'll go with you," Anakin said.

"A clone battalion. *If* he goes," Mace said. "The chancellor needs the highest levels of security."

Palpatine, flying off to the scene of a disaster on a neutral world? Not just a neutral world, but the crown jewel of the Trade Federation, the same organization with ties to Nute Gunray? Obi-Wan shook his head, and in a rare moment of letting his impulses break through, he spoke without a fully considered plan. "Chancellor, you must not go. It's a trap. Dooku is playing us."

All eyes suddenly turned to Obi-Wan. And now he had to coalesce those impulses into clear thoughts, with the fate of the galaxy at stake. "Dooku wants you arriving in a hostile environment, a no-win situation. Think about the optics. This planet is in a state of shock. Its people are mourning. If the chancellor arrives with troops and Jedi and a fleet, it will, at best, heighten tensions. At worst, it could lead to violence. All while leaving him vulnerable to sabotage."

"Master Kenobi, I understand your concerns. But this is a risk I must take," Palpatine said, a solemn gravel to his voice. "I will do anything to put a swift end to this war."

Obi-Wan shook his head again, mind sprinting for a solution that would pull Palpatine back from immediate departure. "A lone Jedi. A single emissary with a small crew of scientists and investigators, representing the good faith of the Republic."

As Palpatine's eyebrow arched up, Yoda let out an audible "hmmm."

"It is the best balance of diplomacy, transparency, and investigation. A Jedi has the training to uncover the truth, the autonomy to make decisions, the abilities to move quickly. And the authority to represent the Republic," Obi-Wan said, the words coming out so rapidly that he needed a large breath. "We are peacekeepers. Even the Trade Federation knows that."

"'Peacekeepers,'" Palpatine said, a slight smile to his lips. "I am not entirely convinced this will work. However, the logistics of my sudden departure will, unfortunately, require a day to sort out. Master Kenobi, if you can convince the Cato Neimoidian government and the Trade Federation before that, then I will concede to you."

"One day." Obi-Wan nodded, then looked around the courtyard. Palpatine. Yoda. Mace Windu.

Anakin.

They all watched him.

"I will come up with a strategy to present within one day."

"In the meantime," Mace said, "we will discuss potential security measures for the chancellor with the Senate. We must be prepared for both paths."

Palpatine looked off cam again, then spoke a few inaudible words. "I have further issues to attend to. But I look forward to your findings, Master Kenobi. We must move quickly."

The Cadesura disaster stole the gathering's sense of ceremony, though when the meeting adjourned, Obi-Wan had hoped to express his pride to Anakin. And given the importance of the milestone, he'd figured his old Padawan would have wanted to have a moment together. But Anakin left so fast that Obi-Wan only caught the blur of his dark cloak on the way out. Thoughts stirred in his mind, war commitments keeping their relationship distant in the short span following the promotion. He'd held on to so many questions for Anakin, waiting for a quiet moment: Was his new arm working for him? Did he have any questions about the responsibilities that came with becoming a Jedi Knight?

What really happened on Tatooine?

But between the rapidly changing intel on the Separatist insurgencies and the sheer chaos of synthesizing military battalions into the long-standing traditions of the Jedi Order, Obi-Wan and Anakin barely had time to breathe, let alone have a talk. Obi-Wan followed the trail of his former apprentice, hustling from the courtyard to the interior, then down the steps over to one of the Jedi Temple's wide hallways. He kept pace, though he never got too close—a range that put him in plain sight just in case Anakin decided to slow down and turn around.

But when it became clear that Anakin's pace was actually increasing, he reminded himself to let go of that personal desire to catch up. Anakin would come find him when he was good and ready. Besides, the catastrophe on Cato Neimoidia remained his top priority, and the fallout from it meant all sorts of complications, not just for the Jedi, but for every system, faction, and government somehow connected to the war.

He just had to find a way to start untangling it all.

Obi-Wan was about to break left toward the stairway leading to the Jedi Archives when he saw Anakin pause down the hall. Despite the distance, he recognized Anakin's body language, and the shift proved massive enough that it stole Obi-Wan's thoughts from the war.

Anakin, so bold in his determination, usually walked with his weight carrying him forward, nearly leaning ahead as if he were chasing the future. But here Anakin stopped and his entire body softened, from the way he held his shoulders to the way his arms hung. His head turned, waiting, and Anakin's smile grew so large that Obi-Wan saw it across the hall.

Then he understood why.

Dashing across to meet him was Padmé Amidala, trailed by a hand-maiden and one of Naboo's security, a woman Obi-Wan recognized as Mariek Panaka. The senator marched directly, wearing a flowing maroon dress with dark-navy trim, a simple bronze headpiece holding her hair tightly in a bun. She took even and controlled steps, presenting the opposite of Anakin's hurried gait, but the same straight path, like magnets hurtling through space to lock into each other. He'd heard Padmé had been visiting the capital planet on Senate business for a few days, though all senators had been on Coruscant more often than not in the weeks following Geonosis. As much as the Jedi shuffled around the galaxy these days, senators seemingly had withdrawn to the Core, dealing with the hows and whys of a potential civil war while the Jedi commanded clone troopers.

Padmé's proximity wasn't much of a surprise, but her stop at the Jedi Temple was a little out of the norm. Unless she planned on attending the courtyard ceremony for the newly promoted Jedi Knights? It may have been as simple as that, given her history with Anakin—a show of respect and gratitude, something thrown off course by the news of Cato Neimoidia.

As for Anakin, well, Obi-Wan had known of his former Padawan's infatuation with the senator for a while now. He understood, having handled his own youthful brush with temptation—one of the few things that still made him equally chuckle and groan when he thought of it. At least until he let the memories drift away into the distance, knowing they'd float back ashore at some point. But here, Anakin's greeting, though stilted and formal, rippled a wave of emotion through the Force, a very specific frequency that Obi-Wan recognized as everything he knew about Anakin consolidated into a flash.

Curiosity. Adoration. Joy, anxiety, fear. All of those rippled off Anakin, but above all came something far more dangerous:

Passion.

And passion was a liability even during normal Jedi operations. But infinitely more so in the context of war.

He expected the senator to go on her way, a short greeting before official business. He also expected Anakin to hesitate a second too long, that boyish infatuation pulling his attention more than it should before his sense of duty returned.

Instead, they stood there. A careful distance apart to be sure, but something was markedly different here. Not that long ago, Padmé had practically brushed Anakin aside when they'd arrived in her apartment following the assassination attempt, right before Geonosis. Yet here, though they held an air of formality between them, they clearly engaged with each other. The senator known for giving impassioned speeches, for her sharp observational skills, for her ability to find a constructive path forward, was lingering to talk with a Jedi known for never slowing down, whether in a speeder or on foot or by any other means.

But there they were, talking politely, smiling at each other. Padmé even took a quick glance around her, a subtle move that no one would notice up close, but it clearly stood out from above—especially because for the briefest of moments, her bodyguard looked off at something in the distance. She reached up, a quick touch at the spot behind his ear where his Padawan braid had been.

Then, as if the gesture flipped a switch in her, Padmé's pose tightened, her chest and shoulders suddenly taller despite her small frame. Anakin too reacted, but not with the expected embarrassment from such a close interaction with the object of one's infatuation, but rather a scan to either side, similar to Padmé's yet nowhere near as subtle.

He soon matched her, returning to a strong stance. Though he towered over her in height, the air of softness surrounded him, and another short conversation passed, words too quiet for even a dedicated observer to pick up. Despite this turn to buckled-down formality, Anakin's bare emotions continued rippling outward. Even as they parted ways, Anakin's feelings left a wake in the Force, a clear silhouette of his presence, something that probably only Obi-Wan would recognize. Far too often Anakin let his emotions dictate the situation, the tempering from Jedi training working only as a leash to the impulses that still ruled his actions. But anything that let a Jedi's guard down for even a moment put the Republic at risk.

Especially one as powerful as Anakin Skywalker. Especially one prophesied to be the Chosen One, to bring balance to the Force.

And Padmé, rather than dismissing it as she'd done in her apartment not too long ago, had amplified their connection. What to make of all of this? She was letting Anakin indulge in his infatuation, though to what degree, Obi-Wan couldn't tell. But there was more to it, and Obi-Wan wasn't sure if he wanted to know where it led.

"Oh." The short word escaped him, an expression as unexpected as what he'd just witnessed. He continued watching Anakin, who took a moment to gather himself before stopping to talk with Jaro Tapal and the red-haired youngling who trailed him. And though they talked longer than he did with the senator, no similar feelings projected from him, not in Anakin's body language nor in his connection to the Force.

"Oh, hello, Master Kenobi," Padmé said with a quick wave. "Is the chancellor still here?"

Obi-Wan must have been so lost in watching Anakin that he completely missed Padmé making her way up the stairs to his location. She stood still, and both her handmaiden and her bodyguard waited equally spaced from her, nearly a precise triangle formation. He nodded to greet the trio, then considered how to answer. "He attended the ceremony by holoconference. But the topic changed quickly."

"Because of Cato Neimoidia?"

"Because of Cato Neimoidia."

"Thank you," she said, a simple and efficient acknowledgment.

Obi-Wan gave another quick nod, still in his same spot as she moved quickly past to connect with Senator Bail Organa across the hallway.

It seemed that many senators were suddenly interested in visiting the Jedi Temple. But galactic disaster would do that, especially when Count Dooku publicly goaded the Republic into sending someone to the site of the bombing, possibly even its leader. Obi-Wan shook the mixture of doubts and concerns from his mind, the question of Anakin's motives pulling him away from the task at hand, though he reminded himself that something like this might not resolve immediately—or could resolve on its own.

It might even require a conversation with Anakin.

But right now, the Republic was at war. The Jedi had to intervene. And if he wanted to prevent Palpatine from falling into Dooku's trap, he needed to convince Cato Neimoidia to accept a Jedi emissary rather than the chancellor.

Obi-Wan let go of his feelings and started toward the Jedi Archives.

CHAPTER 4

ANAKIN SKYWALKER

ANAKIN HAD SEEN THIS BEFORE.

In fact, so many times. The backdrop was always different—in some cases, under the overwhelming harsh suns of Tatooine skies. And in other cases, in the deep vacuum of space.

The experience, though, that always remained true. Speed, lights, obstacles. Turns and g-forces. Whether in a podracer, in a Jedi starfighter, or zipping between buildings on a speeder. Or here, where a few Republic credits to a group known only as the Family gained access to speeder racetracks through abandoned sectors of Coruscant's underworld. Now nothing but industrial fossils, structures and piping and lights that blinked for decades and would probably blink long after the war ended. Paying to use a Family track during a non–race night was something Anakin dreamed about ever since hearing rumors of their existence. And though somewhere out in the stretches of space, clone battalions fought battle droids and emergency medical personnel tried to save lives on Cato Neimoidia, for one night Anakin shut it all out to be with his wife.

His *wife.*

Such a thought, such a *definition* still seemed unreal to him. Though it felt like another lifetime; only recently Padmé had been a near-stranger, someone he'd catch glimpses of as she moved in and around Coruscant, or on the HoloNet. He'd dreamed of her, then he'd tried to push those dreams aside.

And then Naboo happened. And Geonosis.

And Tatooine.

Now, married. They'd barely seen each other since that secret cere-mony and their short few days stolen away together, the duties of a Jedi and a politician pulling them all over the galaxy, leaving their marriage mostly as a spiritual bond. They'd send encrypted transmissions when-ever possible, their conversations timed against the unpredictable for-malities of war and duty, but even then he felt like their relationship was a dream, the most impossible and wonderful dream.

Except she came back to him. Or he came back to her. Not just holos expressing how desperately they missed each other, but tangible feel-ings and real touches that made it all *not* a dream.

And *that* amplified everything in him, making every moment even more precious, all of the good and bad held tightly as if they were the only things that mattered, even in a time of war.

Yet in this speeder, as they hurtled through the depths of Coruscant on a highly illegal and very dangerous makeshift course, this was sup-posed to be their first time together since he achieved the rank of Jedi Knight. Their chance meeting in the Jedi Temple caught him off guard, and it took all of his discipline to *not* throw his arms around her, to freeze the time and space around them so he could feel the weight of her body against his. But tonight, though he'd claimed to take a walk to focus his thoughts, the truth was he and Padmé had planned ahead for this: not just a few evenings out together when their time overlapped on the capital planet, but in the lower levels, where no one would care enough to notice them—a place where they pledged to *not* talk about politics or the war.

Or Cato Neimoidia.

Though she'd agreed to this activity—and paid for the speeder rental—it became clear as Anakin pushed the throttle forward into a near-vertical dive that she didn't live and breathe speed the same way he did, even though she had some piloting experience herself.

"I should have sent Dormé for this," she yelled over the whipping wind, her cowl blowing off her hair. Had she come out in any of her usual embellished stylings, the sheer velocity of the joyride would have ripped it all apart. But here she wore an unassuming outfit: dark trousers and a muted green cowl that easily blended in with the surroundings, and it matched his own, a simple mechanic's coat draped over his Jedi tunic to give the appearance of an everyday laborer and not a Jedi Knight. Anakin hit the final turn, easing up on the throttle to make the back end drift, the angle of their glide providing momentum so that a quick burst of the speeder's booster fired them just through the narrow space.

"I'm taking it easy," he said with a laugh, a final drop over the ledge that earned a scream-turned-laugh from Padmé before slamming the vertical boosters, cushioning their descent like a floating cloud made of metal and wire and alloys.

Like his arm.

Anakin pushed the thought aside, then reached into the Force with his senses, like sonar through the ether to identify where the path narrowed and twisted, even where previous racers lost control and crashed. He hit the brakes to drift into a twist, a series of controlled flips and dives before finally breaking past the uncontested finish line.

The speeder stopped, both Anakin and Padmé lurching forward before slamming back into the seats. "Whew," he said, before looking at his wife.

This was Padmé Amidala, who'd stared down certain death on Geonosis and charged forward with a blaster to reclaim her planet from Nute Gunray, yet here was breathing heavily with wide eyes and a hand across her chest. "I'm so sorry," Anakin started, "are you okay? Was that too much? Was I—"

Sudden laughter echoed out into the industrial bones around them. "Anakin," she said, her voice broken up by the laughter before she playfully smacked him across the shoulder. "That was exhilarating. And I never want to do it again."

He joined her in laughter, then leaned over, bringing them face-to-face. She reached out and took his hand—his mechanical hand—the same way she'd held it during their wedding ceremony.

Her eyes broke, looking down at the interlace between her fingers and his black glove. The pressure of her hold translated from electric synapses into the nerve endings on the remaining stump of his organic arm. Not too long ago, a mere *look* from her would make the hairs on that arm stand on end. Now such a thing was impossible. He squeezed her hand back, the microsecond of difference in sensation between his natural movement and this mechanical replacement still throwing him off. Different from combat or illegal racing, where pure instinct and the enhanced sensory intake of the Force tried to compensate. But here, in a quiet moment with his wife, at the start of a marriage as sudden as the replacement of his arm, a microsecond felt like hours.

"This doesn't bother me," Padmé said, placing her other hand over his glove. "It never will."

"I know. It's just not something I'm totally used to yet."

"It's part of you. Besides." She offered a smaller, more intimate laugh than seconds earlier. "You drove the speeder just fine." She leaned forward, pressing her lips against his, sensations he burned for during all those hours on cruisers and shuttles, when the hum of a lightsaber and the chatter of clone commanders stole his attention. He leaned in to her, their hands releasing to roam elsewhere, leaving them in a timeless space where only they existed.

Until the mechanized voice of a droid interrupted.

"The Family appreciates your business," said BS-1119, the bouncer droid that looked a lot like a reconfigured HK assassin unit. Anakin looked up to see it approaching, twin pistols hanging from holsters bolted onto its mechanical hips and a single pointing finger indicating that they should leave. Despite its threatening demeanor, the droid came off as overtly polite, probably a quirk of a program balancing security and business needs. "You are welcome to schedule another practice ride through one of the Family's industrial courses. In addition, bets are open for upcoming races." From beyond, floating law enforcement droids scanned, and BS-1119 flipped a switch on a nearby control panel on a nondescript wall. "This track is closed. Please pilot your vehicle elsewhere. You must leave now."

"It'd probably be in bad taste for a senator and Jedi to be caught down here," Anakin said.

Padmé grinned and sat back in her seat. "Let's grab something to eat instead of getting arrested."

Husband and wife.

What a strange thought. Despite their marriage, their lives had prevented them from living as such, what with Padmé handling things like the situation with Hebekrr Minor and Anakin bouncing around the galaxy performing as a mix of warrior, guard, medic, and deliveryperson. Married couples did things like take walks, go shopping, have dinner. Not fight a war or negotiate peace and then collide for several hours because their schedules allowed for it.

A sudden frustration burned within Anakin, lashing at the galaxy for keeping them apart. But even their joyride a few moments ago acted as a reminder—his body, his mind, his heart were committed to a life of adventure as much as a life with her. Perhaps if Qui-Gon had never found him on Tatooine, he would be on the podracer circuit now, or have found a life with some other dangerous recreation.

Would his mother still be there in that life?

But that question led to a dark path of further questions. He buried it deep, locking that night away and reminding himself that he was here with Padmé, in a strange life that intermixed combat and justice with quiet moments as husband and wife.

He just wished he could pick and choose *when* each occurred.

"I don't think you need a disguise," Padmé said, her weight leaning in to him as they walked forward into the marketplace. "Without your Padawan braid, no one's going to recognize you."

"Oh, it always got in the way. I don't miss it. Did I tell you when a stray blaster bolt singed it?" That moment from earlier today at the Jedi Temple, when she'd reached up and touched the spot where it had once hung behind his ear—they'd seen each other over holo recently, but that unexpected moment was like the Force challenging them to put on their best fronts. Anakin caught her scanning around before making the move, then the tilted smile that sneaked through, a private acknowledgment that they were pushing the boundaries of their existence in the place with the highest of risks.

It made him burn for her even more.

"I'm actually going to miss your short hair," she said, reaching over to run her hand through hair that had started to grow past the standard Padawan trim. "It was always so nice and neat."

"Maybe I'll just grow it out to annoy you. Have you seen how Obi-Wan's hair flows in the back?" he asked.

"No, please, anything but that," she said, prompting both of them to break into laughter. He'd heard that the underworld's residents were too mired in their own circumstances to be aware of the greater conflicts of the galaxy, and right now, he understood it. With the layers of structures too dense to reveal the sun, life felt encapsulated in a bubble here. In some cases, that might be claustrophobic.

But right now, it meant nothing could touch their existence—not war, not politics, not the rules of the Jedi.

They could just *be*. Because this was as close to those moments by the lake on Naboo as they were going to get for now.

They walked amid the glowing neon, a mix of signage and cheap functional illumination, silence suddenly as natural as breathing. He soaked in the easy joys of just existing next to each other—without guards or holos or fear that something would pull one of them away. They made it to their destination, a large arching sign proclaiming UHMANDASEE MARKET: a place that even the more cultured among Coruscant's surface dwellers would brave for a more authentic culinary experience. Rows of stalls and a few deactivated transport speeders stood, each offering a different level of messy-but-authentic delicacies from all over the galaxy.

Yet even in this context, where they had the space to simply be and enjoy each other's company, he saw that she still observed. It came in the smallest of personal tics—the way her inhale quickened, the way her eyebrow rose, the way her head turned to change her angle ever so slightly.

He saw the marketplace, a confluence of individual culture and industrial underbelly. But he knew her mind—while she saw all that as well, Padmé framed everything within the specific circumstances of who she saw. Not just the cook at the grill, but how a child was at his feet. Not just the artist selling wares, but how the size of her bag showed that she didn't have a permanent home. Not just the masseuse working on a client on a chair, but how the masseuse had supported the broken chair with additional spare parts instead of simply purchasing a new one.

These details escaped Anakin, at least until he tried to process things the way his wife did. The Jedi were selfless, giving themselves to an Order committed to intergalactic peace. But Padmé was selfless in a much different way—an empathy that drilled down to the well-being of whoever she encountered, something tempered with a drive to constructively find a way to fix it. Passion tempered by calculated action, the opposite of Anakin's own sun-dragon heart.

They paused, Padmé pulling back her cowl and kneeling down to smell the flowers sticking out of a small vendor cart. And even then, he knew she considered the vendor's situation, from the creakiness of the old droid watering the bouquets to the flower stand that had been clearly rewelded so many times it sagged.

Perhaps that was why they were meant for each other. Anakin acted like a fiery burst against injustice while Padmé brought a relentlessness to any situation, a constant search for a solution even in the most dire of circumstances.

Passion and purpose, locked together forever in a delicate balance.

"What do you think?" Padmé asked, putting a purple flower with glowing teal crystals over her ear.

"I thought we were staying inconspicuous?"

"You," she said, tucking a matching flower into the breast pocket of his coat, "are not a Jedi Knight. And I am not a senator. We're just a married couple having dinner." She gestured around, and he noticed that several other couples had donned matching flowers as well.

Of course she would scout this out first.

"Yeah," he said, locking elbows with her. "Just like any other married couple."

She rested her head on his shoulder, the glow of her flower tinting her face.

Passion and purpose indeed.

"Come on," she said, pulling away and taking his hand, "there's something I want to show you."

CHAPTER 5

OBI-WAN KENOBI

ALL THE KNOWLEDGE IN THE known galaxy lived in the Jedi Archives. So researching Cato Neimoidia should have been easy. But even though Obi-Wan sifted through details like topography, climate, planetary rotation, government structure, and cultural tendencies, none of that seemed to really provide any particular insight as to *how* he might convince the Trade Federation to accept a Jedi instead of Palpatine. Tutorials on speaking Pak Pak, Republic-generated simulations using data obtained via clone intelligence, and a complete history of the Trade Federation were all part of his hours of study, yet he didn't feel any closer to actually discovering the insight that might break through prejudices on both sides. Methodically sifting through data would do as much good as sitting there worrying about Anakin.

Instead, Obi-Wan tried a different tactic: a simple question that he'd relied on from time to time over the past decade, and perhaps not enough:

How would Qui-Gon Jinn approach the Cato Neimoidia situation?

That led to him moving swiftly to the Archive exit, Jocasta Nu barely acknowledging him, though her assistant Noxi Kell—who'd had an answer for every single question he'd presented—did offer a nod and a wave on his way out.

A short time later, he arrived under the lit buildings of Coruscant's evening at the CoCo District, heading straight toward an establishment that he'd last visited during a seemingly much more innocent time.

"Don't you Jedi sleep?" Dexter Jettster's voice rang out from behind the counter even before Obi-Wan fully stepped into the empty diner, only a waitress droid rolling around to wipe the counters.

"Not when there's a war going on." Obi-Wan's boots squeaked on the still-damp tiled floor. "A war you started, by the way."

The kitchen's double doors flew open as Dex squeezed through, blotches of sauce and grease stains on his shirt as his upper left hand draped a towel over his shoulder. Dex glanced around the space, then behind him. "Hate to break it to you, but those clones were already there, whether or not you went to Kamino. No customers, huh?"

"No. Which is good. Because I need you to be discreet. A dart that looks like a children's toy is one thing." Obi-Wan held up a datapad and a holoprojector. "This requires more care."

"Discreet?" Dex laughed. "I was the biggest information broker across the Core Worlds for years. You think I don't know how to be discreet?"

"Not you," Obi-Wan said, going to the barstool where Dex pointed. Dex settled in across from it, leaning with his top elbows planted while his bottom two hung loose. "They don't teach black-market precautions at the Jedi Temple."

"Admit it, Obi-Wan. You just wanted to make an old man cook one more dish for the night."

Obi-Wan sat down, adjusting his cloak so it didn't catch. "You caught me. Your food is always better than the Temple refectories, though don't tell Master Yoda I said that."

"You're in luck." He whistled. "Plate it for two," he called to the back. Several clangs later, one of the waitress droids rolled through the double doors, a tray balanced on her head. "Good timing, I'm just having my closing-time dinner."

"One for the Jedi; one for you, boss," the droid said, the words laced with sass.

"Thanks, Wanda."

"Dinner" was a relative term, as it looked like Dex's staff simply dumped the day's leftover cake onto plates. The bulk of the Sic-Six-layer cake slices went on Dex's plate, though Wanda did put a single piece on Obi-Wan's plate. "Warmed them up for you, sweetie," the droid said before rolling off.

"Dessert for dinner?" Obi-Wan asked with a laugh. "That'll kill you."

"Heavy proteins for midday dinner. Heavy sugars for closing-time dinner. You're telling me you don't know basic Besalisk physiology?" Dex asked, wiping a dab of white cream from the side of his mouth.

"Sounds like an excuse to eat leftover cake."

"Or perhaps it's that," Dex said, soon followed by his low throaty laugh.

"The boss does this every night," Wanda chirped in from the back. "Says it's better than letting the cake expire."

"The sound logic of an efficient businessman." By now, Dex had eaten two of the six pieces on his plate; Obi-Wan decided to be a little more restrained, taking a single bite off the top layer of orange-colored shavings.

"So, what can I do for you?" Dex asked between bites. "Need me to find more clones?"

"Not unless you're looking to add to your wait staff here." Obi-Wan tapped the holoprojector and out burst a hologram showing the simulated bombing from the library terminal. "What can you tell me about Cato Neimoidia?"

"You're supposed to pay me first before I say anything. I know I've been out of the game for a long time, but that's how I remember information trading works."

"Here." Obi-Wan used two forks to lift the thick bottom layer of his Sic-Six cake and put it on Dex's plate. "Your payment."

"Ah, you know how to bribe a man. Okay, Cato Neimoidia." Dex took in a large breath, flickering lights above causing flashes over the large brown ridge over the center of his skull. "A lot of fog. Trees with glowing oil. Funny-looking mountains. And cities that hang in between them. One less city"—he pointed to the holographic explosion on a loop—"if the HoloNet is accurate."

"Not quite a full city. But yes, it is. And." Obi-Wan took a much smaller bite than Dex's. "Dooku is whispering into their ear that the Republic is behind it."

The Besalisk raised an eyebrow and paused. "Do you think that as well?" he finally asked, the hesitation likely for dramatic effect.

His tone nearly caused Obi-Wan to choke on his cake. "Of course not," he said, indignation creeping into his reply. "No Republic action has been sanctioned to strike neutral systems." It was a serious statement, and yet Dex roared with laughter at it, his bottom-right hand slapping the inside of the counter.

"You don't believe that some Republic system would take this opportunity to weaken the Trade Federation? Somewhere far from the Core, where there are fewer eyes? Your idealism is adorable." Dex grabbed a napkin from under the counter and balled it up. He tossed it over Obi-Wan's shoulder, hitting the cylinder-shaped music player against the far wall. It came to life, neon blues and reds lighting up while a song made up of nothing but percussion instruments started. "If the Trade Federation implodes, a lot of systems could step into that power vacuum."

The point was clear, and any twinge of embarrassment disappeared quickly, Obi-Wan staying in the moment. "I don't know if it matters now, honestly. They have just released a statement agreeing with the suggestion to bring the chancellor to Cato Neimoidia. *Dooku* wants the chancellor to go there."

"Sounds inadvisable. So I can see why the Separatists are pushing that button."

"Exactly. And Palpatine will go unless I can convince them to accept a Jedi in his place."

"The Neimoidians." The hologram of the bombing fizzled as Dex poked at it, then swiped it aside to pull up data on the Trade Federation's purse worlds. "Unique species. Their brains are wired for calculation. Everything is an instinctive risk assessment to them. Some call it cowardly. I think it's a strong survival instinct, percentages and risk. I worked with some, back in my black-market days. Quick thinkers. I'd want them on my side. Picking a side means losing half your customers, though." Dex straightened up, his massive shoulders suddenly looking like mountains as he stood behind the bar. "In most cases."

"So that's it. Appeal to their sense of risk. How do you recommend going about that?" Obi-Wan lifted his plate. "Bring them cake?"

"They don't have a tidy relationship with the Republic, I'll tell you that. And not exactly with the Jedi, either. If I recall, you were involved with some of that."

Obi-Wan's voice dropped his sense of humor. "Nute Gunray is considered an extremist by their government. Senator Lott Dod—"

"There you go again. You Jedi, getting lost in the details."

Obi-Wan tapped his fork against his plate. "So go with cake then?"

"Perhaps." Dex stretched out, upper arms reaching overhead while his lower arms clutched his belly. "It's simple, really. Cato Neimoidia is the base of operations for the Trade Federation. Long memories, those Neimoidians."

"Make them forget." Obi-Wan waved his hand, prompting a laugh from Dex. "I don't know if one Jedi is powerful enough to do that."

"Not forget. Show them that sending Palpatine might invite more trouble than it's worth. And show them that a Jedi isn't going to tear through them like at Naboo." Obi-Wan nodded, his mind reframing options to Dex's new direction. "Remember, it's all numbers to them. It's what got them where they are. See, all of the Republic types think it's their ideology." Dex shook his head with a chuckle. "That's shortsighted. It's a strategy, not politics. Their neutrality is different from the neutrality your old friend preaches."

Obi-Wan had known Dex a long time, going back to a youthful misadventure out in the Unknown Regions. And though they only saw each other occasionally, his old friend knew just how to needle him.

This particular jab was so effective that a grin slipped through, and Obi-Wan raised an eyebrow in subtle acknowledgment.

"What old friend?"

"Oh, I don't know. Dresses better than you. Striking eyes. Mandalorian royalty. Used to call you Ben, for some reason," Dex said with one of his hearty chuckles. "That one. I hear she's quite the savvy politician."

Obi-Wan wasn't going to give him the satisfaction of saying her name out loud, or the fact that the Duchess Satine of Mandalore was maintaining neutrality in the Clone Wars to ensure that her people didn't return to their previous warlike ways. "Ah, the simple foolishness of impulsive youth."

"You keep telling yourself that, old buddy. I don't know, why don't you ask her about neutrality instead of an old slug at a diner?"

"Well, it's simple, Dex. I wanted dessert." To prove the point, Obi-Wan stabbed two pieces of cake, one from each layer, then took them down in one bite. "So suppose I convince them. The Republic sends a Jedi," he continued, still chewing. "Then what?"

"I'd say it starts with the bombing. What was targeted, how was it done, and why?"

Obi-Wan clicked a button on the holoprojector to deactivate it, then tapped the datapad before sliding it over. "I'm glad you asked."

Dex took one glance at the numbers and lists on the pad, then pushed it back. "No, no, no. See, you're looking at the wrong thing here. All you've got is facts."

Another eyebrow rose, though this one had nothing to do with Satine Kryze. "What's so bad about facts, Dex?"

"Without context, facts are useless." The holographic images returned as Dex tapped the pad with his large finger, then started swiping through. "You look at this and you see blast radius, casualty total, potential targets. What is the context?" he asked, tapping his finger with every word of his question.

"The context is—" Obi-Wan took in a breath. "We know the Republic didn't do it." Dex started to retort but Obi-Wan held up a finger. "We *assume* the Republic didn't do it. The Separatists say they didn't. The Trade Federation is neutral."

"Whoever did it is an extremist. Regardless of side. Correct?" Dex asked. His question came with a tangible weight, and in that moment Obi-Wan considered that Dex would have made a really good teacher for a Padawan.

"Fair to assume. And the Trade Federation considers Nute Gunray an extremist."

"Extremism only escalates when it's left unchecked. When you stay neutral in the face of it." The Besalisk gave a knowing grin. "But what if you could turn the Trade Federation into an ally? Make neutrality seem like the"—Dex's chuckle echoed through the space—"*risky* thing to do."

Obi-Wan nodded, the remaining food on his plate suddenly forgotten. Dex was right: Going to Cato Neimoidia, treating things strictly as an investigation to clear the Republic's name—that would only keep the Trade Federation neutral. And that neutrality would in itself enable the war to escalate. "This catastrophe," Obi-Wan said, pointing to the looping simulation of the attack, "may also be an opportunity."

"Oh?"

"Senator Lott Dod acts as a firewall for the Trade Federation. Getting an audience with their leadership is nearly impossible. But this provides us a direct opportunity to speak to them. To be heard. Possibly." He leaned back on his stool, hand over his beard. "Especially right now, while the war is young."

"Now you're getting it. So the first trick is to get them to accept a Jedi. And while that Jedi is earning their trust, perhaps talking them *out* of neutrality. Easy, right?" Dex looked over his shoulder. "Wanda?"

The waitress droid rolled to the kitchen window. "Ya need something, hon?"

Dex took a bite from the remaining cake slices, then looked at the chrono on the wall. "Brew a new pot of caf, please. We're gonna be a while."

"You got it, boss. Cream and sugar in yours, hon?"

"Oh, no," Obi-Wan said. "I prefer my caf straight black."

CHAPTER 6

ANAKIN SKYWALKER

THE VIEW ABOVE LOOKED LIKE stars, though Anakin knew better.

They both did, really, the pinpricks of light being blinking status beacons or glowing signage from higher levels. That was life in Coruscant's underbelly among its endless rows of massive structures. But it was romantic for anyone willing to pretend the lights were stars and the industrial fumes puffing from nearby stacks and vents were fog.

The artificial night sky made the underworld feel like a completely different place—not just a location in the Republic, but a portal to another dimension. In Uhmandasee Market, a new smell came every few meters, though Padmé led Anakin to one very specific rusty stall. They sat on a stack of rusty crates, something that may have even been in that very location since the days of the High Republic. Did things change down here, in a world of nearly perpetual dark, a population only concerned with the next job, the next sleep, the next meal?

Ironic, Anakin thought to himself. Because while he wondered about the culture and safety of the local residents, Padmé focused entirely on the immediate: the franikhad in her hands, metallic foil wrapper preserving its heat. "This is really, really, really good," she said, taking large bites without the decorum usually found in governmental banquet halls.

Maybe it was because none of the handmaidens lingered around to see it. "And," she added, finishing the franikhad in a gulp, "I don't want to know what's in it." She dabbed the napkin against her lips. "You haven't touched yours yet. Afraid it's not going to be close to the real thing?"

"The real thing" being a franikhad, a dish commonly found on desert planets. The term *delicacy* went a little too far; variations existed based on local meats and culture, but nearly every desert planet that Anakin knew of had some form of franikhad—a dish prepared in a makeshift oven dug into the ground to take advantage of a planet's natural heat and lack of water. After cooking, the local meats and vegetables were served in a thin breadlike wrap. He still remembered the exact steps to go from their home to the Mos Espa vendor with a ground oven right next to her stall—and if they'd managed to get a few extra parts for bartering, his mother would take him there for a bonus indulgence, something far tastier than the bland dishes they typically ate. "How did you even find out about this?" he asked Padmé.

"Oh, people in government know where the good food is. They talk. And once I heard Bail compare it to a 'meat griller on a desert world,' I thought of you. We just haven't had a chance to try it." Padmé's brow furrowed with a sudden hesitation. "Ani, I'm so sorry. I know the last time we were on Tatooine . . . I was just so excited to find this for you, I didn't even—"

"No, no, it's not that." He put the franikhad up to his nose, taking in the aroma of spices and meat. It *was* close, close enough that it triggered warm images of the dinner table with his mother. "Those are good memories. And this," he said, holding it up, "is a new memory. With you. It's perfect."

"Something's bothering you, though."

"Sort of. It's not what you think. And it's not this. I just . . ." Anakin hesitated, suddenly feeling like the little boy on Tatooine so flustered at the sight of her walking into Watto's shop that he blurted out the first thing that came to mind. "I have something for you."

"A gift? Ani, you never need to worry about those things."

"It's not much. You know, the Jedi and our rules about possession. I can't give you *things*," he said, opening the pouch on his belt. His fingers wrapped around a disk-shaped gold pendant, its necklace chain dangling as he pressed it into her hand. "But I can give you a piece of me."

Padmé held it up, the harsh light from the vendor's window enough to put the object in full view. "Is this . . . ?"

"My Padawan braid." She traced the braid, now coiled into a spiral and encased in carbonite as it sat within the pendant's simple design. "To new beginnings."

Even in the dim light, Anakin could see the flush come to Padmé's cheeks, and though she'd been known to sway entire systems through the power of words, her mouth remained open yet silent. But she didn't need to say anything.

The look in her eyes was enough. She leaned against him, and even though she put the chain around her neck, her hands still held on to the pendant, as if it could keep them together despite the galactic turmoil constantly around them. "Okay," he said after a minute. She turned to him, inquisitively. "Now I'm going to try the franikhad."

It *was* close to Tatooine cooking—close enough that Anakin considered ways he could discreetly get credits, find a speeder, and enjoy it from time to time. He wasn't sure if war would make all that harder or easier to do.

Then he gave himself a mental kick. Here he was, sharing a frozen joral cream sundae with Padmé in complete anonymity, and his mind wandered back to war. He told himself to lock into the moment, to simply be with her, and he tracked her gaze over to the trio of children sitting next to one of the stalls, scooting a toy podracer crudely constructed out of a pair of cans, string, and a stick.

"What are you thinking?" Anakin asked, though he knew the answer.

"Those younglings," she said, digging into the sundae between them, "I worry about them. Will they ever escape the underworld? Do they know what's out there? Do they realize a war is breaking out?"

He knew it—she was always thinking about how to make things better, just like when she sent Sabé to Tatooine in a quest to free those enslaved there. Thoughts probably churned right now about education subsidies for the underprivileged younglings of the lower levels, about how to use her influence as a senator to speak with local governments for an outreach program, that sort of thing. He knew her heart *and* her mind.

And while that was so much of why he loved her, it also kind of irked him in the moment.

"I'm sorry," she said, catching herself. "We don't have much time together. We shouldn't spend it talking about the war. It's just—" She held her spoon up to her mouth, paused in contemplation. "—Cato Neimoidia."

Of course. For that brief instant, Anakin didn't care who bombed Cato Neimoidia or why; he just wished it would all disappear, that the sunless realm of Coruscant's underworld really *was* a portal to another dimension, one without the Galactic Senate or the Jedi Order. But then guilt quickly draped over that, an understanding of the civilian suffering on the planet, where *right now* emergency medical crews attempted to rescue Neimoidians from the debris.

"I don't know what to believe with the bombing. Or why. The way this war has started, it's not just the violence. It's bad faith and disinformation, misrepresentation under the mask of independence." Her words came at the pace of a public speaker, as if she stood in a floating pod in the Senate chamber instead of sitting with a bowl of frozen joral cream. "I know the Republic gets stuck in bureaucracy, I've lived it. But to claim that—" She paused again, her human side taking back over from the politician. "I'm sorry again."

"Don't be. I want to hear what you have to say."

"It's a trap. I don't know by whom or why, but it's a trap. That's why we got to the Temple so quickly today, to catch the chancellor before he made any decisions. I'm sure the Republic Security Council wants to treat it purely as a military operation, but diplomacy is required for these . . ." Her head tilted, and she gave that thoughtful look, the one where she squinched her nose up, a line forming between her eyebrows. "Now you're just humoring me."

"Well," he said, finally releasing the smile that had been building up. "You put up with the race track. I'm returning the favor."

"No more war. No more politics," she said with a wave of her hands.

"No more racing." An idea sparked in Anakin's mind, a variation on a lesson designed to help younger Padawans focus under duress—but surely it worked now. "Look over there." He pointed across the small courtyard. "Pick something you see. The first thing."

Her brow crinkled at his request but she played along, an exaggerated squint as she observed. "I see . . . a balloon. Trailing that young Quarren. Now what?"

"Keep looking at it. Just stare at it." As she looked, Anakin knelt behind her, close enough that his lips brushed her ear. "All that exists right now is you, me, and that balloon," he whispered.

"Just us," she whispered back.

"Just us," he said, feeling the warmth radiating off her cheek. "And a balloon."

A gust of wind blew, something probably created by a combination of exhaust vents, passing traffic, and barely functioning industrial fans. It contained the stink of so many smells that never should have blended together, and Anakin looked, really looked at the lives of the underworld dwellers.

Other than the lack of sand and heat, it really wasn't that different from growing up on Tatooine.

"I want to help these people," Anakin said. "I don't know how, but I want to do something."

"That's my arena." Padmé craned her neck, kissing Anakin on the cheek. "You just keep us safe so I *can* do something about it."

Still kneeling behind her, he placed his left hand on her shoulder. She reached up and took it, their fingers interlacing even with their awkward position, and though he could have moved, the moment was a perfect encapsulation of who they were—and he didn't want to break it. Not just yet.

"I considered requesting you for escort duty. Since you're a Jedi Knight now," Padmé said, a playfulness to her tone despite the topic shifting yet again to their politics. "But I decided against it."

"Why's that?"

"Because secret dates mean I get to spend time with my husband. Instead of"—her voice changed to a deeper, formal tone—"Jedi Knight, protector of the Republic." Before he could react, she stood up, then took him by his mechanical hand. Flower still glowing behind her ear, she tugged him along. He walked in step with her, away from the rusted crates that doubled as stools and toward the path leading out of Uhmandasee Market.

"Wait, we're not done with the sundae," Anakin said, glancing back at the almost-but-not-quite-finished dessert.

"I think we can let it go. You'll see." Padmé pulled with intensity and picked up her pace. They wove their way through the mix of underworld locals and curious surface travelers until breaking past the perimeter of the market where their speeder sat parked. She opened the storage compartment and pulled out the bag she'd packed right when they picked up the rental vehicle from the dealer several levels below the planet's surface. She held it up to show him, but he failed to catch anything special about it.

It appeared to be just what it was.

"It's a bag. Am I missing something?"

"It *is* a bag. But sometimes what's important is what's inside." Padmé kept her eyes locked with his, a mischievous smile on her face, as she tugged on the bag's drawstrings, opening it enough to pull out . . .

Folded blankets?

But the look in her eye gave all the context he needed.

This was the Padmé he adored, someone who spent most of her days understanding the nuances of countless beings to do right for them. Yet on occasion, a fire burst through, something brighter and more intense than the hottest sun—when she allowed it.

Like now.

She walked to the side of the rented speeder, a barely functioning vehicle covered in dents and grime—a far cry from Jedi starfighters or the elegant designs of Naboo transports—and unfurled the blankets in the back seat. "A lot of quiet places in these lower levels," she said. "You're the pilot. Think you can find us somewhere private?"

CHAPTER 7

OBI-WAN KENOBI

ONLY A CHAIR, OBI-WAN KEPT telling himself. A chair that Qui-Gon never sat in, for a variety of reasons. He'd had a chance to join the Jedi Council, of course, turning it down to remain Obi-Wan's Master. And then that opportunity never returned, Qui-Gon's path splitting off into a different direction before being ended abruptly on Naboo.

It was only a chair. And yet it meant so much more.

Though some time had passed, Obi-Wan still felt a complete spectrum of emotions when he entered the Jedi Council Chamber and looked at the chair designated for him. He tried to let each feeling pass, though guilt was often the last to leave. Of course he wouldn't turn down the opportunity to fill Coleman Trebor's spot, even on a temporary basis; sitting on the Council was among the highest honors for any Jedi. The responsibility itself hadn't proved daunting—after all, he'd mentored the most powerful and headstrong Jedi in recent memory.

The questioning in him came from the title itself. Yoda, Mace Windu, Even Piell, Eeth Koth, and others—all more skilled or more wise than him, something he freely admitted. For them to ask for his input . . . *intimidating* wasn't the right word. Instead, Obi-Wan wondered if he possibly had the proper insight and experience to contribute to such a group.

But he had been the one to suggest a Jedi in place of Palpatine. He had stayed up with Dex devising a strategy to present, something he'd done earlier to the Council and Palpatine. And with their blessing, everything led to this moment.

All Obi-Wan could do was breathe, despite the weight of the galaxy on his shoulders.

"Our intelligence has lowered the estimated death toll to approximately thirty-two hundred. The local government has set up temporary infirmaries for rescued survivors, currently estimated at three hundred. Up to a thousand are listed as missing. And we have received more information to refine our simulation of the blast."

"Signs of Republic involvement, are there?" Yoda asked the holographic armored trooper in the middle of the Council Chamber.

"Nothing specific that we can see. There are no logs of any activity in the sector, not from troop movements, transports, or ID tags of individual cruisers. But getting on the surface to investigate up close will offer more direction."

"Understood. Thank you, Commander," Mace said. "These are the latest reports from the HoloNet." A compilation of news recordings and official speeches appeared in the trooper's place: aerial images of where the Cadesura district used to interlock into the rest of Zarra, now a massive gap between spires on Cato Neimoidia; on-the-ground images of medical personnel sweeping through rubble; the massive makeshift infirmaries in factories and parks as survivors were rescued from the wreckage.

The recording interrupted, pausing before disappearing, only to be replaced by Mas Amedda, the Chagrian vice chair of the Galactic Senate. "Masters," he said, a slight bow to his head, "we are ready for the negotiation."

Obi-Wan steadied himself, the chair never feeling more ill fitting than now.

Yoda tapped his cane against the smooth Council floor, then gestured to the holo.

"May I present Alluv Eyam, minister of defense of Cato Neimoidia." The Neimoidian faded into view to the right of Mas Amedda, burnt-orange robe and matching headpiece signaling his status within the government. "And of course our chancellor is listening as well." Palpatine's image appeared on the opposite side.

"Minister Eyam," Obi-Wan said, nodding. "On behalf of the Jedi Council, we extend our condolences to Cato Neimoidia as well as the Trade Federation."

The Neimoidian nodded, then held up a single finger. "I appreciate your concern, Master Kenobi. However, we are in a state of crisis management here. I request that your proposal be brief. The Trade Federation and Senator Dod have decided to stay out of this discussion, given that Senator Dod has a presence in Republic politics. In full transparency, Separatist leaders have sent us a preliminary report to back up their findings pointing to suspicious Republic activity. Given this, we remain in support of Count Dooku's suggestion and would appreciate Chancellor Palpatine's swift arrival to discuss matters."

Obi-Wan shot a quick look over to Palpatine. Access to anyone within Trade Federation leadership outside of Senator Dod was an immediate victory. Even though the Cato Neimoidian officials concerned themselves mostly with local governance, the planet itself was still the center of the Trade Federation's operations. Winning over their minister of defense and others could be significant for the Republic.

Obi-Wan stood up, the morning light of Coruscant beaming through the projections. "I understand. Simply put, we have assessed the situation and we believe that sending Chancellor Palpatine would be a mistake for all involved. In his place, a single Jedi emissary with a minimal investigative support team should travel to Cato Neimoidia." Minister Eyam opened his mouth but Obi-Wan expected this, and though it would have been polite to let him speak, Obi-Wan continued to lay out all of his points. "The arrival of the chancellor represents both an immediate security risk and an invitation to escalate conflict. Because of his status within galactic politics, he would need to be accompanied by many layers of security, from guards to clones to possibly even Jedi. Not only would this create unease among a population currently in mourning, it might raise tensions with anyone who has prematurely blamed the Republic for the Cadesura tragedy.

"A single action might thus bring the war to Cato Neimoidia. That is the last thing that your people need—not because of any political stance, but because they are dealing with an unspeakable tragedy.

"We propose that this emissary be sent, not simply to assess the damage but also, given the Jedi's training and tools, to undergo a thorough investigation to identify the true source of the attack. At the same time—" Obi-Wan paused to emphasize the oncoming point. "—the emissary would be available to hear your concerns and grievances surrounding the war or its impact on your operations. The support crew would be open to monitoring and only there as specialists to assist the investigation. Such a group would be far smaller—and far more effective—than what the chancellor would require. We offer the resources of the Republic to you—" Obi-Wan took a moment before looking Minister Eyam square in the eye. "—in good faith."

Several seconds passed with only the hum of the holoprojector. Eyam looked off to the side, then tented his long fingers before returning to Obi-Wan. "This is an interesting proposal, Master Kenobi. I see your point."

"We believe such a move would minimize *risk* for all parties involved. I hope you consider the possibilities and see that as well. We want to assist Cato Neimoidia while avoiding any possibility of violence. This is not about the war. This is about the truth."

Eyam again looked away, speaking inaudibly to someone unseen. "You make very good points, Master Kenobi. I have considered the variables of your proposal and I believe you are correct. This is the best way to work with the Republic without inviting unwanted attention or further violence."

Obi-Wan exhaled and stifled the urge to smile. He'd been in many high-stakes negotiations during his life, but none as pivotal as this—not just because of the implications for the galaxy, but also as a representative of the Jedi Council, as a Jedi *Master*. "I thank you for your consideration. Sending a single Jedi requires minimal logistics. We will—"

Before Obi-Wan could finish, a new holographic image appeared.

Count Dooku.

Tension rippled through the Jedi Council Chamber, a tangible shift in the air *and* the Force.

"If I may interject, Minister Eyam," Dooku said, "while Master Kenobi and the Jedi Council speak honorably, might I remind you of the long history of prejudice between the Republic and the Neimoidian people."

"Master Kenobi, I must apologize," Eyam said. "The Trade Federation has invited Count Dooku to listen in on our discussion."

A series of holofigures stood in front of Obi-Wan, the unlikely image of Palpatine and Dooku mere meters apart offering a stark representation of the galaxy's balance of power. But rather than speak, Palpatine turned to Obi-Wan and gestured for him to continue.

All that time with Dex culminated in this critical juncture, cups of caf and long hours never being more important than now. "The Jedi are outside of galactic politics. What is your concern, Count Dooku?"

"'Outside of galactic politics'—I find that statement amusing given that Jedi are leading your clones into battle while you represent the Republic in a political negotiation. Similarly, any investigatory crew that you bring will be under the employ of the Republic and not to be trusted."

Obi-Wan wanted to say, *Get to the point,* but losing his composure in the face of a liar and murderer would instantly hand over victory to a Sith. He held on to the image of Qui-Gon's calm in the face of danger, a centering he relied upon when needed, and spoke directly to Eyam, a new idea sparking in his mind. "I wish to allay any suspicions and fears from you, the people of Cato Neimoidia, the Trade Federation, and"—he looked at the Sith Lord's hologram—"Count Dooku. Thus I will augment the proposal. I will go. By myself. Without any support. The investigation may take a little longer as I am merely one person, but I am willing to trade this to ensure good faith among all parties."

Dooku raised an eyebrow, and Obi-Wan locked his focus on the count even though his instincts wanted to pull away and see Palpatine's response.

"Master Kenobi, I believe the last time we saw each other, you and your apprentice tried to murder me."

Obi-Wan considered reminding everyone that just prior to that, Dooku tried executing him, Anakin, and Senator Amidala in a giant Geonosian arena. However, that seemed politically unwise given the delicacy of the moment. "Consider that a misunderstanding," he bit out. "If you haven't been listening, I have promised Minister Eyam a commitment to the truth. Nothing more, nothing less."

"The truth." Dooku laughed. "What a way with words you have. Truth can be manipulated. How do we know Minister Eyam can trust you?"

Trust. Obi-Wan eyed Dooku—even as a holo broadcast from across the galaxy, he recognized exactly the game being played here. Every single word from Dooku was both a challenge to him and a threat to Eyam, Dod, and whoever else might be listening.

Obi-Wan considered all of that, then launched a counterattack as targeted as a swing of his lightsaber. "You knew my Master. You were *his* Master. So tell me, Count, did you trust Qui-Gon Jinn?"

The mere mention of the fallen Jedi's name shifted Dooku's expression, his eyes softening and mouth turning for a flash before returning to a cold neutral, the first, possibly only crack in Dooku's armor.

"Qui-Gon Jinn was an honorable man."

Now Obi-Wan moved to the offensive, a momentum to his words. "I carry his teachings with me every day. If you trusted Qui-Gon, then know you can trust me as well."

Dooku's eyes darted, a quick movement that probably gauged those around him. Obi-Wan took a moment to do the same thing himself—and caught the smallest smirk on Palpatine's lips. "You make a convincing argument, Master Kenobi. Very well. I endorse this proposal. With two further caveats: You must arrive on an unarmed Republic shuttle, not a starfighter or other vehicle with attack capabilities. And you are prohibited from any communications with either Coruscant or the Jedi Council. Of course," Dooku said, "I have no true say in this, I am merely voicing an opinion. Minister Eyam must make the decision."

"Anything that ensures diplomatic discussions with minimal risk of conflict or violence is appreciated. Count Dooku's caveats make sense," Eyam said quickly, his tone as straight as his words.

Obi-Wan considered the possibility of being completely stranded on
Cato Neimoidia, without any means of connecting with support. He bit
down on his lip, mind racing at options to counter the suggestion, when
Palpatine's voice broke through.

"The Republic accepts these terms. Master Kenobi will depart tomorrow after a day of preparation."

Eyam looked among the different parties on the holocommunications. "We welcome any assistance that may help us in our time of need."

"I look forward to seeing you in person, Minister Eyam." Obi-Wan
bowed his head and was about to signal for the transmission to end
when Dooku spoke up.

"One final detail, my friends," he said, the word "friends" stretching
out with a coarse inflection. "I believe in supporting Cato Neimoidia
during its time of need. As such, I shall send my own representative
from the Confederacy of Independent Systems to ensure that this Jedi
emissary remains"—Dooku smiled in a way that seemed sincere only
on the surface—"honest." And with that, Dooku faded from the transmission before anyone else could respond.

"My research has informed a strategy I suggest we employ for this operation," Obi-Wan said to the remaining members of the Jedi Council.
About fifteen minutes had passed since all of the transmissions ended,
leaving the assembled Jedi free from the interplay of political and
military influence for a more open discussion. "The chancellor is
right—this is an opportunity for negotiation. Considering how all communication to the Trade Federation has gone through Senator Dod
since Geonosis, the fact that he is staying out of this is notable." He took
in a breath, running through all of the points he'd discussed with Dex.

"The Trade Federation has denounced Nute Gunray as the leader of
a splinter group. This bombing, whoever did it, is clearly the act of an
extremist of some sort. These are related symptoms, not a root cause.
Extremism will only accelerate the war, not bring it to a peaceful conclusion." All eyes sat on him, without any objections so far. "But we have
an opportunity now, a unique one, to show the Trade Federation that

remaining neutral in the face of extremism is, in fact, enabling terrorism—and thus, making the war more dangerous."

Yoda watched the space for reactions. Ki-Adi-Mundi tented his fingers and leaned forward, scars still healing across his cheek from his recent encounter with General Grievous.

"I believe the strategy here to be equal parts diplomacy and negotiation, with the key being to understand the Neimoidians as a people. Because their culture is based on a philosophy of risk assessment, we must build a message around the inherent risk of prolonging the war by letting extremism grow. We must remind them of not just the economic risks of instability across the galaxy, but the potential loss of life as the violence escalates. Including, as they have discovered, to their own people.

"I see a mission in two parts: First, gain the trust of the Trade Federation by successfully clearing the Republic, then appeal to their sense of risk assessment to actively support the Republic. That move would take away major logistical resources from the Separatists, all hopefully leading to de-escalation and eventually negotiations rather than more fighting. And above all else, we must show good faith."

Obi-Wan took a breath, giving the Council and the chancellor a moment to process the information. Finally, Yoda broke the silence. "Informative, Master Kenobi. An astute observation, you have provided."

"While you depart for Cato Neimoidia, we have a new matter to discuss: the chancellor's request to prepare Padawans for the field," Mace said with a solemn nod.

"Padawans for the military?" Obi-Wan asked, unaware that Palpatine had asked for such a thing. Padawans had certainly fought in skirmishes alongside the clones—Geonosis saw more than its share, including Anakin. But further blurring of the lines between the Jedi Order and the military? The idea caused enough unease in Obi-Wan that it momentarily overtook the mission to Cato Neimoidia in his thoughts.

"A recent discussion. Interrupted by Cato Neimoidia's tragedy."

"We must act in the best interests of the Republic. We are at war," Mace said, as definitive a statement as Obi-Wan had heard the old Master make. "The chancellor is allowing the Jedi freedom to assess the best way to balance military assignments between Jedi Knights and Padawans."

"Your concern, it is not. Focus on Cato Neimoidia."

The various Council members murmured an affirmation, a vote of confidence in Obi-Wan that explained Yoda's look. He inhaled sharply at this realization, and uncertainty flooded him—not at the ability to do the job that he'd meticulously researched and planned out. But at the trust the Council—the chancellor—placed in him.

Had he earned it?

Obi-Wan let the feeling pass and simply bowed his head. "I will begin my preparations immediately. But," he posed to Yoda, "my former Padawan is still new in his role. Should I speak to him about the chancellor's militarization requests as well?"

"Skywalker is no longer your responsibility," Mace said, the lines on his face shifting ever so slightly. Obi-Wan recognized the look—it seemed to be a constant whenever Anakin and Mace crossed paths.

Even Jedi had interpersonal conflicts, he supposed.

Yoda must have sensed the change in the air, stepping in with his usual softer touch. "Patience and humility, Skywalker and other new Jedi Knights have learned to earn their title," he said. "To show the younglings, their next task is."

A decade had passed since Obi-Wan handled the responsibility Yoda referred to, and he cringed a bit inside. It quickly turned into a grin at the thought of Anakin Skywalker, the person Qui-Gon believed to be the Chosen One, the young man who charged headfirst into Count Dooku's lightning attack, now headed toward the biggest challenge of his life.

"As his former Master, this assignment, you should give him. Warn him, perhaps. So many questions, the younglings ask," Yoda said with a laugh. "So many questions."

CHAPTER 8

MILL ALIBETH

JEDI INITIATE MILL ALIBETH TRIED to keep up. She really tried. "Come on!" her friend Vivert yelled, and even still, they trailed the group of seven younglings ahead of them, with Mill falling even farther behind. Their footsteps echoed through the large stone hall of the Jedi Temple, and she looked up to catch her friends rounding the corner to get to the turbolift. First Ami-Kat-Ayama, a Cerean girl with thick black hair tied up in a bun. Then Alay and Mala Thurya turned, a pair of purple-skinned Twi'lek twins, their familial bond making sure each always pushed the other forward. Then three more younglings dashed ahead and even Felix Yabir, the young Sullustan with shorter legs, sprinted faster than Mill. They disappeared from view, though Mill managed to make the left turn and see the group of Initiates moving quickly, a whirl of voices and excitement that startled the very serious adults on either side of the hall.

Finally Vivert pulled ahead, lingering enough to glance at Mill, as if that single look repeated her words before she sprinted onward. Vivert Stag's curly hair bounced on her pale cheeks with each step and she broke farther away.

Mill took a moment to close her eyes. She was already behind anyway, and she could feel the anxiety creeping in, so she went back to her recent practice of doing the *opposite* of her Jedi teachings.

Wherever she felt the Force, she tried to push it away, quiet it, keep it at bay.

Another voice came through to break her concentration, this one with the robotic ring of a synthesized voice.

"Younglings! Walk, please!"

But the protocol droid failed to move fast enough, its arms and legs out of sync in stilted toddling. Protocol droids lacked speed to begin with, but this one had hit a double case of bad luck. First, it received a fill-in assignment with younglings instead of serving visiting adults from other planets, or the ones from the main government buildings. And the younglings knew this, tricking the protocol droid before it could introduce itself. If it had said its service number, Mill didn't even hear it.

Second, this protocol droid had a loose gyro in its knee socket, slowing it down further. Rumors had the normally quick repair lab within the Jedi Temple being converted into something for the war. Blasters or shields or whatever they might need. She wasn't even sure if that was for the clones or for the Jedi who fought with them now—"general," she'd heard the clones say, which made no sense given that the Jedi were either Masters or Jedi Knights or Padawans. Or, like her, Initiates.

It didn't really matter, because *nothing* made sense these days.

Like how Vivert and the rest of her Initiate friends jogged forward as if nothing bothered them at all. The Clone Wars, they called it, which she supposed was a fitting name since the Republic now used a clone army. But wasn't it a war about . . . systems leaving the Republic?

Whatever name they gave it, one thing was clear—every image, holoclip, or even discussion affected Mill, sometimes making her more ill than the worst bacterial infection. Her whole life, simply being close to violence or suffering left a deep nausea, but it had only gotten worse with each passing day after the Jedi returned from Geonosis.

Actually, "returned" was the wrong word for that. Because many Jedi *didn't* return. Masters, Jedi Knights, Padawans, all manner of Jedi lost their lives at Geonosis. And with that, sometimes even being in certain parts of the Temple caused headaches and queasiness.

Yet today seemed worse than usual. Her friends jumped out of bed, ate quickly, and sprinted down the hall to get to the transport shuttle, their every word stuck on the idea of making their own lightsabers—weapons of war, as the Clone Wars got worse with every passing moment.

It all made Mill's stomach hurt and temples pound.

"Gathering! Gathering! Gathering!" her friends chanted in a group, a joy that she couldn't quite grasp. For several weeks, it was all they talked about: what color kyber crystal they wanted, what type of handle or emitter they wanted to use, or how Professor Huyang was so old that the ancient droid supposedly arrived at the Jedi Temple in a big blue box thousands of years ago before ever teaching lightsaber construction. She'd felt well enough to fake it, laughing or joining in. Besides, lightsabers *looked* neat, and the way they hummed and buzzed, well, that seemed to be the best part of being a Jedi.

But lightsabers meant violence. Violence meant suffering.

And though no one could quite explain why Mill's particular connection with the Force worked this way, suffering made her sick.

"Younglings!" the protocol droid called before holding a comm to its mouth, its shiny green plating reflecting the endless lights of the Jedi Temple. "Attention, Padawan Quinn. The younglings have finished their meals and are awaiting you at the transport to Ilum."

"Understood. I'm rushing to get over there."

Mill knew why the adults seemed tense this morning—actually since yesterday. The only thing anyone talked about in the Temple was Cato Neimoidia. The usual training sessions had been canceled, with younglings handed off to various droids to work on acrobatics or meditation. The older Jedi rushed to and fro, some with their Padawans and some by themselves. "They're sending the Jedi all over. To calm everyone down," Vivert said over breakfast. "Every system thinks they'll be the next."

Next. Mill considered what that meant. She'd tried to shut it all out, to instead focus on what she could do: take a breath, take a step, look at her studies, eat her meal, stay hydrated, all to push herself to the point of getting on the *Crucible* for the flight to Ilum. Once there, she figured, she could at least get away from all talk of the war and the horrors that just happened on Cato Neimoidia.

She did all of that. And she did it all *without* connecting with the Force. That proved to be too overwhelming in a time of crisis.

Mill pushed forward, her friends already down to the landing platform while the protocol droid fell woefully behind. Left foot, right foot, and repeat, and she even managed to get some words out. "Coming," she yelled to her friends, "wait up." She forced a smile, despite the burning nausea in her gut and the pounding in her two Zabrak hearts. She almost made it through until something caught her eye.

She shouldn't have looked. But the glow of the holo-recordings instinctively tempted her focus, pulling her from the path to the docking platform to a small office off to her left, a few robed Jedi gathering around a bright holotransmission.

And then, for the first time, she laid eyes on Cato Neimoidia.

It was only a glimpse, a view from the sky of a long stretch of a city draped in fog. Except this city had a massive chunk missing from it. In its place rose lines of dark smoke.

That was all Mill took in before her feet stopped, her momentum nearly causing her to stumble over herself. Her tan hands slammed to the floor, and the short tail of black hair dropped down, tickling the side of her face, some of it catching on her horns. She thought of other things, anything to block out the images of the collapsed cityscape, and though she was far enough from the hologram that fine details eluded her, it didn't matter.

When she closed her eyes, her connection to the Force brought it all to her unintentionally, like a navigational map of the fallen region except with heatlike signatures pulsing. Not as a display of temperature, but an insight into the pain of a population, a wave of bright oranges and reds silently screaming into the ether of the Force.

"Youngling? Is something wrong? Do you require medical attention?"

"Unh-unh," she said, pushing herself up. By now the other Initiates had gathered at the turbolift to the platform, and she took step after step, the dizzying connection to the Force still causing her to stumble off center. She tried to close off from the Force, but her link proved too strong and it flooded all of her senses.

"I'm going to build a staff," Ami-Kat-Ayama said. "Spin it around. Slice through a line of battle droids like a buzz saw." The mere mention put the image in Mill's mind, as if she were the line of battle droids falling victim to the whirring lightsaber, but rather than unfeeling machines, the sensation of violence rippled through her.

"No you won't. They're gonna shoot fifty blaster bolts at you. And you're only gonna block one of them. Too slow." Vivert twirled, an imaginary lightsaber in her hands.

Felix spoke in his native language, a taunt in words Mill hadn't totally grasped yet but which caused the others to laugh.

"Yeah? Maybe I'll just deflect them over to you. Hit you right in the face," Vivert replied with a laugh.

Mill tried. She tried so hard to keep it together, so much that her knuckles were sore from clenched fists. But the more her friends' banter escalated, the more the violence of their words whipped sensations into her mind, heightening the pain she already felt from the images of the bombing.

Her legs gave out, knees hitting the floor, and though she supported herself with one arm, the last thing on her mind was Ilum and the Gathering. This morning's breakfast ejected out of her, a collective *Ewww* coming from her friends.

"Em-Three-Em-Four! What's going on?" yelled Malera Quinn, the human female Padawan assigned to take them to Ilum.

"It is Initiate Alibeth," the droid said. "It appears that this youngling is quite ill."

"Mill, right?" Malera knelt down, her blond hair draping over one shoulder. She'd met Malera before during other Padawan-led training, but something in her face felt different, lines of concern that weren't there before Geonosis.

"Are you all right?" Vivert came by, too, hand on Mill's back. She forced a smile to reassure her friend.

"I'm fine," Mill said. "I'm ready for the Gathering and to meet Professor Huyang and—" The sudden thought of a lightsaber of all things—an elegant weapon for defense, yes, but a weapon nonetheless—brought the nausea back, but now her head spun as well.

"I'm afraid you are not, youngling," Malera said. She turned to the protocol droid, apparently named M-3M4. "Take this Initiate back to the infirmary. She's going to need a different assignment while we go to Ilum."

Mill nodded, saying the appropriate thank-yous and goodbyes as she got herself up. But inside, she made a new vow to herself:

She wouldn't just quiet the Force. She would find a way to permanently cut herself off from it. Because she couldn't live like this.

CHAPTER 9

OBI-WAN KENOBI

"THERE YOU ARE," OBI-WAN CALLED out. Right before he spoke, he'd spotted Anakin by himself but stayed quiet. The Jedi refectory was nearly empty, so much so that Anakin must have figured no one would notice if he changed the configuration of the holodisplays from a rolling list of schedules and menus to a podrace from some remote world. He waited until Anakin finished and settled into his seat, a simple vegetable soup on the tray in front of him, and gave his former apprentice several seconds to enjoy his setup before barging in.

In return, Obi-Wan used the time to consider the scene in front of him: Anakin trying to bend rules to serve his personal desires. Here, it was minor. Not that long ago, it was far more drastic, and a single memory flashed, summing up Obi-Wan's worries in a few words:

"You will be expelled from the Jedi Order!"

He'd screamed it at Anakin as wind whipped into their eyes, their gunship soaring over Geonosis. In return, Anakin screamed right back. "I don't care!"

But that was the problem. Anakin did care. He cared about so many things—including podracing—that Obi-Wan felt like he was often the safety lock on Anakin's throttle, making sure Anakin kept from going so fast that he'd spiral out of control. Yet now they were peers rather than Master and apprentice, a war severing that protective tether and letting Anakin drift free among his instincts and his passion.

"Master," Anakin said, standing up so fast that his knees banged the table, the soup in his bowl sloshing in reaction. Obi-Wan noticed the subtle gesture Anakin made behind his back, cutting power to the holo-display with the flip of a finger. "I was just catching up on the Cato Neimoidia news and—"

"It's all right," Obi-Wan said, waving his hand as if he was doing a mind trick, though in this case it simply calmed the soup from spilling farther out. "Perhaps peace could be negotiated if we all watched sports and drank ale together. Actually, I've come to talk with you about your next assignment tomorrow."

Anakin looked at Obi-Wan, the smallest twist forming on his mouth before it reset to neutral. "Tomorrow? I thought I was shipping out in two days to oversee aid delivery to Langston."

There it was again. Obi-Wan would have detected it even from across the room, but sitting right next to Anakin, it was unmistakable—the exact same ripple that he'd sensed earlier when Anakin came across Padmé at the Jedi Temple. The cocktail of emotions had a different formula, but came wrapped in the same skin.

She was nowhere to be found. So why did he feel this way?

A very strategic response formulated in Obi-Wan's mind. "Oh, you still are. Tomorrow's is local." His head tilted ever so slightly, measuring Anakin's response. "Shouldn't interfere with anything you have planned."

"Ah. I mean," Anakin started before looking over at where the refectory's holographic projection had been. "We're meeting with the chancellor tomorrow. The newest Jedi Knights, that is. I didn't want to miss it."

"Anakin, you can catch a feed of podrace tournaments on any shuttle or transport. If you know how to do it." Obi-Wan spoke with specific precision, something equally designed to disarm while also dig a little deeper. He paused, letting Anakin take a sip of soup before moving on to a new topic, something just as tactical. "Oh, did I tell you I ran into Senator Amidala at the Temple yesterday? It sounds like she and a few other senators agree with the Jedi using the opportunity to speak to Cato Neimoidia. I haven't seen her since Geonosis, but she looks no worse for wear."

Anakin stood up again, a careful move that avoided any table collisions this time. Then he knelt back to the access panel of the holoprojector, his face completely hidden. "If you run into her again, tell her I say hello. One second," he said, tinkering with the configuration. "Can't let anyone know I was watching podracing." Now Obi-Wan sat and waited, giving Anakin the space to restore the holoprojector settings but also himself the space to process what he'd witnessed, not visibly but through the Force.

Because that same surge came at the mention of Padmé, like a button being pressed. Even without her physical presence, she occupied his thoughts—and the fact that Anakin didn't even try to shield it created a monumental problem, a vulnerability that endangered both Anakin and the Republic.

"Almost got it," he called out. On the one hand, Obi-Wan felt the pull to confront Anakin *now*, about dedication and responsibility and all the other things Mace Windu had just lectured the group on—especially in this moment, when the balance of power across the galaxy was at stake. Infatuation and other trivial matters could wait, and as someone who currently sat on the Jedi Council—even on a temporary rotation—did he not carry the responsibility to ensure that commitment was pure and resolute among the Jedi Knights?

But then a flush came to his cheeks, something that made him thankful that Anakin still tinkered with the holoprojector. Because Dex knew how to see right through his old friend, highlighting Obi-Wan's own hypocrisy in the matter.

And besides, right now Cato Neimoidia was *his* priority, and his personal feelings about Anakin could not interfere with that.

"There we go," Anakin said, popping back up. The refectory's usual mix of information returned to the display, and as if the process reset Anakin himself, Obi-Wan detected no further changes in Anakin through the Force. "No one is the wiser. So, I hear you're off to Cato Neimoidia tomorrow?"

"Word travels fast."

"You know I should be there with you." Obi-Wan had heard variations on that statement before, and in some cases it came with the intimation that Anakin considered himself more powerful, more capable, the obvious solution. In this case, though, his voice, his posture, the concern on his face, all came across as authentic, an unexpected maturity.

What an interesting change in attitude.

"I would much rather have that. But we must abide by Count Dooku's caveats. He has smartly backed the Jedi into a corner. It must be me alone." Anakin's discomfort at the idea painted his entire expression, a stony silence, as if the young man tried to will his way into the situation. "Even though I'm sure the Trade Federation would love to hear your take on the galaxy's best podracers. Perhaps you could even inform them of your favorite underdogs," he said, allowing a smirk to come through.

Anakin returned the smile, building a bridge between the two, perhaps even a silent acknowledgment of their equal status. At the very least, it cracked the tension. "I wish," he started before his voice trailed off. Another surge of emotion came, like a wave but rather than a complex mix of feelings, Obi-Wan sensed . . .

Was that regret?

"I wish Master Qui-Gon could see us now."

Anakin often left Obi-Wan flustered, sometimes with his bravado, sometimes with his stubbornness, sometimes with the way that bravado and stubbornness always *pulled off* the impossible. But this came from sheer surprise.

Anakin barely mentioned Qui-Gon to Obi-Wan. How much did the slain Jedi Master occupy his thoughts?

"I'm sorry, Master, I shouldn't have—"

"He would be proud of you," Obi-Wan said, a pure sincerity in his voice. Qui-Gon, with such belief that Anakin was the Chosen One—whether or not that was true, it was hard to argue with Anakin's accomplishments. "His faith would be rewarded."

They sat in silence for several seconds, the only sound that of cutlery and plates from far across the dining hall, both of them now silent.

Finally, Anakin pushed things forward. As he always did. "I really should fly out to Cato Neimoidia. As backup. I don't trust Dooku. Or the Trade Federation. Or Neimoidians in general, for that matter."

"That's not within the parameters of the mission, unfortunately."

Anakin gave a quiet laugh, then shook his head. "Wait a minute. Are you telling me that Jedi Knights really do still follow all the rules? We thought that was something you told the Padawans to keep us in line."

"Indeed. In fact, I think you'll find that life as a Jedi Knight is much easier when you stick to the rules. Improvising tends to only invite trouble. Speaking of which—" Obi-Wan brightened, and suddenly he found himself trying to contain the urge to chuckle. "You should have a plan for tomorrow."

"What is this mystery assignment?"

"It is something far more challenging, far more emotionally taxing than a simple negotiation, but it is a rite of passage, something notched on the belt of every Jedi." Anakin's face crinkled in curiosity, and Obi-Wan knew he had his young companion exactly where he wanted him. "You must meet with the younglings and pass on your wisdom."

Anakin's laugh echoed through the nearly empty hall, enough that it caught the attention of the group of Padawans in the far corner. "Okay, seriously, what's the assignment?"

"Anakin," Obi-Wan said, placing a hand on his shoulder. "I am being completely serious with you."

Anakin's eyes grew wide and he began to slowly shake his head. "No. You can't be."

"I'm afraid I am. And this can't just be about lightsaber techniques or physical manipulation of the Force. You must teach them the wisdom you've gathered on your journey from Padawan to the trials. And—" Obi-Wan bit his lip to hold in his laughter. "—you must answer their questions. All of them."

CHAPTER 10

RUUG QUARNOM

NO MATTER HOW MUCH SHE showered, Ruug felt the accumulated grime of recent days cling to her body, a stench of decay that refused to let go. Hours of inhaling fumes, getting caked in soot and debris, or desperately hoping that some life remained in yet another uncovered body all made for an endless toil that left a thick film on both her body and mind.

She'd washed, the guard station in Zarra's capital complex offering facilities just as ornate as the governmental offices. Yet despite cleaning up, along with a complete change of clothes and a decontamination of her custom armor, her body felt raw, as if the mists of the surface had burned skin away and exposed every nerve.

She walked across the top-floor hallway by herself, a case in each hand: one for the pieces and modules of her rifle and one for the segments of her custom armor. Ruug always took these back to her quarters, not for safety purposes—every member of the Neimoidian Royal Guard had a secure locker for equipment—but because without them, she simply felt incomplete.

Around the corner, an open balcony allowed Cato Neimoidia's breeze to sting her face. She turned, taking a moment, and though her view of the cityscape was high enough that she could see the trailing plumes of smoke from Cadesura, the flashes immediately below her drew her attention.

One story down sat a flat courtyard, a simple outdoor facility for security-force training. And in the middle of it knelt Ketar, rifle propped against his shoulder. He fired, muted yellow bursts of training bolts zipping across the space toward training battle droids. The bolts absorbed into their light shields, though each droid deactivated upon impact—all except the last, which started marching faster.

"*Vatstu,*" Ketar cursed loud enough to echo into the air, then he stood and approached the remaining droid, rifle up. One shot rang out, then another, then a third, each directly hitting the battle droid. Its body went limp, arms hanging down. "*Vatstu!*" Ketar let out again, though this time it clearly didn't have to do with any accuracy. Another flurry of bolts flew into the droid, but with its shields deactivated, the training rounds burned dark patches on the droid's outer shell.

He fired again and again, the impact knocking that single droid over. Rather than stand down or reload, Ketar flipped the rifle over and started to smash the droid's head with its stock. Chips of alloy broke off, splintering in different directions until Ketar fell onto both knees from frustration or exhaustion or both.

Ruug understood. She'd been around death and destruction a long, long time and even still, nothing had come close to Cadesura. She dropped her two cases over the ledge, then leapt over herself, twisting to land in a roll that safely carried her momentum forward.

The noise caught Ketar's attention, and the young guard looked up.

"You know, I can teach you to vault like that," Ruug said, neatly stacking her cases on top of each other before approaching her partner. "Might be a better use of your time than target practice." She pointed at the now-headless battle droid collapsed beside them. "I think you win."

"It's not target practice," Ketar said, almost too soft for her to hear.

"Yeah," she said, planting herself next to him. "I get it. Sometimes you just gotta blast a droid." She picked up twisted pieces from the battle droid's smashed head. "Or beat the poodoo out of it."

Ketar reached down toward the mess of servos and wiring sticking out of the droid's neck, though he stared off at the mists above the buildings. "I just can't understand it all."

"Hey," Ruug said, one hand on his shoulder. "You don't have to. That's not your job."

"How can you not try to, though?" The rifle fell to the textured training surface, and long green fingers pressed against his closed eyes. "How can anyone justify this?"

Those questions demanded answers. Questions without sense, answers without logic. Questions with *no* answers. They came for everyone who engaged with war for the first time.

Even for someone who'd felt her own compassion broken apart and rebuilt so many times, Cadesura made Ruug interrogate what little faith she had left. Except right now, she couldn't let Ketar see her own fragility.

"Our job is to help people. You did that today." Ruug squeezed his shoulder, yet Ketar remained motionless, face in hands. She debated going into soldier mode: *On your feet! Treat your weapon with respect!* But a catastrophe of this size meant that every single person in the capital, on the planet, perhaps even in the sector processed it differently.

Ruug chose the only thing they could do at a time like this. "Cato Neimoidia is counting on us," she said in a quiet but steady voice.

Though it took several seconds, that sentiment seemed to worm its way in, at least enough for Ketar to meet her face-to-face again, emotions intensifying the color and cracked pupil lines of his eyes. Ruug stood, then held a single hand out, and while she waited, she listened to the sounds of other people walking around the government complex, of speeders flying to and from landing platforms, of the planet's intense winds swirling around them.

And when he was ready, Ketar took her hand. Ruug pulled just enough to boost him up, and though the young man stood taller than she, he seemed as tiny as a newly born Neimoidian in grub form.

"You should get some rest," Ruug said. "We have a lot to do tomorrow. People to help."

"Yeah," Ketar said, face pulled downward. He bent over and picked up the fallen rifle, then slung the strap back over his shoulder.

"I mean it. Get some rest." Ketar grunted an affirmative, though by the time Ruug got to her equipment cases, the training droids had powered back up again. Halfway out, she turned to see him returning to an attack posture, the stock of his rifle against his shoulder while bolts launched just off target. She considered telling him that he should adjust the stock a few centimeters lower for better stability, but chose not to.

Instead, she left him to burn off his frustrations as she considered her own, armor in one hand and rifle in the other.

CHAPTER 11

OBI-WAN KENOBI

THE LAST TIME ANAKIN WALKED with Obi-Wan to a transport, they had been Master and apprentice. Today, though, Anakin seemed like a parent giving their youngling advice before heading to camp for the first time, except this lecture was about Neimoidian culture. Clearly he'd spent the evening either at the Jedi Archives or talking to someone who knew just as much about intragalactic relations as Dex. Both options offered a way to avoid thinking about the actual speech he had to deliver to younglings, so perhaps it was a strategic choice.

As they approached the landing platform, Anakin's tone took a marked shift. He'd been so focused on details about things like "the ruling class only represents a small percentage of a society's culture" and "conflict often comes from a failure to listen" that his sudden demeanor change once they got within view of the transport to the shuttle proved surprising.

"That thing?" Anakin asked with a completely different tone. He stopped to point at the small craft at the end of the walkway; it wasn't the worst thing Obi-Wan could fly—the transport had probably been in service for about a decade, perhaps during Chancellor Valorum's term.

And it had been well cared for, meeting Republic standards for service and maintenance.

But it was a far cry from a sleek and combat-ready Jedi starfighter. Obi-Wan detested flying as it was, but at least Jedi starfighters were maneuverable enough to feel like an extension of one's own body. This ship might not even outrun a maintenance droid.

"To comply with Dooku's requests. No Republic Cruisers within the vicinity. No starfighters with attack capabilities. Just," Obi-Wan said, "getting me from point A to point B."

Anakin shook his head as they resumed their walk. Behind them, a small astromech droid lugged a crate of basic supplies, not just for essential hygiene but also for investigation. "I should be there with you."

"Now, now. Perhaps it will be simple this time."

"Simple? With the Trade Federation? With Dooku likely hiding nearby? With *Neimoidians*?"

"Yes, but, Anakin, you're forgetting one key point."

"What's that?" he asked, his brow furrowed, likely wondering if there was something from his earlier details that he'd missed.

"Whenever it's us, things get complicated. That time with Shaak Ti on Naran-Shiv. That nest of gundarks." Obi-Wan laughed. "*Geonosis.* Maybe the trick is to separate us and things will go smoothly. For once."

"For once," Anakin repeated, his tone lighter but still carrying the weight of the mission with it.

"Anakin." Obi-Wan let out a quick sigh. "We will have to learn how to handle things on our own. This will be a change for both of us."

"You're just upset because you can't have me do the flying."

"That may be." They'd reached the shuttle by now, at least enough that the droid pulled away from them. It maneuvered around them silently, tugging the floating supply crate to the cargo door. "Even still, you have the harder task." They both stopped, the whir of droid servos filling the space as a specialized inventory arm lifted Obi-Wan's gear into the hold. Around them, clones walked in groups to the larger transports, shouts of "yes sir!" mixed in with random jabs about "clankers" and "scrap." Across the way, Obi-Wan spied Quinlan Vos shrugging off assistance from a droid as he packed spare parts into his own Jedi starfighter for launch. Vos noticed, tossing his long hair back before shooting over a wink and closing the craft's equipment hatch. "I don't envy you. Talking to younglings. I'm just off to stop a war."

"I've been studying the Neimoidians," Anakin blurted out despite Obi-Wan's effort to keep things light.

"Clearly."

"There are more details to understand. I should send you holos on negotiating with them."

Pushing boundaries to get his way certainly fit into Anakin's usual approach, but it wasn't like him to do something so . . . academic. This strange appreciation of nuance and methodical details was quite the opposite of his usual preferred approach of aggressive negotiations. Sometimes Obi-Wan had wondered if Anakin purposefully slacked on political studies just to goad the opposition into making the first move so his lightsaber could do the talking.

The other point of view was that this change represented a compliment. Perhaps his former apprentice *did* learn something about the art of negotiation during all their time together.

Obi-Wan chose to go with that, quelling the still-reflexive instinct to snap at Anakin about knowing his place.

Equals, he reminded himself. He was no longer responsible for molding Anakin; that was the galaxy's job now.

"No transmissions. Besides, once I reach Cato Neimoidia, my communications to the Republic will be jammed."

"Only through official means." The comment caused Obi-Wan to raise an eyebrow, and Anakin reached down to his belt. "Remember this?"

Coruscant's sun lit up Anakin from behind, causing Obi-Wan to take a second to squint at the small object in his hand. "Anakin . . ." he said with a sigh; of course he remembered that. A modified comlink, one of RazBohan's high-encryption long-range models, something Anakin tinkered with on the fly during a mission to Taris several months before Geonosis. Taris's nearby sector experienced a constant flood of ion storms to dampen communications, and the only way to boost the signal was sending them through layered data packets. Anakin's engineering proved successful, the result being an inherent encryption for a powerful and secure comlink between the two.

"Look, this isn't breaking any rules. You've pledged to avoid any transmissions to the Council. I'm not on the Council," Anakin said with a shrug. "And you're not supposed to contact Coruscant. I won't be on Coruscant, either, I'm off to oversee medical supplies on Langston. As far as the Trade Federation knows, this could simply be your means of watching, I don't know, the final race of the Fire Mountain Rally in a few days. Tom-Torre's attempting a sweep of the regional circuit and—"

"Anakin, how much sport did you actually watch as a Padawan?"

"Enough to know how to switch the refectory feeds," Anakin said with a knowing grin. "I'm just saying, easy excuses for having a comlink."

Obi-Wan supposed he shouldn't have been surprised, and though he'd never say it, he hoped all those unauthorized viewings of the galaxy's biggest races gave some comfort during Anakin's hardest years. "I'll keep that in mind."

"But—" Anakin pulled out another object, this one a shiny black case. "—with this you won't have to worry. This case will keep it safe and hidden. It's made from a partial phrik alloy. Might even be tough enough to withstand a lightsaber."

"You didn't test it?" The docking bay's light reflected off the case's smooth surface, the dark lines of phrik mixed in with something that probably wasn't quite as expensive.

"I've only got one of them. Hold up your thumb."

"Where did you get this?" Obi-Wan asked, shaking his head but doing as he was told. The device beeped several seconds after encoding his biometrics.

"I have a friend who excels at stealth." Anakin popped the comlink into the case, then touched the side, prompting the case's lid to slide over the comlink. Obi-Wan looked over and around the case as Anakin held it up; it sealed so tightly that it appeared seamless. "See? Now no one will be able to tell what it is."

Obi-Wan took the thin case, which was a little heavier than it looked.

But it could easily stow away among his personal belongings, perhaps even attach to a piece of his equipment as a disguise.

Anakin held up the counterpart comlink, a similarly thin device. "Just for emergencies. I promise I won't call you or track you. You'll follow all their rules." Such a small object for such a large safety net. And he was right—it did technically follow all the rules, and Obi-Wan could choose to ignore the comlink's existence if he wanted to. There was a certain pragmatism to having options, especially if Anakin kept his word on *not* checking up on him.

"All right," Obi-Wan said, putting it in his belt pouch. "But *no* communications from you. I will call you if I need something."

"Hey," Anakin said, palms up for emphasis, "you know me."

Several months ago, those few words might have come with resentment or defiance. But here, a cheekiness came through, and the look in Anakin's eye lacked the usual judgment of the past, and instead arrived with a hint of amusement.

What would life be *without* constantly fighting with Anakin?

Obi-Wan smiled to himself. It would certainly have fewer headaches. "I should go." They stood, eyes locked as a gunship ignited its engines, its rumble loud enough to pause their conversation before it floated off to join its battalion. "Goodbye, my young appren—" He stopped himself before saying *apprentice*. Behind him, the droid beeped to signal that his things were loaded. "Goodbye, my young friend. May the Force be with you." He checked his pouch again to confirm that Anakin's encrypted communicator was safe, then turned to take his leave.

CHAPTER 12

ANAKIN SKYWALKER

ANAKIN WAVED AT HIS FORMER Master, but Obi-Wan appeared to be too focused to see it.

The shuttle hummed as its systems came to life, then the docking bay rumbled with the groan and churn of engines activating, all louder and lower than the Republic's battle-ready craft. The shuttle *was* older, its liftoff process nothing like the smooth jump-in-and-go of the latest Jedi starfighters. Instead, this shuttle—a transport probably built to hold five people and some supplies, tops—growled on the same level as larger troop transports. In the small cockpit window, Obi-Wan sat, his posture straight and both hands on the yoke.

The ship hovered, lifting a good thirty meters off the landing pad before rotating and zooming into the sky, its distinctive *chug-chug-chug* sound gradually disappearing and blending into the never-ending din of Coruscant. Anakin held up his comlink and considered pressing the top button to open the channel, a way to both needle Obi-Wan and verify that it worked. But he put it away, having tested it last night with Padmé in the security of her apartment.

In fact, last night was all about the mission. It wasn't supposed to be—they'd planned on a quiet night in, simply enjoying the fact that they were in the same place at the same time for another night. But Padmé had been in full senatorial mode, and despite Anakin's best attempts to distract her with physical temptations, the bulk of the evening involved understanding the nuances with Neimoidians: as a culture, with the local Cato Neimoidian government, and with the Trade Federation as a larger entity.

Padmé's inability to turn it *off* was something that had already made their early marriage rocky at times, the process of integrating two wholly separate lives and personalities turning out to be a little more surprising than he'd expected, even when they'd isolated themselves on Naboo following the wedding. But he'd complied with her research requests, loading up various articles and texts while she made notes, making him commit key points to memory to pass on to Obi-Wan this morning.

Then they indulged themselves.

Anakin picked joyriding through Coruscant's lower levels. Padmé picked saving the galaxy through diplomacy. It seemed fitting, though perhaps tonight they might hit a happy medium.

Across the way, Anakin saw a pile of junked gunship engine pieces, a stack of them waiting as spare parts or perhaps for scrapping. Maybe a clone technician just forgot them. But he reached out, his mechanical arm up, fingers lightly spread. The very top piston trembled before lifting straight up, and Anakin swept his arm left, then right, then up again before settling it down.

And while the object obeyed his command, it still lagged in both response and precision, like a starfighter's controls with slightly loose wiring. The Force flowed through his body, and this arm was part of his body, synthetic or not. But it still didn't *feel* quite right.

"Can I help you with something, General?" a clone asked. *General*— that still didn't make sense to him given the separation between Jedi and the Grand Army of the Republic. He'd passed trials to become a Jedi Knight, not a military leader. But he figured this was a clone commander: an individual, but still working within the parameters built into his body and mind.

Whether they had the ability to move beyond that, time would tell. Though for now, he found them remarkably *human,* in a good way.

"No," Anakin said, "just here to wish a friend well on his mission."

"Understood." The clone turned around and joined the group lining up at a far transport, all of them identical in their size, voice, and armor except for distinguishing color trim.

Anakin looked back up to the sky that enveloped Obi-Wan, other shuttles and ships coming and going while a few light cruisers hovered low enough to be seen. Then he turned around and headed for the exit. He had younglings to deal with and wisdom to pass on, whatever that meant.

And then one final night with Padmé. Hopefully without politics or war.

Just husband and wife.

CHAPTER 13

RUUG QUARNOM

MUCH OF THE PAST FEW days had been spent below the mist, Ruug and Ketar down on the surface doing everything from clearing rubble to stopping fires before they reached explosive gas lines to administering emergency medical aid. And though her long history as an operative involved murder both up close and from afar, nothing ever quite matched the sheer devastation of what she saw in the fallen Cadesura district.

But the Cato Neimoidian government still functioned, handling the usual business of the local municipality while coordinating with the Trade Federation—and on a public level, the continued posturing with both the Republic and the Separatists. That meant that standard guard shifts still happened, the pair swapping the chaos of the surface for the near-quiet of government hallways.

During that time, Ketar didn't heed any of Ruug's advice on tempering his emotions. Particularly now, when he accompanied his duty with long diatribes about the Republic's responsibility for the devastation, and how Nute Gunray's splinter faction made sense given the long history of prejudice in the Republic. Ruug's response was to let Ketar get it out of his system.

It just went on for so *long*.

"And the Republic," he said, his harsh whisper having grown into something much more audible, "the Republic does not respect any of our culture. Our people. My parents, they—"

"Ketar?" Ruug asked after what must have been several minutes of a continuous tirade.

They stood on opposite sides of the open doorway on simple guard duty, a lifetime away from the endless fires and debris far below, the intricately carved stone walls and exquisite ceiling murals of Zarra's capital complex a stark juxtaposition with the destruction still looping in Ruug's memory.

But here, at least Ketar's rants—which began to border on nonsensical—distracted her. Down the hall, government officials passed, probably out of earshot from their low conversation.

"Yeah?"

"Did you get any sleep last night?"

Ketar straightened, blinking as he adjusted his weight. He peered down the hallway as a Neimoidian and a Muun stopped their conversation and turned to observe.

"Right, right," he said, his voice returning to a volume more fitting for guards standing on duty.

"Well?"

"Well what?"

"Did you get any sleep last night? After those training droids?"

Ketar looked down at his boots, a quiet laugh soon growing into a chuckle. "No."

"You fought even more battle droids, didn't you?"

"Long into the night."

Of course he did. She supposed she should at least commend Ketar on constructively getting out his rage, though doing so clearly left him lacking the faculties of a well-rested, well-nourished Royal Guardsman of Cato Neimoidia.

"I hope you at least cleaned up after smashing any of them," Ruug said, light enough that a smile came with it.

Ketar laughed again, shaking his head—a gesture loaded with enough of an apology that Ruug decided to call it even. In fact, she laughed, too, once again distracting the pair attempting to have a discussion down the hall.

At least their shift ended soon. "No more practice droids tonight."

"Ruug, I want to make a difference," he said, his voice laced with both desperation and defiance.

"Okay, look." Her voice maintained a controlled whisper to *not* give away the fact that they were chatting instead of performing guard duty. "I'll take you down to the surface in the evening. We'll investigate what we can up close. But only if you get some rest after this shift. Go to your quarters, watch a holo. Have an agaric ale. Maybe both. That's an order."

"We're equal rank. Your orders don't count."

"That's an order from the rank of experience and age." And concern, for what it was worth. She shot him a raised brow, and his ensuing grin and nod showed that maybe she'd gotten through to her young friend.

Then a new voice entered the space from within the room they guarded.

". . . simply to ensure that everything the Republic does is trustworthy."

Ruug's history of missions and training had taught her to pick up all the details that identified a situation. Tone. Sounds. Environmental factors. Her mind worked in a constant scan, gathering information to know as much about the current situation as possible. That led to a running log of all of the Neimoidian officials and dignitaries in and about, both with typical Trade Federation business and with local handling of the disaster.

But this voice was unfamiliar, its oily speech already carrying a different kind of cadence. It was female, hardened and spiteful, a gravel to it despite the dignified words it used. "I am honored to support you during this difficult time," she said, the smallest changes in inflections activating Ruug's suspicions.

"We appreciate your presence," Minister Alluv Eyam said. "But we have assurances from the Republic that the Jedi is arriving alone. An unarmed shuttle, not a starfighter."

"A trick. The guise of diplomacy. The Jedi are known for such deceptions." Several meters away, Ruug saw Ketar tense up, his attention pulled from standard guard duties to this conversation. "Don't forget, Count Dooku used to be one of them. He understands their ways."

"Despite the tragedy of recent days, I personally have only had honest experiences with the Jedi."

"Then you are a *fool*," she said, the harshness of her words echoing throughout the room. The footsteps stopped, all of them hesitating. "The Jedi have convinced the entire galaxy of their righteousness. I see through them. Count Dooku sees through them. We will reveal the truth of what happened here. Tell me, Minister, does the Republic have a history of treating Neimoidians with dignity?"

"Well . . . it has been a journey to find the right balance."

"Your diplomacy serves you in your role. I hear you are the best orator in the Cato Neimoidian government. My role is to speak—and recognize—truth. And my job is to help you understand where you should focus your interests. The galaxy is listening, Minister. Now consider what you know of those running the Republic. Do they think your people to be greedy?"

"Well, *greedy* may be a—"

"Do they consider them to be cowards?"

"I don't see what—"

"Do they recognize your art? Your theaters, your music?" the woman asked, each question pushing further into the tone of demand. "Or has it all been swept away, lost in the noise of their propaganda? How much could the Republic actually respect the Trade Federation if their only official interaction is a single consulate office that is hardly used?"

With each passing second, Ruug saw Ketar react in subtle ways—fists tightening, boots shifting, an exhale of grief.

"It has been a challenge at times."

"A challenge. That is one way to look at it." The woman's voice carried a playful lilt, and if Ruug was able to see her, she was sure she'd spot a measure of a grin. "Tell me, who is this emissary of the Jedi?"

"Master Obi-Wan Kenobi of the Jedi Council."

Ruug held up her guard rifle, sliding her hand down to the composite grip to let the light from the inner chamber reflect off the short stub of chromium around the muzzle. She twisted it slightly, then looked at the reflection. There was Alluv Eyam, minister of defense for the planet. And Feldus Spar, another local official, one who had been overseeing relief resources.

And this new person. Pale skin, a lithe frame, no hair on her head, but cruel lines that appeared to be tattoos framing her mouth and temples. She walked, and under a long cloak, the bottom of her dark skirt swayed out in a way that seemed more functional than decorative.

"I look forward to meeting this . . ." She paused, then looked out at the doorway where Ruug and Ketar stood, as if her eyes connected with Ruug's through the exact angle of the reflection. ". . . Obi-Wan Kenobi." The woman's gaze lingered for several seconds, then she broke off from the group, marching directly toward their guard post. "I have overheard someone here expressing frustration with the Republic," she said as she broke the threshold. She walked a meter out into the hallway, then turned, Eyam and Spar moving to catch up to her.

The weight of the woman's look brought a pressure to Ruug's senses, and she felt immediately that something about the situation was off. Had this person been here on some order of standard governmental business—a diplomat from the Separatists, a visitor from Trade Federation executives—everything would have carried a different air.

The woman's piercing stare told a completely different story. Ruug had met people like her before, people who tried to intimidate with their presence alone.

Whatever her game, whatever her intentions, Ruug wasn't having any of it. "Guards aren't supposed to engage with passersby during our duty," she said quickly, meeting the woman's unblinking stare. "It's disruptive."

The side of the woman's lips tipped upward before she made a snap turn, then looked at Ketar. "I appreciate the hard work of loyal guards. My apologies for getting in the way of your tasks. If, however, anyone wishes to discuss the previous transgressions of the Republic . . ." She let her words trail off before stepping back toward the Neimoidian officials.

Ruug turned to Ketar, who stared straight ahead, but something behind his eyes had changed. "I offer a sympathetic ear. And I will be easy to find."

Ruug watched as the woman and the officials walked away, silently cursing them as they departed.

CHAPTER 14

OBI-WAN KENOBI

OBI-WAN HATED FLYING, BUT THIS didn't even really count as flying. Rather than the smooth controls and quick responses of a Jedi starfighter, this shuttle—something so dated that he didn't even know the make and model of it—felt more like nudging a floating box. When he turned the yoke, the shuttle responded a second late; when he boosted the throttle, it accelerated so gradually that no g-forces hit him.

But at least the chairs were comfortable. That was one thing it had over Jedi starfighters, with their cramped cockpits. Given the front compartment's roomy nature, he'd even brought his storage crate up to the front and examined the various tools to help his investigation, things to detect chemical compositions, examine blast points, compare the Republic's simulation with up-close evidence.

And of course, Anakin's case. He held it up, the smooth dark material gleaming under the colored status lights of the shuttle's interior. Would it really take a lightsaber to break through it? It was inconspicuous enough, though, and Obi-Wan opted to adhere it to the bottom of the chemical scanner, something that should easily pass any visual inspection of his belongings.

The shuttle's comm screen blinked to indicate an incoming transmission. "Finally," Obi-Wan muttered to himself before hitting a button. Dex's scowl appeared on his screen, the bang and clatter of the kitchen behind him. "You have good timing, Dex. I'm just about to land."

"Well, you have bad timing. You called during the dinner rush. War is good for the restaurant business, at least on Coruscant. But I have your information. Which isn't much other than to say that there hasn't been a lot of chatter about Cato Neimoidia lately."

"Nothing?"

"Whole system has been clear of bounty hunter activity for a few weeks now. Same with spicerunners. Same with"—Dex laughed—"less savory types."

"So this is a purely political situation," Obi-Wan said with a sigh. "Well, we'll see if negotiations can create a peaceful end to this war."

Further shouts from Wanda came over the audio. Dex glanced over with an annoyed grimace, then turned back to the comm in his small back office. "It might work. Which is better than *It won't work*."

"Thanks, Dex, you're very reassuring."

"Oh, have you seen today's big HoloNet news?"

"No," Obi-Wan said, dread creeping into his thoughts. "I've been focused on mission prep."

"Lemme forward it." Dex reached in and around the cam's view, various beeps and clicks happening. "There you are. Do you see?"

On screen appeared Satine Kryze of Mandalore. She stood in front of the cam, making a speech from what appeared to be a balcony in the Mandalorian capital of Sundari. Despite her animated discussion and grand gestures, the audio didn't come through, with the news anchor speaking over the images instead. "Is Mandalore's proclamation of neutrality a truly political middle ground? Or is Satine Kryze's recent speech part of a secret bid to aid the Separatist movement? We discuss with our expert panel of analysts, next on *HoloNet News Tonight*." Obi-Wan tuned out the talking head, though the caption stood out clearly enough.

MANDALORIAN DUCHESS DEFIES REPUBLIC IN ONGOING WAR.

"I see it," Obi-Wan said softly.

"She's recruiting systems to push for neutrality. It's not going to help things."

Obi-Wan had kept tabs on the duchess as anyone would an old friend, but especially one who rose to power in a political situation as volatile as Mandalore's. Yet most of those updates came in the form of reading summaries of speeches and governmental actions. He rarely saw Satine's face before his eyes, and doing so triggered a wave of emotions he recognized, the urge to dream of a different life, a different galaxy.

But as he always did, he let the thought flutter away, evaporating before ever taking root. Still, he found himself shaking his head, long enough that Dex must have noticed, even with the shuttle's dated comm system. "This is different. Mandalore's entire history has been based on warfare. Getting involved would undo all of the duchess's work to create a new future for her people."

"I sense a little bias here. You're telling me that you wouldn't prefer Mandalore to be on your side for this?" Dex cleared his throat. "Or think about it this way. What if—"

"I don't have time for theoreticals, Dex."

"One question, old buddy: How bad would it be if Mandalore joined the Separatists?"

Obi-Wan looked at the shuttle's computer. Its estimated remaining travel time to get into orbital range was twenty-three standard minutes. "That's not a concern right now," he said. "And we'll address it when it happens. I should go, Dex. I have landing preparations to make."

"And I have dinners to cook. Don't get yourself into any trouble, Obi-Wan. Wanda can't fly out there to help you."

"Well, then I'll just have to have a cup of Jawa Juice with her when I get back."

"I'll tell her that. See you when you return, old buddy." Dex nodded and waved his top left hand, then the screen blinked off, resuming a display of fuel and speed details.

Obi-Wan wanted to meditate—wanted a clear and level head to prepare for the formalities and negotiations ahead. But based on the flight time remaining, he allotted himself a few minutes to consider Dex's thought experiment.

What if Mandalore came to the Republic's aid? And Obi-Wan had to work with Satine?

Would that be a greater challenge than Mandalore pledging itself to Dooku?

Obi-Wan let thoughts flow through him, dwelling on them enough to process but without ever stewing on them. Though when he considered what might happen if, of all people, *Anakin* stumbled upon his history with Satine, he found himself smirking.

And he allowed himself to hold on to the briefest moment of amusement.

CHAPTER 15

ANAKIN SKYWALKER

A VACUUM IN THE FORCE.

Anakin had felt this in recent weeks, random pockets throughout the Jedi Temple—and *only* the Jedi Temple—where the Force cut off for a mere instant, like those rare occasions when a patch of air stood perfectly still despite being surrounded by an outdoor breeze.

Those pockets were fleeting, tickling his senses long enough to get his attention before dissipating into the flow of the Force. It had emerged more in the recent weeks, and he'd figured it simply had to do with the turmoil they *all* felt at the outbreak of the war.

So it was quite strange to feel it here, of all places: a small training room in the Temple, a place mostly used for Padawans and Initiates.

He'd arrived a few minutes early, mentally prepping for the challenge of speaking to younglings. And as he walked in, another group bounded out, younglings across all ages, from ones whose legs stumbled over each other to an older Zabrak girl. They all passed, though Anakin found himself reaching into the Force, trying to make sense of the odd sensation. It echoed a long-lost feeling in *himself,* touching on something from his own early years when an overwhelming loneliness drove a fury that nearly wedged between him and the Force itself.

"Master Skywalker!" one of the younglings shouted, interrupting his contemplation. And then another, and then another, and suddenly he faced a pressure quite unlike anything, his focus returning to the present.

The younglings were listening.

In fact, their attention seemed so rapt that it only increased the pressure on Anakin to say something brilliant. He'd been able to recall and recite all of the details Padmé impressed upon him, informing Obi-Wan about things like Trade Federation governmental structure, Neimoidian cultural quirks, and how to say "hello" in Pak Pak. And yet his memory fizzled while trying to speak in front of younglings, the speech he'd prepared completely blanking on him.

This turned out to be *much* more difficult than all the other times he'd been assigned to teach younglings—explaining piloting safety, showing basic lightsaber forms during a training session, even escorting Jedi Initiates to Ilum for the Gathering. Those were all physical tasks, establishing the basics of Jedi training and culture.

But this was . . . personal. And complicated.

"What I learned on the way to becoming a Jedi Knight," Anakin started, visualizing the speech he'd written on a datapad. All of the powers available through the Force—physical miracles, sensory impossibilities, mental alterations—and yet none of those gave him the snap recall for this presentation.

He really should have brought that datapad instead of attempting to improvise.

Ten younglings in front of him, all eyes trained on him regardless of age or species. "Sorry. Let me start again," he said with a half smile. "What I learned on the way to becoming a Jedi Knight. Humility. Trust. Focus. All of the tenets of the Jedi Order. But most of all, I learned about myself."

"Master?"

"Yes, youngling," Anakin said, pointing at Cath Erangris, the young Mon Calamari girl with a thick white hand up.

"What's hum-all-tee?" she asked in a squeaky voice.

"No, it's 'humility.'"

"That's what I said. Hum-all-tee."

"Wait, wait, wait," he said, palms out. Anakin managed to stifle his frustration, a reminder to himself that he was supposed to be some sort of *role model* here. Of course, Obi-Wan would have laughed at the idea of him trying to explain humility. "Humility is when you don't think you know everything. I mean, when you know you should ask for help. As in, there's no . . ." His lips pursed, and he tried to *not* allow his exasperation to overtake him.

"Can we see your lightsaber?"

"Oh! What color is your lightsaber?"

"I bet it's green."

"Shhh! You're supposed to be listening!"

"No, it's blue."

Anakin stepped back as the younglings spiraled out of control, their discussion turning into a competition about who had watched more holos of Mace Windu showing training moves with his purple lightsaber.

"Whoa. Hey. Younglings?" Their collective chatter grew louder and louder, and each time Anakin called for their attention, they stirred themselves into their own conversations, like he didn't exist. He sighed, head in hands, and was just thankful that neither Obi-Wan nor Padmé was around to see this. The younglings eventually settled on their own, and once a dip occurred in their volume, he seized the moment. "Younglings . . . look, let's save the questions for the end, okay?"

Some of them snapped back to attention, the younger ones lost in their own world. "What I learned on the way to becoming a Jedi Knight," he started again. "Humility. Trust. Focus. All of the tenets—"

One of the younglings yawned, throwing Anakin off.

Several seconds passed, most eyes locked on him, and in return Anakin bounced between each of their gazes. Anything he'd planned was completely gone, and instead he was left with a roomful of younglings and zero words of wisdom to pass along.

He'd have to figure out a way. But really, this was what he excelled at on the battlefield. Surely he could handle a speech to younglings. "I would say, it's not what I learned. It's *who* I learned it from. Across my entire life. When I was young, I had a friend on Tatooine, his name was

Kitster." Anakin paused, thinking of the young boy with shaggy black hair and a confident grin, the endless pranks that he'd either played on Anakin or convinced Anakin to partake in; he took a moment, sending a wish into the Force that Kitster made it off Tatooine as well. "He helped me find joy during a difficult upbringing, showed me that we could find something worthwhile in even the barest of sand dunes. My mother." He paused, the echoes of that night on Tatooine still fresh, and Anakin looked over at some passersby to hide his expression. "She taught me compassion. She taught me to fix things. She encouraged me to be curious, to want more, to find a way even when the Republic's laws weren't there for her." His memories turned, not to the violent bloody final moments in the huts of Tusken Raiders, but tucked in bed, the sun-dragon myth once again playing in his mind. "Heart. She was all heart, and she wanted me to feel that way as well, to believe in my heart.

"My Master, Obi-Wan Kenobi."

"He's on the Council," one youngling said.

"That's right. He's helping out for now." Anakin left it at that, given that even *he* didn't fully understand who was rotating in or for how long during the recent chaos. "Duty. Honesty. Hard work. He was a great example of that. See, this is the thing—every single person you encounter in your life, you can learn from them. Even if you only see them from time to time. My friend Representative Binks. You know Representative Binks from Naboo?"

Several of the children nodded. "He walks funny," one youngling said.

"He taught me loyalty. And to never judge people. You say he walks funny. But to him, that's just how Gungans walk. As a Jedi, you'll encounter many different people—during your training, during your missions. Politicians, locals." A smile formed on his face, something that might have given him away in other circumstances. "Royalty. Some of them you'll see again and again, and other times, your paths will only cross for the briefest of moments. But you can learn from every one of those encounters. Because every being in the galaxy has something to offer. Sometimes—" He sucked in a breath. "—it just takes a little bit of patience to find it."

The room sat quiet, the silence of children waiting for more. One youngling, a Chalhuddan with horns just beginning to sprout, slowly raised their hand. "Master?"

"Yes."

"That's a lot to remember," they said.

"It is," he said, and his laugh was contagious enough to cause the others to join in. "If you can't remember any of that, try this. I had a friend once, his name was Qui-Gon Jinn. You may hear about him from time to time. He was a great, wise man. He *cared*. And he questioned. He once told me, right before one of the biggest moments of my life, to 'feel, don't think. Trust your instincts.'" Anakin felt the weight of observation behind him, and he turned to see Mace Windu taking a quick peek before moving forward, a familiar scowl on his face. "Sometimes, things like that, you might already know it. But it helps to have someone you trust give you *permission*. Understand?"

A collective "mmm-hmmm" came across the younglings, and relief washed over Anakin. His original speech would have gone on three or four times longer than his impromptu list of people who'd shifted his life's direction. And yet this seemed like enough.

Still, he had time to fill. "All right," he said, arms out, "let's try questions again—*one* question at a time." All the younglings raised their hands. "Please?"

Thirty minutes—and some cheap acrobatic tricks—later, the younglings filed out one by one as the *long*-overdue Padawan arrived to gather the Initiates. Anakin gave a wave to each one, sometimes followed with a "bye" or a "thank you."

The last one exited, and Anakin looked at the chrono on the wall of the small training room—he still had to go to the chancellor's office for the rescheduled formal introduction of the latest Jedi Knights. Such a task barely blipped in his mind; many would have found meeting the ruler of the free galaxy to be a monumental occasion, but for Anakin, it would be a watered-down version of the occasional breakfasts or walks he'd had with his longtime friend. Did the others even realize that the chancellor had enjoyed casual conversations with him ever since he arrived on Coruscant?

If not, Anakin decided discretion seemed the smarter option. He received enough grief with rumors of "the Chosen One" spreading around, at a time when Padawan competitiveness came out in all kinds of passive-aggressive ways. It didn't matter, really; he knew his friendship with Palpatine was genuine.

Which meant that Palpatine wouldn't take offense when Anakin barely paid attention during the formalities. Because his mind would be elsewhere:

On the final night Padmé would be on Coruscant.

Instead of waiting for the ceremony later, Anakin let his mind indulge right then, wandering into a dream—not the dreams of sleep, when nightmares and visions often collided, but a waking moment when possibilities seemed endless.

When a night with Padmé wouldn't always be a fleeting moment slipping through their fingers. Anakin gave in to the indulgence of the moment, imagining a galaxy beyond that, where he could do everything he was meant to do *without* any of the restrictions of the Jedi Order. A simple freedom to exist, to do the things Anakin *and* Padmé excelled at, yet free from scrutiny or judgment or limitations that forced them into wearing disguises in Coruscant's underworld.

Perhaps someday it would be possible. Someday, they'd be able to see each other every day.

But for now, the reality of the situation was that they had one night. He blinked, returning to the moment. Now what would they do? Stealth remained critical for two people such as them, and there *was* the allure of staying in and letting things naturally unfold between them. But spending time out together was such a rare occurrence, something to possibly indulge in if they did indeed have the means and—

"Master?"

Anakin looked down, one of the younglings back to grab a small bag left behind. "Oh. Hello again. Um . . ." His mind raced for the most appropriate way to close this out as quickly as possible. "May the Force be with you."

"Okay. See you tomorrow."

"Right. Uh-huh." By the time the youngling crossed the threshold, her words registered. "Wait, what do you mean 'tomorrow'?"

"The mission. We're coming with you."

"Um, you must be mistaken," Anakin said, reminding himself to use a gentle tone and let the youngling down easily. "I'm off to Langston. We're delivering—"

"Medical supplies. I know. See you at the shuttle tomorrow."

The youngling turned on her heel, then sprinted off to catch up with her Padawan leader. Anakin took several steps forward past the doorway before stopping. The group of younglings disappeared down the long hallway, leaving Anakin to wonder if Obi-Wan was right:

Dealing with younglings was *much* harder than stopping a war.

CHAPTER 16

OBI-WAN KENOBI

DESPITE HIS VARIOUS DEALINGS WITH the Trade Federation over the last decade—including the toothless trials of Nute Gunray—this marked the first time that Obi-Wan stepped onto Cato Neimoidia's soil.

Well, not exactly soil. That remained some distance below him, and instead Obi-Wan walked out of his shuttle's small loading ramp to a landing platform not unlike those on Coruscant: a long oval connected to a bridge that led into the city itself. On either side, further landing platforms of various sizes sat, from small spaces reserved for governmental use to a large port for commerce traffic, making this corner of Zarra more of a transportation hub than anything else. Despite the functional nature of the space, the surrounding structures represented the ornate aesthetic of Cato Neimoidia, a land bridge arc juxtaposed with rows of towers with intricate carvings up and down their walls.

At the oval's lip stood a group of Neimoidian leaders. He recognized Minister Eyam from the other day, though he wasn't sure if the others were local representatives of Cato Neimoidia or if they belonged to the greater Trade Federation contingent. However, two things were certain. First, Senator Lott Dod had kept his word and stayed out of it, which made it more likely these were local officials.

Second, standing behind them was someone new, someone who didn't seem to fit the picture. He angled his view, moving slightly to avoid drawing attention to his scouting efforts. Certain details clearly stood out, from her pale skin to the intensity of her glare. She waited in a familiar pose, one that Anakin often adopted as his default stance: legs apart, arms behind the back. But here, the mystery woman clearly held a constant scowl on her face despite the hood over her head, her focus tracking Obi-Wan from the moment he emerged.

"Master Kenobi. Welcome, emissary," Eyam said. "I'm pleased to make your acquaintance in person." The sleeve of his long purple robe draped off his outstretched arm as he spoke. High winds kicked up, flapping the sleeve and blowing the tails of his outfit, though his ceremonial headdress remained in place.

"*L'a heeting*," Obi-Wan said with a slight bow, greeting the Neimoidians with their native Pak Pak as a sign of respect. "The Republic sends its sympathies and condolences. The tragedy of your people has captured the hearts and minds of many in the Republic, and we will do everything we can to discover the true culprit behind this attack." A G2 droid scooted by, then beeped a request for permission to go aboard his craft. "That's fine." He gestured inside, then waited for the droid to come out carrying his crate of supplies. "I travel light. But I think you will find that I have nothing to hide."

"Shall I do the inspection?" the woman asked, finally stepping forward. She pulled the hood off to reveal a hairless head, and her limbs remained obscured by her long cloak.

"Whomever you prefer." Obi-Wan leaned over and pressed the latch to unlock the lid.

She brushed past the Neimoidian dignitaries, her shoulder pushing into theirs; Obi-Wan took the opportunity to give her another look and confirm his suspicion.

Republic forces *had* seen her before, identified only as an authority within the Separatist army—a leader of some sort to be sure, though different from the recent emergence of General Grievous and unlike any other military commander they'd encountered. Her background, her skills, even her name required further digging, and now the unlikely bonus of this Cato Neimoidia investigation enabled Obi-Wan to see who she was—and how much of a threat she might be.

The woman walked past him without a word, then knelt down to look at the open crate and reached inside. "Republic credit chips," she said, holding up the small stack of emergency currency. "The minister will provide you with all of your accommodations. You have no need for currency here, so the local government will safely bank this for you. You will, of course, receive it back with accumulated interest when you leave."

"I appreciate the favor."

She dug further and removed each item, giving a visual inspection before setting it back inside. Obi-Wan watched, his own awareness keeping his heart rate and breathing steady while he waited for the inspection to pass. She reached the final item, the chemical scanner with the comlink secretly attached to it.

"This is interesting," the woman said. She stood up, her cloak flowing back down to rest, and she presented the device in front of the gathered Neimoidians. "I've never seen such elaborate plating on a scanning device."

"It was custom. A gift from a friend. Consider it," Obi-Wan said, "a bit of a lucky charm."

She tapped a finger against the underside where the alloy case attached before coming back to Obi-Wan, holding it up as they met face-to-face. "It's very pretty. I didn't know Jedi cared for such flamboyant things."

"Sentimental value."

"A sentimental Jedi." The woman smiled, the harsh lines of her tattooed face bending in unnatural ways. "I think we'll be friends."

"Perhaps you can have it when I'm done with my investigation."

"It would be a lovely accessory. And look, it's even my color." She put the device back into the crate, then clamped the lid shut. "The Jedi is clean," she announced, her long cloak whipping out to reveal a hint of a skirt underneath as she turned on her heel.

"Come, emissary," said Minister Eyam. "We will send your belongings to your quarters. This shuttle"—he gestured to a small transport craft on a connected smaller platform, one likely used for city-to-city vehicles—"will take us to the disaster area."

They walked in silence, though Obi-Wan noticed the mystery woman matched his exact pace stride for stride. "I'm sorry," Obi-Wan said, "I didn't catch your name."

"Ventress," she said. "Asajj Ventress. A pleasure to finally meet a Jedi. Count Dooku speaks so highly of your Order."

They started with the formalities—a basic tour of the government offices and the most notable landmarks of Zarra: the brightly lit mix of business and artistry, from the hanging towers below the capital's biggest stone archway to the open-air Grand Theatre of Judgment where trials and debates took place. The cityscape looked truly gilded from the air, designs and architecture unique to the culture and unlike anything else Obi-Wan had seen in his journeys across the Republic—elegant and sophisticated in ways far different than, say, Naboo, while still taking advantage of the planet's unique natural wonders, structures jutting out in directions simply impossible elsewhere. The tour itself was short-lived, and soon they soared through the rolling fog of Cato Neimoidia, a long descent that revealed just how high up the rocky spires of this world were. Though he had watched holos showcasing the topography of the planet, none of it did justice to the overwhelming girth—no wonder they had the ability to anchor entire cities.

"It's quite majestic, isn't it? Have you ever seen anything like it?" Obi-Wan said, a strategic question to goad the mysterious Ventress into revealing more about herself.

"Not in person."

"I have not either. I've traveled to planets with all forms of environmental oddities but nothing quite like this."

She shook her head with a breath, then straightened up. "Let's dispense with the pleasantries. You wish to ask me something, Kenobi?"

Her direct line of questioning caught Obi-Wan's diplomatic sensibilities off guard. Perhaps that was by design, given her demeanor. "I'm trying to be polite." Obi-Wan tilted forward in his seat. Around them, the Neimoidians remained silent, though he was certain they listened. "Unless *you* feel you have something to hide. Something," Obi-Wan said, suddenly all of that experience strategically arguing with Anakin proving fruitful, "that makes you untrustworthy?"

Ventress's head tilted as she bit her bottom lip, a huff of amusement coming out just enough for Obi-Wan to hear. In fact, the other passengers may have missed it. "While my Master has great respect for your Order, he also understands that it is the political tool of the Republic. If you recall"—she gave a knowing nod—"that is one of the reasons he left it."

She referred to Dooku as "Master." Was that an intentional representation of hierarchy within the Separatist leadership? Or a slip revealing something further?

"Fair point."

"Because of that, he has sent me to oversee your investigation and interactions with the Neimoidians—" She sucked in a breath, holding it as if to tease him. "—to ensure that there is no evidence of corruption." Her eyes locked with his, a menacing leer that felt as much a dare as a threat.

Fortunately, Obi-Wan had dealt with worse. He did, after all, see Anakin through some very turbulent teenage years. "Well then," he responded with a tense calm, presenting an equally lengthy pause. Then his tone retreated, going back to the standard diplomat's voice as if he were simply talking to another politician on Coruscant. "I look forward to working with you," he added, putting his hand out to shake, "in good faith."

She looked at his outstretched hand, then back up to read his face. He responded in kind with a polite smile and waited without any movement, like an AI holo awaiting input before animating its canned response. "Likewise," she finally said, taking his hand.

The damage was worse than Obi-Wan had expected. They started with an aerial view, constantly circling as the Neimoidian inspector explained the disaster simulation they'd created to get a sense of how the entire structure fell: speed, angle, tilt, how fires from the initial explosions spread to other areas, the way those fires then weakened other structures prior to impact. And though Ventress presented a cold and unmoving front, he noticed that the air shifted around her when the inspector described the way bodies were flung out from the structure during its nosedive to the planet's surface—and, in very pragmatic terms, when he described the radius around the structure in which corpses had so far been recovered.

And that was just the first pass.

The closer they got, the more unsettling the visuals were, from the still-smoking fires to the imploded buildings, the crumbled remains of their gold plating reflecting the licks of flames. "By estimates, we have recovered about a third of the bodies so far."

"Were there any survivors?"

"Yes. Luck was on their side. Our analysis team wants to discuss their circumstances with them to see if they can identify a pattern, some type of safety parameter we can build into our infrastructure." He looked down, his green skin turning more ashen as his eyes closed. "But most of them refuse to talk about it."

"Look," Ventress said, interrupting the discussion. "Stop the shuttle."

The flight paused, hovering in midair. Ventress took out a scope, then stood by the cockpit. "There it is," she said. "Come here, Kenobi."

"What is it?" She handed over the scope and pointed at an angle off the flight path. Obi-Wan brought the scope to his eyes, the target area already highlighted in a bright-green box within the display. The scope zoomed in, its internal computer interpolating details about the damage so fast that Obi-Wan couldn't digest it all. But the visual highlight was enough. This clearly was the remains of a strut built to secure the city block between spires, a charred burst indicating the center of an explosion.

"The blast points," she said, and as if by design, five further green boxes lit up, each framing clear burn marks. "How many do you count?"

"Six." Six blast points, each precisely laid out with exact spacing and angles to one another, probably calculated by computer. The destruction on the shredded end of the massive strut blanketed over a lot of the finer evidence, but Obi-Wan had seen enough in his time—including his few weeks being around the clones—to understand that Ventress was right. And bounty hunters, pirates, mercenaries—while it remained possible that they could do something like this, the odds of that felt low, especially after Dex's report.

"Six blast points, distributed specifically to maximize damage given the load on the strut. I would consider this military precision. Wouldn't you?"

"Perhaps," Obi-Wan said, one eye on Eyam in the front of the craft. "Droids can be precise as well."

"That they can. Such an astute observation. I can see why they call you a Master." She turned to Eyam as well. "And this is just a single strut. Who knows what we'll find elsewhere?"

Though an exhale of frustration fought to come out, Obi-Wan caught it, and instead offered the scope to Ventress in a controlled gesture. "This certainly requires more investigation."

"Indeed." She took the scope back with a harsh tug that pulled on his fingers.

"If there are no objections," Eyam said, "I would like to land and show you the destruction on the surface level."

"Please do. It is imperative that I see the entire range of destruction before I start my investigation. I promise I will get to the bottom of this." The shuttle chair creaked as Obi-Wan shifted in his seat to look directly at Ventress. "Perhaps through mutual cooperation, we can find some common ground between our governments."

"Cooperation?" Ventress settled back into her chair, legs crossed and arms folded. Light from outside reflected in the shuttle's cramped quarters, and Obi-Wan caught a glint of metallic reflection by her hip before she adjusted her cloak. "Certainly. If you can win me over."

CHAPTER 17

ANAKIN SKYWALKER

CHANCELLOR PALPATINE PACED IN FRONT of the group of standing Jedi Knights, Anakin on the far end.

"You are our greatest hope and our guardians," he said, Coruscant's infinite stream of building lights visible behind him through the window spanning the length of his office. "Particularly now, the Republic needs you more than ever. Fighting a growing enemy is a challenge. Not just physically, but philosophically, morally. You represent the best chance for lasting peace throughout the galaxy. You are Jedi," Palpatine said, his voice taking on a grim sheen, as if the accumulated talking and tasks of the day wore him out, "Knights of the Republic."

The group gave mild, polite applause, a smattering of noise that barely rose above the sound of the ventilation. They each waited, the same group as yesterday save for Cyruss Okent, who had already been assigned to join a clone battalion fighting a sudden strike on Bracca, and Palpatine gestured out to the hallway. The short ceremony now concluded, the Jedi marched in pious single file, Palpatine receiving each one with a "Congratulations, and thank you for defending peace and justice."

Anakin was third from the end, and though he and the chancellor enjoyed a less formal relationship, a guise of etiquette felt necessary here. "Thank you, Chancellor," he said. "May the Force be with you."

"Master Skywalker. Please do wait a minute," Palpatine said, pausing the line. "I need to speak with you about Master Kenobi's mission to Cato Neimoidia."

"Yes, Chancellor," he said with a slight head bow, his voice as docile as a youngling acknowledging his teacher.

D'urban Wen-Hurd gave the final acknowledgment of the group before shuffling out. Both Palpatine and Anakin watched her leave, waiting for the double doors to slide shut and seal them in the room, alone.

"You are concerned about Obi-Wan?" Anakin said as Palpatine walked over to the small tray of refreshments delivered for the brief meeting. Outside the massive transparisteel window, Coruscant's sunset started to transition the day's oranges to purples while lines of speeder traffic whooshed by.

"Caf?" Palpatine asked, pouring himself a cup.

"Sure," Anakin said, thinking he could use a little perk before seeing Padmé. "A single shot of cream."

"There you are, my young friend," Palpatine said, putting a cup on the visitor's side of his broad desk. "Sit down, sit down." Palpatine eased into his elaborate chair with a slight groan, then sipped on the small white mug in his hand. "Now, tell me, how is Jedi Knighthood?"

Anakin took the cup, a blink of confusion on his face. "I thought you wanted to talk about Obi-Wan's mission."

"I simply wanted to catch up," he said with a raised eyebrow. "It is so rare these days to find time for quiet conversation, don't you think? But if you want to discuss Master Kenobi, I am happy to."

The right thing to say—the *Jedi* thing to say—would be to shrug it off and instead chat about the upcoming aid mission to Langston. But the chancellor was no ordinary politician or Republic dignitary; he had been there for Anakin since his early days with the Jedi, seemingly always tuned in to Anakin's turbulent feelings. In moments of loneliness or frustration, Palpatine popped up in the timeliest manner—a chance hallway meeting or crossing paths at the landing platform.

Or scenarios like this, when they would happen to be in a meeting together and Palpatine would find a way to grab a few extra minutes with Anakin. Not always with caf, but sometimes. That open hand of friendship always encouraged an honest conversation, the feeling that "how are you?" was a true inquiry and not just a default greeting. Especially since they'd both been busy, the chaos of the war's quick escalation throwing him all over the galaxy.

Not to mention time spent on Naboo to get married.

"Has anything troubled you lately? We haven't even had time to discuss the happenings of Geonosis." Palpatine took a sip and shook his head. "How fast life changes these days."

"Actually . . ." Anakin started. The words formed in him, wanting to push out without any regard for secrecy, to tell someone *besides* Padmé about the horrors of that night on Tatooine. Someone older, wiser, who clearly cared for his well-being.

Someone who didn't judge.

Which was why he couldn't tell any Jedi about it. Not even Obi-Wan.

"Anakin, I may be a busy man, but for the next few minutes, I am here merely as your friend. You can tell me anything." Polite creases formed around his mouth as Palpatine smiled. "Please, feel free to confide in me about whatever concerns you. You have permission to be honest, and I will not judge. While I do work with the Jedi, I am not beholden to their rules."

"Right before Geonosis . . ." Anakin started before pausing, but it wasn't a hesitation. Instead, it was as if all of those feelings and memories competed to get out, causing a logjam in his throat. "My mother died."

Palpatine's lips parted, his brow tilting in concern. "My boy. I am so sorry for your loss."

"She didn't just die." The words broke through, a storm raging with them. Flashes from that night flickered by. The way the lightsaber pierced the wall. The dance of the flame over his mother's cold open eyes. The *thump* from the severed heads of the Sand People hitting the ground. "She was *murdered*. And I—" Anakin stopped himself, letting it all formulate. Before that night, Anakin *thought* he knew pain. His first few days in the Jedi Order, the undying ache of missing his mother compounded with the sorrow of losing Qui-Gon Jinn—all of that magnified the way the Jedi seemed to talk and act with an intentional calm distance. Those dark times were a speck of dust compared with the endless desert of that night, that moment when his mother's body went limp, unable to finish her final word.

Rage. Despair. Disbelief. None of those words aptly described the unseemly primal explosion he felt in that moment. Even now, just *thinking* about it allowed such a beast to crack through his defenses until he took a steadying breath and pushed it back so words could form. "I killed them. The Sand People." Unlike that moment in the Lars homestead, Anakin wasn't expelling grief through searing words and falling tears. This came out calm, tempered—equal parts admission and confirmation. "They took her life. And I took theirs."

Palpatine set his caf mug down with a clink, then reached over, the warmth of his palm resting over Anakin's mechanical one. Though the hand was made of wire and alloy, he felt the connection in ways so different from most of the moments in his life. "They killed your mother. Your *mother,*" he said, his weathered voice slow and deliberate. "Of course you wanted revenge. How could anyone *not* when facing such an injustice? It seems like simple mathematics to me."

No, this was not an admission. This was a *validation*. And he knew—he *knew*—that the chancellor would give it. Because he always understood in ways that the Jedi couldn't.

As if reading Anakin's mind, Palpatine sat up and quickly asked the perfect question. "How many Jedi actually care about other people?"

Anakin started with his reflexive response. "Attachment is forbid—"

"I know the dogma. But, be honest. Let's take, say . . ." Behind the chancellor, a Republic Cruiser emerged from below the window line, hovering upward until its ion drives came alive in a burst, powering the ship into the sky. "Master Windu. He is perhaps the Order's greatest warrior, most powerful Force adept. But do you really think he cares about people?"

Like a button pushed in his mind, Anakin saw Mace's glare, heard his condescending monotone speech, felt the air of judgment that naturally came with him. He knew the Jedi Master would do anything to complete the mission, to dedicate himself to seeing justice in the Republic.

But did he *care* about anyone?

"Not," Anakin said slowly, "in the same way you or I do."

"You see? Master Windu can go on for hours about shatterpoints, but perhaps that *lack* of empathy is his very own shatterpoint." Palpatine gave a weary grin, his eyes offering an empathy that Anakin so rarely felt in his life. "You care, Anakin. You have an immense heart. Don't let the Jedi take it from you. Your heart makes you a better person. It makes you a *stronger* person."

Though the words didn't directly reflect the tale of the sun-dragon, it touched on it just enough that Anakin pictured his mother, sitting on the edge of his bed. Had he been alone—not with the chancellor, not with Padmé, not with Obi-Wan—he may have cracked. But he wouldn't let himself right now, and instead he pushed all those feelings inside. "I'm worried about Obi-Wan," he blurted out, changing the subject to the most obvious choice.

Palpatine laughed quietly and picked his mug back up. "You see? You are a person who cares."

"I should be going with him. How can they send me to escort an aid drop-off when Obi-Wan is going alone into enemy territory?"

"Ah. Don't call them the enemy. Cato Neimoidia is neutral, after all." Palpatine took an extra-long sip of his drink, the pause long enough for a new storm to gather in Anakin's mind. The *enemy*—of course they were. All framing of neutrality and politics disappeared, and instead, all he thought of was Naboo a decade ago. Though he rarely came face-to-face with any Neimoidians, he saw their machines of war up close. And Padmé, she had nearly lost her life, her planet in a desperate quest for liberty.

If there was an enemy, it would be them.

"Despite their ties to Nute Gunray—and *his* ties to the Separatists," Palpatine said with a sigh. Anakin tried to temper his feelings, but the mere mention of Nute Gunray fanned the flames. "But you are right. Master Kenobi should have brought you. Unofficially, as backup."

"If you thought so," Anakin asked, "why didn't you say so?" The question was blurted out in a way that he immediately regretted, his feelings getting the better of him. Palpatine didn't seem to take offense, and instead smiled again as a response.

"A valid question. You see, I only have the authority to approve the framework of the mission. Perhaps if the Jedi and the military were further integrated, I might have more say. The execution of it comes down to the Jedi themselves. They set the mission parameters."

"Count Dooku set the mission parameters," Anakin said, his feelings settling.

"Mission parameters can always be changed—in politics, military missions, or life—and the truly wise know when to make those changes. Ah." He straightened up, finishing his caf. "I have taken enough of your time. Your first lead assignment as a Jedi Knight is tomorrow, is it not?"

"Yes. And Initiates are going to be on it." Anakin decided not to finish his drink. His hands rested across his lap, a formal pose as he tried to ground himself from the whiplash of emotions. "It's concerning."

"I understand. I personally requested that change. Not just on your mission, but many missions."

"Younglings aren't ready."

"That may be true." Palpatine tented his fingers as he swiveled his chair sideways. The chancellor looked outside, the color of sunset tinting his face. "But this war may last longer than we hope. And as the younglings grow into Padawans, they must feel comfortable around the clones. We must prepare for every possibility. I hope they do not have to face the horrors of war. But I would rather them be prepared than not. Wouldn't you?"

"Yes, of course," Anakin said reflexively, though doubt still tugged at him. Obi-Wan had spoken with concern about lines blurring between the Jedi Order and the military; bringing younglings into the mix seemed to push that even further.

"Anakin, you should set that aside for one evening. Rest up," he said, "and enjoy your time before your first mission. It is a milestone. You should be proud. I know I am." They stood up in unison, then walked slowly back to the entryway, as they'd done possibly a hundred times now since Qui-Gon brought Anakin to Coruscant. "Do you have any special plans to commemorate your achievements?"

Plans—whether or not Padmé came up with anything concrete to do, he'd find out soon. The specifics of the plans didn't matter, though he hoped they'd avoid politics on their final night. What mattered was spending time with his wife before the galaxy tore them apart yet again.

Someday he might get used to it. Or someday, maybe they wouldn't have to do this dance anymore. "It will be quiet," Anakin said as the large double doors slid open. "I plan on meditating."

"Of course," Palpatine responded with the same reassuring smile Anakin had seen for the past decade. "As a Jedi Knight should."

CHAPTER 18

OBI-WAN KENOBI

THE REST OF THE DAY played out with a frustrating level of bureaucracy during the up-close investigation on the planet's surface, Obi-Wan putting his tools to good use—all while the mysterious Asajj Ventress stayed close by, shadowing him in her hood and cloak. She offered little input during that entire time, stoically observing. He'd considered asking her opinion on debris trajectory from the explosion or the decay of lingering chemical compounds but it didn't seem necessary; she clearly came with an agenda, even if that agenda only involved trying to intimidate Obi-Wan into a mistake of some sort. He took his recordings and scans, made his analyses, and brought them back to his quarters, acting as if nothing bothered him.

After that came a diplomatic reception, as if the context of a societal-shattering disaster never took place. Obi-Wan sat and enjoyed a well-prepared meal, local cuisine courtesy of Zarra's finest professional chefs. Yet despite the mix of exquisitely cooked dishes and fancy table linens, the conversations continued around matters of the bombing, a desperate plea for answers wrapped up in the guise of a dinner party.

All the while, Ventress kept a measured distance from Obi-Wan, always seated three or four chairs away. But when she spoke with others, her eye seemingly never wavered from tracking him, and even as he retired to his quarters for the evening, he stretched out with the Force, scanning for the presence of someone following him the entire time.

It didn't happen, and he let himself indulge in a meditative rest for an hour, a mental and physical restoration to better fuel his inner discipline for the task ahead. Scanners hung in pouches on his belt, and he draped himself in his long cloak to better blend in with the dark, foggy evening. Then he stepped out the window, a simple escape guided by the Force.

Shortly after, he acquired a small craft through persuasion slightly aided by Force trickery. That level of rule bending didn't sit well with him, but his resources were limited, particularly since Ventress had confiscated his credit chips and it was imperative that zero electronic records tie the Republic back into this. Without physical currency, he instead worked with the realm of simpler minds. The personal vehicle lacked the comforts of a Neimoidian shuttle, but it got the job of flying him down to the disaster zone done.

Not that the data he'd collected earlier was bad. But given Ventress's constant presence, a deeper look at the situation was necessary to verify his findings and collect new data.

In the dark, the thick fog wove in between the fallen urban sprawl to create a near-black atmosphere, only interrupted by some still-smoldering fires and the occasional clusters of orange glow from bioluminescent oil oozing from Cato Neimoidia's native surface trees. Obi-Wan let the Force guide him, his instincts pulling him toward blast points and debris, taking samples to refine calculations that would hopefully provide deeper insight into what really happened. Whether a stunt or coincidence, Ventress's move with the scope earlier today focused suspicion on the Republic, and it was up to him to dispel any assumptions. He examined the area for well over an hour on his own, the constant data from scanners creating a continuous refinement of the Republic's simulation on his datapad. He'd unfolded his chemical scanner, the phrik-alloy case detached and hidden in his quarters, then began identifying the gaseous compound from still-noxious fumes when something interrupted his concentration.

Or someone.

Movement. Quick, nearly silent, but enough for it to cause a detectable blip in the Force.

Obi-Wan curled the scanner shut, then slipped it into his belt pouch, though he remained crouched, staying still to avoid creating any sound. While his ears picked up only the wind and the howl of local wildlife, he needed more, and he took the calculated risk of turning with controlled movements, keeping his weight steady to not kick out any flecks of gravel at his feet.

He pulled out Jedi macrobinoculars, a smaller scope than what Ventress used earlier—enough to easily carry around but without the computational capabilities found in her equipment. The internal screens came to life, gears whirring as he zoomed and panned to find the source.

Then he saw it. Or rather, her.

A Neimoidian female. The tall frame and long fingers gave it away, along with a general sense of identity detected through the Force. But not a typical member of the Trade Federation, not the usual stately, regal robes and headdresses. And not the standard helmet and shoulder armor of the guards, or the bulky armor of Neimoidian heavy troops. This silhouette appeared somewhere in between, light enough for movement but plated enough to withstand heavy fire. It was a commando's outfit, built for a balance among movement, stealth, and protection.

She held a small device in her hands, possibly very similar to Obi-Wan's scanners and tools, though she worked with a soldierlike methodical cadence, completely different from the strange sense of competition he got from Asajj Ventress. She moved the device up and down, focused on a single point before leaping up onto a ledge, landing with a balance that held steady even with the ledge crumbling away. This repeated several more times, an impressive nimbleness to her movements despite clearly not being Force-powered.

The figure stood up, jolting with a forward purpose that made Anakin seem like a lumbering tank in comparison. She climbed and vaulted over cracked structures, a gracefulness to her swift movements made extra impressive given that a large sniper rifle was strapped to her back, and her finger tapped what might have been a comlink at the side of her head. Obi-Wan panned the macrobinoculars to follow, wondering where she might be going, when the snap of a twig caught his attention.

He stood, in one movement buckling the macrobinoculars to his belt while drawing his lightsaber. The blue blade sprang to life with a *snap-hiss*, its cool glow illuminating the space. Obi-Wan stretched out, sensing all of the echoes of life around him, filtering out the insects and wildlife to get to . . .

He turned, no longer needing the scope to see the figure from earlier on the second story of a half-destroyed building. Except rather than scanning materials or debris, she now knelt in firing position, her sniper rifle trained on him.

Obi-Wan had raised his lightsaber into a defensive position when he heard something new behind him.

"Freeze, Jedi."

CHAPTER 19

ANAKIN SKYWALKER

AN AID MISSION.

Anakin kept telling himself that over and over. He was supposed to be on an aid mission with the 302nd Battalion, arranging logistics with Commander Theo for distribution to an embattled mining district on the planet Langston, just outside the Oggustus Nebula. Langston's mining industry produced a full gamut of materials, but the abundance of nyix made it a coveted resource for shipyards, and it was no surprise that the droid armies tried to seize it early on in the war. With devastation hitting the biggest cluster of mining towns on the northeast section of its largest continent, Anakin should have been thinking about maximizing efficiency. Some areas would need food. Some areas would need bacta and first aid. Some would need shelter and infrastructure. And others simply needed help rebuilding, along with defensive preparations should the Separatists strike again.

So many of the tasks required mind-numbing repetition, from cataloging the cargo manifest to reviewing drop points to planning distribution teams based on environmental hazards. Lists upon lists, all to handle the endless crates of medical tools, rations, and other supplies needed for a region that suffered an early major battle of the war.

Yet Anakin cursed D'urban for offering to take the lead with Theo. It seemed like a selfless gesture on her part, given that several thousand supply crates required sorting into shipment groups. But now he realized that she'd tricked him.

Because no amount of training prepared him for *this*.

Trapped in the tunnel of lightspeed on a blistering path from Coruscant to Langston, Anakin stood there in front of the worst mistake of his life:

Four younglings waited in front of him, an endless barrage of "Master Skywalker!" echoing off the walls of the cargo hold.

He was supposed to be on an aid mission. Not trying to control the sheer unrelenting chaos of . . .

Babysitting.

"Hold on, I can't answer all the questions at once."

This was worse than the morning at the Jedi Temple. In the Temple, a sense of decorum existed, the venue providing the familiarity of rules and guidelines. But here, on a ship with only two newly promoted Jedi Knights—and a bunch of clones *not* trained for helping—four younglings might as well have been sixty, a rapid-fire blend of so many voices repeatedly yelling "Master Skywalker" at once. Even finding a centering rhythm within the Force seemed impossible amid the noise and tugs in so many different directions, a confusion so very different from the battlefield.

The sound of a lightsaber burst past the voices, a green training blade sparking to life. "No, we're not using those right now," Anakin said. "I'm going to collect all the lightsabers if anyone ignites another one."

"Show us your lightsaber!"

"How many battle droids have you destroyed?"

"I bet he almost killed Count Dooku himself."

Anakin wanted to bury his head in his hands and scream, all of the discipline he'd trained into himself melting away at the sheer illogical nature of younglings. Somehow, they got the younger batch of younglings on this trip, all just old enough to be corralled on a cruiser. With proper supervision, of course.

Except . . . weren't there five younglings?

One youngling's training lightsaber lit up, leading to a push and a skirmish and yelling, all in the seconds Anakin took to scan for the other youngling, the older Zabrak girl. "Stop!" Anakin yelled. "A lightsaber is not a toy."

The youngest of the bunch, a Firrerreo named Connis Dav, stood with trembling lips, tears welling up.

"What I mean is," Anakin said, his voice calm, "this weapon is your life. You have to treat it with respect."

"Show us!"

"Yeah, show us!"

He sighed, giving in to the fact that he wouldn't be winning any teaching awards for this lesson. "Okay, look. Everyone stand in a line over there and *don't move.*" His lightsaber burst into full view, the shimmering blue blade longer and brighter than the younglings' training versions. "It is a weapon of precision and elegance. It requires the utmost control."

Now what? He was improvising about lightsabers and he'd run out of things to say, unless he went into the wiring schematics. *This* really was where D'urban Wen-Hurd would have done a much better job than him. Because she used two short shoto blades, her training involved a unique form of lightsaber combat that emphasized daggerlike slicing and acrobatics—a demonstration that would be much more entertaining than Anakin's technique.

Then an idea popped into his head. "And when you can really control it, you can do this." He passed the lightsaber from his mechanical hand to his organic one, the trick he had in mind too risky to do without feeling completely in sync. His hand opened up, fingers letting go, but the lightsaber remained. He took a step back, a deep connection with the Force enabling a hold on the weapon as muscle and nerves were grabbing it, and it floated in midair.

"Whoa!" the younglings cried out.

Why didn't he try this earlier? Anakin dipped a finger and it twirled left. Then another finger and it twirled right. It then lifted up and down, a colorful light show in the form of the legendary weapon of the Jedi Knights, and he even added a somersault over the floating lightsaber before sucking it back into the grip of his mechanical hand.

Then he shut it down. That was something he could trust that hand with.

The younglings applauded, raving with "did you see" and "how'd he do that" and other exclamations. That seemed to win them all over for now—except he was still missing the Zabrak girl. He looked all around the cargo bay, and between the crates and passing clones, he spied her. She'd been there all along, just sitting in the corner by herself. "Younglings," he said, "now I would like you to meditate on what you just saw. For, um, ten minutes."

"Awww," they groaned, but as a group, they collectively sat and closed their eyes. Maybe simple tricks were all that was necessary to get them to listen. If not, then D'urban would have to grab the spotlight for the next round. She owed him that.

As quiet set in, Anakin's ability to concentrate returned for the first time since stepping in front of the younglings. But with that focus came an odd sensation—and in fact, he realized that he should have recognized where the Zabrak girl was all along.

Because the vacuum in the Force that he'd sensed throughout the Temple circled all around her.

"Are you all right?" he said, approaching the Zabrak. She opened her eyes and the vacuum disappeared, the currents of the Force resuming their normal flow. He should have remembered her name; they'd all been introduced hours earlier. But he went with honesty here, kneeling down in front of her. "Hey, it's okay. You can talk to me. I'm sorry, but I've forgotten your name."

"Mill Alibeth."

"Mill, I'm Anakin. Is something the matter? Hyperspace can make you nauseous the first few times if you're new to it."

"It's not that," she said, shaking her head. "It's something else."

Mill appeared to be the Zabrak equivalent of his age when he left Tatooine, perhaps a tiny bit older, and likely past the age of simple Force tricks being impressive. "Well," Anakin said, "we're gonna be here awhile. So if there's something on your mind, you can tell me." Now, this was improvising—handling younglings of any type was as foreign to Anakin as Padmé's political negotiations—but he couldn't contain his instinctive urge to care, to try to help.

"I . . ." Mill started. She huffed out a sigh, then looked at his eyes. "You promise you won't get mad?"

"I promise. You can count on me."

Mill leaned forward, close enough that Anakin felt her breath. "I don't know if I belong in the Jedi Order."

Anakin took in several slow and controlled breaths, so many things flashing through his mind. Qui-Gon's certainty in stating "he *is* the Chosen One" before the Jedi Council. The peace parade on Naboo, standing proud with his newly shorn Padawan hair. Endless bickering with Obi-Wan. Padmé. So many thoughts about Padmé.

Tatooine. The Sand People.

His mother.

All of those things tied intrinsically with his decision to leave home and join the Order. And yet, through it all, he, too, never felt like he quite belonged—and this was the first time *anyone* had ever said it.

Mill's breath quickened, a tremble coming to her voice. "I'm . . . just kidding. Forget I said—"

"I understand," Anakin said in a controlled, calm voice.

Because he did.

"Tell me more, youngling."

"I . . . feel the Force," she said, her hand balled into a fist. "But it's overwhelming. I *know* the Order can do good. I know the Jedi are guardians of peace. But . . ." She turned, Anakin now facing her tight black tail of hair. "But the war. The fighting. The violence. I feel all of that through the Force. I can't explain it, but it's too much. And I don't understand why the Jedi are peacekeepers and all of the other Initiates can't wait to get their weapons. And we're in the battlefield, with soldiers?"

"Justice sometimes requires a heavy hand."

"But from the Jedi? I just—" She turned back to Anakin. "It doesn't feel right. I—the other day, I . . ."

"It's okay, youngling. You're not in trouble. I appreciate your honesty. What happened yesterday?"

"The Gathering." She bit down on her lip, as if she replayed the events in her mind. "I was supposed to go. But the bombing at Cato Neimoidia. I just . . . *couldn't* think about lightsabers and crystals. I don't even want my lightsaber. I just want to help others. I don't . . ." Her eyes dropped for a second before they locked back onto his, as if her body required a confession. "I don't know if I want to feel the Force."

Suddenly, it all made sense. The vacuum in the Force, both yesterday and here. She wasn't in meditation.

This youngling was trying to quiet the Force. Possibly even cut it off.

Anakin knew. He recognized it, because for a very brief moment during his darkest, loneliest days shortly after becoming a Padawan, with his peers lacking compassion for him and Obi-Wan constantly flustered and his heart yearning for the comfort of his mother, a spike of anger shut him off from the Force.

For a flash, it did the trick. It tempered his feelings, it quieted his mind, it soothed his fears. But then it was gone, not nearly enough. Because while that avoided connection, it also pushed him further into a corner, and it was at that moment he realized that he needed to reach *into* the Force rather than avoid it.

Anakin looked at the other younglings, still sitting in a line in meditative poses, though the occasional jabs and giggles came from them. Palpatine's words about getting the Initiates *used* to war replayed in his mind; in front of him, Mill turned, Anakin sensing a cloud over her, an internal shame likely for questioning the Order.

Anakin also understood that part all too well. "I've always felt a little out of place. My entire life. Even with the Order."

"You?" She looked at him, eyes wide. "But aren't you the Chosen—"

"Don't believe everything you hear," Anakin said with a laugh, though he groaned inside. Not *again*. Half the time, people said it to him in awe. The other half, in jest. And on occasion, in condescension—usually from Mace Windu. No matter how much he succeeded, no matter how much he proved himself, things always seemed to come to that, and not in the way Qui-Gon intended. Qui-Gon saw it as a path for Anakin; whether or not that played out, he didn't know. But everyone else seemed to think it was a title, like a sports champion. He shook his head, going to a better place. "My mother once told me, 'Always believe in the strength of your heart.' And she was right. Whatever things people said about me, their assumptions, it doesn't matter. What you believe in your heart is your path. When I *questioned* the Force—even disconnected from it—that is what brought me back. That is what brought me *through*." Anakin took her hand with his mechanical hand. She looked at the glove, a look of shock on her face that came and went.

He understood. Not everyone knew about his new limb.

"I know how you must be feeling. That you don't fit in, or your path feels elusive. That it's difficult to master your connection with the Force. But that's part of the journey. Your journey. And you will find—"

"General Skywalker."

"Sorry," he said to Mill before standing up. Captain Sparks patiently waited for him, helmet with bright-yellow lines tucked under his arm. "Yes, Sparks?"

"Sir, Commander Theo needs you on the bridge. Apparently the intended drop zone has been damaged to the point that we won't be able to land. We'll need to find someplace new."

"Understood. I'll be right there." He turned to Mill, then looked at the younglings, the white-skinned Mon Calamari peeking at them with a single yellow eye. "Listen. Controlling your link to the Force is something that takes time and practice. Some struggle with it more than others. But do me a favor?"

"What's that, Master?"

"Don't try to run away from the Force. Lean *into* it. Reach into it. Control it." Anakin tried his best at a reassuring smile. "If I could learn to do it, so can you."

She nodded, though it wasn't clear whether his words really crystallized in her. At least not yet. "As for the war . . . the Jedi do a lot of good for the Republic. Sometimes, 'aggressive negotiations' are just as important as bringing medical supplies. I know that's confusing, but it's true. Both can benefit the galaxy. I understand you. I've been where you are. So be patient and we'll talk more later. All right?" Mill nodded, her features softening, Anakin empathizing with the simple need for *someone* to listen. "But for now?"

"Yes, Master?"

"If you *really* want to be handy"—Anakin pointed at the Initiates who pretended to meditate but really kept poking at each other—"take care of the younglings. You're the oldest."

"But—"

"Hey." Anakin offered a smile, something to break the heavy mood. "You said you wanted to help others, right?"

CHAPTER 20

RUUG QUARNOM

RUUG REALLY, REALLY HOPED KETAR would not let the moment get the best of him.

Especially since this Jedi now held a glowing laser sword in front of him.

"I said 'freeze.'" Ketar's voice came over their shared comm channel, just a fraction of a second off from the real-life view she had in her sniper scope. The Jedi emissary stepped back in slow and controlled movements, and though his weapon was still up in a defensive position, his posture showed a complete lack of aggression.

Ruug had heard plenty about the Jedi Knights, of course. Anyone in any military had. But most of her time in the Neimoidian special forces involved black ops usually in the Outer Rim, protecting—or sabotaging—supply lanes, blockades, and other missions where the needs of Neimoidians and the needs of the Trade Federation overlapped.

Which meant it usually didn't involve the more proper nature of the Jedi.

"I heard you. And I am abiding," the Jedi said—a man by the name of Obi-Wan Kenobi, if she remembered correctly from the overheard discussion during their shift earlier today; nothing official had been passed to them. Guards handling grunt work apparently weren't on a need-to-know basis. Ruug held her rifle steady, though she glanced down at the spectrometer at her feet, the small display showing that it had finished processing its chemical residue scan. She reached down and quickly attached it to her belt before returning to the unfolding scene. "But—" He projected his voice out much louder, and despite the lack of light, she saw his silhouette turn her way. "I mean you no harm."

He spoke directly to her, not Ketar.

The Jedi took one hand off his blade's hilt, holding it palm-up, then methodically backed up several steps, his angle twisting to likely keep an eye on both Ruug and her young partner.

Ketar shifted, and in the scope, light from the laser sword reflected lines on his face, a clear hardening underneath the angled brim of his standard guard helmet.

"I am not your enemy," the Jedi said, this time in a calm and quiet voice meant probably for Ketar.

Part of being an elite commando meant reading people, seeing their actions before they happened through any possible tics or tells. Here, the Jedi offered a calm neutrality, and though this might have been due to their supposed mystical powers, Ruug got a hint of sincerity from the situation. Still, nothing was certain, especially not under current galactic circumstances. "It's illegal for anyone to be below the fog without a permit at this time of night," she yelled. "Especially in an investigation site."

They stood still, the hum of the Jedi's weapon captured clearly over Ketar's comm channel until the howl of the planet's wildlife broke through. Fog rolled over the wrecked building, though the glowing blade emitted enough light to remain visible in her scope without any thermal vision or other augmented views.

"I don't have a permit," the Jedi shouted back, "but I am conducting an investigation."

"We know who you are," Ketar growled. "You're here to cover up the evidence of the Republic's sabotage." He stepped closer, his pistol up, and despite the dim conditions, the barrel of the weapon showed a clear tremble. "You're trying to get away with murder. And destruction."

"I am on an invest—"

"Liar." The entire cycle of emotions constantly burned through Ketar since their first visit to Cadesura, and investigating on the surface didn't change anything. Anger. Grief. Despair. Concentration. And then back again. Right now, the Jedi emissary may have encountered them at the exact wrong moment in the cycle, and Ketar's voice clearly showed where his mind was. After their guard shift today, he'd promised to get some rest before their evening investigation, something she'd offered to Ketar to keep him constructively occupied instead of blasting training droids. Though based on the sudden shift in his demeanor, she had a sneaking suspicion that he'd sought the company of the Separatist agent instead of taking a nap. "You are here to—"

"Ketar," she yelled. She knew enough about Jedi to understand that their weapons cut through anything, and if her partner didn't realize that, then she'd fill him in later. For now, she needed to dial down the situation. "Patience. He deserves a moment to speak. You, Jedi—you better have a good reason for being here."

The Jedi glanced her way, a thoughtful look visible through her scope, and his voice carried that through as well. "I am on an investigation on behalf of the Republic, at the invitation of the Trade Federation. I am of the firm belief that this disaster was not caused by the Republic and my goal is to prove that and find the true culprit."

"You were down here earlier with the others." Ketar shook the pistol at him. He must have talked with Dooku's agent, because even Ruug didn't know that. "Why sneak here at night? With no oversight, no of-ficial escort?"

"My investigation . . ." He searched for the right words, and Ruug appreciated the careful consideration being applied here. "My investigation required more time. Given the level of bureaucracy accompanying me, the window for an efficient process was shrinking. It was critical to scan and assess tonight given the rate of decay for evidence in such a harsh environment."

Bureaucracy. Ruug wondered if that meant the Separatist woman. She seemed the troublemaking type.

"Do you actually believe this Jedi?" Ketar yelled over to her.

"The actual guilty party doesn't matter to me," he continued, maintaining a calm and deliberate voice. "I believe the Republic is innocent. But if it turns out to be some unknown faction claiming to serve the Republic, so be it. Or if it was done on behalf of the Separatists. All I want is the truth. And—" He paused, then pointed at her with his free hand. "—I can see you are investigating as well. I watched the way you studied the remains. It appears this is what we both want. So perhaps we can work together." The hand holding his weapon stretched up in a controlled motion, raising it high for both Neimoidians to see.

The shining blue blade quickly snapped back into the hilt, leaving them in near-dark. A new light appeared, a personal lamp beaming from Ketar's shoulder that changed the complexion of the scene. A swift change in the shadows caught Ruug's eye, enough to show that the switch in light might have caught the attention of . . . something. Ruug changed her scope to thermal vision, the clarity of the real-world view becoming pixelated burnt figures against a blue backdrop. The Jedi slowly lowered his hilt to place it on the cool ground of the planet's surface. "I work in good faith." He raised both hands, then stood and took two steps back.

And then she saw it. Her shoulders tensed, locking the rifle into a steadying position, and her finger readied for the right moment, the right shot.

"This is a token of—"

A flash erupted from Ruug's rifle, and through her scope, she watched as the Jedi didn't flinch, didn't even move. The blaster bolt whizzed a meter over him, soon followed by a beastly howl that rang into the night.

With that, Ruug swung her sniper rifle onto her back and began bounding down, landing on debris that crumbled upon impact and vaulting forward over chunks of broken buildings. She hit the surface floor running, hurdling over obstacles while her focus shifted from the Jedi to the large furry creature with four stumpy legs writhing on the ground, yelping in pain. Had it been upright, it would have towered over Ketar and the Jedi. But here, it needed help. "I need a medpac," she yelled. "Ketar, get out some rations as well." Her feet pounded, dust clouds floating up and mixing into the fog with each step, and she charged past the Jedi over to the fallen beast.

"Feed it the rations while I patch the wound," she yelled, taking the medpac from Ketar in mid-stride. Ketar moved to the animal, its girthy belly heaving with each breath and large ears tilting forward. "Korgee beasts are gentle but they get hungry. There you are, girl. We'll get through this." It caught the aroma of the rations, and soon it nibbled out of Ketar's hand while Ruug addressed the shoulder wound with bacta and laser sutures. "This whole mess has affected the local wildlife. It's not their fault their food chain has been disrupted. Normally they're very docile," she said as the Jedi came over as well, one hand on the creature's forehead, and seconds later its whine became a controlled, steady breath. "They lose their minds a little when they get hungry."

"You're saying I was its dinner?" the Jedi asked.

"Never doubt the appetite of a korgee beast," Ruug said with a laugh. She moved over, giving it scratches under its neck, loose hairs tossing into the air. "Or the amount they shed. You're a good girl, aren't you?" The korgee beast nudged the sniper with its black nose, then looked at the Jedi before Ketar tossed an open ration into the distance. It limped away, the scent of the food drawing it from the trio.

"My name is Obi-Wan Kenobi," he said in a soft voice as he watched the korgee beast trail off into the mists of Cato Neimoidia. "I am the emissary from the Jedi Order, representing the Republic."

"Ruug Quarnom," she said, exhaling as she got back on her feet. "And I have much less exciting credentials than you."

"But perhaps more liked by animals."

"My enthusiastic friend here is Ketar Nor. I'm supposed to be training him." She gave a short laugh, and Ketar replied with a sour expression. And from Obi-Wan's raised eyebrow, she caught a bit of empathy at the give-and-take of their relationship.

"Do all guards carry sniper rifles and custom stealth equipment?" he said, gesturing at her formfitting maroon-tinted armor.

"If they're good enough." Ruug pointed at the dormant laser sword still sitting on the ground. "While I certainly believe in the idea of neutrality and independence, I also want the truth." She picked up the hilt, taking a moment to assess how such a small piece of craftsmanship carried so much energy, even weighed more than she expected. "And I, too, believe in good faith," she said, handing the weapon back to its owner.

Obi-Wan took it before nodding in approval, eyes locking with Ruug the entire time. Though, she noticed, he avoided the glare coming from Ketar.

CHAPTER 21

ANAKIN SKYWALKER

ANAKIN RAN, HIS EYES SCANNING.

His boots thumped against the metal deck plate of the cruiser, passing by as Theo and Sparks addressed a group of the 302nd next to the stacks of bacta crates slated for distribution down on Langston. Clones prepped the mission, but they wouldn't be any help to him right now.

Not unless they'd been babysitting.

Still, he asked. And they'd replied with a simple "Not recently, sir."

"Have you seen Mill Alibeth? The Zabrak youngling?" Anakin asked another helmetless clone down the hall, who merely shook his head. His search continued, sweeping through the ship's security cams, methodically working his way through. Finally, in a small storage room, he'd located D'urban Wen-Hurd, showing off her acrobatic lightsaber techniques with her shoto blades; she must have run out of ways to entertain them as well. Except Mill wasn't with them. "Where's Mill?" Anakin asked, the question coming out more like a demand than he'd intended.

"She is meditating," D'urban said, after landing from a gravity-defying sprint along the wall. She withdrew both her blue and green blades then tossed her long hair back, adjusting the large glare-reducing spectacles strapped around her head. "Storage room off the main corridor."

"Master Wen-Hurd! Master Wen-Hurd!" the younglings yelled in unison, leading to a sigh that caused Anakin to smirk. It was *her* turn to deal with this.

Of course, Mill's meditation corner happened to be the last place Anakin looked, and by the time he found her, his breath paced at a light huff. He took a moment to center himself, both physically and mentally, then spoke to the meditating youngling. "Mill?" he asked softly.

"Master?" she said, opening her eyes.

"Are you connecting with the Force? I didn't sense any disruptions."

"Trying to let it in. But it's more like . . . keeping it at bay." Her gaze dropped to the floor. "There's a lot of talk about battles here."

"I have something to show you. You should come with me." With that, Anakin turned, his robe swirling with the movement, and he motioned her forward. "We have to catch the transport before it goes."

She sprinted to catch up, then tried to match his steps. Except he marched with focus, so much that he didn't realize she lagged until they were halfway to the launch bay. Not only did she struggle to keep up with him, she also stayed quiet the entire time, awaiting instructions.

Of course. The younglings trusted him on a level beyond Padawans.

"We're going to the surface. I was just about to head out when I got an idea."

The hallway let out into the loud launch bay, shuttles awaiting loading as troops jogged back and forth or pulled supplies or checked weapons. "What's that, Master?"

"Listen," Anakin said, kneeling down to look at her face-to-face. "I understand how you feel. I was brought to the Order when I was a boy, not a baby. I had a life, friends. My mother. It's a little different from what you've been through, but—" He exhaled, trying to find the right words to connect with her. "I understand that conflict. What you feel like when you're being pulled in different directions. The way you *feel* the Force, but you hear it differently than what they tell you at the Temple, and that's scary. It makes you want to hide from it. I understand all of it." The last few days flashed through his mind, from the joyride with Padmé to his talks with Obi-Wan and the chancellor—the most important people in his life. "I'm still seeking *my* path. But I thought getting you on the surface might help you see with your own eyes. To witness the different ways the Jedi serve the Republic. It's not just lightsabers and fighting." He flagged down the trooper leading this particular transport, a clone known as Sister that he'd met on assignment shortly after the secret wedding. She took off her helmet, rows of tightly braided hair falling down over her armored shoulders.

"We're loaded up, General. The supplies are already on the surface. We've just gotta distribute them. Hop aboard when you're ready," she said. Sister pointed to the clone troopers waiting in the transport's open hull, standing still in a line. R2-D2 rolled up to them, beeping chirps of annoyance. "Your droid is impatient, sir."

"Yeah." He reached out to gently tap R2-D2 on the dome. "He gets that way." He turned back to Mill. "So what do you think? Up for a ride?"

Mill looked at the transport; Anakin traced her gaze and saw it locking directly on the clones. "We're not soldiers. Why are we leading them?" Despite her question, she took a step forward. R2-D2 scooted alongside her and Anakin walked to keep pace. Sister put her helmet back on, lights reflecting off its magenta and blue vertical stripes, then she gave them quick salutes, which Mill tried to imitate in return.

Such a question had never come into his thoughts before, perhaps because he'd simply gotten thrown into the fray at Geonosis. In fact, it seemed like many Jedi fell into immediate lockstep with the clones, the war demanding so much of them that no one pondered who they were, why they were here. What little he knew of the clones came from the battlefield, though he'd found them to be intelligent, loyal, and often funny—in many ways, anything *unlike* what he expected. "Try not to think of them as soldiers. Or clones. In many ways, they're just like you and me. Trying to do some good in the galaxy the best way they know how. Now," he said as she looked up to him, "let's go help some people."

CHAPTER 22

OBI-WAN KENOBI

DESPITE THEIR ROCKY START, RUUG led Obi-Wan to new areas to investigate, going far beyond the massive struts that marked severance points, all the way to areas that showed collateral damage from the initial blasts. She pointed out irregularities in the blast radius, how the struts splintered differently—evidence that could mean several different things about the types of explosive compounds used. She also pulled out her own datapad of compiled evidence, including material traces that had since evaporated into the fog and wind of Cato Neimoidia's surface. That, along with his own accumulated scans and sensor readings, gave him an entire day's worth of material to comb through—and, unfortunately, no Republic computers for processing. But he'd figure that out later.

The entire time, Ketar stayed silent, an air of suspicion coming from him while they talked.

In their fourth hour of investigation, Obi-Wan knew his body was reaching the point of physical exhaustion. "I do not know much about Neimoidian sleep cycles," Obi-Wan said, "but I should return and get some rest soon if I'm going to be of any use tomorrow."

"That's not a bad idea," Ruug said. She held up a small vial and poured its contents over the mix of metal, concrete, and stone, something that appeared to be a chunk of strut blown into the side of a building. It bubbled, releasing a neon-yellow mixture through the air, visible just enough for her to hold up a scanner to it. "Chemical reaction. I'll send over the results once it finishes."

"You've done good work without hauling a proper lab with you," Obi-Wan said, scrolling through his datapad.

"I may not have any of your Jedi powers, but experience does close the gap in some scenarios. Ketar," she said, handing him a device out of her armor's chest pocket, "run process four-C on this with an exposure time of six seconds."

"Understood," the young guard said. He brushed past Obi-Wan as if he weren't even there, then began tapping on his datapad.

"Surely you didn't learn all about chemistry and explosives in basic training," Obi-Wan said.

Though Ketar stood behind Obi-Wan, he knew the comment caught the guard's attention.

"I'm just a guard," Ruug said, standing up to stretch her back, "trying to teach people like Ketar why our work matters."

"That is a guard uniform?"

Ruug squinted at her datapad, though from the way her head tilted, he guessed she considered his question more than her scanner's results. "You're inquisitive, Jedi."

"Part of the job."

Ruug let out a quick laugh. "This"—she patted her maroon body armor—"was part of the job, too. Neimoidian special ops. Explosives. Infiltration. Sniper. But now just a guard." She put away the last of her devices and nodded toward their shuttle.

"Looking for a quieter life?"

"Not necessarily. But sometimes important people think you should be quieter. And there are various ways to accomplish that." They walked in silence, the only sound coming from the crunch of dirt and debris beneath their boots.

"It sounds like you are not satisfied with the Neimoidian involvement with the Trade Federation," Obi-Wan said—an honest comment, but given how accommodating Ruug had been over the last few hours, the words came as their own form of bait.

"Ah. That's a very . . . binary view of things. You Jedi do enjoy your rules." Obi-Wan bit his lip at that, and rather than be defensive, he decided to let Ruug continue. "I believe in the idea of the Trade Federation. When the Republic fails to recognize your homeworld as anything but an asset in shipping and commerce, you become a commodity. And a statistic. I'll not let my life be a line item in a shipping manifest. With the Trade Federation, Neimoidians finally have a voice. History shows the Republic barely acknowledged our existence until the Trade Federation. The *way* governments operate, though, that always changes."

Ketar spoke up, perhaps for the first time in an hour. "Why shouldn't we support the Separatist cause? We know our worth—and it's much more than the Republic claims."

Obi-Wan caught a hint of a smile on Ruug's face, though she clearly tried to hide it. "We're not talking about the Separatists here. Cato Neimoidia is neutral," Ruug said. "The Trade Federation is neutral."

"Neutrality in the face of oppression is further oppression," Ketar said. Which Obi-Wan agreed with, to some degree. But probably from the opposite perspective as Ketar.

"Is it oppression? Or is it independence? A freedom to choose?" Ruug asked, almost like a teacher leading a student to an epiphany. But Ketar hesitated, the bite to his attitude settling as he considered the question.

They walked a few more steps in silence before Obi-Wan spoke up, despite the fact that the question wasn't directed at him. "I would say it depends on context," he offered, something for both of them to consider in different ways.

They both looked at him, though with very different points of view written on their expressions and postures. "I agree," Ruug said. "Context defines everything."

"I have a friend who thinks like you," Obi-Wan said, the smirk on his face probably not visible in the dim Cato Neimoidian night.

"I can believe in the Trade Federation without liking its leadership over the past ten years. And I can recognize the systemic issues within the Republic but still think that some people within it are reasonable. Even," she said with a chuckle, "a Jedi."

Ketar shot back another comment about how Republic culture was more dangerous than Republic law, and Obi-Wan recognized Ruug's responses to it all—not the specific words or rebuttals, but the way she tried to equally acknowledge and shut down Ketar's ire, well . . .

He'd had some experience with that in his life.

This discourse continued back to their shuttle, a small guard craft that offered little more protection or maneuverability than his own "borrowed" craft. And while they bickered, Obi-Wan caught sight of a strange hovel beyond an alley of the dilapidated block, one more thing to check out before his way back. He considered asking them to come along, especially considering Ruug's additional equipment.

But something about Ketar's mood told him he should leave well enough alone. And the small bunker itself gave off a suspicious feel, a frequency in the Force that created an invisible disquiet, along with the fact that the entrance to it sat remarkably clear despite rubble strewn about everywhere else.

"I'll head back to my ship," he told them, giving them a farewell wave. They parted ways and boarded their craft, Ruug nodding in acknowledgment while Ketar stared straight ahead behind the cockpit window. He started his walk ahead, waiting for their shuttle to lift up and disappear into the fog.

When he concluded they'd flown far enough away not to detect his movements, he took out his macrobinoculars and switched to thermal vision, a safety check of the shed's surrounding area for any starving korgee beasts that might be lurking for a human-sized snack. With the coast clear, he started forward, and though fatigue weighed down both his thoughts and movements, this seemed too anomalous to pass by.

CHAPTER 23

ANAKIN SKYWALKER

"THE FIRST TEN CRATES GO to the neighborhood at sector N-seven-A-I," Anakin said to the helmeted clone trooper in front of him. "Then meet up with Captain Raptor at Fong-Tim Square to split the remaining batch into groups for smaller distribution."

"Right away, General." The clone saluted, then turned to the Juggernaut transport packed with more medical supplies than clones.

"And be careful of the sand. I've seen worse but this still gets in the transport's gears." Anakin smirked, thinking of home. Podracers levitated off the ground, but he'd certainly worked with his share of wheeled and treaded vehicles during his time. How the Jawas kept their sandcrawler rolling, he'd never quite figured out. Langston's largest continent was mountainous, but with high winds and seasonal torrential rain. Communities sat at the base of mountains, but the weather mix also created an accumulation of blue-tinted sand just thick enough to be annoying, yet not quite a way of life.

Still, it got in the joints of his mechanical hand, even when he'd covered it with a tight-fitting glove. The convoy away, Anakin removed the glove and tried to blow some of the grit out of his knuckles. "See," he

said to no one in particular, "no one believes me but it gets *everywhere*."
He blew again, the cool of his breath tickling the adaptive hardware that
translated into a sensory feeling, then shook his arm while flexing his
fingers. Little bits of sand trickled out, and Anakin could practically
hear Padmé laughing at him like she had not that long ago, when they
were hidden away in the Naboo countryside following their wedding.
On that afternoon, they'd stood barefoot at the lake's edge, and even
though Naboo's tranquil countryside proved idyllic, the grains of sand
caused a squirmy feeling, a constant shifting to get comfortable.

Padmé noticed, of course, but because she always strove to understand others, she'd offered something that encapsulated everything
about her: "After a few days on Tatooine, I get why you hate sand so
much," she'd said with a laugh before turning more thoughtful. "We
come from different places, Ani. It informs so much of how we see the
galaxy."

That moment was the only good thing to ever happen regarding
sand.

And here, as he flexed his fingers, he could feel the grit between the
servos, adding onto his already out-of-sync feeling, any motions coming with the annoyance of something stuck in the wrong place. He
sighed, putting his glove back on—this would require a complete oil
soak for the hand later when he had access to the cruiser's repair station. But for now, he'd deal with it.

Around him, clones still moved back and forth, some chattering to
one another about the most efficient way to mount supplies on the floating dollies and others remarking on reports of various skirmishes
breaking out across the Mid Rim. Anakin looked back over the horizon,
a cluster of shattered homes in the distance. Mill was supposed to have
accompanied clones on a local drop-off, but the troopers appeared to be
coming back without her.

He was about to intercept a group of clones with yellow trim painted
across their helmets and shoulders when his emergency comlink
beeped—the counterpart to the one he'd given Obi-Wan. "Obi-Wan.
I'm here," he said, grabbing it from his belt.

"Anakin? Anakin, can . . . hear me?"

"Semi-loud and semi-clear. Weren't you going to stick to 'mission parameters'?" Silence came over the comm, and Anakin didn't know if his joke got stuck somewhere in the digital bits sent across the galaxy or if Obi-Wan simply dodged the question.

But then the comm broadcasted a laugh, a short burst that seemed to be the most his former Master could let loose. "Outside of parameters—well, I suppose I've learned something from you after all. Listen, I need your help. I'm sending you an upload of scans and data. I have my suspicions about what it means, but I don't have any way to process it."

"Send it to me. I'll have Artoo look at it."

"No, Artoo interfaces with Republic networks. This can't have any official traces. It needs an information broker."

Anakin waited for the oncoming clone troopers to pass him by before responding. "General," the lead soldiers said with a salute without breaking stride.

"Information broker?" Anakin asked, his voice quieter. "Is this what you do in your free time? You know, you could watch podracing with me instead, I won't tell the Jedi Council. The Athio Seven Hundred is coming up."

Obi-Wan responded without reaction. "We need to act quickly. Contact Dexter Jettster on Coruscant in the CoCo district. He will send you a secure channel to upload. Tell him it's from me."

"Wait, doesn't he own the diner? How does that come into play?"

"Dex will take care of it. I need a fast turnaround. I have less than a day to put together my findings."

Static popped over the comlink, and with that, Obi-Wan was gone. Something didn't quite add up, and even though Mill was still wandering somewhere among the dilapidated buildings, he owed it to Obi-Wan to get this done as soon as possible. "Trooper," Anakin called out. The clone group stopped, all turning around. "Is the shuttle ready to go back to the cruiser?"

"Not yet, sir," one of the clones replied, pointing to the transport. "We're still unloading supplies."

Anakin looked back to the area where Mill had ventured out. "I'll need to get back soon. And a secure comm channel. In a private room."

"Right away, sir. We'll make preparations." The clone responded without question, without any hesitation. As a Padawan, Anakin's requests and commands would have come with the need to double-check with clone commanders or Jedi Knights. But here, there was the obedience of hierarchy, something that created a direct chain of command.

What a strange position to be in. Anakin reminded himself of what he'd told Mill, that the clones were just people trying to do their part—and staying cognizant of that would be necessary given the power of rank.

"Anything else, sir?"

"Not from you. I just gotta go pick up something I lost." Anakin walked forward, and though Mill's presence usually echoed a low-level anxiety, he didn't get any ripples like that. And that in itself might have meant that Mill had found a focus, an unexpected calm.

Strange.

"I'll be back soon," Anakin said.

"Understood." The trooper saluted, his posture straightening. "General."

CHAPTER 24

MILL ALIBETH

STRANGE THAT HERE, AMID THE devastation of the war, Mill felt at peace.

Not when she looked around at the broken buildings. Or walked alongside armored soldiers who all looked exactly the same without their helmets. Sure, they had little differences—hair, scars, some even had tattoos.

But still. All those same faces and voices, all with massive rifles. And they were so *obedient*. Anakin had revealed that he'd grown up enslaved, and now he was a Jedi commanding clones bred for war. The whole thing unnerved Mill.

Yet when she'd asked the clones to leave her here for a few extra minutes, she'd been given space and suddenly the universe made sense to her. In fact, she cracked open the door to the Force. And rather than it flooding her, she found herself in its currents, letting it guide her to kneel down, open her medpac, and stretch out her feelings just like they taught her at the Temple. The family of Gharal siblings remained quiet, perhaps not too trusting of the large soldiers that roamed their neighborhoods. The scars of violence proved to be too unsettling, despite the fact that their loud shuttles and huge transports carried supplies.

With this family, though, only two things mattered—the cough of an infant too young to speak, and the leg of the eldest sibling, where something had caused the normally scaly light-gray skin to turn soft and oozing. For the infant, the Force guided Mill with the proper time to smack its back between its two shoulder scutes after it coughed, ejecting the dust that had tickled its throat.

Connecting with the Force, it turned out, had its advantages.

As for the eldest, it would require something more. "I have bacta," she said, tapping the canister at her feet. Though Initiates only learned rudimentary first aid by her age, one thing she'd discovered was that bacta often did the healing part on its own. It was the fear and pain that needed to be managed.

Mill approached her, a thirty-year-old girl named Rokura, who was a mere adolescent given the long life spans of the Gharal. "Scared is," Rokura said, and a tremble ran through her thick neck ridges, sweat caking her thick black hair. "Limb pain feel. Bacta help not enough." Mill nodded, understanding the broken Basic. Above her, blaster bolts had torn holes in buildings—if the buildings still stood. Some of them didn't, only their foundations remaining. Dust tossed in the air, harsh enough that it got in her hair and tickled her horns. On her arms, flecks of Langston's sand covered her tan wrist.

In the Jedi Temple, even on the cruiser, war seemed so far away, but here it almost drew Mill out. Rokura moaned in pain, the infection in her leg likely making her delirious. She trembled when Mill put a cool cloth to her forehead, kicking out at the youngling. The commotion stirred the baby, a cry that quickly turned into coughing but settled with a few breaths, the debris and grit no longer in its lungs.

One thing at a time. Mill closed her eyes and looked through the Force. The city's residents appeared in swirling colors—not quite the level of suffering she'd felt on Cato Neimoidia. This was calmer, like they'd gotten used to their situation. But here, Rokura spiked in her vision, shades of red in the form of a Gharal girl.

Mill put a hand over Rokura's head, then breathed, and in that breath, an instinct arose, as if the Force were a warm blanket and Mill draped it around Rokura's ravaged body. "I will help you," she whispered, without prompting or thought. And as if on command, the Gharal's trembling stopped, her breath steadying.

Mill blinked, an awakening similar to snapping out of a deep sleep. It took several seconds for her to return to the present, recent actions already a hazy memory—she knew what happened, but the how and why seemed inscrutable. But Rokura still needed practical aid; Mill stood up and applied bacta in swift movements. The wound fizzed as the bacta's microbiotics activated immediately upon contact. "She'll need to be still for a few minutes," she said to the family before going back over and putting her hand over Rokura's forehead again. "Rest," she said, in a clear direct voice, her eyes closed, letting herself sink deep enough into the Force that all of the surrounding distress lit her senses like beacons within a thousand-meter radius.

Then she heard a voice through the ether, a chanting-like rhythm. "Mill . . . Mill . . . Mill."

"Mill!"

It was Anakin.

Shaken out of her trance, Mill stood up, the tails of her Jedi tunic tinted by layers of Langston's blue dust. R2-D2 chirped and whirred next to her, and though she didn't yet understand the astromech, it felt like a lecture about paying attention.

"Master Skywalker, I—"

"We need to go. Why didn't you come back with the clones?" He squinted, finally realizing the scene around him. Next to Mill, Rokura's siblings scooted back in the shadow of the tall Jedi.

"They needed help," Mill said. "And they were afraid when the clones were here. They had just seen the clones fighting battle droids a week ago, and the battle did this—" She gestured to the broken buildings around them. "—to their home." She pointed down at the resting Gharal girl, now with closed eyes and deep regular breaths. "She needed bacta. And something to settle her nerves."

"You did this?" Anakin asked, kneeling down to inspect the situation more closely.

"I'm sorry, Master Skywalker. I know it was disobeying commands, it's just . . ." How could she possibly explain this strange ability, the way hurt and agony became part of her field of vision like a thermal sensor on a scope? "They needed help. And they were scared. They've already lost their parents in the fighting."

"We need to go. But," Anakin said softly, "you did the right thing."

"You're . . . not mad?" Mill didn't mean to respond with such surprise. But even the Padawans she'd been around seemed so stuck on the rules. And *that* came from all the older Jedi.

But Anakin was different. She knew this from their first conversation.

"The Jedi aren't perfect. And sometimes we have to work around that." His head tilted, a thoughtful look on his face. "You connected with the Force?"

"I let it in, yes," Mill said with a nod, almost an affirmation to herself.

"Do you see now?" Anakin asked, taking her hand. And she did, in a way. Not the way Jedi used the Force to jump really high or knock things down. But the connection between living things, the way they were all tiny specks across the same massive universe—for the first time in possibly her entire life, she understood.

Mill nodded, prompting Anakin to smile. "I knew you would. Now, before we leave." He pointed to the open medpac on the ground. "Anything else they might need?"

CHAPTER 25

OBI-WAN KENOBI

SUNRISE ON CATO NEIMOIDIA LACKED the colors usually found on other planets. Each planet's unique atmospheric conditions and chemical makeup had given Obi-Wan some stirring views in his time, bright and bold colors that looked like the Force had taken hold and burst into the physical realm in the form of brilliant splashes across the sky.

But this planet was draped in fog, and the early morning on the surface may as well have been Coruscant's lower levels—shadows and structures combined with thick mist to absorb most of the light, turning things mostly into an ashen gray outside of the occasional orange glow from trees.

It provided good cover as Obi-Wan sneaked down to get a closer look at the strange bunker he'd discovered right when Ruug and Ketar took off. There were, of course, plenty of half-shattered buildings of all sizes, so another one the size of a speeder garage shouldn't have seemed out of place. But this one, the way the double doors sat neatly together without a trace of damage, it all appeared a little too intact for something that had withstood the massive shock wave of the structure crashing on the surface.

Not to mention the unusual wake of the Force he sensed from the bunker. It had come and gone in a flash, but all of that together pulled at him to explore further.

A bunker that, of course, had been locked during that late night. A sealed door was always a cause for greater concern.

Now he returned, various scanners and sensors packed with him. More important, he'd picked up several hunks of raw meat from a local market. He waited behind the shed, sitting quietly on a cracked retaining wall, then stretched out in the Force to scan for any korgee beasts.

It didn't take long to sense the region's natural wildlife.

Obi-Wan tossed the first hunk of meat in the direction of the nearest korgee beast. Then another, a mere ten meters out.

The third, right in front of the shed's door.

Obi-Wan assessed his surroundings, first with his eyes and ears, then with the Force. With things clear, he reached back and thrust his hand forward into the air, a telekinetic propulsion whipping through the space and causing a massive V-shaped dent in the door. The dim surroundings lit in a brilliant blue as Obi-Wan's lightsaber gave a *snap-hiss* and came to life. He pierced the hinge on one side of the door, melting it through until it snapped off, then gripped the door through the Force and pulled the corner with the severed hinge down, the metal groaning as it bent. Sweat formed on Obi-Wan's brow, the door piece stubbornly warping slower than he would like, and it gradually twisted until it created a hole big enough to crawl through—and damage that looked close enough to be impact from wildlife to cover his tracks.

One more scan around showed the area to be safe outside of a sniffing korgee beast, and Obi-Wan considered the animal's rough distance to the bait one more time before climbing in.

His boots landed on the metal floor with a clang, the space empty enough to carry the sound. Little light made it through, so Obi-Wan activated his lightsaber again to get a better look.

On one end sat a large locked case about a meter wide. Obi-Wan tugged at the lid for good measure. On the other, a small comm station appeared to be set up—a portable configuration sitting on a makeshift table along with a battery source, perhaps the kind usually manufactured to go in starfighters. It was enabled, though, and between the clean setup and the system's status lights and power indicators, it clearly had been established recently. Obi-Wan activated its interface, though the data log was blank. He almost began searching its database for deleted records when he noticed a small datapad plugged in to its side.

The datapad lit up, a card-sized device too small for its own screen that instead projected out a hologram of information. Obi-Wan blinked several times to make sure he read it correctly.

Then he read it again.

And again. He checked details one more time before scrolling through different tabs of information, but rather than provide a clearer context to the findings, every passing word and number only amplified the mounting sense of dread growing in his gut. He took a breath and centered himself; after all, he had a job to do.

And the Republic was counting on him.

The display showed an analysis of bomb debris, explosive blast patterns, and structural damage—all side by side with the same type of equipment used by bomb squads in clone battalions. Schematics scrolled by with matching images, real-world evidence juxtaposed with designs from the Ministry of Science. Each successive screen of information broke down the connections in more detail, creating further links to the Republic.

The anxiety in his gut grew, though he let the feelings pass and considered the bigger picture: If this data made a Jedi Master feel so much unease, it surely would be damning for a Neimoidian audience mourning a catastrophe. That thought propelled him back to constructive action, his mind starting to consider ways forward. Though things certainly looked bad for the Republic, many different ruses could be at play. The data itself could be falsified, the comparisons might be disinformation, the culprit may not have actually had ties to the Republic.

Though several different paths forward played out in his head, they all started with the same first step.

He'd brought along Anakin's comlink for an emergency. This constituted exactly that. He pulled it off his belt and sent a signal far across the galaxy to Anakin.

"Obi-Wan. This better be good. We just got the younglings to settle down."

"Anakin," he said, "I have one more thing for you to send to Dex for analysis."

"Didn't I just send you Dex's findings?"

Which was true. But those findings came in the form of results from various scans and measurements, more for processing than anything else—simply hints, not the hard, clear evidence he held before him.

"This is different. Tell him the entire war may hinge on this. He can't get this wrong."

Anakin's cheeky tone hardened, and Obi-Wan could practically see his eyes narrowing in serious thought. "What have you found?"

"A datapad. Of unknown origin. Tucked away in a hidden bunker on the surface. Its contents show a clear link to Republic materials and protocols."

"It's false," Anakin said quickly. "It has to be false. Someone is trying to trick you."

"That's what I need you to prove." Obi-Wan opened the access port on the back of the datapad, then connected it to the comlink. "I'm sending you everything on here. Do not tell anyone about this. Not the clones, not the Jedi Council. This information cannot have any possibility of getting out until we determine its source and validity."

"Are you sure? Keeping this from the Council?"

Such a question surprised Obi-Wan; it was a reasonable thing to ask, though having Anakin of all people ask it caught him off guard. Perhaps his former apprentice *was* maturing after all. "The information is too volatile. The local government already has suspicions. We must keep any official communications out of this until we have definitive proof that it's falsified."

"Understood." Anakin went silent, though the transmission channel remained open. "What will you do with the datapad?"

"I'm not sure yet." Leaving it here wasn't an option; it had to be safeguarded. But he couldn't carry it the whole time, not with the possibility of encountering guards and officials. "Every choice comes with an inherent risk."

"What if—" Anakin paused, his voice lowering. "What if you destroy it?"

Obi-Wan wanted to be shocked at such a suggestion; extreme measures like that dipped into the deceptive ways that led to the Separatist mentality in the first place. But the truth was he'd considered such a thing. In a time when Jedi planned military operations, Padawans became soldiers, and a clone army appeared out of nowhere, all of the clear delineations of roles, of protocols, of morality itself suddenly disappeared, leaving only a fuzzy definition of what right and wrong were supposed to be. "I have thought about it," he said, as much an admission to himself as to Anakin. "Especially since I'm sending you the data. But no, we need to keep the original intact." He switched off its glowing holographic projection and assessed the device itself. "I think it's small enough to fit into that secure case you gave—"

"Wait," Anakin said. "Nothing is coming through on my end."

"Blast it." Obi-Wan looked up at the bunker's ceiling, though the layers of debris, mist, mountainous arches, and the still-suspended cities of Zarra probably caused more interference than a simple layer of metal. "I'll need to get off the surface. Stand by while I get back up there."

"Okay. I'll be waiting. Keep that safe until you can send me a copy."

"Agreed. I'll get up there as fast as I can. Kenobi out." The comlink beeped, then Obi-Wan took one last look around the bunker. The communications terminal, the locked case—all of it would have to wait for further investigation. Right now, his priority was getting back into comm range.

Obi-Wan considered the few pieces of bait he had remaining for the korgee beasts. He kept one in his pouch in case he encountered any wildlife on his way back to his craft, then threw the remainder by the door. Within seconds, a shuffling noise stirred in the debris down the cracked alleyway, and Obi-Wan departed, reassured that the local wildlife would cover his tracks.

The last time Obi-Wan was in a bar, he nudged a young man to go home and rethink his life, then severed the arm of a would-be assassin. And while that hadn't happened too long ago, the war had stopped giving any meaning to time, making the immediate task seem excruciatingly infinite while the days counted quickly. How had they gone from greeting Senator Amidala in her apartment to being thrown into the middle of war, with all of its skirmishes and subterfuge, in such a short period? Indeed, the war had escalated so fast that quiet moments to ask how and why they got there proved rare.

So when they arrived, he took advantage. Obi-Wan sat at the bar, allowing himself a moment's peace to consider it all. Once back on Zarra's streets, he'd successfully transmitted the data to Anakin, who promised to get in touch with Dex as soon as possible. He'd then hidden the device in the secure case with the comlink before leaving for the less glamorous part of Zarra. Only now did he have time to ruminate: the war, Dooku, the clones, the mystery data. And he gave himself time to have a drink. If the locals knew who he was or why he'd come to the planet, it didn't seem like they cared, at least not in this particular pub that Ruug had suggested.

Perhaps it had to do with its location, a neighborhood buried far off by one of Zarra's struts and far from the center of the government's ornate buildings and brightly lit commercial district. In this small, stuffy room, a mix of Neimoidians and offworlders sat shoulder-to-shoulder, a thick burning cloud of some type of smoked spice trailing through the air. The wall of chatter blanketed sound enough that he almost didn't notice Ruug sitting down next to him, still in her commando outfit but without the outer layer of maroon armor.

"Your apprentice isn't here?" Obi-Wan pointed at the empty stool next to him. "I saved two spots. He seems like he could use a drink. Or two."

"I needed a break," she said with a laugh. "He's a bit moody these days. What's your word for them?" She flipped a coin at the bartender, a different currency than the standard Republic credit chip.

"Padawan." Obi-Wan had asked the question as a means of casual conversation, though it came with the benefit of stalling as he weighed bringing up what he'd seen earlier. Ruug carried herself differently than Ketar and definitely Ventress: weary, weathered, but held by a strong moral compass. Would that be enough for her to accept the revelation of the mystery datapad *without* an overreaction? He bit down on his lip while considering the alternatives—including the possibility of simply not telling Ruug. "My own apprentice actually was recently promoted. He's off on his own now, trying to save the galaxy through willpower alone."

Ruug laughed as the bartender slid over a drink so roughly that it spilled out onto her long green fingers as she caught it. "How long until reality hits him?"

"He may be even more stubborn than Ketar."

She shook her head, taking down half her drink in one gulp. "Lucky us, right?" she asked. "He's a good kid. Just caught up in all"—she gestured around them—"this. I'm trying to keep him away from Ventress. She's a little too eager if you ask me."

"I'm not terribly fond of any agent of Dooku's."

"See, at least you're honest with me," she said, taking a smaller sip. "I have findings for you."

"As I for you."

"Well then." Ruug held up her remaining drink. Obi-Wan clinked his glass against hers, and they both took a sip. "It's not much to go on. Further scans. We've lined up some more security recordings with the simulation to try to identify the exact chemical mixture for the blast radius, explosion heat, that sort of stuff. Take a look." She slid a datapad his way, though he didn't pick it up, instead focusing on his drink. She looked his way, then back at her own glass, then back at him. "I do . . ." she started before looking all around the room. "I do have a lead."

Obi-Wan immediately thought of Anakin, somewhere across the galaxy getting information from Dex. Obi-Wan said he wanted the truth; he'd said that to Ruug, to the Jedi Council, to Palpatine, to *Dooku*. But right now, he didn't necessarily want the truth, he wanted Anakin to report that the information on that datapad was falsified somehow, or out of context, or something that would not link the Republic to such morally bankrupt standards.

And Ruug—was her lead the same information? Was that possibly even her bunker?

"It is *only* a lead. I need to run further analysis. Getting discreet access to the labs right now is difficult."

"Is it definitive?"

"We'll find out." Ruug looked down at the amber fizzing liquid in her glass. "I don't want to bias your investigation. So, forget I said anything. For now. Could be nothing. What about you?"

"Nothing to make a strong case, either way." He pulled out his own datapad, the one with Dex's report on scans and measurements, and made the decision right then to omit any mention of the *other* one hidden in his quarters, the one with potentially damning evidence. "Trace elements found in common explosives. Blast zones representative of seven different types of explosive designs. Destructive capabilities found on the black market but also common in many militaries. And my research shows no chatter about Cato Neimoidia among bounty hunters or spice miners," he said, leaving out any details of making any transmissions.

"That's forensic evidence. You don't have any leads?" Ruug asked with a heavy sigh.

They looked at each other, noise from the pub creating a tornado of sound. Glasses clinking, people of all different species shouting, laughter and claps coming in from all corners of the cramped room. Somehow, life moved on here, even though each of these people probably felt the toll of Cadesura. He asked himself one final time if he should mention the mystery datapad, and once again he resisted.

Not with what it revealed, nor how he found it. He simply needed more time.

"Not that I can speak of, no."

"Then that's it," she said, shaking her head. "Thousands dead, unfathomable damage, and all we have are some chemical readouts and a lead that may be nothing."

"I have full faith in the truth," Obi-Wan said. Though at that moment, such a claim felt like a bit of a stretch. "We just need to trust each other."

Ruug gave a quiet chuckle. "Oh, I forgot, you Jedi are peacekeepers. I admire your optimism. To trust," she said, holding up her nearly empty glass. "I have a bad feeling about this."

Obi-Wan raised his in return, then spoke softly, almost as much for himself as for her. "Without trust, we have nothing. Without truth, we have nothing. We *must* have faith in it." And that was as much a part of him as his connection to the Force.

"Truth. I'll let you in on a secret. You know who forges that truth?" Ruug asked, the ridge above her left eye raised. "People like me. You never see us, but that's what we do. I've killed bad people and I've killed good people. People who deserved it and people whose only mistake was that the Trade Federation felt they got in the way. You know what I've realized?"

"What's that?" he asked, finishing his drink.

"Almost everyone deserved it. To some degree. The group blocking shipping lanes in the Outer Rim. Maybe they're doing it to claim a bigger stake for the right reason, to help overturn some injustice that affected their planet. But the other side? That blockade delays the shipment of medical supplies to a planet facing famine. Populations that will never meet, all hurting one another, without ever thinking about it. We're connected, every one of us in the galaxy." Ruug's finger circled the rim of her glass. "For every gain, someone else has a loss. Justice doesn't really exist. Not for everyone."

"I'm sorry you feel that way," Obi-Wan said, sincerely and without bite. Part of him understood her, he really did. He had seen planets, systems, entire populations deal with injustice. Her words carried a logic, and he recognized it. He simply chose not to give in to the cynicism.

But they had lived very different lives.

"When my government told me to kill"—she tapped a finger against the bar—"I killed. Because almost every one of my targets deserved it. One way or another. But not the people on Cadesura. They were living their lives. Cato Neimoidia is neutral." Her body slumped over the bar, red eyes squeezed shut. "Cato Neimoidia is neutral," she said again.

"We will get to the truth." Obi-Wan's mind returned to the mystery datapad, the damning evidence. He wanted to *will* it into something that cleared the Republic, but a shift came in him, a recognition that Ruug was right. The truth was bigger than just the Republic's needs. "If it turns out to be difficult and ugly, then we will still turn that into jus-tice. We just need time."

"Then what? That doesn't bring back the people who fell to the sur-face. Does that honor them? Does that do right by them?"

They sat in silence, empty drink glasses in hand, as Obi-Wan consid-ered the path ahead. "No. It does not. But I believe justice finds a way. It has to. Otherwise, why are we even here? We choose to do right, even in the face of so much wrong. Because there is no other way."

A good minute passed before Ruug tossed another several coins onto the bar and gestured for a refill. The bartender looked at her and she held up two fingers. "In theory, you're right. But I've seen it firsthand." She stared straight down at her folded arms. "This galaxy, it tries to break you."

"We can never let it do that. We must have hope."

Another two glasses slid down the bar. She caught both and took one down in a single gulp before handing the second to Obi-Wan. "Unfor-tunately," she said as she waved to the bartender again, "I became numb to hope a long time ago."

CHAPTER 26

ASAJJ VENTRESS

KETAR PROVED HIMSELF EAGER TO listen to anything Ventress had
to say. Which she understood. All of his pain and rage bubbled under
the surface, searching for some type of release.

It was fortunate for him that she had come along. Fortunate that she
had encountered Ketar and his more prickly partner when she did.

Fortunate that Ketar found her shortly after their shift.

She'd listened, of course. Walking with him, sitting with him, letting
the young man vent his fury about Cadesura, about the lives lost, about
his suspicions about the Republic. He didn't prove to be an expert at
science, though, letting his emotions make illogical conclusions about
explosives and further conspiracies. Such diatribes were as irritating as
they were amusing, but she stayed quiet, using the mere act of silent ac-
ceptance to earn his trust.

But now she would take action, turn the tables. He probably wouldn't
even realize it.

They stepped through the mists of Cato Neimoidia, a deliberate journey from where she landed her ship to the bunker, something she'd set
up even before she announced her presence to the local government. It

wasn't the most direct or efficient way, but Ketar simply followed her, mostly in silence, as he took in the devastation of Cadesura's fallen neighborhood. Ventress made sure to point out when they'd passed something that might specifically needle Ketar's rage, asking questions about a crushed museum or the markers left where bodies had been discovered, the whole journey taking several times longer than it should have.

That was all by design.

"I understand your concerns. And your anger," she said. "I wanted to—"

They stopped, the most unexpected sight in front of her.

"What's this place?" he asked.

Ventress squinted, a quick assessment of what had happened. And then she saw it, one little giveaway that prompted the corner of her lip to curl up.

Kenobi had visited, hadn't he?

"The Confederacy set me up with equipment," she said. "I've stored it down here." They approached the building, each step revealing further details under the full moonlight.

Ketar knelt down, then reached to the ground. He held up small tufts of fur, then pointed at the splashes of blood on the bunker before drawing his pistol. From behind the structure, a korgee beast waddled out, still chewing on a piece of meat, its large ears forward. "The wildlife," Ketar said, "it must have hunted its prey here." He gestured to the massive dent in the front door as they got closer. "Looks like it collided with the door when they fought."

The creature locked eyes with Ventress, though she held a hand out, each step taken with cautious approach while it sniffed the air. It swallowed its meat, then moved tentatively closer to her. Ventress reached out through the Force, tapping into a rarely used sense in her, a simple communication to tell creatures that she was safe.

Large brown eyes the size of fists looked her way, then softened. Ventress removed her hood, then scratched the beast on the side of its nose, fingers entangled in whiskers. "I understand the drive to survive," she said before looking around to scan the area. Other than hints of further wildlife, she didn't detect any presences. "It is not its fault. Here." She reached into a belt pouch. "Enjoy some rations."

Ketar caught up to them, though he kept several meters' distance. "Their environment has been disturbed by the crash."

"I imagine it was quite disruptive." Ventress paused, then stepped over to the broken door. "Curious," she said, her finger tracing the area where a distinct circular puncture showed the scars of burning and melting.

Clever, Kenobi.

"What's that?" Ketar asked.

"Oh," she said, "nothing. I am simply marveling at the strength of these beasts." Ventress petted the creature once more and it turned, bounding off into the night, only a few stray tufts of fur trailing behind. "It appears this bunker is no longer safe from the local wildlife. Come, I could use your help."

They climbed through the opening, which offered just enough space for a single person. Ketar snapped on the light from his shoulder, and Ventress assessed the situation. Most of it looked intact, though there wasn't much there to begin with. The comm system still appeared capable of transmitting, and the case in the corner appeared sealed— a firm tug on the lid showed the same.

What was missing, though, was the datapad.

She looked around the comm station, checked the corners, but the light equipment in the bunker ended the search quickly. She'd planned on giving the information to Ketar, a means of pushing him over the edge he precariously clung to. Her plans would have to change.

But her goal—that remained.

In fact, this might prove to be even more useful in pushing Ketar.

"I want you to consider this: What if there was a way to ensure that Cato Neimoidia never supported the Republic again," Ventress asked, walking over to the secured case in the corner. "What would that be worth?"

"Almost anything," Ketar said in a quick response.

"*Almost* anything?" Ventress tilted her chin up and gave a shrug. "Or anything?"

"It depends on the risk." Ketar crossed his arms, the motion partially blocking his shoulder lamp. "My people have suffered greatly."

There it was, that heralded Neimoidian risk assessment. Such an inherent trait seemed beneficial in most situations. However, when passions ran high, all it took was a few choice words to change things by 1 percent, possibly 2.

Sometimes, that was all that was necessary.

"Let us consider that. Of all the Neimoidians in the galaxy, is this their greatest injustice? Or is it the long history of quiet prejudice they have faced?" Ventress looked him in the eye, then gave the thought several seconds to sink in. "Individuals died with Cadesura. Your people have faced a different battle long before, all across the galaxy. People like—" She stepped forward, now only an arm's length between them. "—your parents?"

Ketar blinked several times before his eyes fell to the floor.

"You could get justice for Cadesura. Or you might think bigger than that. Think about the entire planet. The Trade Federation." Ventress turned her back to Ketar, one arm up. "Every Neimoidian in the galaxy."

She waited, his silence telling her that her words dug in deep.

Now was the perfect time.

"I have something to show you," she said, stepping over to the locked case on the floor. A biometric scanner glowed to life, a single green line running over her palm before the locking mechanism whirred and clicked. She lifted the lid, and the illumination from Ketar's shoulder lamp cast shadows as he came closer to it. He looked inside, a sharp gasp indicating he realized what it contained.

"Oh, don't worry. These explosives have nothing to do with the tragedy of the Cadesura bombing, I assure you of that." This was the truth, though Ventress wondered how deep her claws were in him at this point. He may have believed anything she said at this point, truth or lie. She leaned over behind him, a direct strength to her next words. "What this does offer is the opportunity to make sure Cadesura is never forgotten."

"I . . ." he said, a tremble rippling through his body, something Ventress detected despite his guard armor. "I don't understand."

"A betrayal of this magnitude needs someone to stand up for what is right." She let him have a moment, the power of mere words exploding into possibilities on display in Ketar's expression. "Consider this a tool to do just that."

"Do what?"

"Make a statement. Of some sort." Ventress already had a suggestion in mind, but she drew her words out with intention, as if this were a sudden burst of inspiration. "Perhaps the Republic consulate office in the east wing of the capitol complex. It is a single-person room that is rarely occupied. Did you consider why it is always empty?"

"Rosbuen Frisk, the regional diplomat? She covers multiple systems. She's elsewhere most of the time."

"Doesn't that frustrate you? The Republic cares so little that the assigned diplomat simply visits for a day as a formality. Rather than a true sense of duty." She nodded, a gesture to suggest confidence in the idea, but really, the move had a much more calculated purpose.

It gave Ketar permission to consider it.

"A single explosive," she continued, "at that office. A statement without risk."

"A bomb . . ." Ketar slowed, as if dozens of thoughts were encapsulated in that single word. "I don't know. I need to think about it."

"Of course." His hesitation marked her victory. Because it showed consideration rather than outright rejection. All she needed to do was give him the proper space and motivation to turn that into something more. "You must calculate what you're willing to sacrifice. In the meantime, we should finish here and move this somewhere secure from the local wildlife." She glanced over her shoulder, then back at Ketar. "We wouldn't want them to get hurt. Besides, there's something on the surface I need to find."

"What's that?" he asked, still staring at the explosive material in the case.

"You said you find that Jedi to be honest. Honorable, even though you disagree with him."

"He seems that way, yes. Ruug trusts him. And I trust her."

In the dark, Ventress smiled, a grin so large that she would only allow it given that she stood behind Ketar. Beneath her cloak, her hands instinctively reached for the lightsaber hilts that hung by her hips, weapons that would soon come into play. But not here. For now, they'd stay hidden, obscured by draped fabric. "Let's find out what he really brought with him to Cato Neimoidia, shall we?"

CHAPTER 27

ANAKIN SKYWALKER

ANAKIN CLICKED THE BUTTON AGAIN, prompting a single beep.
And again, nothing.

"Come on, Obi-Wan," he muttered to himself. He paced around the small room, a makeshift office tucked to the side of a random hallway in the cruiser's lower level. From the window, he saw the loading bay, troops walking back and forth, groups of clone troopers in green helmets passing by further troopers in armor with gray patches and lines. At the end of the bay, a shuttle landed, a different group with yellow-trimmed armor unloading, empty supply crates in their arms. And behind him, Mill sat outside the door, waiting patiently—she didn't ask why he huddled in there, but she agreed to wait.

Anakin wasn't even sure why he kept her around when she could have easily been dispatched to the other younglings. But from the little time they'd spent together, he'd gotten the sense that she'd learn more around him than with the rambunctious Initiates more interested in Force trickery than what was happening down on Langston.

At the very least, she had way more patience than those younglings. "Where are you, Obi-Wan?" Anakin said to himself, clicking the button on his comlink again. The beep came and went again, a call with no answer. Anakin held up the device, talking to it as if it were a standard communicator. "Come in, Obi-Wan. This is your really annoyed former Padawan."

But of course, those words wouldn't transmit across the galaxy. Not until Obi-Wan picked up on his end. Anakin supposed that he might have been tied up in something important, or he may have simply forgotten the communicator in its secured case.

Whatever the reason, a problem still existed in the form of some really important data—some really *damning* data—and simply standing around waiting for the fallout drove Anakin mad. Anakin checked the comlink's transmission logs again and made sure that Dex's report was received by Obi-Wan's device.

Which it was.

Which meant that Obi-Wan now had confirmation that all of the data he'd discovered on Cato Neimoidia's surface was authentic. Where it all originated remained undetermined. But all of the technical links tying details directly to the Republic . . .

They were real.

And Anakin didn't know what to do about that except pace around the room, repeatedly hitting the button on the comlink. He glanced over at the door, which remained shut, Mill outside. They were supposed to be meeting up with the rest of the younglings for a lesson on local maps and how the climate of a planet influenced its topography and thus the way the society built its community. A valuable lesson, to be sure, both from a cultural and tactical perspective.

But really, Anakin needed to hear from Obi-Wan.

For now, the best he could do was leave him a message. He clicked the button twice, and a chirp with a higher tone beeped to indicate it was recording. "Obi-Wan. Where are you? I've just sent you the findings. It looks bad for the Republic. The information on the datapad is authentic. It's real. There has to be a reason. I don't know how or why, but there has to be. We need to get to the bottom of this." He clicked the button again to transmit, then leaned back against the room's console, arms crossed.

How could someone frame the Republic so easily?

As if the Force had been listening in on the moment, Anakin's comlink finally beeped. He looked at the door one more time, then figured Mill could wait another few minutes. "Well, you sure took your sweet time. I thought we had a galaxy to save."

The low hiss of the communicator's open channel continued, though no voice came over it.

"Obi-Wan? Obi-Wan, can you hear me?"

"You see?" A voice spoke, someone who was definitely *not* Obi-Wan Kenobi. The female voice was raspy and oily, two short words loaded with menace. "He brought a communicator with him."

"Who is this?" Anakin yelled. "What have you done with Obi-Wan?"

The comlink beeped a low tone, dropping the connection dead. Anakin stared at it, gripping the device in the palm of his mechanical hand, as if he could penetrate through the wiring and composite to reveal the true nature of who was on the other side. He almost hit the button again to send a hailing signal, but thought better of it—in fact, right now this comlink was the wrong kind of evidence.

With that thought, he tossed the device into the air, drew his lightsaber, and in one move slashed it in two. It fell to the floor, each half landing with a clink, steam coming from burning orange-yellow seams.

"Master Skywalker?"

Anakin looked up to find the door ajar and Mill poking her head through.

"I felt your—" Her lips pursed and nose wrinkled as she searched for the right word. "—concern."

"It's okay, Mill," he said. Fists formed at his side, and his jaw clenched, thoughts turning into fears turning into so much more. Who could he go to? They weren't supposed to be in contact. He couldn't reach out to the Jedi Council. Obi-Wan had told him to stay away.

And now someone had all of the information that might cast blame on the Republic. That someone *had* to be the agent Dooku had sent to Cato Neimoidia.

"Master? Are you all right?"

Anakin looked at Mill, the tan skin and horns of a Zabrak but the eyes of universal youth. That moment down on Langston seemed so profound, the intersection of spiritual awakening and a commitment to righteous choices, and yet after all of that she was still just a youngling. Curious, uncertain, and maturing.

She would grow into herself—and her abilities—to make her own choices. But for now, she relied on her elders, as he used to.

"No," he said quietly. "I'm not all right. And I lied. Things aren't okay."

"Can we—" she started before catching herself. Then she looked to either side, each direction down the long hallways of the cruiser, before stepping in the room and letting the door seal behind her.

Smart, Anakin thought.

"Can we help Master Kenobi?"

"You heard," Anakin said.

"Well, you kind of yelled it."

Back on Tatooine, he had a choice to make. With Obi-Wan in peril, wounds still fresh in his heart from burying his mother, different paths were laid out before him: go and help Obi-Wan or stay on his home planet as Master Windu dictated.

But in the end, he didn't make a choice. He was a Padawan, still operating under so many layers of guidance—and Padmé had been the one to decide for both of him.

However, now he was a Jedi Knight. With the authority to make decisions. Even ones people didn't like. Except it turned out that even Obi-Wan bent the rules from time to time.

He might as well start now.

"Let me think." Anakin began pacing around the room, ideas snapping into focus. They couldn't include the clones in this; that visual might trigger a far greater conflict—that was Obi-Wan's entire reason for going alone. Same thing with the Jedi. Any officials with any type of ties to the Republic would cause problems. No, this had to be discreet. And swift. "When you were helping that family down on Langston, did you happen to see any vessels with hyperdrive capabilities? Maybe in the neighborhood around there?"

Mill's expression turned puzzled with a scrunched face. "There are a number of them in the landing area. They're not really being used right now. They're too busy trying to rebuild from the battle."

That moment of decision. In a previous life, it meant waiting for permission, for guidance: Obi-Wan telling him what to do and when to do it, or Padmé using her status to make a decision for them. But here, now, the choice was his. He could stay on the cruiser, finish the distribution assignment on Langston, then head back to the Jedi Temple in a few days. Or he could go down to the surface now, let Mill guide him to an available ship, and fly to Cato Neimoidia.

What was proper versus what was right—it *was* right, after all. Even Chancellor Palpatine believed he should be out there alongside Obi-Wan. In fact, only the rules of the Jedi stood in the way.

This was Anakin Skywalker as a Jedi Knight, finally with the freedom to choose his path. And he was going to take it, to protect Obi-Wan Kenobi—and maybe even the galaxy.

"Can you show me where these ships are?"

"Sure," Mill said, "but what for?"

Anakin looked down at the long corridor, a handful of clones passing by with nothing more than a salute. "It's like I asked you the other day— you said you wanted to help people, right?"

CHAPTER 28

OBI-WAN KENOBI

THE DAY HAD NOT TURNED up any further leads, despite a full morning and afternoon on the surface. The local officials let him investigate alone, and Ventress was nowhere to be found, but even that unexpected freedom of movement failed to prove any more fruitful, producing only further gathering of scientific data that was ambiguous at best. Obi-Wan had returned to Zarra, pressure accumulating from two ticking chronos: Ruug's lead, whatever that was, and the potentially disastrous information sitting on the mystery datapad.

He had only been gone from his room for ten, possibly fifteen minutes—a simple walk to clear his mind, the rhythm of movement enough to ground him while sharpening his mental acuity. Yet when he turned the corner of the hallway in the palatial government offices, a problem immediately jumped out. He walked at a normal pace, conscious of any possible surveillance as he returned to his quarters, but it became clear as he approached:

The door was ajar.

He stopped in front of it, examining everything from the sliding mechanism to the embedded electro-mechanical lock. When he pushed at the door itself, though, it barely moved, the usual motion sensors failing to trigger. The lock sat devoid of any status lights, as if something drained the power—or cut it—from the entire system. He pushed, his palms shoving hard to nudge the panel open enough to let him slide through, but once he got inside, he saw a bigger problem than a busted door.

On the floor was Anakin's supposedly impenetrable case, separated from the scanner that acted as its cover story. Obi-Wan knelt down, remembering Anakin's claim that the alloy "might even be tough enough to withstand a lightsaber."

And here that hypothesis had been put to the test. Because the case itself was punctured, a burn mark that Obi-Wan was quite familiar with. Strategically placed to be able to split the case in two without harming the contents, a precision that would require . . .

Training in the Jedi arts.

A Jedi controlled panic, recognizing the onset of such an urge and then tempering it with both physical and emotional control. But considering the contents of the case—a single comlink and a small datapad that might change the fate of the galaxy—brought Obi-Wan the closest to panic he probably would ever get.

He scanned the room, a desperate search for both devices, but with the simplicity of the space, it was clear that both had been taken. He picked up the pieces of the case, taking a closer look to confirm his suspicion about the lightsaber burns. The rest of his things lay right where he'd left them, from his other equipment to his storage crate. Only this, with the evidence in plain sight.

Obi-Wan stood in the middle of the room, his mind plotting out the different steps forward. So many variables came into play—who stole the equipment? Who had they shown it to? Was it contained to Cato Neimoidia or had it gotten bigger, dragging both the CIS and Republic into this?

Who would have access to and training in lightsabers?

Footsteps came from down the hall, gradually approaching until they stopped outside his door with a firm step. "Master Kenobi," a guard said. "Your presence is requested."

Had the culprit resorted to stealth, the comlink and the datapad would have been recovered without giving away what was afoot, and yet here, everything was placed with as much precision as the lightsaber cut itself. All of it came with clear intention, from the way the case opened to the fact that it sat in plain sight.

This wasn't about evidence.

This was a message.

"Master Kenobi," the guard repeated. He turned around, only to find that two other guards accompanied the speaker, all with weapons drawn. "We will need your weapon as well."

Minister Alluv Eyam looked at the gathering, a small group to fit in an office about half the size of Palpatine's but with more ornate decor, the wall of shiny and glowing sculptures standing on the polished stone floor a far cry from the muted tones and occasional artwork of the chancellor's office. Obi-Wan walked in, escorted and with his lightsaber now in the possession of one of the guards. Across the way, further officials sat, an elevated podium that established hierarchy despite the fact that this wasn't a trial. No obvious recording devices stood in place, though those types of things could be hidden easily within walls or statues. Assuming never proved to be a good strategy, so Obi-Wan instead merely wondered if Senator Dod and the rest of the proper Trade Federation leadership listened.

Or, possibly, Count Dooku.

Around the room stood another set of guards, and behind Obi-Wan sat several officials that he hadn't met before.

Ruug was nowhere to be found. And perhaps more important, neither was Ventress.

"Master Kenobi. Thank you for coming on such short notice."

Eyam's tone remained cordial, and Obi-Wan weighed the different ways to respond. Whether the officials had seen the incriminating evidence was unclear; at the same time, feigning ignorance might appear, at best, patronizing.

At worst, deceptive.

And despite some of the twists and turns caused by Anakin's communicator and the mystery datapad, all of Obi-Wan's decisions sparked from a purity of design, a commitment to finding a way to de-escalate the war, to save lives, to abide by the Jedi creed of peace and justice.

Yet despite his best intentions, he may have accelerated the greatest crisis the Republic had ever seen.

Obi-Wan elected to go with a straightforward response. "Thank you, Minister Eyam. When I arrived on Cato Neimoidia, I promised that I would do everything in my power to identify the perpetrator of the crime. I do have several leads at the moment, along with a wealth of forensic data. I hope to have findings for you sooner rather than later." Voices murmured around the room, and Obi-Wan waited for them to settle down.

"We appreciate all of the efforts you have made, Master Kenobi." Eyam nodded, and though the guards still stood at attention, no air of aggressiveness came from them. Obi-Wan wondered if perhaps the motivation for this gathering stemmed from the administration performing a simple status check rather than any disturbing findings.

"I promise you a thorough and detailed report in the coming days, free from any political filter or other undue influence."

More whispers floated through the room, gathering momentum until the collective voices reached a crescendo that caused Eyam to call for order. Through it all, Obi-Wan maintained a straight, stoic posture, though he called out to the Force, gauging the emotions swirling throughout the space.

"We understand that you are still gathering data," Eyam said. "However, further evidence has recently come to our attention."

Suddenly, the mood in the room shifted, a palpable change that led Obi-Wan to accept that the worst may have indeed happened. And he would have to react accordingly to preserve any chance of peace. He simply nodded at the minister's statement, his eyes scanning the room, when several clicks echoed through the space.

The door behind the podiums slid open, revealing two figures.

Ketar.

And Ventress.

But not Ruug.

"Because this evidence," Ketar said, a ferocity to his words, "clearly shows that the Jedi emissary has not been completely honest with us."

He walked in, a small folded cloth in his hands. Everyone in the room turned, angling this way or that to get a look at the cloth, but Obi-Wan already knew. He knew from the unblinking glare on Ketar's face, from the smug derision on Ventress's lips. He knew because the message had stared right at him from the floor of his quarters, a message in the form of broken pieces only possible via precise cuts from a lightsaber.

Whose lightsaber, he still didn't know. But as Obi-Wan met Ventress's look under her hood, his suspicion grew.

"While this Jedi *Knight,*" Ketar started, a derisive mockery in the word, "was among us, I knew something was not correct. After all, doesn't the Republic have a long history of treating Neimoidians as second-class citizens, as walking transactions and nothing else? So why would this be any different?" He unfolded the cloth in his palm, plucking out the missing comlink resting on top of the datapad Obi-Wan had recovered on the surface. Ketar held them up high, one device in each hand. "Deception is the way of the Republic," he said, his voice so piercing it sparked an uproar.

Eyam stood, arms waving to calm the commotion that had overtaken the space. But just as the noise began to settle, Ventress spoke up. "We found the Jedi's secret bunker on the surface," she said, activating a holoprojection of the structure he'd visited. Images cycled through until it stopped on a close-up of the door.

Specifically, the lightsaber burns on the hinges.

"In my time working with Count Dooku, I have come to recognize the mark of a Jedi's weapon. He did, after all, leave the Order because of concerns of corruption. And this"—she gestured at the image—"is clear evidence of Obi-Wan Kenobi trying to seal off the bunker." Which, of course, wasn't the purpose of the burn, but Obi-Wan knew such a clarification meant little right now. The visual was enough to identify his presence, regardless of truth. "And why would he hide such things? Why would he"—the image switched and showed the bunker as a burnt-out ashen shell—"burn such a structure? Clearly, to destroy the evidence."

With that, Ketar held up the datapad and comlink again. Except this time, each activated.

First, the datapad projected a hologram of information, side-by-side comparisons between bomb details forensically pieced together and schematics of Republic bombs used by the clones. Then the comlink played audio for everyone to hear.

"Obi-Wan. Where are you?" Anakin's voice came out. "I've just sent you the findings. It looks bad for the Republic. The information on the datapad is authentic. It's real."

"I can explain," Obi-Wan said. "I understand what this looks like, but you must listen to me, I want the same thing you do. I want peace and I want truth. Please, give me more time." But his words had no effect on the audience. The technicalities—that the bunker already existed, that the datapad was already there, that communications went to Anakin on Langston and *not* the Jedi Council on Coruscant—none of that mattered. The optics were well against him. Ketar—and Ventress—simply needed an opening.

"So, this Jedi," Ventress said, "comes to *your* world. Violates your rules. Hides the evidence you so desperately seek. And then transmits it to the Republic. He has not just broken trust. He has smashed it to pieces, then swept it away."

Ketar walked in front of the officials, still holding up the two devices. "We're fortunate that the Confederacy sent Asajj Ventress to oversee the Jedi emissary. Without her, who knows what he might have gotten away with?"

The room gave way to shouting, words and fingers pointed at Obi-Wan with a distinct fury where anything presented by Ketar and Ventress amplified the raw pain of Cadesura. Eyam shouted everyone down, then stood up.

"The emissary of the Republic has been charged with hiding evidence and violating the conditions of his stay during a catastrophic time. As such," the minister said, "he will be tried for his crimes in the Great Theatre of Judgment, open to the air and mist for all of Cato Neimoidia, for all of the *galaxy*, to see. Guards?"

Six guards marched in from the back entrance—Ruug among them.

Obi-Wan looked at her, and while most of the guards wore stoic determination, Ruug's mouth and eyes showed creases of concern.

"Should he be found guilty, the emissary's punishment will be swift.
Until that time, he will be detained." Eyam took in a breath and gauged
the room. Ketar continued to glower, a spark ready to ignite at a moment's notice. Ventress watched with cool detachment, arms crossed in
a frozen pose.

As for Ruug, the worry on her face grew with each passing second.
Was it for Obi-Wan? Was it for her people? Was it for the galaxy, whose
gears were about to turn yet again?

"Obi-Wan Kenobi, Jedi Knight, emissary of the Republic. Let it be
declared here: You are an enemy of the state." Eyam stood and flicked
his wrist forward. "Guards, take him away."

CHAPTER 29

ANAKIN SKYWALKER

THE CLONES COMPLIED WITH EVERY request.

They didn't bother to ask why Anakin wanted additional medical supplies or access to a shuttle. Instead, he got a simple "Yes, sir" followed by a quick departure to retrieve the crates, stopping only to answer Mill's question about whether the additional supplies would be missed.

"We always load an excess of three to five percent of materials in case anything is lost or damaged on the way," the trooper explained, which worked for both of their purposes, and he even pointed to one of the four *Eta*-class shuttles sitting unused in the docking bay. "Whichever one you prefer, General."

No explanations. No justifications. A simple chain of command, one that left him with countless troops ready to do whatever he deemed necessary. The sheer number of possibilities exploded through Anakin's mind, the temptation of simply getting whatever he wanted done. But that quickly became tempered with a discipline, one that reminded him where his responsibilities lay.

Padmé. The Chancellor. Obi-Wan. The Jedi. The Republic. Though after Padmé, things shifted around based on situations, pushing him one way or the other. In many cases, they all aligned—Padmé, after all, was a key member of the Senate, which worked with the Jedi and for the Republic.

Prioritizing one often trickled down to all of them.

Even now, with this makeshift plan, it all chained together. If he went to be Obi-Wan's backup, it might assist in Obi-Wan's goal of de-escalating the war. If the war was de-escalated, then the Republic would be safer. If the Republic was safer, then the Jedi would be needed less, and the Senate would have fewer emergency sessions.

And if those things happened, then Anakin and Padmé would have fewer things trying to pull them apart.

Really, that was all that mattered. Galactic peace, Obi-Wan's safety, Palpatine's stability, all of those things were important. But when layer by layer was stripped away, the only thing that truly mattered to Anakin's sun-dragon heart was Padmé.

He would do anything to protect her, even if that meant shifting the entire axis of the galaxy.

Or in this case, going to help Obi-Wan on Cato Neimoidia. Because *someone* had gotten their hands on the most important data in the galaxy.

The clone returned, the blinking lights of the launch bay reflecting off the gray stripes painted across his helmet. He gestured to the three supply crates on the now-deactivated repulsorlift dolly, then walked away when Anakin dismissed him. R2-D2 rolled slowly up to the inventory, then beeped a comment that roughly came across as "Do I have to carry all of that?"

Mill looked at the droid quizzically, and Anakin offered a quick translation before replying. "Some of it. But I'll need you for something more important."

R2-D2, in fact, did not carry any of the storage crates. But the astro-mech droid *did* pull the repulsorlift platform beneath the three boxes of medical supplies. They walked through the broken neighborhoods of

Langston's mining district, a cluster of domed buildings designed to work with the heavy winds at the base of the nearest mountain—signs of a civilization that had thrived just a few weeks ago before the Separatists decided to make it a battleground. Wisps of blue sand blew, causing a thin veil of color to come and go, enough for Anakin to bury his gloved mechanical hand under his cloak. His eyes, his hair—he was used to sand in that. But the joints and gears that were now part of his body, those needed protecting.

Decades of architecture and infrastructure had been transformed into mounds of rubble and half-standing buildings; walls had complete chunks missing due to rockets or blasterfire. And while Mill's demeanor reset itself during their short time back on the ship, she took tentative steps, a strained look on her face in the form of thin lips and concerned eyes.

Mill led the way quietly, allowing Anakin to take in the scene, the multispecies population showing a combination of resolve, fatigue, and despair. Anakin saw it, from the younglings playing blitzball in the nearby lake to the elder Aqualish sitting in the remaining doorway arch of an otherwise vaporized building. And if he saw it, then Mill must have sensed it as well.

"Look at this." She broke free from their pace, then ran over to a pile of debris, a mix of dented stone and twisted beams, all marred by the blackened scars of blasterfire. "Do you see it?"

Anakin caught up to her, still uncertain about what caught her attention.

"Even here, with all *this*"—Mill spread her arms wide—"life can grow." She pulled several pieces of jagged debris out of a rubble mound, much of it already covered in a layer of Langston's sand. The chunks rolled to the ground and settled, and Mill blew the remaining sand away to clear off the space. "There," she said, a single wildflower now visible. It reacted with a sensitivity greater than most flowers Anakin had seen, its petals tilting upward as they encountered the sun's beams. "A little bit of help." She turned, catching Anakin's sudden grin. "What? Clones don't look for flowers, huh?"

"They probably don't. But it's not that." Anakin gestured at Mill to keep leading the way, thinking of Padmé putting a flower in her hair just nights ago, and wondering if she'd kept it or if it had already withered away. "I know someone who would appreciate this. That's all." He pointed over the horizon, a path opening into a wide thoroughfare for the community. "Should we start asking around?" Anakin asked—a practical question, but also something to distract Mill from her obvious queasiness. "The town's spaceport is over there. There were a few local craft sitting around." He dragged his finger across a nearby wall, a layer of sand coming off onto his black glove. "Probably covered in dust."

"No," Mill said, "we should keep going."

R2-D2 complained, but Anakin motioned for him to settle down. "Don't tell me you're getting tired." He laughed at the droid's sassy reply. "What do you mean a long walk? We don't even know—" Anakin stopped and watched Mill, and though the youngling carried the burden of being affected by everything she felt around them, she walked with purpose, turning immediately down a smaller alley.

"Hey, Mill? We're in a business district," Anakin said, catching up to her. "Plenty of shopkeepers here who probably own a ship for one reason or another. Why don't we just announce ourselves?"

"Because. They need these supplies."

"Mill, we can't help everyone we encounter. That's just not practical. And I really need to get going."

The young Zabrak turned, a surprise fierceness in her eyes. She suddenly looked taller, and her jawline clenched with a burst of confidence. In that moment, Anakin saw so much of a reflection in her—not just of his instinctive stubborn pull to his own moral compass, but also of Padmé's ability to both empathize *and* be pragmatic about it.

One look told him who "they" were.

"Rokura and her siblings lost their elders in the attack. They need *something* to get by without the family business. I don't know if they'll use these supplies. Maybe they'll barter them." Mill turned and resumed walking, each stride picking up the pace. "But this'll help. Shouldn't we give them that? After what's happened to them?"

Anakin turned skyward with a sigh, exasperation, but also a hint of amusement slipping in. R2-D2 chirped back a *what are you waiting for?* series of beeps, and Anakin shot the droid a look.

"Yes, Artoo," he said, patting the rolling droid on the head. "I know she's right."

R2-D2 squawked again, almost as if the droid laughed at him. Then he whistled, a question in electronic form.

"Yeah, I agree. Padmé would like her, too."

The transaction took longer than Anakin would have liked given the circumstances, but he quickly saw that Mill made the correct call. The supplies now with the group of Gharal siblings, Anakin powered up their family ship—an ancient hyperdrive-capable *Dynamic*-class freighter called the *Norriker* formerly used for hauling select bins of Langston's rarest ores, small purchases for specialized manufacturing. But now the ship sat idle, two generations of the family killed in crossfire and collateral damage, leaving it to become a rental-by-barter craft for a Jedi Knight on an unauthorized mission.

Mill waved goodbye to a limping Rokura, then met with Anakin as he ran a diagnostic check. "They know I'll return it as soon as I can?"

"They do. They also said to take your time—no one's flying anywhere right now."

"Hopefully," Anakin said, looking at the readouts on the panels for power balance among speed, shields, and auxiliary operations, "this will be over in just a day or two. I'd much prefer that." R2-D2 chimed in with a sarcastic comment about needing some downtime, and Anakin refused to dignify that with a response. "As for you," he said, "call Theo from the shuttle and tell him that I've gone to investigate something. They'll send a pilot to bring you and the shuttle back to the cruiser. You do know your way back, right?"

"That's not necessary, Master."

"Why's that?" Anakin asked, running initial diagnostics on the hyperdrive's energy stabilizer. "D'urban will make sure you get back to the Temple soon."

"Because I'm coming with you."

He stopped toggling the switches and swiveled his chair around. "Excuse me?" This was why he'd never, ever consider dealing with a Padawan. He *knew* how stubborn they were; that was him mere months ago.

"Master, I would rather do something that might bring an end to the war instead of digging for kyber crystals."

"The Gathering is much more than just getting a kyber crystal. It's a—"

"I know, I know. I've heard the Padawans say 'you find yourself on Ilum.' I don't care. The other younglings want weapons. Adventure and fighting. Big jumps. You're going somewhere that might put an end to the war."

"Cato Neimoidia is no place for a youngling. Not right now."

"And how do you know that?" she asked, hands now squarely on hips.

"Because," Anakin said, ducking underneath the control panel. He pretended to check wiring, but really, it was to buy time to come up with an answer. "It's a tense political situation."

"Why do we do this? Are we just swinging a lightsaber and lifting boxes? Or are we building peace?" She got down on his level, determined scowl now face-to-face with him under the console. "Peace across the galaxy. Peace in yourself. You asked me if I wanted to help people, well, that's what I'm going to do. With you."

Her words echoed a memory, so many years ago when Qui-Gon Jinn told him to stay in the cockpit of a starfighter as the Naboo attempted to take back their planet from the Trade Federation. Of course, he kept his word about staying in the cockpit. "Qui-Gon told me to stay in this cockpit, and that's what I'm going to do," he'd told R2-D2 at the time, with the same conviction Mill used now. And he'd kept his word, all while doing what he thought was right—what his heart told him to do in order to help the people he quickly grew to care about. He'd stayed in the cockpit; it was the surroundings that changed as he flew into space.

"I'm not changing your mind, am I?" he asked.

Mill sat down in the *Norriker*'s passenger seat, then adjusted the ponytail behind her horns. "Not a chance."

CHAPTER 30

OBI-WAN KENOBI

EVERYTHING SLOWED AROUND OBI-WAN, A trick of the Force to accelerate the way his mind processed the situation. He blinked, his eyes closed for a fraction of a second, yet enough for thoughts to ripple through his mind as he considered the options before him. Six guards approached, each with standard rifles—except Ruug, who apparently was allowed to use her configurable sniper rifle, the barrel withdrawn into a shorter-range module for closer combat. Ketar and Ventress held their positions, the young Neimoidian still with Anakin's comlink and the incriminating datapad. The officials both in front of him and in the audience behind him stayed seated, though all gave off a palpable tension.

His lightsaber hung on a guard's belt behind him. That part didn't bother him.

The rest?

Given all of his training with both a lightsaber and the Force—and really, the two represented a single intertwined flow—a pure combat situation here would not be that difficult, and the situation played right into one of his favorite fighting techniques. There'd been worse, and

Obi-Wan figured that even this collective group of guards failed to match the threat of, say, the bounty hunter Jango Fett with his arsenal of Mandalorian weapons and tools.

Ruug had specialized training, of course. The rest, though? Just guards. Should it come to violence, he felt confident in his abilities.

But he had a different goal than simply defeating an opponent. His entire purpose here was to clear the Republic's name and lobby the Trade Federation away from neutrality—perhaps not into complete alignment with the Republic, but at least to a level where economic sanctions against the Separatists were on the table. Such a discussion had already been a long shot, and the recent revelations made it far more challenging. Using his lightsaber to deal with guards would make it impossible.

And then there was Ventress.

Was she the one with the lightsabers? How did she factor into all of this?

Had it just been the guards, Obi-Wan might have decided to simply put his hands up, relinquish his lightsaber, and strategize a plan from that. But given the unknown variable of someone—Ventress or not—capable of wielding such a specialized weapon, that raised far too many questions to surrender on the spot.

Any threat with lightsaber skills meant that protecting *his* lightsaber was his top non-diplomatic priority. And his only option here was to do his best at imitating Anakin Skywalker:

He needed to *improvise*.

Obi-Wan opened his eyes, each of his moves playing out with specific purpose.

First, he called his lightsaber to his hand, its blue blade erupting from the hilt. As expected, the guards readied their rifles.

Next, he waited. Someone had to take the first shot. And only seconds passed before it came.

Not from one of the guards. And definitely not from Ruug.

The first shot came from Ketar, who had dropped the devices and drawn his pistol. His eyes flared as the bolt exploded out of the gun, a bright red that only intensified the color of his eyes.

That was all Obi-Wan needed.

Next, he shifted the angle of his lightsaber, tilting it slightly in antici-pation. With the bolt less than a meter away, his arms tensed, muscles coiling up before releasing with a small and direct push forward. The bolt impacted the lightsaber, a pressure driving against the weapon be-fore it kinetically redirected, a confluence of velocity and angle that led the burst of energy in an entirely new direction.

The bolt soared through the room, flying between the helmets of two guards to directly impact the control panel of the back door. It tore through the panel's outer covering and circuitry, ending with a brilliant spray of sparks—a contained sprinkle of fireworks that petered out into glowing debris falling to the floor.

The door slid open, its locking mechanism destroyed. Two of the guards turned to face the now-open exit, and while Ruug kept her rifle trained on Obi-Wan, she didn't fire. Ketar took several more shots, which Obi-Wan deflected into the safest areas possible. The immaculate masonry of the room would have to be collateral damage here.

Ventress, though, still didn't move.

Obi-Wan gave himself to the Force, and his body rode the ensuing wave, legs and arms moving infinitely faster than their normal pace. He ran and vaulted over the front podiums and landed in motion before slipping between the guards. And though each of them focused on the spot where he used to be—even Ruug—Obi-Wan thought he caught the corner of Ventress's eye, a simple tracking glance as he crossed the door's threshold.

Halfway down the hall, he returned to normal speed, still moving at an athletic pace but now clear of immediate danger. The first part of his ad hoc plan was met; he'd escaped the room to safety without hurting anyone. But now?

"Go, go, go," a voice cried out. It might have been Ketar, though Obi-Wan wasn't sure. In fact, he wasn't sure where to actually go—curious bystanders started to peer down the hallway, office workers and govern-ment employees of all kinds.

He ran at normal speed, attentive to the way overexertion of the Force's physical gifts might affect anything from strength to coordination. The way the Force surrounded him as he moved informed his decisions and calculations; an extra burst down the long hall *was* feasible, but doing so might briefly drain him.

No, right now he needed to rely on his own body, at least until an opportunity presented itself.

"I'm on the target," another voice yelled. That one was distinctive. "Stand back, give me a clear shot."

Ruug.

Which, Obi-Wan guessed, meant she'd switched her rifle to sniper mode and zeroed it in on him.

He stretched out with the Force one more time, not for any physical gifts of strength or speed, but to slow the world down and appraise the situation:

Directly in front of him, civilians stood in the hallway, many shrinking back from the reality of the scene.

Around him was a tunnel. The tunnel may have had elegant carvings in the walls, lines of shiny minerals embedded into subtle carvings amid the bleached white stone, but regardless of aesthetics, the hallway remained nothing but a tunnel with a start and an end.

To his right, though, were a series of windows open to overlook the massive courtyard Minister Eyam had called the Grand Theatre of Judgment, an open-air arena of sorts. But more important, adjacent to it sat several more nondescript buildings farther into the complex, places less exposed to public view. *Those* buildings had flat ledges and rooftops between the spires and slopes of Cato Neimoidia's architecture.

That would help.

Getting there required a precise leap at an exact angle to grip onto the buildings hanging down from the arch above, something that tapped into the way the Force augmented a body's natural ability to leap. He considered the current placement of all the beings around him, from the guards behind to the civilians in front. A Force-assisted burst of speed right now might leave his body exhausted, unable to tap into what he needed to scale such heights.

However, Ruug had her sniper rifle trained on him. And Obi-Wan was pretty sure that, as someone who'd earned her grizzled weariness and commando armor, she didn't miss her shots.

That left a choice: trust his body's capabilities under duress or trust Ruug.

Time snapped back into reality and he dashed forward, lightsaber blade drawn back into its hilt, and took one quick glance back. While Ruug had one eye in her scope, the other eye shut for focus, he sensed her reactions, her purpose, her inner moral compass.

There was no conflict in Ruug. She knew exactly what she was doing.

Obi-Wan trusted that her certainty came from the right place.

"Shoot the Jedi!" Ketar screamed, his voice cracking. "Shoot him now!" Blaster bolts rang out, though without the boom of a sniper rifle. Obi-Wan knew the fire came from the muzzle of a pistol, not Ruug's specialized weapon.

"Stand down, Ketar!" Ruug yelled. "There are civilians in the way!"

About twenty paces remained until he reached the open window. Nineteen. Eighteen. Seventeen. Each step came with precise measurements, an internal calculation both physically to get him there and mentally gambling on Ruug's decision.

"I've got a line of sight!" she said, her voice projecting far enough for Obi-Wan to hear everything.

Ten. Nine. Eight.

Obi-Wan took one last look behind him. The Force rippled around him, and Obi-Wan put his faith in it—and in Ruug.

Five. Four. Three.

Obi-Wan's angle shifted enough to prepare his body to leap. He felt the Force surrounding him like an ocean current and also powering the physical response within the fibers of his muscles.

The sniper rifle erupted, a fraction of a second later than it should have—at least if Ruug had intended on killing her target. Instead, her extra breath gave Obi-Wan the exact amount of time he needed to leap out the large open window, the rifle bolt whizzing right below his feet as he ascended.

"No!" As the Force pushed Obi-Wan's flight, Ketar's voice trailed him. Obi-Wan turned his head just briefly enough to make eye contact with the guard—and Ventress who, for whatever reason, moved at a casual pace behind. He soared upward, gripping onto an exhaust pipe below the rounded glass dome of a restaurant, shocking the patrons looking down over Zarra's governmental district. He burst forward, clinging to holds and ledges from the hanging buildings until he made it over the more accessible rooftops of the capital.

His hands let go and he dropped, Cato Neimoidia's fog making his hair and beard damp. His boots landed on the ledge of a building, and a second jump took him to the roof. Blaster bolts came from the direction of the government offices, the fire whizzing past him in scattered angles.

Figuring out who shot at him—and whether Ventress was involved—required the luxury of time, something he didn't have thanks to a fleet of seeker remotes rising to his elevation. They propelled forward, and Obi-Wan set out on foot again, switching from Anakin's improvisation to his own specialty.

He needed a plan.

CHAPTER 31

RUUG QUARNOM

As soon as she called out "I'm on the target," things kicked into motion, and Ruug knew exactly how Ketar would react even before the trigger was fully pulled. The cross-traffic of civilians gave cover to her story, though she hated the fact that they were potentially in the line of fire—and she was furious at Ketar for brandishing a pistol when terrified innocents stood in the way, government employees who had nothing to do with the investigation or any ongoing tensions with the Republic, political or otherwise.

As for Obi-Wan, Ruug had tracked enough targets to predict where they headed. This marked the first time such a target had Jedi abilities, but the same logic applied. An open window. Plenty of options.

An easy escape.

Ruug's job was to make it look good. Risk assessment was an inherent part of Neimoidian culture, the counterpart to their inherent ability to calculate—except in this case, the risk was whether or not she'd accidentally take down a Jedi. The odds clearly showed the path as the marked escape route, and the combination of Obi-Wan's current speed and what she'd witnessed mere moments ago created reasonable assumptions for her approach. All it took was a fraction of a second, a mix of practicality and instinct, and Ruug sent the deadly bolt whizzing barely beneath Kenobi's feet as he vaulted up with a supernatural ascension.

Even for an experienced sniper like herself, such execution caused her to exhale with relief.

"He was in your sights!" Ketar yelled, and though she'd expected this outburst, she still acted with indignation at the way he lost his composure.

"Stand down, Cadet." Ruug matched Ketar's volume, well aware that everyone watched. "Remember who is the veteran here."

"I don't care, you had the chance to kill the Jedi and you didn't take it."

He'd spent time with Ventress, that much had been clear, despite Ruug trying to steer him away. Just days earlier, his grief seemed so overwhelming. And now he came up with evidence out of nowhere—without even informing his partner—and his urge to fight training droids had evolved into full-blown murder, despite civilian danger.

Ruug replayed the last few actions in her head from the chase out into the hallway to the moment Obi-Wan vaulted upward. And through it all, he had moved swiftly and carefully around any civilians. That spoke volumes about the Jedi's integrity, and it gave her something to establish moral superiority in front of other Neimoidian guards. "Would you prefer me to rain blaster bolts on every innocent person in this hallway? Sacrifice them for whatever vengeance you seek?"

Ketar's scowl spoke just as much about what *he* was willing to do. And just how far someone or something had pushed him in such a short time.

Ruug cursed herself for not taking Ventress more seriously during their meeting while on guard duty.

"This would avenge *our dead*."

The fact that Obi-Wan had communicated with one of his Jedi brethren hadn't surprised Ruug. His analysis had to come from somewhere, and the equipment he'd brought certainly didn't seem powerful enough to run the computations and processes necessary to generate his findings. The datapad, however, was another story.

He didn't deny it. He said he needed more time. And at the bar, he'd hesitated a few times when they talked about leads, like he was about to say something then changed his mind. So while he did omit the truth, he likely ran his own risk assessment in doing so.

Still, she was just as mad at him as she was at Ketar.

"Kenobi was on to something. Ransacking his things impedes the investigation."

Ventress stepped in front of her, walking uncomfortably close given the circumstances. "Perhaps you have your own bias in this situation."

"I'd call it experience."

"Experience? Or has guard duty softened your ability to make diffi-cult judgments?" Ventress locked eyes with Ketar, her expressions say-ing more to the young man than her words. "I thought you Neimoidians excelled at—" She took in a breath before turning back to Ruug. "—risk assessment."

This agent of Count Dooku carried a sinister glint in her eyes, one that probably worked in intimidating many she encountered, possibly even the officials in the other room. And in the case of Ketar, it probably drew him to her.

But Ruug had seen far worse, *done* far worse, to let a few side-eyed glances scare her off. "I'm not playing your game," she said in a firm tone and with a shake of the head before looking back out at the ledge.

Ketar huffed, turning to the sky. "Where's that transport?" Comm chatter with the other guards revealed that seekers pursued the Jedi, but Ruug already knew that a handful of lightly armed aerial remotes wouldn't be able to stop someone with Obi-Wan's abilities. No, he must have had a plan and a purpose, and if he really did intend to try for a peaceful resolution, then he wouldn't be jumping on a shuttle to Corus-cant.

That meant that Ruug needed to get to him first.

"Thirty seconds inbound," a voice from the remaining guards called out.

Ruug unlocked the side module on the rifle's handguard then shifted it toward the base, activating a retraction of the elongated barrel. Inside the weapon, further mechanics churned for a quick second, switching internal plasma calibrations to work at closer range. She swung the rifle across her back, the strap holding tight to her armor. Ketar readied his pistol, things clicking into place as he replaced his ammo clip. Three other guards moved behind them, ready for the transport.

"I'll take the next one," Ventress said, giving space as the small floating platform came into view. Ruug ignored anything and everything from Ventress as she stepped onto the windowsill, the drop below far enough that it came with an inherent trust as she stood next to Ketar. The octagonal platform slowed to a stop a step away from the open window, and Ruug stepped aboard, the platform dipping under their weight. She grabbed the handrail to steady herself.

Ketar did not, instead only looking up and pointing toward the direction where Obi-Wan had disappeared.

CHAPTER 32

OBI-WAN KENOBI

THE SEEKERS KEPT PACE WITH Obi-Wan as he leapt from rooftop to rooftop, using the Force to help steady himself on harsh angles or slippery materials. Blaster bolts zoomed by him, the remotes failing to target with much accuracy, though Obi-Wan's ignited lightsaber made the occasional deflection.

All of this bought time for options, a stalling technique rather than pure escape. His ship had been confiscated, though jetting off would send the wrong message right now anyway, the appearance of guilt when he wanted discussion. He had no means of communication with Anakin, and while he often disagreed with his former Padawan, sometimes the mere act of debate and counterarguments produced a solution.

And running indefinitely wouldn't help anyone.

As he moved, he scanned the area and considered his priorities. The most important thing remained getting an audience with the Trade Federation, and though they already leaned toward not believing him, it marked another chance to plead for de-escalation. And given that Neimoidian culture made trials public, recordings of his arguments would likely make it out across the galaxy, broadcasting a message to slow down and think rather than play into any hands that wanted rapid conflict.

Barring any of that, he still needed to find a way to escape.

The last time he'd been in a similar situation—captured, isolated, and with few options—the best idea hadn't come from himself or Anakin; instead, Padmé demonstrated a level of forward thinking that bested the Jedi, using a hairpin to quickly undo her shackles while Master and apprentice bickered. She'd likely been thinking about how to escape from the moment the Geonosian guards hauled them into the arena and the beasts emerged from their gates. That provided all the time needed to execute her plan.

Obi-Wan didn't have a lockpick. But he *did* have a lightsaber, one that guards would take away the moment they caught him. That made safeguarding it key—and given that he was being chased, protecting it became the current objective. He turned a corner as shouts from below echoed upward. The pulsing hum of hover platforms grew louder and louder, each with a number of guards on it. The seekers elevated, likely to give the guards better line of sight, and Obi-Wan considered the spaces around him:

Several buildings reached skyward, and above those hung another block of the bridge city, structures built downward in an arch that aided in his escape. Overpasses connected some of these, enabling foot traffic in all directions.

Directly below one of those, in fact, sat the open courtyard for public trials.

And above that, an elaborate tower, something that appeared too thin to actually offer any public functionality. Still, it *looked* ornate, curves and reflective glass embedded into an architectural marvel.

An idea emerged in Obi-Wan's mind as he recalled a wall where he'd found datachips hidden by a Jedi long ago on the planet Lenahra. He turned, changing the angle of his sprint to move toward the tower. More voices shouted, calls for guards to close in on him from all angles. Obi-Wan tapped into the currents of the Force, feeling the burst of energy rippling through his body as it elevated him halfway up the tower, well out of the sight lines of the approaching guards. With several seconds of cover, he found a small cutout beneath a window ledge, something that seemed more decorative than functional. His hand- and footholds maintained, he grabbed his lightsaber from his belt, then flipped it upside down and jammed it against the wall. The blade activated, now an elongated energy knife digging directly into the side of the structure, and as he jostled the hilt to clear a radius, melted ore oozed out. The weapon went quiet, its blade retracting without ever being visible after carving a space just deep enough to keep a small object secure from prying eyes.

Like a lightsaber hilt.

The weapon lodged and hidden, Obi-Wan once again launched himself with the Force, propelling forward as if the tower had merely been a tool for his escape rather than a hiding place for his lightsaber. He landed on an adjacent parapet, civilian observers ducking in fear at his appearance. He swerved around them, then resumed running, though this time he purposefully let his speed dip. A floating platform of guards approached in the distance, along with two behind him. He hesitated, more for appearance than anything else, his search for places to turn simply a way to burn off the seconds until capture.

Two seekers emerged, elevating before jetting forward, and though Obi-Wan no longer had his lightsaber to deflect blasterfire, he held up both hands and reached through the Force to grip the machines and smash them into each other. Their crumpled chassis dropped, a trail of spark and smoke left in their wake.

The action provided good cover for his true intentions, a show of defense that masked the fact that he intended to be captured. Behind him, boots slammed on the stone path, followed by several shouts, all melting together into a verbal mix of aggression. "Cover me," Ruug yelled, and Obi-Wan turned to see her sprinting toward him, a pistol drawn out while her usual rifle sat across her back.

A line of guards formed behind her, with rifles aimed directly at Obi-Wan. On the other side, the farther guards landed and mirrored the formation. Obi-Wan put his hands up, then glanced upward at the tower, a quick flick of the Force to feel that his lightsaber remained secure in its spot. "Don't move, Jedi!" Ruug yelled, and though her volume increased, her voice carried a level tone. She slowed her approach, pistol trained on him as she got closer.

"Hands behind your back," she said, her voice low enough that he barely heard it over the altitude's winds and the humming repulsors of the floating guard platforms.

"I appreciate what you did in the hallway," Obi-Wan said without resistance.

Ruug holstered her pistol and pulled out a pair of energy shackles. She moved without speaking, first binding Obi-Wan's left hand, then the right. "Why didn't you tell me about the datapad?"

"I needed to know if it was authentic or not."

The binders clicked into place, a pressure now gripping Obi-Wan's wrists. "If you wanted me to trust you," she said, "you should have been honest with me."

A low hum vibrated from the shackles, the frequency of their energy subtle enough that perhaps only he picked up on it. "You're right. I apologize for that."

"No laser sword," Ruug said, lowering her voice even further as the guards approached.

"I'm improvising. Listen." Obi-Wan relaxed, shifting into a defeated posture clear enough for others to see. "Yes, the datapad points to the Republic. But we don't know *why* yet. Presenting it as fact without context could escalate things beyond repair. I need a chance."

"They sound like they've made up their minds."

"A chance is not a guarantee," Obi-Wan said over his shoulder. "Nothing is absolute, except for not taking that chance."

"Well then." Ruug patted him on the back. "I'll do my best to help."

"You!" Ketar called, the single word practically a taunt, and though every rifle from the armed guards pointed at him, the young Neimoidian clearly moved out of step from the group. A tension rippled through Obi-Wan's body, and he reached out, dipping into the currents of the Force to sense whether Ketar was close to pulling the trigger. "Did you really think your tricks could help you escape?"

"Stand down, Ketar. He is under arrest. I have apprehended him."

"*No.*" Ketar moved forward, stepping into Obi-Wan's peripheral vision.

But Ruug moved to block him, her shoulders now nearly touching his. "He is a prisoner. He will stand trial in the royal court of Cato Neimoidia. Your job here is done."

"She is correct," Ventress said, appearing from behind the row of guards. She pulled back her hood, though her cloak remained wrapped around her as she walked forward. "The Jedi will submit. It is what they do. But I do have one question for you." Ventress extended a pale finger at Ruug. "Where is his lightsaber?"

To this point, Obi-Wan had placed his faith in Ruug, starting with their initial encounter on the surface of Cato Neimoidia and continuing all the way to her intentionally ill-timed shot in the hallway. Now he waited for something more subtle than anything involving blasterfire.

What would Ruug say about his weapon?

"Damaged, possibly destroyed. If you check the surrounding grounds, you will likely find its remains," Obi-Wan said, giving Ruug a lead to work with. "Your seekers shot it out of my hand."

"'Damaged, possibly destroyed.' What kind of Jedi are you if mere remotes can destroy your weapon? I thought you were a Jedi Master."

"Being chased by guards and seekers at high altitude is not part of standard Jedi training."

Ventress clicked her tongue as she began pacing around him. "Quite convenient if you think about it."

"I can confirm," Ruug said, moving to step closer to Ventress. "I saw it happen. You can check the holo security recording, though it happened up there." She gestured to the tall adjacent tower. "I'm not sure the cams have the angle."

"Are you certain that is what you saw? And you are not under the influence of a Jedi mind trick? Only the strong can resist that." The two nearly collided in front of Obi-Wan, Ventress staring Ruug down. But Ruug's orange-red eyes never blinked, never lost focus, in a way that shouldn't have surprised him. Someone with possibly decades of commando experience likely couldn't be intimidated.

Especially someone with a strong moral compass.

"I'm certain," Ruug said, taking a step forward until she was nearly face-to-face with Ventress. "Check the security recording."

They stood, only the wind swirling between them as everyone held their positions: the guards, Ketar, and Obi-Wan. He watched, the only movement between the two women coming from the rhythm of their breathing. Ventress looked Ruug up and down, then eyed Obi-Wan without turning.

"As a representative of the Confederacy of Independent Systems, do you have a problem with what I've done?" Ruug finally asked.

"I trust your judgment," Ventress said slowly. She took several steps back, arms out, then walked up to Obi-Wan just as guard rifles nudged him to move. She leaned in close and spoke directly in his ear. "I was pleased to see your work up close, Master Kenobi." She reached up and tousled the long locks of hair dangling over his neck. "Count Dooku was right. You're quite impressive."

CHAPTER 33

ANAKIN SKYWALKER

THE *NORRIKER'S* CONSOLE BEEPED AGAIN.

And yet again, Anakin chose to ignore it.

"Shouldn't you check that?" Mill asked. "It's beeped six times now."

Seven times, actually. The first time, Mill had been in the back trying to learn how to speak astromech with R2-D2. They tunneled through hyperspace, the swirling bright mix of blue and white flashing over the cockpit. Going through hyperspace in a small freighter with questionable integrity made for a completely different experience for the youngling, and though Anakin relished feeling the rattle of the deck plates and the rumble of the propulsion systems, the difference between official Republic equipment and the way everyone else lived caught Mill off guard.

"It's nothing," Anakin said.

"Beeping usually indicates something . . ." Mill leaned forward over Anakin's shoulder and squinted. ". . . bad, right?"

In this case, it *was* bad. But not bad like "mechanical failure" or "low fuel." This was a comm signal, and though Anakin wouldn't know who it was exactly until he opened a channel, he had a sneaking suspicion that it came from a clone commander.

That was the problem with making it up as you went along—most of the practical logistics simply never came up. Obi-Wan had plans built upon strategies built upon guidelines, even when he had to come up with something on the fly. Padmé worked much in the same way, and Chancellor Palpatine, well, he wouldn't have gotten to where he was today if he hadn't set up his plans in advance.

The three most important people in Anakin's life all worked efficiently and methodically. And then there was him, like the sun at the center of that solar system pulling them all out of balance with his impulse-driven decisions. Padmé never gave him grief about it, but he'd started to recognize what her half smiles meant when an idea popped into his head.

Obi-Wan, on the other hand, always made a comment at the end. It usually came as a one–two punch, the first hit being a scold for not listening, the second being astonishment for Anakin pulling off whatever little miracle he'd attempted.

And on very rare occasions, Obi-Wan would follow that with a bit of gratitude.

"Bad is relative," Anakin said.

"Is this something I'll learn as a Padawan?"

"Not likely. How much pilot training do you have?" Mill's head tilted and she raised one eyebrow. "Okay, fair point. Well, every control panel is different, but there are a lot of similarities." The beeping started again, a simple red light flashing over the navigational chart. "Like that particular beep and light, that's someone trying to reach us over the ship's comms."

"Someone? You mean—"

"Most likely," Anakin said. "It makes sense. I mean, the Three-Oh-Second and D'urban weren't exactly going to ignore that we didn't come back."

"I thought you took care of that."

"I may have skipped that part in my plan. Hey," Anakin said, pointing at her with a laugh, "*you* were supposed to go back to the cruiser. I just made up the rest as I went along. They must have figured out who we bartered with and gotten this ship's comm codes."

"So, maybe just tell them what we're doing? The clones listen to you."

That was true. Ever since attaining the rank of Jedi Knight, the clones had fallen into place. And even if D'urban was involved, perhaps some blustery vague talk could temporarily smooth it over. "Okay," Anakin said, "let's try it your way." He clicked the flashing button and a small beam shot up above the console, the holographic image forming into existence. Anakin's hopes lay with Theo, Raptor, or Sparks, but a worst-case scenario of an annoyed D'urban Wen-Hurd was doable.

What he got, though, moved the needle beyond worst-case scenario.

"Skywalker," the voice said with familiar disdain before the image fully assembled. "Where are you?"

"Master Windu," Mill said with a gasp.

Anakin resisted his urge to roll his eyes.

"Master Windu." Anakin kept his tone flat and diplomatic, the typical default he reverted to whenever talking to any Jedi—even Obi-Wan, though their last few conversations felt like they'd started to evolve past that. "I'm sorry, your transmission broke up."

"Skywalker. Repeat your destination."

Which he couldn't reveal. He couldn't even play coy with it; the smallest hint would likely push the Council toward suspecting his destination. With Obi-Wan in a dangerous situation and any word of Republic involvement likely to dial tensions up even further, the Senate, chancellor, and Jedi all had to stay out of this.

Not just for Obi-Wan's sake. For the sake of a war that threatened to spiral out of control.

He needed to think fast.

"We're on our way to . . ." He let his words fade out while he rotated the small knob for the comm's frequency stabilizer. "There's a lot of interference right now. Ion storms. But I have the youngling Mill Alibeth with me. She is safe. I'll check in as soon as we land."

"What was that?" Anakin twisted the knob again, static interrupting the signal and causing lines to jab in and out of Mace's hologram. Over his shoulder, Mill laughed, and Anakin turned to shoot her a *be quiet* glance—not out of scolding, but to keep up appearances. But they locked eyes, and her grin became infectious, so much so that he put his gloved hand over his mouth to prevent his near-laugh from transmitting across the galaxy to the Jedi Order's most revered fighter.

Because even though Anakin excelled at improvising under duress, that applied only to combat situations. In this case, his actions came off as no more than a childhood prank on the Jedi's most powerful warrior. Which was pretty funny in itself.

"Repeat. Your. Destination."

"Understood, Master." He let go of the knob and the transmission stabilized. "I have the youngling Mill Alibeth with me. She is safe. Please send my apologies to the Three-Oh-Second and D'urban Wen-Hurd. We got pulled away after discovering an urgent issue on Langston and this ship's comms aren't stable."

"*Skywalker.* Where are you going?" Mace Windu always spoke with quiet intensity, but now the venerable Jedi Master's frustration manifested into an emerging growl. In all of the challenges that Mace had faced down recently, from taking down Jango Fett with a single lightsaber swipe to staring down an overwhelming wave of super battle droids on Dantooine, he'd done so with such calm and control—and yet here, a simple comm trick managed to get under his skin.

Anakin gave himself a silent pat on the back. He'd definitely have to tell Padmé about this.

Assuming they all survived.

"Commander Theo," Mace said to a clone off cam, "get me a tracking lock on this transmission."

"Right away, sir," the clone responded.

"We're hitting a huge ion storm now. I will check in as soon as I—"

Anakin cut off the transmission there, Mace's burning eyes and tight scowl suddenly disappearing.

For several seconds, the only sound in the ship came from the frequent rattling of deck plates, a regular *tink-tink-tink* that tapped an almost musical pattern as the ship flew through the brilliant tunnel of hyperspace.

Finally, Mill broke the silence. "Well," she said. Anakin looked up to see the whites of lightspeed reflecting off her tan cheeks and pale horns. "That didn't go good."

"Don't worry," Anakin said. "You're not in trouble. If anything, I'm going to be the one in trouble. But that's all right." The panel showed the navicomputer's flight path to Cato Neimoidia, about half a day's journey left, though possibly longer given that the shuttle might fly apart at any minute. "I'm used to it."

R2-D2 rolled in behind them, whistling a lecture at him. "Takes one to know one, Artoo." The droid whistled in return before swiveling its head and looking at Mill.

"Are assignments always like this?" Mill asked as she settled into the passenger seat.

"I don't know," Anakin said. He leaned back into his seat, the torn leather crinkling as he sank into the worn padding. "I've only been a Jedi Knight for a short time. Artoo?"

R2-D2 beeped, this time without the sass. "Show us everything you know about Cato Neimoidia." An affirmative series of chirps came through, followed by a holoprojection of the planet.

The console beeped again, an incoming transmission that Anakin didn't dare answer. He reached over to mute it, and as he did, he noticed some of Langston's blue sand was still stuck in the straps of his glove.

Sand. It got everywhere.

The beeping continued. Anakin could only assume that it was Master Windu, who had more than enough patience to keep this up for the entire duration of their journey. But even if he realized their ultimate destination as Cato Neimoidia, the Council would abide by mission parameters and avoid any confrontations. That was the difference between them and Anakin.

Anakin smirked at such a thought.

He clicked the button to the left of the flashing indicator, setting the Norriker's incoming transmissions to silent for now.

Consequences could be dealt with upon returning to Coruscant. But with Master Windu already irritated, they'd better save Obi-Wan, because if they came back empty-handed it might be worse than losing his arm.

CHAPTER 34

OBI-WAN KENOBI

FOUR PLAIN SMOOTH WALLS SURROUNDED Obi-Wan, lacking the opulence of most of Cato Neimoidia's other architecture. Micro lights must have been embedded within the top of the wall, providing an ambient illumination to the green-gray holding cell, and the door itself appeared to be a simple metal slab with a locking mechanism, probably something capable of withstanding significant brute force or blasterfire.

Not that Obi-Wan had any intentions of escaping. He'd been in far worse situations, and in every case, a solution presented itself. Even that nest of gundarks, though he'd had Anakin with him then. That harrowing escape had been filled with claws and teeth, dirt and chaos, yet once they'd stopped arguing about who went first, Obi-Wan and Anakin had fought and moved effortlessly on their way out, equal parts collaborators and single fighting unit. Even when Anakin was younger, they moved in sync, as if their verbal jousting was a necessary part of their relationship, balancing their natural instincts for combat.

But now nothing tethered them—the very mission came with the order of isolation. Every step here kept him alone by design, and even when he had the choice, he chose to keep Anakin at arm's length.

The thing was, every single time he tried to keep Anakin away, he found a way in. That was simply who Anakin Skywalker was.

Years ago, when Anakin was still early in his Padawan time, Obi-Wan had been assigned a minor investigation to a dead star system, something so ancient that the remaining dwarf lingered at near-absolute-zero temperatures. He'd intended to fly there alone despite his discomfort about piloting himself due to the strange quantum fluctuations and gravity wells. But halfway through the hyperspace journey, he'd heard the strangest noise coming from beneath one of the panels by the port-side thruster:

Snoring.

Obi-Wan had lifted the metal access panel, only to find twelve-year-old Anakin stowed away, having fallen asleep in the warm ambience and rumbling metal above the sublight drive, the heat reminding him of a Tatooine evening. "I didn't want to stay at the Temple," he'd said before explaining his elaborate plan to hide on board. "Besides, you said you promised Master Qui-Gon you'd protect me."

Which he had.

"Since you're here," Obi-Wan had told him with a sigh, "you might as well take a look." And when they'd arrived at their destination, he'd taken it as an opportunity: the rare privilege of viewing such a scientific impossibility doubling as a good reminder of the Jedi Code regarding attachment and letting go, a lesson that over time, even stars burned out.

Out there, in the most lifeless regions of space, Anakin had simply found a way to find him.

Obi-Wan and Anakin. Anakin and Obi-Wan. The mentor who took careful, measured steps; the Padawan who charged forward with explosive power and, it seemed, ridiculous luck. Despite their age difference, despite their rank difference, despite their *personality* difference, they always got the job done.

But that was under the guise of Master and apprentice. This time was different. They were equals now, their link purposefully broken. Too many gears turned in the galaxy right now, and everyone in the Republic slotted into a specific purpose to help end the war. They had responsibilities, and the *mission* depended on them staying apart.

Obi-Wan laughed at the mysterious twists and turns of the Force. Their first time truly apart—not as easy as one off to a remote system while the other handled tasks on Coruscant, but pulled in completely different directions—and of course every plan that he'd tried to conjure up came with the caveat of "if only Anakin were here."

If only Anakin could discover more about Ventress. Or tap into the Neimoidian public broadcast system to provide more context to the masses. Or help Ruug out with her lead.

Or investigate further, finding some possible way to identify a false-hood about the datapad. That was what Anakin did: find a way. They didn't even need to directly attack the situation together, but Anakin's resourcefulness, stubbornness, impulsiveness, his sheer *Anakin*-ness, felt necessary at this point.

Without it, Obi-Wan may as well have been flying blind or missing a limb. Or in this case, possibly damning the Republic to consequences too great to contemplate. While dishonoring the memory of thousands of dead from Cadesura. And quite possibly, making himself complicit in the whole thing.

All because he did this without Anakin, without their constant push-ing and reining in of each other's boundaries, and Obi-Wan wondered if Qui-Gon had foreseen all of this—not just his own loss at the hands of the vicious Sith Lord on Naboo, but the fact that Qui-Gon would forever tie two opposing forces together, their partnership always edg-ing toward spinning out of control but always, *always* finding a way to make a happy landing.

It took *not* having that intrinsic link to Anakin for Obi-Wan to finally see how much they needed each other. Not just on a strategic level, but to keep each other in check—Obi-Wan's tactful diplomacy pulling in Anakin's impossible drive, and Anakin's overwhelming *everything*-ness removing a layer of Obi-Wan's measured, clinical thinking.

If he survived this, perhaps he'd even tell Anakin someday.

Though really, it might work better if he didn't. Anakin's ego didn't need any more feeding.

And besides, he needed to get out of this first. Obi-Wan tapped into the Force, trying to sense if his lightsaber remained where he'd planted it. But without knowing exactly where he was in relation to that tower, such a search proved fruitless. He resigned himself to the fact that his weapon wouldn't be accessible until the trial actually occurred in the courtyard. Until then, all he could focus on was what he might say to sway those who listened: the local government, the mourning Cato Neimoidian public, the Trade Federation leaders. Most likely the Republic—Palpatine, the Senate, the Jedi, all of the HoloNet—even if it was on an intercepted signal. And quite likely Count Dooku and Nute Gunray.

What might convince every single one of those different factions that somehow, somewhere, there was *more* to this? And in the end, peace was the best solution?

That *wasn't* something he'd discuss with Anakin. He'd just rely on Anakin for the rest of it. But if his former Padawan learned anything from his promotion—or at the very least, Geonosis—it'd be to understand that the responsibilities of a Jedi Knight actually involved *listening*.

In the quiet confines of the cell, Obi-Wan found himself doing something as silly as wishing things were different, when he needed Anakin most.

Obi-Wan let that feeling pass, knowing that any energy put into those thoughts would likely be wasted. He sat on the floor with nothing but himself and four walls, cross-legged and straight-backed, then closed his eyes. His sense of self released, giving in to something much greater than an individual body and mind, all in search of wisdom and a solution to an impossible problem.

CHAPTER 35

ASAJJ VENTRESS

THE BULK OF ZARRA'S ARCHITECTURE was ornate, all intricate curves and immaculate carvings, much like the tower by which they chased Kenobi.

All such a waste of resources, a façade to shield the population from the realities of a cruel life.

Here, in an industrial district just west of the capital, Ventress felt much more at home. Everything from the streets to the small storage room she'd rented for a handful of credits felt completely functional, nothing extravagant or excessive. Her surroundings offered her a simple means to get the job done.

Which was why she only had one thing in the room. She opened the door and the room's internal sensors detected her as she walked inside. Ketar followed behind her, but once automated illumination filled the space, she turned to find him examining his blaster.

"Something wrong with your weapon?" Ventress asked.

"I think so." He held it out as if targeting within his sights, then checked the alignment on its small scope again. "I had Kenobi lined up. He must have gotten lucky."

The bravado in his words caused Ventress to laugh, something that clearly stunned the young guard. She admired his confidence, a trait that was likely amplified by the surge of fury and despair he'd felt since the Cadesura incident.

But of course, it was foolish. "I am certain that a single blaster is no match for a Jedi Knight. If Kenobi was trying, you would have known." She walked in front of him. "Had you survived, that is."

Ketar turned, his permanent scowl seemingly even more pronounced. "How would you know? You're just a diplomat."

"Oh. Is that what you think?"

"Isn't that why you're here? To observe the Jedi emissary?" he asked, his voice echoing off the simple metal walls that offered a completely opposite take from the exquisite Cato Neimoidian governmental complexes they'd spent time in.

She paced the room, considering the challenge presented by his questions—not because they were difficult to answer, but because there were so many choices. Ventress weighed the possibilities, how she might get the most out of his naïveté. Her goal had been clear ever since Count Dooku ordered her to fly to Cato Neimoidia, and with Kenobi about to face trial, exposing the two-faced nature of the Jedi Order and the Republic was well on its way. Dooku's instructions lacked specifics, though, something he often did—and Ventress understood why. This was not just a test of her physical gifts or her Force abilities; he wanted to see her strategize, improvise in the face of opportunity.

And this was an opportunity. Ventress promised herself she'd make the most of it.

"Just a diplomat," she said, stepping away from him. With her back turned, she listened, gauging his reaction as the next seconds unfolded. With one hand, she drew back her long cloak, and with the other, fingers gripped one metal hilt attached to her belt, the curve of its form against her palm. She unlatched it and stayed steady, holding the weapon in front of her. "Or perhaps more." A brilliant crimson glow emerged from the hilt, the distinct explosive discharge and ensuing hum now filling the room. "Do you see?"

Behind her, a quick shuffling noise told her that Ketar did *not* expect that, and now he even held his blaster up. He really *was* obedient after all; when she'd told him to stand guard outside Kenobi's room during her search, she figured he must have taken a peek. But no, he must have stayed in the hall the whole time, completely missing her lightsaber slash on the secure equipment case. She allowed herself a quick, short grin before returning to neutral and facing him.

"I understand the ways of the Jedi. And I come prepared to defend myself. They are volatile, unpredictable. Stealthy." She took two more steps toward Ketar, the blade close enough to reflect off his pistol's metal body. "Untrustworthy."

"You have their weapon."

"That is one way to look at it. But you have a pistol. How many people in the Republic have a pistol? How many people in the Outer Rim, in Wild Space, have a pistol? A weapon is a weapon, regardless of training or skills. Take a closer look." She angled the red blade his way, the tip of it now close enough that he winced at the heat burning off it. "Ask yourself, have I broken your trust in any way? You saw the datapad. You saw the comlink. You heard the transmission from Kenobi's partner confirming the evidence. This was all here, waiting for you. I've lifted the veil for you to see. Haven't I?"

In a gradual, slow gesture, Ketar lowered his pistol, though it remained in his hand.

In return, Ventress deactivated her lightsaber, its deep red no longer tinting the space. "Now I want you to think about your partner."

"Ruug?" Ketar asked, a puzzled look on his face. "What about her?"

"Do you trust her?"

"Of course I trust her," he said. His gaze fell to the floor, a headshake that showed this struck a nerve.

Count Dooku often spoke of the importance of opportunity, of knowing when to force a moment out of nothing, then take it before it slipped away. Now was one of those opportunities.

"Ruug's looked after me ever since I joined up."

"Interesting," Ventress said, her head cocked at an angle. "Since you joined. I can understand that. But what about since *Kenobi* arrived? Any behavior that might seem out of character?"

Ketar slowly turned his head to Ventress, the room's harsh flickering light tilting the shadows cast by his helmet over his cheeks.

"She's tried to keep you away from me, hasn't she?"

"She," Ketar started, "knew I'd been exhausted. She was just encouraging me to take care of myself. Because Cato Neimoidia needs us."

Even as he said the excuse, Ketar's tone gave away that he was reconsidering it all.

Ventress had him.

"The Jedi," she said, "are known to be able to influence the emotions, even thoughts of others. Has Ruug acted differently since Kenobi has been here? She is a decorated commando with elite training and a custom weapon, and yet . . . what happened when Kenobi ran?"

Ketar's mouth opened, and over the buzz of the room's lighting, she heard a low guttural sound as he tried to form words. Ventress waited, more than happy to let him come to the conclusion himself.

"She missed," he finally said.

"Loyalty," Ventress said in a slow, controlled cadence, "can be exploited."

Ketar took a single step back, a reaction out of impulse rather than decision. And now Ventress would move in for the finishing blow. "If you trust her, then you will do whatever it takes to break the hold that Kenobi has over her. To break the hold that the Jedi and the Republic have over Neimoidians. You can do this, Ketar. You can be the one." Just as he had fallen back, she moved forward, keeping a very specific distance to stay in his space, in his line of sight. "How do you think Kenobi's trial will go?"

"The evidence is damning," he said softly.

"Damning. That is different from certainty, isn't it?" At this point, Ketar might have agreed with anything Ventress said, but her words continued their assault, chipping away at his thoughts and concerns until she led him like a youngling following a toy. "The Jedi are powerful. Their ability to sway minds is unfathomable to those that don't understand their kind. Think of their Order—indoctrinating children fresh out of the womb, and their parents? They simply *let* them leave. Forever. Think of what Nute Gunray said about his encounter on Naboo, the frightening speed and power. And now they suddenly transition from 'peacekeeper,'" she said with a derision, "to soldiers commanding the military? Is that not concerning to you?"

"It is." Ketar's voice came out as a mere whisper.

Ventress sensed it, not just from the emotion rippling off him, but from the way his entire body tensed, the way his lip curled, the way his eyes stayed shut as the questions pierced through him. He was on the edge of giving in to her, something that happened so easily that she almost laughed at it. Count Dooku wanted to test her, and yet this was no challenge at all. Cadesura had created a creature seeking faith in something, regardless of what it was.

All she had to do was be there for him.

"You care about your people. Your planet. The Trade Federation. Then what risks are you willing to take to ensure their safety? To make a statement that will forever sway them away from the Republic?"

With Ketar's eyes still closed, she walked over to the case of explosive materials and put her hand on the biometric reader. "Or perhaps more than a statement." It beeped and whirred, locking mechanisms undoing before she lifted the case open, stacks of a pliable and very volatile orange compound just waiting to be wired into a detonator.

"You must calculate the risks," Ventress said, "and then make a choice."

Ketar opened his eyes, and Ventress stared right back at him.

CHAPTER 36

ANAKIN SKYWALKER

THE LAST TIME ANAKIN TRAVELED in disguise was before he and Padmé were married.

They'd dressed in simple refugee clothes, a poncho over a patterned vest for him, and an outfit light-years apart from her usual regalia for her. The intention of those days was to hide, but what they found became something greater—an overwhelming yearning that consumed both of them. It seemed a lifetime ago, though it had been far more recent, and while he now cringed at some of the things he'd said during those idyllic moments, the way words had tumbled out of his mouth without proper social graces or any sensible filter, he wouldn't trade any of it.

Because for all the awkward exchanges and regrettable attempts at impressing her, each of his mistakes—and hers—chipped away at their mutual defenses until they saw each other for who they were.

And it all started with a simple poncho, much like the one he wore now. Except this time, his outfit wasn't selected from various materials made available to a Jedi and a senator. Quite the opposite, in fact; with the worn coverings they'd procured along with the *Norriker*, Anakin and Mill played the role of down-on-their-luck merchants hoping to sell wares on Cato Neimoidia, a planet known for welcoming every opportunity for even the poorest merchant.

They left the public landing platform on the edge of Zarra, and their clothes may as well have been dirty washrags compared with some of the others coming and going in the port. Lush robes, glittering jewels, tailored formfitting suits—all of it spoke of an expensive class of travelers who partook in higher levels of business typical of the Trade Federation, where the systemic levers behind merchants and laborers were pushed and pulled—for the right price.

Those people looked down on, even ignored the ones who got their hands dirty building the merchandise or packing the minerals or selling the wares. Which made it the perfect disguise for two Jedi in search of another Jedi.

"There're a lot of guards," Mill said as she glanced around. Anakin must have become desensitized to the Trade Federation's mechanical armada by now, because even though the port's guard stations saw clusters of battle droids, their presence failed to intimidate him. Instead, the sight of them provoked an instinct to whip out his lightsaber and slice through them, but he tempered his impulses and considered their bigger threat: the armored Neimoidian guards, the ones who might be searching for suspicious activity.

"Ignore them for now," he said, and they entered a densely packed area of well-dressed travelers of all shapes and sizes, so many species eager to do business with the Trade Federation. Coming here meant paying high prices to take in the view from Cato Neimoidia's luxury hotels and spas, especially the buildings hanging downward from massive arches of their bridge cities. "As long as they ignore us in return, we'll be fine."

R2-D2 offered an annoyed beep at the constant starting and stopping as they waited for cross-traffic to clear up, repulsorlifts carrying suitcases or people simply too caught up in their own business to offer basic politeness. The droid threw a set of curses at a female Muun who bumped into him, but the tall, thin woman didn't give them a second glance. "Easy, Artoo," Anakin said. "You never know who might actually understand you here."

"So are you going to tell me why we're here now?" Mill asked after several more steps.

Anakin shot her a puzzled look. "You know why we're here. You volunteered to come along."

"No, I know I'm helping you. And I know it's something about Master Kenobi. Something that's *not* fighting with hundreds of clones. But what?"

Anakin rose onto his toes for a view toward the exit, craning and angling around taller beings than humans. Except this really was just a stall tactic to avoid the question. She was right, though. The youngling understood that in general, they were here to find Obi-Wan, discover who'd stolen his comlink. The nuts and bolts of that, though, remained vague—partially because he hadn't figured out exactly what to do once they landed.

But partially because he wasn't sure how to explain the mystery evidence. It wasn't quite a rescue mission, and the politics of the situation mucked up the neat boundaries of what needed to happen. Could he just say that it felt *right* being at Obi-Wan's side when things might go sour?

"It's complicated. Politics aren't things younglings should think about. *I* don't even like thinking about it much."

Cato Neimoidia's air was thick, the fog making it harder to breathe the instant they stepped out of the air-conditioned port building. Mill inhaled sharply and stopped in mid-step. The flow of foot traffic moved around them as if they were a rock that somehow interrupted a river rather than two people taking in a disaster.

From their vantage point several stories up, the gap in Zarra was jarring—the capital city stretched over the horizon, rocky spires and other formations acting as foundational anchors between blocks and districts. Yet a massive hole was visible to the upper left, as if the Cadesura district had simply evaporated from existence. Had they stood closer, the collateral damage of the explosions probably would have been visible in the remaining underlying infrastructure. But from this distance, it was simply gone. Transports circumvented the disaster area, still taking residents and visitors from one block to another. Anakin squinted, an internal judgment coming on about the people all around them, the people resuming their normal lives and taking transports to work as they floated over such devastation.

Except when Mill paused, he did, too, and he took in the scene around him. What he knew of the Trade Federation, of Neimoidians, had all come from the way the HoloNet portrayed them, the way Senator Lott Dod blustered, anything and everything Nute Gunray had ever done. While the Neimoidians coming and going no longer paused at the shock of the missing Cadesura district, they moved forward, some purposefully avoiding a look in that direction, others looking at it for too long.

Their mourning had nothing to do with Nute Gunray's actions.

For the city's residents, lives pushed forward, but the way each of them took in such a tragedy was a personal internalized experience that Anakin could only interpret from their expressions—or lack thereof.

Mill, on the other hand, wore her feelings on her face. "I think," she said, "I'm getting better at this."

"What's 'this'?"

"Feeling . . . this." She gestured at the space all around. "I can sense their suffering. But it's not like I'm drowning anymore. I can handle it." She reached over, taking Anakin's gloved hand. "Thank you. Everything you've shown me is far greater than getting a lightsaber crystal."

Maybe he should have stayed with the Initiates who were impressed with lightsaber tricks and floating objects. Playing an afternoon entertainer was much easier than trying to understand this youngling, someone who didn't quite fit the Jedi mold but was changing before his very eyes through lived experience, seeing the way things worked outside the comforts of the Jedi Temple.

Anakin took in a deep breath of Cato Neimoidia's muggy atmosphere and finally attempted to answer Mill's earlier question—without a plan. He'd just say it. "You want to know what we're doing here? Obi-Wan, my old Master. He's here trying to clear the Republic. He was supposed to *not* contact anyone. Not the Council, not the Senate. Not me. But he needed help on something he found. Something that might incriminate the Republic. And I gave him a secret communicator for a worst-case scenario. It's just"—Anakin bit down on his lip—"it's now a worser-than-worst-case scenario."

"Why's that?"

"Someone else has the communicator." He stepped forward, both Mill and R2-D2 shortly following. "And with that, the data implicating the Republic. We've got to find Obi-Wan, find that data, find a way to explain *why* it seems authentic."

"Do you think the Republic is free of blame?"

Just like that, Anakin's good feelings evaporated, a surge of irritation—any questioning of the Republic meant questioning him, the Jedi, Palpatine, *Padmé*. But he stifled the feeling, stuffing it deep down before it might turn into something worse. "I don't think that's possible. The Republic is trying to stop the war. The chancellor would have known about an operation." He looked at Mill, trying his best *not* to be scolding. "Why would you think that? You're a Jedi."

"If the data seems authentic, I just think it's important to ask. Don't you?"

Padmé questioned words and intentions, always looking for ways of addressing what lay underneath the surface of what people presented. Obi-Wan questioned the details, always trying to get down to a true understanding of what happened—and even if he doubted the motives of individual politicians, his allegiance to the Republic never shook.

Their questioning always drilled further down. But questioning the bigger picture, the thing that held them together? Anakin took a moment to contemplate such a thing. "I didn't." Individuals made wrong decisions. But the institutions in their life? He wanted to say that of course they were trustworthy, that they were the foundation that *everything* was built upon. How trustworthy they were, though, depended on the people in them. As long as morally sound people—like Padmé, like Palpatine—steered those institutions, they'd be safe. Keeping those people in power, though, meant finding and confronting bad actors. Especially the ones in the shadows. "Not until this moment. I like to think that only good people make decisions for the Republic. I suppose it's possible. Corruption is possible." A different type of anger sparked in Anakin. What if the data *was* authentic? Someone working on the inside, but why? War profiteers, or someone looking to betray the chancellor? If corruption did exist somewhere within the Republic government, it had to be rooted out and eliminated.

This was something he'd have to discuss with Palpatine at some point. But not now. Right now, his mission was Obi-Wan and the missing equipment. "You've given me something to think about. Look at that, I'm learning something from you. We'll call it even now."

Mill smiled, a welcome sight given their location and the surrounding situation. "I thought you were supposed to be the mentor."

"Me?" Anakin laughed. "I don't think I was put in this galaxy to teach."

They made their way to the bottom of the port's entrance, the dense crowd gradually thinning out as they broke into their separate paths. Above them hung buildings from a colossal arch, a waterfall from there coming straight down into a large circular fountain in the garden in front of them. And in that water, a hologram appeared, followed by a flourish of music—the Neimoidians' own version of the HoloNet News. Not surprisingly, the bombing remained the lead story. First, images of the smoking wreckage from the surface. Then search-and-rescue teams working through the rubble.

Then Obi-Wan with a lightsaber in an official-looking room.

"That's not good," Anakin said. Without turning away, he reached over and tapped R2-D2 on the dome. "Artoo, do a sweep of the area. See if you pick up on any further information about what's happening."

R2-D2 let out a quick flurry of chirps.

"Well, not *just* eavesdropping. Run some scans, too. See if anything seems out of the ordinary."

Two short whistles of acknowledgment came before the droid rotated and rolled away, leaving Anakin to focus on the HoloNet. The scenes changed quickly, the news anchor narrating over it: ". . . the Republic's Jedi emissary Obi-Wan Kenobi appeared before local officials at a hearing related to the Cadesura catastrophe. But the presentation quickly turned violent as Kenobi drew his weapon and attempted an escape." It cut to a rooftop chase, Obi-Wan running at a normal speed despite pursuit behind him—and a clear set of guards in front of him. "The Jedi used his special abilities to attack Cato Neimoidian seeker remotes before tactical guard teams apprehended him."

Things didn't add up here. Obi-Wan's lightsaber didn't appear in the later images despite it being in the first shot. And though he had patrols on either side of him, Anakin saw multiple escape routes off the terrace—to another roof, to a passing vehicle, or up a tower. Obi-Wan worked more methodically than Anakin, but those options would be obvious to any Jedi used to thinking far beyond two-dimensional escape routes.

Of the guards who apprehended him, one wore specialized armor. And another person approached, a pale woman who was clearly not a guard, but the image didn't provide enough clarity for further detail. Could this be Dooku's agent?

"What should we do?" Mill asked.

Anakin bit down on his lip, thoughts racing while he tried to take in this sudden new set of unexpected variables. The way Obi-Wan ran still felt off, and Anakin considered the possibilities until only one felt right:

He let himself be captured. Possibly even hid his lightsaber securely elsewhere.

That was Obi-Wan Kenobi. Always negotiating until the last minute.

"We should find him. This might be part of his plan." Anakin turned as R2-D2 whistled, rolling back to them at full speed. "But even if it is, we should let him know that we can run point for him. Let's start—"

R2-D2 interrupted again, beeps and boops demanding his attention. "Okay, okay. I'm listening. What is—"

The droid didn't let him finish, and instead beeped out details in an insistent rhythm before projecting a local map, with a red dot blinking at them.

"What's that?" Mill asked. "Is that Obi-Wan?"

"No," Anakin said, kneeling down to examine the location— something about a hundred meters away, tucked between a pair of buildings in what appeared to be a commercial district, possibly restaurants. "It's a bomb."

They made a pair of sweeps around the bomb, Anakin and Mill using their Jedi perception to sense any individuals radiating any strong fears or disturbances. At the same time, R2-D2 rolled in a perimeter check, scanning for additional explosives. They met around the corner from the bomb, Mill waiting for the astromech to return while Anakin inspected the explosive material and wiring.

"The good news?" Anakin asked when they reunited. "It doesn't appear to have a timer. I'm pretty sure it's remotely activated. It's a sloppy job—the wiring is loosely soldered, the formation of the explosive isn't precise. It's some kind of orange compound, I haven't seen it before but—"

R2-D2 beeped impatiently.

"Of course I know you can figure it out. We'll need to document the details to send to the Republic. But it shouldn't take too long to disarm. The bad news is it's still a bomb."

R2-D2's dome rotated as a headshake, then a set of beeps made Anakin's face turn into a grim frown. "You're right, Artoo." The droid was certainly never one to dance around bad news. "That is worse."

"What's worse?" Mill squinted, as if that might make it easier to understand the beeps of astromech droid language.

"He's found two more." Anakin caught Mill's expression shifting to wide-eyed amazement, prompting a short laugh from him. "Never underestimate Artoo." He knelt down as R2-D2 put out a projection of the suspected locations. "He says that based on their locations, they might be part of a series. An explosive chain by design." The fingers of his gloved hand rubbed his chin, the tactical decisions here refusing to easily conclude in a clear path forward. Obi-Wan needed help. His equipment needed to be found. The Republic needed to be cleared. And these bombs needed to be defused. But by when?

No good answers existed, the only certainty being that the bombs existed and that Obi-Wan would face a trial of some sort tomorrow.

"Obi-Wan says one of my biggest problems is I don't know when to ask for help," Anakin finally said, looking over at Mill. "This might be a time to ask for help."

"You mean contact the Republic?"

"Yeah. They could send a battalion out here in time for the trial. If we locate all the bombs and transmit their locations, they can nullify them and rescue Obi-Wan in one fell swoop." Anakin's lips pursed at the next thought. "I hate making Master Windu right, though." R2-D2 chimed several tones, an affirmative that clearly stated his opinion. "It's the fastest way to do it. You think you can get a clear signal?"

"But wait," Mill said. "We can't do that."

"Because it would make Master Windu right?"

The joke went over Mill's head, barely breaking the cadence of her words. "If the evidence already looks like the Republic did the bombing, sending in clones will only make it worse. Even if their goal is to help."

The image of Republic gunships swooping through Cato Neimoidia's bridge cities came to Anakin's mind, clones off-loading in rapid, precise succession across both governmental docking ports and civilian facilities. "You're right. They would see it as an invasion. And possibly turn to the Separatists for help."

"And they might execute Master Kenobi."

Anakin nodded. "And they might execute Obi-Wan," he said grimly.

This was *not* going to be like Geonosis. No swarm of Jedi would come in to tip the scales in battle, no endless waves of clones would fly in to wipe out the opposition. This mission, in whatever form it had now taken and however unofficial it was, relied on Anakin's decisions alone. And it started with his promise to Obi-Wan—a promise that could be bent but not broken. Because it came with the respect of Obi-Wan's understanding of the situation on Cato Neimoidia. His entire goal was to steer the war toward peaceful negotiations. That had to be why he let himself get captured.

But getting to Obi-Wan was simply unfeasible if they had to spend the next day locating and defusing bombs. This was a choice, one that carried all of the weight and responsibility of being a Jedi Knight. Slow, even breaths coursed through Anakin as he closed his eyes and weighed the different outcomes here. Find Obi-Wan and risk the bombs? Or find the bombs and risk Obi-Wan?

What Anakin had told Mill earlier, what his mother had told him years ago about the sun-dragon and trusting your heart—the problem was that Anakin cared deeply about both things. And he could only pick one. A different Obi-Wan memory came to the forefront of his mind, as if the Force nudged it into his consciousness as a bit of right-place-right-time recollection. "What do you think Padmé would do were she in your position?" he'd yelled as they soared over the endless Geonosian dunes.

Anakin remembered what he said. Not just the words, but the way the feelings processed through him, the wind stinging against his face, the smell of burning fuel and fired rockets all around them.

The connections between Anakin and Obi-Wan, between Anakin and Padmé—they were both his reason and his guide in their own ways.

Padmé would do her duty. And here, Anakin would do his—while putting his faith in Obi-Wan to do what he needed to do. With a backup plan in his own way, of course. He was, after all, still Anakin Skywalker. His heart would never change, no matter how much his wife and his former Master tried to temper his impulses. He stared down this impossible situation, the tug in two different directions, and he made a silent vow that he simply would find a way.

"Artoo," he said, "we're going to take care of the bombs. Try to locate the others. We've got less than a day."

"What about Obi-Wan?" Mill asked.

"We'll work as fast as we can. And if we succeed, we'll still have time to get to Obi-Wan. If not"—Anakin stood up, his mind and body already coiled and ready to spring into action—"we'll be there for him when he needs us most."

CHAPTER 37

OBI-WAN KENOBI

SEVERAL HOURS INTO OBI-WAN'S MEDITATION, a noise brought him back into the moment. A beep, then some mechanical grinding, followed by a heavy clank that echoed throughout the cell. He remained seated on the floor until the door began to slide open, the light from the outside casting a silhouette. The figure met all standard Neimoidian proportions, but carried itself with a different posture from the usual Neimoidian guards. This one had the weight of experience on its shoulders.

It was Ruug. Holding up some sort of device.

She looked up, then over each shoulder, then clicked the device. It fired off two quick beeps before she stepped inside, the door shutting behind her. A single finger went to her mouth; Obi-Wan took the hint and refrained from saying anything until she indicated otherwise.

A thin orange beam projected from the device, expanding out in all directions to scan the floor before hitting the bottom corners and moving upward. It crawled up the walls and made it to the ceiling, where all four sides approached a center point, collapsing the beam until it became a single dot that vanished.

"There," Ruug said, pocketing the device. "Temporarily disables the surveillance."

"Are you here to break me out?" Obi-Wan asked, standing to meet Ruug face-to-face.

"I don't know. Depends on what we figure out." She sighed then looked around the cell. "We don't have a lot of time."

"Where is your young friend?"

"Ketar? I'm sorry he keeps shooting at you." Ruug laughed, which made Obi-Wan laugh. "He's young and impulsive, but his patriotic intentions are true. I just wish he slowed down before pulling any triggers."

Obi-Wan didn't try hiding his smile at that. "I've said that before. Too many times."

"They're a handful, right? But it's the only way they'll learn."

"Mmm," Obi-Wan said with a nod before taking this into a more serious direction. "I suggest keeping him away from Asajj Ventress."

Ruug's eyes narrowed, a clear shift in her shoulders and posture at the mention of Ventress. "I've tried. But I know she's found him. Or maybe he's found her. There's something off about her. She arrived under the guise of a diplomatic overseer. But everything she says has a clear purpose. One that I don't agree with."

"I don't trust her."

"Well, I could say the same about you." Ruug's words stung, but Obi-Wan knew he deserved it. "It's just you and me here. No seekers, no Ketar, no Ventress. So I want honesty and I want it now: Why didn't you tell me about the datapad?"

"It's what I said before: I needed to know if it was authentic or not."

"Then tell me you had a lead. Let me ask you this—if the datapad pointed at the Separatists, would you have kept it from me?"

"That is a hypothetical—"

"*Vatstu*, don't give me that. Your own personal biases kept that information from me. And here's the thing, the really absurd thing that could have saved us a whole lot of headaches. Maybe even prevented you from being in this prison cell right now."

"What's that?"

"I told you I had a lead and I needed a few days. Which was *exactly* what you should have said to me. Well, I got my confirmation from my sources and my lead points to the Separatists." Ruug took out a datapad from her back pocket and tossed it at him. Obi-Wan caught it and began scrolling through its screen.

The information sat neatly organized, formatted section by section in a table: The explosive patterns and incendiary traces exactly matched the Separatist blazer bombs seen in the field, only scaled down into a personal scale. The clamping brackets, the mounting tools, even the bomb placement all matched exact specifications used by Separatist droids.

It was as detailed as the report he'd recovered on the surface, if not more so. "You're certain this is authentic?"

"Absolutely. I'd bet my life on it."

"You're betting mine on it," Obi-Wan said, handing it back to her.

"That too."

A wave of emotions flooded through Obi-Wan, a sense of relief and a depressurizing calm that dissipated the anxiety of the last few days. Despite all his training and abilities, something of this magnitude still weighed on him more than he wanted to recognize, let alone admit, given the sudden change he felt.

"So the Republic didn't do it," he said, as if stating it made it all more real. "But one thing doesn't make sense. That transmission from my Pada—" There it was. He almost said it again. "My partner. It had confirmed the authenticity of the materials. Granted, with the context still a mystery. But my source, I trust him with vetting these types of things. It's unlike him to be this wrong, on this type of scope."

Ruug looked at him, her head tilted as if she stared right through him. Her large eyes didn't blink, didn't even move until several seconds passed and her expression dropped. "You don't get it, do you?"

"Apparently not. What am I missing here?"

Ruug huffed out a sigh, then began a slow pace around the room. "You're thinking like a Jedi. Within the rules of the how the Republic operates. Or how you *think* the Republic operates."

"What is that supposed to mean?"

"There's the way governments work for the people. And the way they work for themselves. I told you, people like me shape the truth. I've done missions without any authorizations from heads of state. I've murdered people by making it look like a complete accident. These things happen. This galaxy is a brutal, cold place with no logic or compassion. I've seen it," she said, thumb tapping against her armored chest. "And once you see it, you can't un-see it."

Though she didn't explicitly say, Ruug's words opened up a new path of thinking, an ugly underbelly of possibility that existed outside the realm of Jedi dogma and Republic law. Obi-Wan took in a short inhale, one that nearly knocked him off balance. "The data . . ."

"Now you're starting to understand," Ruug said, her voice dry, almost apologetic.

"You're absolutely certain about your findings?"

"Like you, I used someone I trust. I tracked what I could against archives from the governmental data center. It's ironic, looking up this information," she said with a headshake. "The biggest makeshift infirmary is right next to the data center where all the bombing information is stored." She pulled out the small device she used to disable surveillance and checked it. "This is about to go down a deep hole with no clear answers. So we need to be honest with each other from here on out. Agree?"

"Agree. We may be the only two people in this operating on good faith."

"Which means every side is relying on us to get this right. Whether they know it or not."

"Whether they *like* it or not," Obi-Wan said, his voice steady.

"That's right." Ruug shook her head, eyes dimming into a grim expression. "No more seeing it as Republic versus Separatist. That's too simple, too binary. Evidence points to each side. Which leaves only one possibility: Someone is playing both sides. In secret."

Everything Obi-Wan had hoped to achieve with this investigation— from the moment he spoke with Count Dooku among the Jedi Council— suddenly changed, like a holorecorder quickly rotating on its subject to reveal a completely different image. His mind began churning, the way ideas spun off further ideas for an endless chain of possibilities.

"Who would want to escalate on both sides?" Ruug asked, practically reading Obi-Wan's mind. "Who benefits from that? Mutually assured destruction helps no one, not even the lawless. They need a framework to exploit."

"It would not be the Trade Federation." Obi-Wan thought of Satine, her speech on neutrality urging a policy of non-intervention to maintain peace on Mandalore. "Nor a neutral system. The longer this goes on, the more it inhibits anyone's ability to deal from a neutral stance."

"This was a systemic strike. Not something that could be done by a rogue agent. Or even something like the Bounty Hunters' Guild. You've seen the blast points, the damage analysis. It's too precise. I've worked with bounty hunters," Ruug said with a chuckle, "and precise is *not* part of their standard operating procedure. So the question is, did they emulate Republic and Separatist protocols or were both engaged in secret ops unknowingly commissioned by the same party?"

Obi-Wan reached out into the currents of the Force, sinking into it to let it carry him . . . somewhere. But it didn't. The normal sense of *flow* that came with connecting to the Force felt dissonant here—interrupted, chaotic, blocked, an unexpected fight required to get through the thick cloak draped over it.

The dark side.

Since the war erupted, the Jedi had been sent all over the galaxy, a mix of fighting Separatist forces while playing diplomat to rally local systems to maintain their loyalty to the Republic. But every now and then, when Obi-Wan had a quiet moment, he found himself drawn back to a *different* moment on Geonosis—not the battle that spiraled out of control, endless clones and droids and Jedi massacring one another. But a quiet moment beforehand, the only face-to-face exchange he ever had with Dooku, count of Serenno and leader of the Separatist forces.

He'd spewed lies, a blatant attempt to draw Obi-Wan in, even daring to invoke the name of Qui-Gon Jinn. But somewhere in that obfuscation, one statement held true, something Obi-Wan felt certain in his bones:

"The dark side of the Force has clouded their vision," he'd said.

The dark side, yes. But a single Sith Lord holding such sway, without any hint detected by the Jedi? Impossible. The Jedi were nearly ten thousand strong, an interconnected web of beings in tune with the Force, and such a disturbance to the flow of life would be obvious.

No, these machinations must be something else—a symptom of the dark side, but surely not its epicenter. Obi-Wan focused on that while Ruug checked her device again. "Perhaps the culprit is not important," he finally said, his mind working to take steps ahead of whatever nudged the galaxy into further conflict. "Perhaps what is important is that both sides see *how* they are being weaponized against each other. And with that awareness, the urgency to find common ground will be ever greater."

Her device beeped, its tip changing from orange to a blinking red. "We're running out of time before surveillance resumes. Do you believe the best chance for peace is for you to bring this information back to the Republic right now?"

"Are you offering to help me escape?"

"If that's in the best interests of my people, then yes."

Obi-Wan hesitated, stroking his beard in contemplation. "What will happen if you are caught assisting me?"

"Best case?" Ruug's laugh said more than enough. "They arrest me for treason. Worst case—well, I suppose I wouldn't be alive long enough to know what they'd specifically do."

"I understand," he said, watching the blinking red light on her device. "Do you still believe in the ideals that drive your government?"

"You can always believe in the cause," she said, "even if you don't agree with the leadership." The device's light accelerated its beeping, and she moved to the door, sliding it open enough to peek outside. "You must choose."

The paths before Obi-Wan came with no easy answers. If Anakin had been here, they could have collaborated, somehow involving one of his daring escapes to sneakily inform the Republic while Obi-Wan used his trial as his only chance of public explanation, possibly negotiation. But that wasn't the case here; he was a lone emissary of the Republic, and his goal was peace. Escaping now would cast the Republic in an even worse light, and though the odds appeared slim for any diplomacy to sway Cato Neimoidian officials, they still came with a very harsh—but hopeful—truth.

Slim was better than none.

"I will remain here for now."

"You're sure?" She stepped out, fingers gripping the door. "The path out is clear. Surveillance will resume soon. We must go now if you're leaving."

Obi-Wan shook his head. "I hope you'll be there tomorrow," he said, "in case I need some help." His hand waved at the door, the Force nudging it closed. All around him, subtle clicking noises ticked through the room, the sound of audio and video surveillance reactivating. Ruug's muffled voice came through the thick walls, likely a casual greeting to a passing guard.

Though the floor was cold and uncomfortable, Obi-Wan resumed his position for deep meditation: seated, legs crossed, mind and body open to the Force.

CHAPTER 38

ANAKIN SKYWALKER

SEVEN TOTAL BOMBS.

It took all day and then some, but R2-D2 felt reasonably confident that he had identified all of the bombs and their locations. While Anakin and Mill set out to defuse the first one, R2-D2 examined the locations of the next two. A simple extrapolation using the droid's computational skills—combined with, Anakin admitted, R2-D2's strong instincts for being *right*—built out options for five, seven, or nine bombs, all attached to landmarks of local significance: an elaborate statue that reached up and touched the floor of a transparisteel restaurant hanging down from an overhead arch, a building that by official standards was the oldest in Zarra, an immaculately constructed tower adjacent to the large official courtyard of Obi-Wan's trial, and others along those lines. Each seemed to be something that might have caught a simple glance from a traveler, but carried more meaning to local residents—and for someone from the Republic, they represented a crash course in cultural legacy and history, details that the Jedi Archives somehow overlooked.

The bombs surrounded the government offices, and R2-D2 projected a map, lines crossing to make the target quite clear that these explosions were designed as a message.

Because at the center of it all lay the courtyard where Obi-Wan would be on trial, the so-called Grand Theatre of Judgment. And all of the targets themselves stood within viewing distance—in fact, the tall tower loomed over the large square, which promised a public holo viewing of the trial.

Whoever the terrorist was, all of this played out as some sort of twisted representation of the Republic. Were the bombs intended to go off before Obi-Wan's trial, to push his verdict straight to guilty? During the trial, to frame his statements in destructive chaos? After his trial, as punishment of some sort for whatever way the verdict broke?

Every option seemed possible. And these were things Anakin often left to Obi-Wan to figure out. Anakin was more of the "impossible deeds with a lightsaber at high altitudes and long jumps" type of Jedi Knight. But Obi-Wan's thoughtful analysis and strategic mind would have put this puzzle together. Something else was at play here, though who they were and what their exact purpose was, he still wondered.

R2-D2's analysis remained on the purely technical side: the explosive capabilities of the bombs, the type of compound used, the range of the detonator sensor. But that didn't necessarily dive into criminal psychology. And while Mill gained more control over her abilities with each passing moment, her unique sensory vision didn't help with this task. Though—as Anakin noted with a little bit of pride—she picked up the technical bits of bomb disarmament fast, despite having a completely different upbringing from Anakin's own early days fixing things in Watto's junkyard.

By the time they finished the seventh bomb and scouted a tiring radius all around the governmental district, the droid claimed with 93 percent probability that they'd covered all the possibilities. Percentages were usually the realm of C-3PO, and Anakin assumed R2-D2 rounded the numbers as he sat with an exhausted Mill, day having turned to night. With the chrono ticking until crowds would gather for Obi-Wan's trial, Anakin had to decide between trying to get to Obi-Wan now or indulging in what little rest they could.

But practicality won out. They might not find Obi-Wan in time, and if that was the case, they'd have to help him at the trial. Which meant they needed to be ready. After moving the ship from the public port to a less conspicuous warehouse district on the outskirts, they found a spot underneath a bridge in a quiet sector halfway to the governmental district, a place where commerce blended with residential housing. They sat against stone, R2-D2 keeping watch. Mill slept, leaning against Anakin, her thin black ponytail draped over his shoulder. Exhaustion took her over, and even if Anakin wanted to keep pushing forward, she would have passed out, having nudged her body to the limit.

As for Anakin, he wanted to keep one eye open the entire time, but R2-D2 nagged him to rest, beeping messages about how his timing and strength would be off if he was too exhausted to fight or run. While the astromech droid kept a running scan on their surroundings, Anakin closed his eyes—and though he tried to get into a restful meditation, something deeper and more regenerative than sleep, his mind kept turning back to the mystery of the bombs.

Not so much who planted them, but why were they all connected? And what was the meaning behind each target?

No answers arrived during Anakin's rest, though the mental space allowed his spirit to recharge a little bit. Mill, though, still seemed to fight with exhaustion, and perhaps the emotional whiplash of going from a simple training assignment to fate-of-the-Republic tasks wore on her more than she wanted to admit.

By the time they'd gathered their bearings and emerged from their hiding spot, the population of Zarra walked with purpose to the main square. If Anakin hadn't known differently, the scene would have felt more akin to a local festival or holiday celebration. The only shift came from the attitude of the attendees. While something more joyous would have laughter and singing, the citizens moving past Anakin, Mill, and R2-D2 carried a collective weight on their shoulders, many wearing frowns or looking at the ground—and most draped in deep-blue clothes, which Anakin took to be a mourning custom.

Though Anakin didn't speak Pak Pak, the tone of the conversations conveyed enough. Anger, blame, regret, longing—all of those things came through simply from the volume and rhythm of the words between people. Some of the city's non-Neimoidian residents did express their sentiments in Basic, and they didn't hide their thoughts about what they wanted. And if Anakin wasn't sure, Mill's expression reflected their mood, her empathic abilities chipping away at her already exhausted body.

"Stay strong," he said to her as they walked. She looked up and nodded, and he hoped a reassuring smile might buoy her sagging spirits, the physical toll of all this colliding with the emotional wave from the emerging crowd. Her ability to control her connection with the Force had grown significantly, and what would have once crippled her now moved in step with her, an extension of her abilities rather than a hindrance.

Sink or swim, he thought. And Mill swam stronger than he would have ever hoped given the way their first encounter went.

Even though the trial centered on Obi-Wan—and by extension, the Republic—it became clear that it didn't matter who was involved. This community had sustained a deep and irreparable wound; grief and trauma were on trial, and the people wanted justice in whatever form they could take it.

Their mourning *demanded* it.

"I can feel it. Like walking through a stream." Mill took steady steps and her eyes focused ahead, the nausea that ate at her before seemingly transformed. "Not just what they're feeling, but *how* they're feeling it. They have lost friends. Family. Partners. Children." She looked up at Anakin, a ray of sun lighting her brown eyes. "This comes outside of the war. Their pain is no different from that of the people on Langston. They don't deserve this."

"That can't be our concern right now." Anakin paused, wondering if that sounded heartless. It wasn't meant to; Padmé would have cared about the civilians the same way. But all of that had to be tempered with the mission. "What I mean is, we have a duty to do right by the Republic. To the chancellor, to Obi-Wan."

"What about them?" Mill asked. For the first time, a rise came to her voice. "What do they deserve?"

"They deserve the truth. And if anyone can find the truth, it's Obi-Wan." Anakin stopped and surveyed the scene. The seven bomb locations were all visible, all forming a perimeter around the central location of the trial. He paused, and though urges pulled at him to just get on with it, to ignore whatever complaints Mill had, something pushed back, settling him down easier than whenever he butted heads with Obi-Wan.

"Hear them. Each of these people. They may not matter to governments when the galaxy is at war. But they should matter to us."

Anakin nodded, closing his eyes to *listen*. He didn't use the Force, didn't attempt anything akin to Mill's abilities. He simply took in what he'd heard, the voices and emotions coming out from generations of mourning all pulling toward the town square.

Mill was right. Regardless of what happened in conference rooms and political centers across countless star systems, the individuals who suffered the consequences were often overlooked, ignored. And though some of them cursed at Obi-Wan, at the Republic, Anakin reminded himself that those words simply funneled their pain into something tangible.

Obi-Wan's job would be to redirect that with the truth. And Anakin's job would be to help him. For the Republic—*and* these people.

CHAPTER 39

MILL ALIBETH

THE PROCEEDINGS PLAYED OUT ON a giant holographic display, like a sporting event rather than a war trial. Mill steadied herself, every roar and surge of emotion swaying her. "That's Senator Lott Dod," Anakin said as a holographic Neimoidian in fancy robes took up the space and began speaking. Mill's lips twisted in confusion, prompting Anakin to continue. "He represents the Trade Federation in galactic politics. They've committed to remaining neutral in the war, have disavowed Nute Gunray. Cato Neimoidia is the center of their operations. But here, he's promised to stay out of any investigation."

Dod's brief, calm talk did little to soothe the crowd, though. "I am abiding by the commitment I have previously made," he said, the crowd continuing to chatter over his projected voice. "My presence is as an observer. I am in orbit above Cato Neimoidia with fellow Trade Federation officials. We leave this in the capable hands of those with the best perspective: the leaders of Cato Neimoidia itself."

Mild applause rippled through the square, and Mill looked up at the person who'd become a mentor to her over the last few days. He stood, his jaw tight beneath an unblinking stare. And though Mill was capable of picking up emotions from everyone around her, Anakin Skywalker remained a mystery.

Not because his emotions were hidden. No, it was that they were *all* there, each one fighting to be seen and heard, like every color thrown on top of one another to blur themselves all out.

"Bring out the prisoner," a voice said over loudspeakers, and the hologram switched from Senator Dod to a live view of the courtyard setting, the whole thing floating above the spectators in the square. A judge oversaw the proceedings, an older female Neimoidian in ceremonial robes and headdress, wearing a silver-lined sash that probably indicated her official rank. Obi-Wan Kenobi came out in shackles, walking with a steady pace and a calm look on his face even though guards pushed him forward with the butts of their rifles.

"This is where we have to split up," Anakin said. He knelt down and looked Mill straight in the eye. There it was again—that whirlwind of emotions that seemed to both orbit and permeate Anakin, unlike any other Jedi she'd ever encountered. Perhaps unlike any other being in existence. What lay beyond that, at the eye of his storm? The past few days had exposed her to so many different types of people in such a range of circumstances that her unique ability evolved into instinct. She found herself being able to filter the waves of emotions and reset herself like a muscle. It grew stronger and more controlled, rapidly becoming something that connected her with the Force without overwhelming her senses.

Except with Anakin.

"Listen," he said, "stick to the plan. Know what to look for. We'll rendezvous when the time is right. And trust in the Force. But more important"—he nodded, as if he were saying this to himself—"trust in yourself."

"Understood, Master."

"I'll see you soon, youngling."

With that, Anakin moved swiftly, like he rode a wave that carried him through the crowd of people. Several seconds later and Mill couldn't have found Anakin if she tried. She pulled her dirty, torn hood over her head and set out in the opposite direction, doing exactly what he'd instructed:

Look for a way out.

Voices broadcast overhead, official declarations that reviewed the recent days, from Obi-Wan's arrival to the events that Mill watched as a holographic replay—the confrontation in the Cato Neimoidian office, the chase along the terrace and parapet, his eventual capture. But she ignored the details, not needing them, and instead focused on the things Anakin emphasized to her.

First, there needed to be a path that provided solid cover and easy stealth, with the ability to switch things up should they need to lose guards.

Second, as few obstacles as possible. Which Mill took as "find a stretch with the fewest guards."

She searched, using the Force to provide a deeper perspective to her space in the ways that so many in the Temple had taught her over the years. And the more she sank into the Force, combining her natural abilities and reading what the Force told her, the more she felt like each step forward increased her capabilities—and her understanding of herself.

She was glad that she'd skipped the Gathering. A lightsaber didn't find the way, not in a situation like this.

The broadcast continued, a lengthy speech going step by step over the rooftop chase, and Mill moved as fast as she could, only to hit a wall of emotions that stopped her in her tracks.

This massive wave of pain all came from the south side, and as she closed her eyes to let the Force color in her true vision, she saw it. Not the damage of the people watching the trial, but injured Neimoidians and others, lying down in a huge makeshift infirmary. The voices of the trial faded away as Mill gave in to the vision, the burning-red silhouettes of each and every person filling up her mind's eye until she finally forced herself to return to the here and now.

She opened her eyes and found herself some ten meters from the infirmary, a white tent draped over a shoddy frame, as if the Force had unconsciously pulled her there. One breath, then two, then a third went in and out, a calming technique that reconnected her mind and body, and she noticed a detail that might just save herself, Anakin, and Obi-Wan.

R2-D2 rolled up behind her, the droid's beeps sounding like they chastised her for leaving him behind. "I'm sorry, Artoo," she said, patting the droid on the dome. "Can you scan for any guards? I don't see any. I don't *sense* any. I only sense patients lying down."

An internal whirring came from the droid, sounds that Mill didn't quite get, followed by droid language that she didn't quite understand. But the rhythm of it told her enough.

R2-D2 agreed. There weren't any guards nearby.

"I don't think they're guarding this infirmary," she said. The droid beeped some more, and Mill took slow steps forward. "They might not be guarding *any* of the infirmaries. Are they doing this to let them recover in peace? Or does the military just . . ." Her voice trailed off, though R2-D2 waited patiently. "Just not care?" Her pace quickened, and the droid soon followed, the sound of wheels rolling over gravel. "Come on. Let's find out before Anakin does whatever he's gonna do."

CHAPTER 40

OBI-WAN KENOBI

OBI-WAN STOOD IN THE MIDDLE of the courtyard, hands shackled in front of him, a gust of wind whipping through the hair dangling down his neck. Minister Eyam spoke in a steady, low cadence, and Obi-Wan committed himself to listening with an open mind, despite the urge to rebut falsehoods or misrepresentations.

"Let us remember the recent history between the Neimoidians and the Republic," the minister said, his voice echoing into the open-air space. "Note that I am not speaking of merely the Trade Federation. I am speaking of Neimoidians as a people. We are often overlooked in that aspect. In fact, let me ask our emissary—when you hear the word *Neimoidian,* what do you think of?"

This was a trick question. Obi-Wan had been in enough negotiations to know that questions like this were verbal minefields—the smartest, best kind of trap because Eyam *was* correct. Nearly all Republic citizens associated Neimoidians exclusively with the Trade Federation, barely looking past things like shipping routes, particularly for those that worked in the Outer Rim. He *wanted* to say something about their people, their culture, but the truth was he'd only read about it the other night. He didn't actually *know* it.

He chose his words carefully. "Independent," he said.

"Ah," Eyam said with a hand clap, "I like that. Yes. Independent. Neutral, in fact. Immune to the shouting between the Republic and the Separatists. But the problem lies here. You say 'independent,' and while many Neimoidians do work for the Trade Federation, not all of us do. Yet here you associate our people with a government that represents most, but not all. So while the Trade Federation itself is independent, and most Neimoidians support that independence, you have demonstrated one of the fundamental issues here, Master Kenobi:

"You have linked the two together. Is that because of what the Trade Federation does, because the Trade Federation's business *is* commerce itself? Not minerals or technology or vehicles or *weapons,* not things Republic leaders can purchase or regulate, but something that acts as an impediment to their reach? Surely if the Trade Federation produced spacecraft at the volume of, say, Corellia, it would be recognized for something tangible, something you could point to and say, *Ah, for the greater good of the galaxy.* Perhaps that is why the Republic tends to keep Neimoidians at a distance—and why it is so hard for Neimoidians to be recognized as individuals."

The words sank in, a *truth* to them that came with clarity. But why spend the opening of this trial discussing history?

Obi-Wan's eyebrow rose as he put it together. Eyam knew, perhaps Senator Dod knew as well, that the galaxy *was* listening. This, in fact, might have been the most power Neimoidians ever held in a single instance, and they were going to use it to show the Republic exactly how they felt.

"Neimoidians have a rich, beautiful culture. Look around us—we are surrounded by it. The intricate carving of the goddesses Aven and Maradaine as they tell the Unraveled Tale. The Tower of Light—as much an architectural wonder as it is a work of art. The Museum of Neimoidian Contributions—the oldest building on Cato Neimoidia, a celebration of how our people's skills have benefited the galaxy. Yet are these discussed in Republic classrooms as they cover galactic culture? Not at all." The minister shook his head. "To the Republic, we are a monolith. A people of business." He took another pause, though this time he broke past the façade of calm objectivity. His eyes squinted and his voice rose.

"A people of *greed*. A people of deception. Perhaps . . . not even a people."

Minister Eyam spoke with an orator's rhythm, changing his pitch and pace in a way that precisely engaged with anyone who listened. And though the crowd in the square stood some distance away, they swayed to the rhythm of his words. Obi-Wan sensed their collective grief evolving into a more tangible anger, something that carried enough momentum through the Force to pull his concentration. They sought retribution in some form, someone to absorb their community's pain. He took a quick breath and told himself to focus. Just as the galaxy listened to Eyam, soon it would be his turn.

"Was our tragedy caused by someone from the Republic? We will hear both sides of the case. But one thing that must be considered: What were the conditions that caused such a tragedy to happen, that put Cato Neimoidia in the crosshairs of someone else's war? Had the Republic recognized Neimoidians as a people rather than tools of transaction, would their relationship with Cato Neimoidia and the Trade Federation be different? Would they have enacted greater protections to worlds such as Cato Neimoidia as the conflict unfolded?" Arms raised, he gestured outward, upward, each movement creating another wave of noise from the crowd. "Would Cato Neimoidia even still be a target? As we determine the innocence or guilt of the Jedi emissary, perhaps this context is even more important." A wave of noise came from beyond the walls, the crowd's uproar rolling over the structures and buildings around them. The minister waited for the noise to settle, a space for his words to take root. "What is on trial here is much more than a single act of terrorism. Let us hear from the Jedi emissary."

The judge excused Minister Eyam, then looked directly at Obi-Wan. A rifle muzzle jabbed into his back, nudging him forward until he stood directly in front of the judge. And though he spoke directly to her, Obi-Wan took great care in knowing that his words were being listened to by governments all across the galaxy.

Everything that had happened led to this point, this negotiation.

Obi-Wan considered all of the gears of government across countless systems, how his words might impact chances of either peace or war.

"You are right, Minister Eyam. History does not lie, and I cannot condone the longtime actions the Republic has made in dismissing the Neimoidian people and its colonies time and again. I cannot justify the ignorance, the way the Republic has seen the Neimoidians as assets of the Trade Federation rather than sentient beings. You have every right to be angry; you have every right to want a better life for your people and your children—you have earned your voice, as a people and for those represented by the Trade Federation. I understand the need to be heard, but I urge you now: Being heard requires truth and faith in return. So I ask you to judge the truths I will present in good faith. Otherwise, this war will consume us all."

Outside, the mass of hostility gradually trickled into quiet. Obi-Wan hoped the more humble and philosophical tone of his words countered the bluster of Eyam, statements that might spur reflection rather than whip up a frenzy. He chose his words carefully, a blanket to drape calm over the storm. "You have lost loved ones. You have lost children. I cannot bring them back. But if you listen to me right now, everyone here, everyone watching this holocast—in the Republic or in a neutral system or aligned with Count Dooku's movement—we have a chance to stop this war." His last few words projected with emphasis, as if he had said them strongly enough that they could have ordered both sides to put down their weapons. "I repeat, we have a chance to stop this war. So no more lives are lost." Seconds ticked by, the crowd quieting to a point that Cato Neimoidia's winds blew louder than the gathered mass. "I will now detail my findings in full, proper context."

Obi-Wan reached out through the Force for any sense of how combustible the crowd was, but grief turned out to be their default emotion, which meant how they took the next part of his speech would be completely unpredictable. He considered his words, so carefully planned, and committed to trusting that the right people would recognize his attempt at good-faith negotiation. "I have seen the evidence," he started, his voice clear but quiet. "I have seen it, in my own investigation as well as data gathered by others." Was Ruug nearby? He hoped so—and he hoped what he was about to say met with her approval. "It is true. There is evidence that points to the Republic. The information on the datapad

I uncovered was authentic; this bombing's details match materials and protocols used by the Republic. The evidence shows this, and I will not lie for political purposes." From afar, the clamor of the crowd started again, and Obi-Wan knew that his window of opportunity to make his point would quickly close. He needed to strike with precision here. "I ask you to wait and listen before you judge. Because there is more. Further evidence, evidence pointing to the Separatists. Just as the datapad showed materials and protocols matching Republic bombs used by the clone army, I can confirm that Cadesura was also attacked using materials and protocols matching Separatist blazer bombs." Voices from outside created a communal din, an acknowledgment that things had taken an unexpected turn. "Please. You must see the truth. There is something else at play here. Something that is trying to escalate the fighting. Someone or something that is making gains off *all* our suffering. That is the cause of this tragedy. And the culprit is still at large. Extremist groups are already involved with the war. Your own government has sworn off the actions of Nute Gunray as an extremist faction. And now this bombing, with materials drawn from both sides—and indeed, placed to *look* like both sides, so both the Republic and the Separatists can fight even more battles, fire even more weapons at each other." His voice took on a rhythm, something not that different from the soar and pause of Eyam's cadence. But this was not calculated theater; Obi-Wan let the urgency of the moment guide him, every word a step toward his ultimate goal.

"There is only one solution for all of us, on all sides: de-escalation. And there is only one path to de-escalation: The Trade Federation cannot stay neutral in this war. Neutrality in the face of extremism only gives the extremists more space to breathe. It must be extinguished before more lives are lost, and the only way to stop it is to de-escalate the war. My name is Obi-Wan Kenobi, Jedi Master and emissary of the Republic, and I have presented the facts to you in good faith. I now invite you to return that good faith; join me in recognizing this threat— a threat not just to the people of Cato Neimoidia, but to the Trade Federation, and to stability across the entire galaxy. If the Trade Federation aligns with the Republic, we can use this tragedy as a first step to coming together and negotiating peace with the Separatists."

More noise came from the crowd outside, but by now the voices mixed too densely to decipher what type of reaction was playing out— just that the reaction existed. Obi-Wan gave himself equal odds at taking steps toward peace and throwing an accelerant on the galaxy. If Anakin were here, surely he'd have a witty remark for Obi-Wan to roll his eyes at.

"And now we will hear from the Royal Guard of Cato Neimoidia," the judge said. "Please present your evidence."

Behind Obi-Wan came the sound of a door sliding open. Boots hit stone, creating an even and steady cadence as the guard entered the courtyard and moved forward.

Obi-Wan didn't look. He knew who it would be.

Ketar's voice came laced with venom. "This 'emissary,'" he said with an unexpected pious tone, "from the Republic speaks of truth and good faith. And yet, here is the truth: Obi-Wan Kenobi of the Jedi Order has come here under false pretenses. He has lied to every single person in this square, every single person on Cato Neimoidia—every single person mourning a dead brother or sister or child or parent or friend. He is lying to you—and cleverly concealing that lie in a truth about the recovered datapad." The young guard held up the device, its holographic details fully projecting. "*This* datapad. The one implicating the Republic. And yet, you claim there's further evidence of Separatist materials in the bombing. Where is your source implicating the Separatists?"

The pure, technical truth was that Obi-Wan wasn't sure. He'd hoped Ruug was around somewhere watching the proceedings and acting as a form of safety net for him. But he didn't know the answer to that question, and regardless, he was in no position to reveal her involvement. "I must protect my source. Perhaps if I had a few more days—"

"So," Ketar said, a certain *joy* in his interruption, "an anonymous source, no physical evidence, and only his word to go on. Let me tell you something about the word of the Republic." Ketar deactivated the bomb data holograph, then looked directly at Obi-Wan. "Now, our Jedi friend likes to talk about good faith, so let me speak on that. We know that to the Republic, Neimoidian physiology is often misunderstood, often mocked. We know that the Republic sees Neimoidian culture as business assets, sees us as cogs of galactic commerce and nothing else. But all of us here, on Cato Neimoidia, know that Neimoidians are much more than that. Every single one of you knows a Neimoidian who is a scholar. Or an artist. Or a historian. Or a philosopher.

"Neimoidians like my parents. Who *were* artists, in fact. Oh, like many Neimoidian artists, they didn't make their living that way. As much as our society celebrates artists, our reality within the Republic requires our culture's most celebrated to work"—Ketar looked over at the overseeing officials—"in expected ways.

"Which they did. They worked to optimize the computer systems that supported transactional databases. But their true passion was found here, on Cato Neimoidia, all the way on the surface. The luminescent oils found on the trees below the mist—they painted with those. A rare skill. That delicate touch to preserve the oil so the glow changes with light and temperature rather than fading away. When I was a child, they showed me the natural wonders of our planet. Their work was so esteemed in our sector that they were even invited to show it at Coruscant's Festival of Stars. I remember . . ." Ketar paused, his gaze dropping and voice softening. "I remember the piece exactly. The way the oils lit from black to brilliant colors to white, an ode to the magic of hyperspace travel.

"Now I'll explain to our Republic emissary, transporting bioluminescent oil is not easy. That is why so much of this art stays here, on Cato Neimoidia. But they were determined. They took all necessary precautions to protect their work from the rigors of hyperspace and atmospheric entry. Yet when they got there—the first Neimoidians to present at such a prestigious event—how do you think Republic officials treated them?"

Obi-Wan knew exactly where this was headed. And with that realization, he could feel the screws turning, even without the low murmur of the surrounding crowd.

"A unique artistic vision, only possible by Neimoidians living here on Cato Neimoidia. And on Coruscant, they were given the runaround, even doubted about its authenticity. After all, as you can guess, the Republic only views Neimoidians in one way. And on the third night of the festival, when they were finally given a quiet corner to display their work, it was vandalized overnight." Ketar's eyes closed, his hands balled into fists. Such a tale had nothing to do with the Cadesura disaster, yet Obi-Wan knew that the trajectory of the Clone Wars might tilt on one family's tragedy. "It turns out that those on Coruscant may not know Neimoidian artwork, but they are *very* familiar with Neimoidian slurs. Slurs that I will not repeat here.

"My parents left early, discouraged by how Coruscant treated them. And though it's a relatively short trip back to the Colonies, they decided to use that extra time to explore other regions they had yet to see. Through Republic-protected hyperspace lanes."

Ketar met Obi-Wan's eyes, an unblinking stare that told him how this story ended. "They never came home. Pirates raided their shuttle. In the Republic's so-called law and order, their trustworthy hyperlanes turned out not to be so. Only a single distress call made it through." He reached behind him and produced a small disk in his palm; his other hand tapped a button on the side and out projected what Obi-Wan assumed to be the family painting, a swirl of dots and lines with colors moving in the most impossible ways.

Even in a small holographic form, Obi-Wan recognized its unique beauty. And though shame wasn't a feeling Jedi encountered very often, he distinctly understood it here.

"Look at what the Republic's promises have done to my family. Their pride. Their safety. Our *stability*. The biggest HoloNet stars in the galaxy get paraded around with armed escorts. Cato Neimoidia's most talented artists? Nothing." The hologram faded away, Ketar putting the projector back in his pocket. "You may be asking why this matters here, and I'll tell you why. Because we have heard talk about 'good faith' today, and all our lives. Good faith?" Ketar asked, his voice escalating. "From the Republic? It has never existed. Never. And now I will give you one very real, very relevant example of this." The last word came at a full yell, one that caused even the judge to wince. "One last try: Who is your source implicating the Separatists?"

Ketar's question hung in the air, enough time passing that the noise from the nearby crowd grew in volume, a sound that synthesized both the venom and the desperation of their anxieties, of this moment. Obi-Wan considered his last discussion with Ruug. In theory, he *could* name her. Would that be enough to sway the judge, the crowd, even Ketar? And what would that do to Ruug? She'd said herself that helping him put her life at risk.

Did he have the right to do that, even with the galaxy at stake? Would he sacrifice Ruug for this?

"Well, Kenobi?" Ketar asked.

He did not.

He would not put her in harm's way.

"I cannot reveal my source right now. If you give me more time, I'm certain something can be arranged."

"This Jedi"—Ketar maintained his intensity, hands turning into fists at his side—"dodges questions, lies about equipment, *destroys evidence.* He speaks of truth? Here is the truth of Obi-Wan Kenobi: He does not view Neimoidians as equals and he, like the Republic dealing with my parents, wants all of us to live quiet, inconsequential lives, so that they may abuse us from the Core Worlds, so they may continue to treat us as assets. He wants the Republic to *own* Neimoidians, to take away our freedom." Ketar circled until he stood directly in front of Obi-Wan, then stepped toward him until they were face-to-face, eyes unblinking. "To that, I say he is guilty. Of conspiring against Cato Neimoidia. Of covering up evidence. Of breaking his promises. And of a much larger crime, one that he shares with the Republic: devaluing every single Neimoidian in the galaxy. I have two words for him and the Republic, and I will speak them not in our beautiful Pak Pak, but in Basic, in *his* tongue:

"No more."

In that moment, Obi-Wan realized the massive miscalculation he'd made. He'd put all his faith in facts but completely ignored the power of emotion in swaying the masses. No matter what he might have said, what evidence he might have presented, nothing would connect with a mourning people like one of their own playing to the power of displaced grief.

He tried to interject, trying to get something in to express his sympathies, to emphasize the importance of strong galactic relations and stability. But it was no use, and any momentum he had dissipated, absorbed into the roar from outside, one that moved with enough fervor that it nearly shook the ground of the bridge city.

"The Neimoidian government is known for its swift and decisive justice. And though some cases require many more days to reach a decision, this particular case is clear." The judge pointed directly at Obi-Wan, the tips of her ceremonial purple headdress blowing in the wind. "Does the defendant wish to say any closing words?"

Obi-Wan adjusted in his boots, his posture straight and eyes clear as he looked directly at the judge. "I have presented the truth." For hours, he'd crafted his backup plan, playing out every detail and option with the sole intent of not using it. The power of truth was supposed to win out, and its failure caused Obi-Wan to breathe out a defeated exhale, the sheer *strangeness* of raw emotional swings creating a brief but tangible bout of exhaustion. "And now I put my faith in you. I await your judgment."

Several seconds of silence passed as the judge raised one hand, a calming pause that radiated like a blanket over the proceedings. With nothing to compete against her words, she spoke with a clear and exact diction: "The emissary from the Republic is found guilty of conspiring against the laws of Cato Neimoidia, of being in collusion with the Republic in the tragedy of Cadesura, and of attempting to hide evidence of that crime." Behind Obi-Wan, approaching guards began a rhythmic stomp, and he tensed himself as Ketar walked in front, putting himself between Obi-Wan and the judge. Obi-Wan glanced up at the tall structure where his lightsaber sat embedded in a wall, the so-called Tower of Light according to Eyam. "Take him away to await sentencing."

A far door opened to his left, which he assumed led to a holding cell. And ahead of him, Ventress appeared on the dais. Though she remained slightly hidden behind Eyam, she looked directly at him, making eye contact before tilting her head.

Then she pointed at the guards closing in behind him.

He sensed his weapon, as easily as if it sat in his palm. Should he pull it now?

No, he thought. Making a commotion now would likely defeat what little goodwill he'd earned in his speech. In fact, it might play into Ventress's—and Dooku's—plan. Obi-Wan decided to leave his lightsaber for now and go quietly, adapting any plan to what lay ahead.

Except the marching stopped, their steady approach paused, replaced with a single *thunk* followed by the clatter of a dropped weapon. Obi-Wan turned to see the lead guard on his knees, hands to his throat. Foam leaked out of the corners of his mouth, and he gurgled before collapsing sideways.

"The Jedi has poisoned the guards!" Ketar's voice soared through the space, and Obi-Wan spun around to find Ketar with pistol drawn.

And above him, Ventress remained, arm still pointed outward, though she slowly brought it down. The corner of her mouth curled upward and she nodded at Obi-Wan, though he didn't have time to guess at her plan, not with Ketar's weapon drawn.

"This is not my doing," he called out as loudly and clearly as possible. "We need medical assistance right now!"

Emergency medical personnel, however, did not arrive. Instead, several further guards sprinted in from the far tunnel.

"The Jedi is trying to subvert our security!" Ketar shouted again.

"Please, hurry, this guard needs medical attention!" Obi-Wan's voice was nearly as loud as Ketar's. "If you release me, I can help—"

"Stop your lies, Jedi. You are a liar and a murderer!" Ketar's arm stiffened and his eyes narrowed. In that moment, Obi-Wan reached out to the Force, sensing his lightsaber.

It was to be a last resort. Pulling it meant unleashing something that could not be undone. He had to choose carefully.

From the side came the sound of other guards rushing. Obi-Wan turned to catch sight of them rushing to their fallen comrade, but before he could even take a single step, the sound of blasterfire rang out.

The bolt soared past his waist and singed the ground some three or four meters behind him, burning a gash into the stone. Specks and chips of stone spiked into the air, and a scorched odor hit his nose. "He's making his move!" Ketar yelled. All eyes turned to Ketar, including Obi-Wan's, and Obi-Wan noticed a subtle shift in the way Ketar held the pistol.

The young guard changed his angle, so slightly that only the most perceptive observers would take note. As that happened, another guard fell to his knees, choking in a similar way, and just as that happened, two more bolts fired from Ketar's pistol, both landing near Obi-Wan but avoiding any direct hits.

With that, it became clear what Ketar's plan was. Taking out Obi-Wan in front of the guards, the judge, indeed the galaxy via the broadcast—that might fail to rally support to his purposes, whatever they were. But with his scattered fire, the choking guards, and false claims of Obi-Wan's actions, Ketar framed Obi-Wan as the aggressor without any direct combat.

And from the dais, Ventress moved, her arm briefly held up in another point before dropping. She turned and disappeared behind Eyam and other local officials.

The click of rifles unfurled all around him. A quick look saw weapons lifted one by one, and it didn't matter that his hands were still bound.

Seconds ago, he'd sought the most peaceful, most diplomatic solution possible.

Now, with Ketar's fear and rage driving the proceedings, combat felt inevitable. And it was his duty as a Jedi to redirect that violence in a way that minimized harm to the mourning populace, and indeed to a galaxy on the edge of ripping itself apart.

He didn't want to use it. Not in this way. But Obi-Wan knew his lightsaber would be necessary. He shut his eyes and let the Force flow through him, igniting perceptions far beyond his physical senses. Murmurs from the crowd danced like raindrops in an ocean, individual strikes that melded into the greater flow.

The energy shackles around his wrists deactivated, circuits crunched through the Force to turn the bindings into deadweight. At the same time, he stretched his senses upward, far up the tower to pull his lightsaber free.

In his slowed perception, another blaster bolt discharged, a burst of red starting to escape a guard's muzzle. Milliseconds after it came the others, a gap that felt like minutes in this state. As this played out, the lightsaber hurtled through the air.

It approached, a speed pushed forward through a combination of gravity and the Force pulling it.

Obi-Wan's legs tensed, ready to fly straight up the instant he was reunited with his weapon. The vector of the hilt projected in his mind, along with a calculation of how high he would need to vault up after catching it, when to snap his hand open, when to time the arrival in his palm with the immediate move to form a defensive pose. All of that came together into a single instant, a plan ready to execute with perfect precision, when something else arrived, breaking all of Obi-Wan's careful timing.

CHAPTER 41

ANAKIN SKYWALKER

OBI-WAN SURE LOVED TO GIVE speeches, almost as much as he hated flying.

Perhaps that was why they worked well together. Whenever Obi-Wan went into negotiation mode, Anakin rushed forward and balanced that with a lightsaber, usually sparing all of them from Obi-Wan's attempts to talk everyone down.

Because sometimes, talking didn't work.

In this case, though, it bought Anakin some time. He'd started in an alley upon parting ways with Mill, then found a good spot to leap up, story by story, until he made it onto a neighboring roof. Though a few citizens took in the trial from the roof as well, Anakin moved swiftly enough behind ventilation ducts and in the shadows of the buildings hanging from the overhead arch to remain undetected. He did make the mistake of peering down over the edge, and while heights weren't anything new to him, those usually came from the building above a surface.

Here, Anakin saw the edge of the bridge city and the long drop through the mist.

He shook off the flash of vertigo and leapt forward until he got to the side of a building adjacent to the courtyard. From a short windowed ledge behind some decorative flourishes, he watched Obi-Wan finish his speech—a very good speech, in fact, one that would play well on the HoloNet—before the young guard stirred things into a frenzy. Despite being far above the crowd, their emotional fervor became obvious, the way they moved to every point the guard said.

He knew even before it was done that Obi-Wan's speech, as strong as it was, would fail in this situation. And as the guards dealt with the ensuing confusion, Anakin perched himself, trying to tune in to what Obi-Wan was planning—he planned *something*, though the choking guard clearly swerved the situation—while also dealing with the very practical matter of rifles being drawn and ready.

From afar, he picked up a ripple in the Force—not something that he necessarily heard with his ears, but the slightest bit of movement around the nearby tall tower, a site where they'd disarmed a bomb the day prior. It didn't matter, though, because something more critical was about to take place here. Anakin gripped his lightsaber, thumb ready to trigger the blade's ignition, his senses reaching into the Force.

He perched behind the ledge, ready to go. In his mind's eye, he could see the blaster bolts leaving the rifles before they physically did: the speed, angle, and exact trajectory, which his lightsaber would easily deflect.

He leapt, a fraction of a second before the first rifle discharged.

At that instant, many things happened at once, though Anakin experienced them with slowed perception. His boots landed in front of Obi-Wan, who still had his eyes closed in meditation. His lightsaber ignited, the blue blade coming to full length right before his feet touched the ground. The blaster bolts burst into existence and flew out of the muzzles.

And over his shoulder came something completely unexpected:

The sound of a lightsaber coming to life.

Anakin turned to see what this surprise threat was, only to find Obi-Wan's lightsaber flying toward him at full speed. He swung his own lightsaber to deflect the oncoming weapon, but its rapid twirling velocity caught him off guard. Though he blocked enough of the blade to direct it to the ground, it still nicked him on the side of his right shoulder. "Ow!" he yelled with less dignity than he would have liked, and as Obi-Wan's lightsaber fell to the ground, its blade withdrawing, Anakin ignored the burning pain and kept blocking the oncoming rifle fire.

The mechanical arm again. If his mind and body worked in complete sync, his arm *should* have deflected Obi-Wan's lit blade right into his former Master's hand, allowing them to step into effortless side-by-side defensive combat.

Instead, Obi-Wan merely looked at him, mouth agape, while Anakin deflected rifle blasts.

"Anakin! I had a plan!"

"Sorry, Master." The lightsaber blade moved effortlessly, guided by an instinct that both listened to the Force and controlled it. Blaster bolts flew away in all directions, most of them zipping upward to eventually evaporate into nothing. Through all of it, Anakin stayed in control enough to kick Obi-Wan's lightsaber toward him. "You gonna join in or do I have to do all the work?"

"I suppose I should say it's good to see you." The hilt on the ground trembled before flying into Obi-Wan's open palm, its energy blade coming back to life. The back door slid open, announcing the arrival of more guards, and Obi-Wan and Anakin stood back-to-back, sur-rounded by the screech of blasterfire and the hum of their whirring lightsabers. "I make plans without you now, you know."

"That's your first mistake." Despite the hail of incoming fire, Anakin moved effortlessly in sync with his former Master. "You said things al-ways get more complicated when we're together. But they also work better."

"Battle droids," Obi-Wan yelled, the playfulness leaving his voice. Anakin glanced up to see two small floating transports, each carrying ten curled-up battle droids ready for deployment. "We need a way out. Do *not* hurt the guards."

"Not even the one running his mouth about the Republic?"

"*Especially* not him."

Anakin wondered just why Obi-Wan would single that particular nuisance out for protection, but that would have to be discussed after everyone stopped shooting at them. "Cover me, then follow me."

"You're giving the orders now?" Obi-Wan said, lightsaber swooping left and right with precise motions.

"You're gonna have to learn to trust me."

"I always welcome new experiences."

Just a few months ago, the exact same words could have been exchanged between Anakin and Obi-Wan, either in a quiet moment or in the heat of combat. But they would have been laced with condescension and resentment. Somehow, this change in rank, this balancing of roles, this *recognition* of each other, transformed their verbal jabs from bitter conflict to friendly competitiveness.

Were they still the same people, just addressed differently? Those were things for Obi-Wan to ponder. All Anakin knew was that he preferred the version of Obi-Wan with an actual smile to the one with a perennial frown.

"Try to keep up." With his left arm, Anakin gripped his lightsaber and reached back before hurling it toward the landing battle droids. The clicks and whirs of their deployment sequence were interrupted as the lightsaber flew in an arc launched by human muscle and guided by the Force. Anakin bent the trajectory to his will, and he didn't need to look back to confirm that the spinning blade sliced precisely through the clump of battle droids. The hilt snapped back into his gloved palm, mechanical fingers gripping it before he changed hands and pointed to the way he arrived. "That way. We're going up."

The Force powered him through, a short instant burst carrying him across the courtyard in a blink. He launched upward, landing on the same ledge he'd used to creep into the scene. He twisted behind a ventilation duct and knelt down, and a second later Obi-Wan was next to him. Another transport flew overhead, landing in the courtyard before the sound of more unfurling battle droids came. The young guard's voice echoed throughout the space. "Where are they?" he screamed. "Find them!"

"Roger roger," a mechanized voice stated.

"Well, I suppose Master Windu will know where I am now," Anakin said. "Don't worry, I didn't contact the Jedi Council. He called me. Or tried to, anyway."

"You came on your own?"

"Sort of. I have help."

The *clank-clank-clank* sound of the battle droids' rhythmic steps started. "Activate scan boosters."

"They'll find us soon," Obi-Wan said. "We need to move."

"Yeah," Anakin said, "I'm working on that." He squinted, first doing a visual scan for any signs of Mill, then tapped into the Force to bring him greater details. "You know, I'm going to start tracking how many times I've saved you. Today, the nest of gundarks, the Moggonite bounty hunter on Vaced."

Obi-Wan adjusted, looking around the corner. "I'll have you know that being captured by that swoop bike gang was entirely part of the plan."

"Like here?"

"If you paid attention today, I was on my way out of here. You, in fact, bumped into *my* lightsaber. So this doesn't count." He glanced at the charred line on Anakin's sleeve. "Are you all right?"

"Me? Of course." He flexed his arm as proof. "I'm always all right."

"Aren't we all," Obi-Wan said, his voice softening before returning to its normal spark. "Well, where to?"

"I'm looking for . . ." Anakin considered his words here. At some point, he'd have to explain the fact that he took a youngling on this particular rogue journey. But those complications could wait. They had to get out of there first. "My partner."

"Your partner?"

"Yeah. You'll like her. Her name's Mill." He closed his eyes, reaching into the Force, searching for her presence. Though they hadn't known each other that long, their shared experiences had built a bond tangible enough to identify, even from a distance. And while he failed to pinpoint her exact location, her presence acted as enough of a beacon to get a general direction. "That way. Let's take the rooftops. And stay as stealthy as possible. We have a ship docked on the outskirts, away from the primary transportation hubs. She's finding the best path to it."

"No, wait. I need to find *my* partner."

They hesitated, more floating platforms of guards and battle droids arriving. Orders were shouted in a variety of directions, and the sound of battle droids unfurling echoed throughout the space. Anakin turned, only to find Obi-Wan scanning the horizon. "Who is this?"

"Her name is Ruug. She's a Neimoidian guard."

"A Neimoidian? Helping their civilians is one thing, trusting them is another."

"Anakin, let go of your feelings about them. She's former special ops. I have full confidence in her. We've been working together. You will understand if we cross paths. Except I don't see any sign of her. She is," he said with a small head shake, "very good at hiding, though. It doesn't matter right now. I need to change your plan."

"Are you trying to pull rank on me?"

Obi-Wan shook his head, his mouth forming a thin line under his beard. "Our investigations have shown that this bombing had both Republic and Separatist ties. There's no simple solution and I suspect something much worse at play here. But to prove it, we need to recover the evidence from the Cato Neimoidian data archive. We can't leave without it." He looked at Anakin, a gravity in his eyes that Anakin had rarely seen. "Anakin, you must believe me when I say that the balance of the galaxy is at stake. If we get this evidence, if we expose the fact that other parties are exploiting the Separatist conflict, we may convince both sides to stand down and negotiate before it gets worse."

"Obi-Wan," he said with a gentle nod. "You don't have to convince me. I heard your speech. You should go into politics."

Obi-Wan's neutral scowl changed, tilting into a full and rare grin. "I hope to give far fewer in the future. Once we get that evidence."

Anakin pointed toward a rooftop path, several buildings in a row of various heights that offered little challenge to Force-wielders. Any bystanders would have seen silhouettes leaping from ledge to ledge, building to building, moving so swiftly with billowing tunics that they may as well have been Cato Neimoidia's native birds in flight.

At the peak of a rotunda, Anakin put a hand up and they remained perched while he once more tapped into the Force to search for Mill. "Give my partner a minute. She's supposed to send a signal when ready." He tracked Obi-Wan's gaze to the now-distant capital plaza, noise from the square still audible. "In the meantime, there's something I need to catch you up on."

CHAPTER 42

RUUG QUARNOM

HEIGHT. COVER. CLEAR LINES OF sight. Those were the only things Ruug needed. She'd done enough sniper coverage in her time with the Neimoidian special forces to adapt to whatever her environment presented. In the case of this trial, Ruug chose the Tower of Light, the landmark close to where she'd apprehended Obi-Wan. She broke into the bottom floor, offices that had nothing to do with the tower's architectural significance as a standout example of Neimoidian cultural achievements. The service lift took her up most of the way, then back stairs brought her through various maintenance levels and storage. She'd finished the final leg through unofficial means involving an ascension gun and old-fashioned climbing.

She knelt, legs twisted to brace herself in a steady position as she assembled the deconstructed rifle from the case on her back, something she used to stay inconspicuous among the public. Extensions and modules twisted and locked into place, things she'd customized over years to adapt to her grip, her posture, the specific length of her arms, and her evolving armor set. The small power pack hummed to life, and she shut one eye to stay focused on what her scope showed her:

First, Obi-Wan. The poor Jedi Master, he really tried. And she warned him, not out of any bias but out of pure practicality. She understood the reasons that drove him, the need to intervene before any further disasters might accelerate the war. And here he was, trying to turn evidence of a mysterious third party into a plea for peace.

Admirable. Noble, and in many ways, quite logical.

But it would fail.

He continued his speech, a clear and genuine desperation in his statement, but that wasn't why Ruug knelt in her position. She zoomed out, then surveyed all around, checking for any signs of disturbances or trouble. Most of the square's blue-clad crowd watched the nearby holoprojection in perfect stillness, their collective mourning over recent events drawing their attention to Obi-Wan in a way that tilted the scales against him.

But at the back of the square, one figure moved through the dense population. Worn rags draped over the figure, though it moved with purpose, a strength to each step that made the outfit a clear disguise. As it turned, Ruug zoomed in enough and captured a frozen image on her scope to reveal a human male, hair on the verge of shaggy, and determined eyes that stared in a way different from Obi-Wan.

Her curiosity kindled at the mystery figure. Except her attention got pulled back to the trial, Ketar now taking full attention. She zoomed in her scope, watching his mouth tremble and eyes squint, his hands turning into fists at his side as he recounted his family's woes. She understood his anger toward the Republic—and in many ways, it felt justified.

But not this way.

Ruug's fingers flexed as she adjusted her grip on the rifle, scanning space again. In the corridor right outside the courtyard, a line of guards approached, standard-issue weapons in their hands. And in the distance, floating platforms appeared on the horizon; she zoomed to reveal the shape of battle droids curled up in storage positions.

Obi-Wan would be found guilty. Through no fault of his own, he'd already been judged.

She heard Ketar challenge Obi-Wan to reveal his source, to name

Ruug. But she already knew he wouldn't. As she tried to explain, people like her created the truths that people like him defended.

Ruug wasn't afraid to lose her life. She wasn't afraid to be named, even to reveal her own sources, who'd sliced into the Cato Neimoidian archives to analyze the data. Not if it could tilt the axis of the galaxy. But she'd seen enough to know that it really wouldn't have made much of a difference, outside of some extra shouting by different parties. Everyone's fate had already been decided.

That was the difference between someone like her and someone like him: Obi-Wan Kenobi was too good for a galaxy at war.

And then the most unexpected thing happened:

A guard started choking.

Obi-Wan's frantic look, Ketar's drawn pistol, and all of the ensuing chaos showed that something was going awry. And on the dais above them, Ventress departed swiftly, disappearing through a back exit. Ruug pulled back the stock on her rifle, prompting a hum that warmed up the internal heat-regulating system for high-powered sniper bolts. As she did, Ketar yelled loud enough to echo to her perch, and guards drew their rifles at Obi-Wan. Sharp winds blew around her and at her from the small ledge, and while her boots ground into the ledge to keep her steady, a crackle came from the stone just below her. She pulled away from the scope for a glance and saw . . . something.

That clever Jedi. Kenobi's laser sword.

It rattled in its lodged hideout, powered by those magic Jedi powers, then leapt out and flew through the air with unnatural speed. Ruug tracked it with her scope, a clear trajectory toward Obi-Wan's hand.

Then everything happened at once. Guards opened fire. The mystery figure somehow vaulted in and landed in front of Obi-Wan, sword blazing. Obi-Wan's own weapon ignited in midair before hitting the ground. Battle droid carriers landed. Ketar screamed, an incomprehensible jumble of fury that projected at a volume loud enough to capture his emotion, if not the specifics.

Ruug's scope dodged around, trying to take in the chaos, though by the time she zoomed out, something had sliced the battle droids in half and the two Jedi had departed. The guards swiveled around, ill equipped to deal with the speed and capabilities of Jedi, and Ketar stomped around the space, waving his pistol and shouting at anyone who might listen.

Because the Jedi were gone.

Ruug zoomed out even farther, then looked for any kind of movement that might give away where the Jedi hid. Then in the upper corner of her scope, she saw what looked like a blur whizzing across the view. She tracked it until they paused, holding her hand steady to keep the view clear as she adjusted the view to bring them in:

There they were, Obi-Wan and his Jedi partner.

Ruug blinked to make sure she actually saw what was unfolding correctly.

Were they . . . laughing?

Another sound came whooshing across, a small fleet of seekers that must have detected the movement along the rooftops, likely from their advanced surveillance processors. They pursued in a V-shaped formation, priming up the small cannons that the Trade Federation added themselves. Behind them sailed in two floating platforms of battle droids, and even as they followed at full speed, the droids began to unfurl into standing position.

Two blue blades appeared as Obi-Wan and his apprentice stood back-to-back, lightsabers swinging in precise motions nearly too quick for Ruug's eyes. She'd seen a lot in her time, but never a Jedi Knight involved in full-on combat, and the stories of their frightening martial abilities with their legendary weapon proved to be true. This was far different from Obi-Wan's escape at the hearing.

And yet the sheer volume of blaster bolts eventually chipped away, switching the momentum as the battle droids joined in behind the drones. As the battle droids closed in, the seekers elevated, creating different angles of attack against Obi-Wan and his companion, dodging in quick jerks against the Jedi deflections.

If there was a time for Ruug to act, it would be now.

She lined a single seeker into her sights and took in a breath, then pulled the trigger.

CHAPTER 43

OBI-WAN KENOBI

THE BLASTER BOLT FLEW IN from far above, though the Force slowed down his perception enough for Obi-Wan to track it: It soared from an unknown origin to its collision point, absorbing into one of the airborne seekers and overloading it into an explosion.

Ruug.

Two more shots came, their echoing bursts crackling through the air. A pair of seekers burst, smoke trailing them as they dropped. Then four rapid-fire shots, each taking the heads off battle droids. A sliver of opportunity presented itself, enough that a few precise blaster deflections managed to tip the scales in their favor.

Though Anakin probably would make a comment later about how he had it handled anyway. And true, Anakin *had* gotten out of worse cases before. But every situation came with its unique circumstances, and just because one had escaped a jam before, it never provided any guarantees for further victory.

A sliver was, however, all Anakin needed to turn a slight advantage into a decisive victory, and within seconds the smoking remains of battle droids lay before them, some still trying to communicate with a central command in their distinctive lifeless cadence.

"No you don't," Anakin said, twirling his lightsaber before stabbing downward. "What was that?" he asked, pointing in the direction of the sniper fire.

Obi-Wan looked at the tower, pausing to appreciate its architecture with attention he couldn't give earlier. It *was* a marvel, a melding of structural impossibility and artistic genius, from the way that it curved at angles that seemed physically impossible to the ornate carving that told one long story of their culture's creation myth.

And, it turned out, a good sniper position. One that, according to Anakin, had nearly been destroyed by a planted bomb. "A gesture of good faith." Obi-Wan put up a hand and held it for several seconds; whether or not Ruug still watched, he wanted the actions honored. Anakin knelt down, inspecting the remotes—standard seeker technology based on Arakyd models, but these carried specific augmentations to attach weapons to the sensors. He picked up one of the pieces, squinting into the gaping blaster-caused hole and the exposed wiring underneath, so consumed by the inspection that he nearly jumped when Obi-Wan put a hand on his shoulder.

"Anakin," Obi-Wan said, and Anakin's posture immediately set for a defensive statement, an ingrained reaction to all the lecturing rained down on him during his Padawan years.

"Sorry, Master. Trying to see what we're up against. In case—"

"I am genuinely thankful you are here." Obi-Wan's voice came out soft and genuine, and despite the chaos of the situation, he marveled at the grown man in front of him—how everything since Geonosis both stretched time out and compressed it into an instant, changing both of them.

For once, Anakin was left without an immediate rebuttal. He turned from the damaged droid in his hand to look out at the horizon of Cato Neimoidia's capital, the missing section from the fallen Cadesura district visible from their location.

As if on cue, a flare went up near the industrial quarter. Anakin pointed to it and nodded before bursting forward. "Well, don't thank me yet." The remaining seeker body clanked on the ground, debris spitting out from its damaged body upon impact. "That's my partner. We should go."

Obi-Wan looked at the area with the flare, then considered the tower where Ruug's cover fire originated. "*That* tower was the bomb target?"

"Yeah. And six more. Non-military targets. Non-financial targets. If it doesn't affect their strategic defenses or economic standing, why target them?"

Voices shouted from the floor level beneath them. Both Anakin and Obi-Wan ducked down, leaning out only enough to see guards fanning out followed by the heavy footsteps of super battle droids. "Let's move," Anakin said, turning. He took several steps forward but then stopped. "Come on, what are you waiting for?"

Obi-Wan knew Anakin was right, and they *should* go. But figures broke into view: Ketar, pistol drawn and looking all over for something to shoot at. Behind him, a fleet of guards and further battle droids.

He squinted and looked above them, searching the skyline for any sign of Ruug, when he felt Anakin grab his arm, completely focused on the path ahead. "We need to go *now*."

With luck, Obi-Wan wouldn't need to find out the answers to those questions.

"Right, right," he said, and together with Anakin headed out with some measure of Force-assisted speed. "On the move."

They ran across rooftops, vaulting over exhaust stacks and sliding down slanted terraces, occasionally stumbling into people on balconies while making their way toward the flare. Every few buildings, a seeker or two would float up, alerted by their presence, and whoever was in the lead waved a hand, crushing the remote's guidance system and internal processor. Each time, they turned at a hard angle, leaping to a different building to throw off any potential trailers.

As they ran, Obi-Wan relayed Ruug's story, including her finding of the Separatist evidence. In return, Anakin paused to point out each of the bomb targets. They jumped, a constant momentum forward as they moved over and around the obstacles in their way.

"How precise was each bomb's construction and placement?"

"Sloppy," Anakin said, arms gripping a ledge to climb. "The wiring was a little loose. The explosive material wasn't packed tight."

Obi-Wan shook his head as he followed suit. "It can't be the same bomber as the Cadesura disaster. The details showed military expertise. We ran simulations."

"Well, your speech about extremists. A copycat bomber?"

"Dooku's agent," Obi-Wan mused aloud. "What role does she play in all this?"

"There's not much intel on her," Anakin said as they moved quickly. "The clones know more *of* her than about her."

They reached a ledge, a marked difference from the intricate designs of Zarra's capital area and surrounding commercial district. Instead, the farther they pushed to the edge, the more the structures changed into more utilitarian architecture. This pattern continued as dashing across rooftops became simple runs over flat surfaces, and getting to the flare's origin became a tour into the parts of Cato Neimoidia no one ever talked about. It all felt functional, likely a place for manufacturing and storage, warehouse rows and several buildings of high-rises; through the Force, Obi-Wan sensed an array of beings in them, and logic put together that these were the poor and working class of the planet, a mix of Neimoidians and offworld beings who served the ruling class of Zarra.

No matter how rich a planet or society, *someone* always had to do the grunt work.

They moved swiftly to the edge of the rooftop and immediately below, the open space filled with large tents, the makeshift infirmaries that supported the ill, injured, and rescued from the catastrophe. "I don't see any guards," Obi-Wan said. "Not even battle droids. But keep an eye out for any more of those seekers."

"I don't think we'll encounter any. My partner was supposed to find us a low-security area." Anakin pointed to an alley between buildings, a short hooded figure standing there.

And behind her in the shadows, the distinct red, blue, and white lights from R2-D2's dome.

"Good to see an old friend."

"Better yet," Anakin said, "an old friend that can transmit your data to the Republic. Let's figure out a way to get him to the data center." He leapt down and sprinted over to the hooded figure before Obi-Wan could reply.

An instinctive exasperation prompted a quick sigh before Obi-Wan decided to follow Anakin's lead. Would Anakin *ever* not do that?

CHAPTER 44

ANAKIN SKYWALKER

ANAKIN WANTED TO BEAT OBI-WAN to the alley.

Not because it was a race or anything along those lines. This represented a more practical need. He landed on the ground, then rushed over into the alley where Mill stood in the shadows. R2-D2 shook with beeps of greetings before rolling forward to greet Obi-Wan. That gave enough time for Anakin to connect with Mill. "Listen, I haven't told Obi-Wan about you yet."

"What?" Mill asked. Her eyes grew wide under her hood. "Am I going to get in trouble? He's on the Council—"

"Hello, Artoo. Glad you could come help us out." Chirps and whirs came from the droid in return. "I heard. You're quite the bomb-finder. Are you . . ."

Anakin didn't need the Force to detect Obi-Wan's eyes turning their way. He stood up, back still to his former Master, and by now, Mill had to be close enough to give away who she really was.

"A youngling?"

Mill looked up at Anakin, and Anakin responded with a nod. The young Zabrak removed her hood, and in the low light of the alley, the silhouette of her horns and ponytail became clear.

"Anakin." Obi-Wan's voice turned into the familiar scolding. "What are you thinking? This is no place for a youngling."

"Master," Anakin started before intentionally pausing and regrouping, stifling his instinct to argue. "Obi-Wan." Some time ago, such a switch could have been construed as a sign of disrespect. But here, his quieter voice projected different intentions.

He addressed a colleague now, without the formality required with a mentor. And Obi-Wan's face softened, the harsh lines ready to unleash another lecture about protocols and safety loosening up into a willingness to listen, if not necessarily understand.

"This is Jedi Initiate Mill Alibeth," Anakin said. "I know it seems strange—risky—for her to be here. But I'm asking you to trust me on this." Mill moved beside Anakin, standing with straight shoulders and tall chest. "She's quite capable."

Obi-Wan's brow crinkled in concern, as Anakin had seen so many times before. But it usually preceded a sigh of exasperation followed by crossed arms and a shaking head. Those reflexive motions didn't arrive. Instead Obi-Wan stood in simple contemplation, focus moving between Anakin and Mill. "You are a Jedi Knight now for a reason," he said, his words even and careful. "I will defer to your judgment." His head tilted, a smile sneaking through. "I see you learned something talking to all those younglings."

"Don't worry," Anakin said, "no way am I taking on a Padawan."

Several toots and blips came from R2-D2, the astromech droid bouncing back and forth.

"Understood. We'll hurry," Anakin said. "Mill, what do you have for us?"

She took a step forward, her façade of confidence melting away back to the same youngling who'd been with him over the past few days: skilled, intelligent, and naturally talented, but only starting to grow into herself. She gestured at the buildings around them and over at the makeshift infirmary behind Obi-Wan.

"There aren't many guards here. If any," she said. "Artoo?"

R2-D2 projected a map, a rotating model of the neighborhood around them with a red line winding around and forming a large curve to get to a dot.

"And this path will take us through the unguarded areas." Mill traced her finger over it, stopping at the bend in the curve. "There may be some activity over here, but I think between Artoo and our senses, we can move by it quickly."

Several more staccato beeps came from the droid. "They're closing in," Anakin said.

"What did he say?" Mill asked. "I'm . . . still learning to understand droid."

"He's picking up patrol chatter that shows activity to the far east of us, over by where the trial took place," Anakin said.

Obi-Wan looked over his shoulder, then took a step forward. "Youngling, how do you know the details of guard locations? Have you tapped into the Neimoidian security network?"

"No, Master, I scouted forward." She looked up at Anakin, who gave a simple nod of encouragement. "I have an ability."

"To sense patrol movement?" Obi-Wan asked aloud before his voice dropped to internal musing. "That could be a tactical advantage on the battle—"

"No, not that. I sense *pain*. Master Skywalker is helping me learn to control it." Obi-Wan raised an eyebrow his way. "I can see the distress of the patients here. They're rescued from the disaster site. Or recovering after damage from the bomb itself. Physical pain. Or emotions. I give in to the Force and I see it, like you might see heat on a thermal scope."

"Interesting," Obi-Wan said, stroking his beard. Anakin knew the gesture and the tone of voice; some people would use that word as a polite dismissive, but Obi-Wan only did so when his curiosity sparked. "Can you soothe them?"

"I . . . don't know. I've only tried once, on just one patient. But I noticed a pattern with all of the infirmaries they've set up." She pointed again to the large tent. "They're not guarded. It's only medical staff here."

Anakin closed his eyes and reached into the Force, sensing the space around them. "She's right. At least here. Artoo, enhance your audio, see if you can pick up the types of droids." R2-D2 beeped an affirmative, then went silent before turning his dome and chittering at Anakin. "Artoo says that based on what he knows of droid movements, it sounds like medical droids. No battle droids."

"I don't know if they're giving the patients peace to heal. Or if—"
Mill gulped before staring straight at the tent. "If they just don't care.
Like they just get in the way."

Anakin was about to say something about how of course the Trade
Federation would treat victims as assets, but Obi-Wan spoke first. "It is
not up to us to judge why this is the case. There could be a cultural history in place here. But this does give us an advantage. Youngling," he
said, kneeling to put himself on her level then tilting his head up to
meet her eye-to-eye. "It is a unique gift. You should embrace it. And I
have a challenge for you."

"A challenge?"

"Before we leave Cato Neimoidia, I need to get to the governmental
data center and retrieve evidence. It is right next to the largest of these
temporary infirmaries." Obi-Wan looked up at Anakin. "My *friend*
found it ironic," he said, before turning back to Mill. "Between you and
Artoo, I believe we can get there undetected."

"Then let's get going," Anakin said. "The quicker we move, the
quicker we can get back to the original plan and fly off this planet."

The projection from R2-D2 shifted, its rotation stopping to zoom out
and show a new location, this time with a green line that followed the
same path for about half the journey before turning left instead of right
at the bend.

"The Force brings us together at the right moments," Obi-Wan said,
nodding at Mill. "He's right. Youngling, lead the way. And let's try to
stay in the shadows. No more rooftop business for us; those seeker remotes will be looking."

"You could just say that we're lucky she's here."

"Anakin, you keep believing in luck."

"I didn't say I believed in luck." He patted Mill on the shoulder,
prompting a smile on her face. "But that doesn't stop us from being
lucky." Mill set off down the alley with her hood back over her horned
head, R2-D2 rolling behind her. Anakin followed, and Obi-Wan kept
pace with him, a quick but quiet walk.

.   .   .

From the sky, Zarra glowed with elegant structures and lush topiaries. In all of the areas that Mill identified, though, it might as well have been the industrial sector of Coruscant. With most of the infirmaries pushed to the outskirts of the bridge city, moving toward the data center proved quite easy, the medical droids and nursing personnel too wrapped up in immediate concerns to care about any detected movement. They'd made it about halfway across R2-D2's projected route when Mill suddenly stopped.

"What's wrong, Mill?" Anakin asked. She took another step forward, though her hands pressed against her head. He moved to support her weight, and though she tried to push him off, whatever suddenly ailed her plucked at her strength.

"I sense something."

Obi-Wan came up alongside them, soon followed by R2-D2. "Scan the area for guards or threats," he said to the astromech, though he gave her space to breathe. R2-D2 beeped in acknowledgment, then rolled several meters away before a small sensor dish emerged from the droid's round dome.

"Is someone approaching?" Anakin asked.

"No. But they're nearby. It's fear. Suffering. Rage." She pressed her hands against her temples then began glancing around, each movement seemingly a struggle. She opened her eyes and stared Anakin in the face. "I can't shut it off. It's so overwhelming that . . ." Anakin took her hands but looked around as well.

"Is it the infirmary over there?" Anakin said, pointing to the adjacent warehouse converted into a local trauma ward.

"No. I sense them, but this is different. And it's so much that I sense it everywhere. And I think it's just one person. But the pain they're feeling . . ."

Mill's voice trailed off, but R2-D2 took up the space, beeping fast enough to cause the droid to tilt back and forth. "A bomb?" Obi-Wan asked. Light came out of the astromech's optical projector, and a map emerged into existence, a simple red X marking a location not too far from them.

"Come on," Anakin said, picking up Mill. Obi-Wan took the lead, moving quickly with R2-D2 rolling behind him and Anakin on lookout while carrying Mill.

"Something's not right," Mill said, her head leaning into Anakin's shoulder.

"Anakin!" Obi-Wan yelled from around the corner of a forgotten building, its doors and windows shuttered with large metal plates. He stood with the open air above, the gray skies of Cato Neimoidia casting a pale light over them until Obi-Wan's lightsaber added a tint of blue. He cut a hole with precision, moving the blade in a square without cutting it too deeply. Anakin understood the specific movements: Obi-Wan didn't want the energy of the plasma blade to accidentally set off any explosives.

Obi-Wan stepped back, then put his hand out, fingers spread widely, and through the Force he extracted the square-shaped metal slab before dropping it into the empty alley.

"There it is," Obi-Wan said before waving Anakin over. "Does this look like the bombs you found yesterday?"

R2-D2's optic lens rotated, along with the hum and vibration of an active scan. Anakin set Mill down and knelt beside Obi-Wan to look inside the abandoned building. "It does," he said, his initial hunch confirmed, but studying it closer to be certain. "Same orange material. The wiring follows the same design. And the igniter unit is the same. So's the remote signal processor. And the explosive form—it's about the same size. And," Anakin noted, "it's still sloppy. But this," he said, gesturing around them, "doesn't make sense. The other bombs were all within a radius of the trial. All of those targets meant something to this community." Anakin shook his head, then glanced around for a full view of their surroundings. "This is just an abandoned warehouse. It makes no sense."

"Agh," Mill let out, hands to her head. She stood up, pushing Anakin away when he tried to help. "No, I need to fight through this. This person is near. Somewhere close by." Her knees buckled but she grunted, steadying herself. "I won't let this overwhelm me. I can control this."

A series of quick chirps and whistles came from R2-D2, rapid enough that Anakin put his hand on his lightsaber hilt.

"How did you disarm this before?" Obi-Wan asked.

"Complete manual rewiring. It takes a little bit of effort. The bomber may not be precise, but they had a good teacher. Keep an eye out," Anakin said, reaching in to remove the bomb from its mounting struts. "I need to be careful with this."

Gravel ground beneath Anakin's boots as he pulled the device out. Obi-Wan stepped back to give him some space as he set the armed device down on the alley's stone paving.

Anakin turned to him, then quickly looked at Mill, who gritted her teeth as she pushed her way to straighten up. "It's coming closer. The anger."

"Then I better hurry." But as soon as he leaned over to begin the disarmament, a voice shouted out.

"Step away from the bomb, *Jedi*."

Anakin whirled around, his lightsaber pulling into his hand and igniting in a single move.

By then, Obi-Wan's weapon reflected blue across his face as well, but he held out a single hand, motioning Anakin to slow down.

And Anakin listened.

He eyed the guard standing across the street from them, the young Neimoidian who gave the fiery speech during the trial. Both of his hands held something—the left, a pistol drawn on them, and the right, a small device, finger on the trigger.

"Ketar," Obi-Wan said, his voice slowing. "Enough people have been hurt. Put the detonator down and let's talk."

"You won't get through to him," Mill said. "He's in a state of rage. I can *feel* it."

Anakin looked at the space around him, searching for vulnerabilities. Despite being more ordinary and in slight disrepair, many of the surrounding structures were still the rounded designs typical of the culture's aesthetics. But in terms of immediate help, the environment provided no tricks.

It would just take speed—a burst to rush over and slice the detonator. Or he could push Ketar down with the Force, hopefully knocking the detonator out of his hand. Or pull the detonator as he would any object on the ground. Those all came with the same risk: If Ketar realized what was happening, his thumb would hit the button and set off the bomb.

A thought crept into his mind, one that he pushed out as soon as it arrived: If he had Count Dooku's mastery over lightning, one zap would likely be enough to shock Ketar fast enough to knock him out and safely free the detonator.

"Anakin, let me talk to him," Obi-Wan said under his breath, as if he knew that Anakin was already considering ways to rush him.

"You heard Mill. You're not getting through to him right now."

"I'm going to try. Give me a chance."

Anakin nodded, letting Obi-Wan do what he did best, but he didn't like the odds—or have the patience required to let this play out. Obi-Wan's lightsaber retracted and he put both hands up. "You see?" Obi-Wan said. "We are calm. We are here to talk. I spoke of good faith before, and I intend to keep it." From the side of his mouth, he spoke quietly. "Disarm yourself."

"I hope you know what you're doing," Anakin said, drawing his plasma blade back into its hilt.

"Ketar," Obi-Wan said, "were those your bombs around the Grand Theatre of Judgment?"

"You!" he said in a low, icy tone. He stared at Anakin. "You must be the one from the communicator. Did you take my bombs?"

"That was me," Anakin responded. "Still couldn't figure out why you picked those targets. I don't know, I thought that was some nice architecture—"

"Some of the finest in our culture's history," he said, his voice seething.

"Master," Mill said, "you're pushing him. I don't know if this is a good idea."

"Look at you, look at the way you mock us. The same as long as I can remember, the way the Republic treats Neimoidians, the way they treated generations of my family. Why would I destroy pillars of Neimoidian culture? Because *then* the Republic might finally see we are more than asset traders. Because they would *see*"—his voice rose—"the smoking remains of everything the Jedi emissary blew away."

"I guess he was framing you," Anakin whispered.

Obi-Wan nodded, then turned to the young guard. "Ketar," he tried again, "I understand your grievances against the Republic. You're not wrong. But please listen to the evidence. We did *not* cause the catastrophe on Cadesura. You can help us. Ruug trusts me. You can trust me, too."

"Don't speak about my partner. You've corrupted her."

Obi-Wan took a step forward, hands up as he tried a different tactic. "You can take the lead on the investigation of my evidence," he said, specifically omitting Ruug from that detail. "You could be a hero to both the Republic and the Separatists—your actions could be the one thing that drives the galaxy to peace. You want to help your people, you want to help the Trade Federation, this is your opportunity. Please, work with me and take it." Obi-Wan looked over at Mill. "What are you sensing?" he asked under his breath.

"Anguish. Confusion. He's still very angry. But you've—"

"Enough chatter between you. Stop plotting against me. I am in control here." A discharge came from his pistol, and Anakin reached into the Force to project out its trajectory and final landing spot.

A warning shot, with no target. He let it fly past them, and Obi-Wan similarly didn't move. It seared into the building's wall, leaving a black pockmark, debris crumbling to the ground.

"Yes, Ketar," Anakin said. "This is your show. You're in control."

"Don't speak of Ruug anymore. I know all about your Jedi powers."

"Ruug has made her own choices," Obi-Wan said. "I have not influenced her at all."

"Then she is a traitor to Neimoidians everywhere."

"Ketar," Obi-Wan said, trying to reframe the discussion. "Listen to me. No one has to know about the bombs you planted. No one has to know about *this* bomb, right here, next to this infirmary." Though no one said it, Ketar's plans suddenly connected in Anakin's mind—if this was all about framing Obi-Wan for disrespecting the Neimoidian people, then the targets would all be things that mattered to their culture and community rather than to the Trade Federation as an organization.

Buildings and statues of cultural significance—and the unguarded wounded.

"These bombs can be erased from history. And instead, you can be the one who said that you wished to take the first step toward peace. Use my evidence, I beg of you. You can be the hero the galaxy needs right now. This will give you everything you want. Greater recognition of the Neimoidian people. A resolution to the greatest crime Cato Neimoidia has ever seen. And vindication for your family bloodline."

"Another good speech," Anakin whispered, and though Ketar probably couldn't see it, Anakin caught the corner of Obi-Wan's mouth curling upward.

"Something's happening to him," Mill said. "His emotions are like a cloud of different colors."

"Now's my chance, while he's distracted." Anakin glanced over at Obi-Wan, who remained still. "He's unstable."

Ketar slowly slid the pistol into his hip holster, a gesture that got all of their attention. But the detonator still sat in his other raised hand—that part didn't change. His free hand went up to the side of his helmet. Details remained too quiet to hear, but *someone* talked into his ear.

"Someone's on his comm," Anakin said, "I should take him now."

"I hope it's Ruug," Obi-Wan whispered. "No, he's still got the detonator. One move and he blows it up. We're not *that* fast."

Whoever called Ketar finished, and the guard reaffirmed his stance, red eyes wide. He took a step toward them as he drew his pistol back out. "You claim I would be a hero," he said. "But bringing the Trade Federation closer to the Republic would make me a traitor. We will not be forced under the thumb of Republic rule. Ventress told me all about you Jedi, the way you manipulate people. The way you control their emotions. I've already seen what you've done to Ruug. How you twist the truth. How the Republic gives you free rein to do as you please. I said it at the trial and I will say it here again:

"No more. You tried to hide your crimes. I will make that impossible."

"Ventress," Obi-Wan said, a rare curse under his breath before returning to full volume. "The spirit of cooperation is necessary for galactic peace. We must come together to stop this outside group that has unleashed havoc on your homeworld. Please look at my evidence. The Republic is not to blame here."

"You're wasting your time." His voice took a grim turn, and his fingers flexed around the pistol grip. He looked up with a startling unblinking clarity in his red eyes. "You don't understand."

"Oh no," Mill said with a gasp.

"I don't care who bombed Cadesura." His words combined with growing fury. "I don't know and I don't care. That was never the point. The only thing that matters is what happens now. The Republic has looked down on Neimoidians for far too long. Neutrality is not the path here. The only way to save my people is for them to join Count Dooku's movement. Count Dooku will save the galaxy. He may speak highly of your Order but he also understands the true nature of things."

Anakin could feel Obi-Wan's burn at the last sentence, a clear indicator that yet another variable was in play. "Ventress has been in your ear as an agent of Count Dooku. Give me the same amount of time you've given her. I offer you only words."

Anakin put his hand on his lightsaber hilt, just in case.

"He's too far gone. Whoever spoke to him on his comm, it's pushed him over the edge," Mill said, stepping behind Anakin.

"It was Ventress. She's manipulating his idealism. Perhaps we should run. Escaping the blast radius is our only chance," Obi-Wan whispered. "You pick up the youngling. Artoo will need to use his rockets."

"There has to be another way. The infirmary. We have to save them." Anakin grabbed at the Force, slowing down everything around him to seek some solution that might save *everyone*. The best thing he could think of was a coordinated Force pull, two at the same time from him and Obi-Wan—one on Ketar himself to yank him forward, and the other on the detonator. That might get it out of his hand cleanly enough for him to—

"No more words," Ketar yelled. "Step away from my bomb."

Or he could turn and sever the bomb's wires in one lightsaber swing and hope that was enough. He knew what wires to pull. This would be less precise than the other bombs, but the Force would guide him. Obi-Wan could take care of the rest.

"Anakin, we must run. The blast radius is set, but if we survive, we can get to the data center and show the evidence to the Republic."

"No, I'm coming up with a plan. We're going to save everyone."

"This is war. In war, there are impossible choices. We *must* get the evidence to the Republic."

"I tire of your stalling. Get away from my bomb." Something shifted in Ketar's stance, as if he'd reached some kind of epiphany. "No, it doesn't matter." A new steadiness came to his voice. "I don't need to survive this."

"He's calm now," Mill said. "Like something turned off all his emotions. All his colors went dark."

"That's not good," Anakin said. He put his hand up, the Force acting as an extension of his own hand. He'd just about felt the detonator through the ether when a crackle popped from high above, cutting through the air like thunder.

CHAPTER 45

OBI-WAN KENOBI

THE DETONATOR DROPPED FROM KETAR'S hand and bounced off the ground, a blaster bolt fired with enough velocity to burn a complete hole in the palm. Ketar looked at his hand, his red eyes growing even larger when another shot rang out. The guard buckled, one leg suddenly giving out and he collapsed to the ground, howling in pain.

Obi-Wan looked up and behind them, the remnants of the bursts still echoing across the sky.

"Did you plan this?" Anakin asked, the fallen detonator flying into his open palm. A second later Ketar's pistol took flight, landing in Anakin's other hand, though he quickly tossed it aside. He turned, searching the surrounding buildings, and he'd moved to grab his lightsaber before Obi-Wan gestured to pause him.

"No," Obi-Wan said, scanning rooftops for Ruug's presence. "I believe this was more of that good faith I talked about. In the face of an impossible choice." Where was she? Obi-Wan tried the most logical direction based on the way the blaster bolt arrived, a specific angle and speed. He found no traces, though after several seconds his ears picked up the clomp of footsteps over rooftop metal. Each clang gave away the location. Someone was running at a clip that would make even Jedi envious despite the lack of Force abilities. "You should disarm that bomb."

"On it," Anakin said.

"How are you, youngling?"

"He's hurt," she said, "but that rage is fading."

Obi-Wan nodded, his hand instinctively going to his beard as he thought through his options. It didn't take long for the footsteps above to turn into a series of huffs and thumps, and then he finally located Ruug: Sniper rifle strapped to her back, she climbed down a series of ledges before attaching a grappling hook to the side of a tall curved wall and rappelling to the surface. The hook retracted its claws and caught up to her as she slowed down, taking in the scene: Jedi to her right, a wounded Ketar to her left.

Obi-Wan walked up to the Neimoidian commando. "There's another bomb. My appren— fellow Jedi is disarming it. Did you know about the series of bombs Ketar planted?"

"Only what was discussed here."

"His hate for the Republic runs deep. And it has been stoked by Dooku's agent."

Ruug nodded and looked up. "She's close. I saw her ship."

"I believe she was in coordination with Ketar over comms."

They both turned to look at the fallen guard, quietly writhing in pain. The heat from the blaster bolts must have cauterized the wounds, much like a lightsaber, as little blood oozed onto the ground below him. Ketar looked up, and through the pain of his wounds, he tilted his head and focused on Ruug. "Traitor," he yelled, spit flying with his words.

Ruug took steps forward toward her partner, but paused and looked back. "This is your call," Obi-Wan said. "Unless you want the Republic to be involved."

"No. I own this. I wasn't there for him. Ventress was." Ruug's normally inscrutable face broke, regret appearing in the form of narrow eyes and a tight jaw. "What have you done, Ketar?"

"Traitor," he yelled again, "people like you will be the end of our kind."

"I hope this is Ventress speaking, not you." All of Ruug's talk of tough decisions, killing for her government, and her brutal commando life seemed to exhaust her. But here, one simple sentence from Ketar cracked her stoic exterior, working its way past any defenses until she simply stared at her fallen partner, silent.

"She has shown me the path. She promises that Dooku will *not* exploit Neimoidians like the Republic has." Obi-Wan wished he could show Ketar what Dooku had said on Geonosis, how underneath the eloquent words and welcoming smile came deceptions both subtle and overt. But he respected Ruug enough to leave this to her.

"Think this through. How do you know he will keep his word?" she asked, kneeling down. Obi-Wan watched as she tried to reach him, as if logic might break through where empathy failed. "Even if he does, how do you know that everyone underneath him will as well? The Separatists are an evolving organization, filled with competing priorities. Including Nute Gunray. Their future is uncertain."

"So you throw in with the Republic? With the Jedi?"

Ruug paused, then looked back at Anakin and Mill as they worked on the bomb. "The Jedi tried to help our people. You tried to murder them. That's unforgivable. There's no possible justification for this. Regardless of what Ventress told you, *you* planted the bombs." She pointed at him. "As Cato Neimoidia mourned, you made that choice."

"I tried to save our people. While you collaborate with the enemy."

"No." Ruug's posture changed, the pain of earlier now turning into an anger that tensed her shoulders and balled her fists. "I find this Jedi to be honest. And I'm willing to listen to honest people. But I will always carry the best interests of Neimoidians."

"You have sold out your people."

"This bomb would have murdered civilians!"

"Keep telling yourself that. Take the easy way out." Ketar spat at Ruug's feet, the glob a mix of saliva and blood. "History will remember you as a traitor. Finish it. Kill me now. Complete your betrayal. What are you—"

Ketar's diatribe ended with Ruug sending a fist into his face. "We're not changing each other's minds." She stood up, that split-second gesture marking the difference between her and Obi-Wan: He would never have given in to an impulse like that, even if knocking out Ketar had a practical purpose.

Anakin, on the other hand . . .

"Do you judge me?" she asked, eyes locked with Obi-Wan's.

That question tied into many different outcomes, and he weighed the possibilities, the way each might ripple out. "You are in a position that I cannot fully appreciate. These are your decisions to make. However," he said, "if you need any assistance, you may ask. From the Republic, or from myself. As a friend." He turned to check on Anakin, who still worked on bomb disarmament.

"He has identified me as a traitor. And—" She inhaled slowly. "—I suppose I am. I aided a declared enemy of the state. And he knows it." She took several steps closer to him. "He's the *only* one that knows it."

"Ruug," Obi-Wan said, "consider your options. Carefully."

"If I finish the job, I have his confession recorded. He will be rightfully blamed for the bombs. Perhaps that will further the discussion on extremism." She looked at Obi-Wan. "And further your push for negotiations. It only supports your argument."

"You will murder your partner, though."

"Oh, I've killed so many. In combat. Up close. On a mission. Collateral damage. Accident. The guilty. The innocent." Ruug's gloved hands pushed against the sides of her face. "It doesn't make a difference how. I've taken their lives. What's one more—especially if it de-escalates the war?"

This was not Jedi business. Obi-Wan's mandate was to investigate the bombing and, if he could, to persuade the Trade Federation into opening negotiations with the Republic. The conflict between Ruug and Ketar lived in a bubble exclusively their own, especially with Ketar's bombs nullified. Somewhere, perhaps Ventress watched with interest, but Obi-Wan suspected her as the type whose words pushed her own agenda forward, regardless of who got caught up in them. She likely didn't care if Ketar lived or died.

"I taught him. I mentored him. And I hoped to temper his rage by showing him how we do the work. I underestimated Ventress." The toe of her boot dug into the ground. "Or perhaps, I overestimated how much he listened to me."

Obi-Wan intentionally stayed quiet. Her words didn't invite an opinion, and in this case, letting her talk it through might bring her to a better conclusion.

She knelt over Ketar's prone body, his eyes closed above his wheezing breath. She focused on the wounds she'd created moments ago, from the sniper rifle she'd described to Obi-Wan as "an extension of my own body" while they worked together on the surface.

Did that mean she felt every visceral impact that her weapon caused?

From across the way, Obi-Wan heard Anakin talking to Mill about the bomb, though they kept a respectful distance. Ruug remained still, only blinking as she stared at her fallen comrade. Seconds ticked by, fingers turning into a shaking fist at her side until one hand brushed the pistol holster on her belt.

"This is how it's going to be," she said.

And Obi-Wan waited.

Her hand hovered, fingers flexing over the weapon, her long gloved forefinger tapping against the grip.

"I might regret this. But we're here now"—her pupil slits sharpened into focus—"and I can't change anything."

Her hand moved and Obi-Wan took in a sharp inhale.

It reached past the holster, shifting farther to the back of her utility belt before pulling out standard-issue energy binders, the same kind she'd placed on Obi-Wan not too long ago.

"I need a medpac," she said with a heavy sigh. As she cuffed Ketar's limp hands, she inspected his wounds more closely. "The path to Neimoidian prosperity is through peaceful negotiation, not bloodshed. We know this. Our brains are wired to calculate this." Obi-Wan reached into his own belt for a small tube of emergency bacta. "This cycle of violence must end," she said, taking the bacta from him and applying it on the burn damage on Ketar's hand and knee. "He's lucky we're next to an infirmary."

"Ruug," Obi-Wan said, helping her turn Ketar onto his back. "I still believe we have a chance for de-escalation. We need to get to the data center and download the evidence of Separatist involvement. Then show the Republic that someone is clearly playing both sides."

"I can help you," she said, pulling on Ketar's arm before lifting him over her shoulder. They walked in step, Obi-Wan letting her lead the way back to Anakin, Mill, and the bomb. "Are all of Ketar's bombs disarmed?"

"We got most of them yesterday. Only this one's left. But I'm almost done. It's safe. And stable. I just need more time to disable it."

Ruug looked at the trio of Jedi surrounding her, and on her shoulder, Ketar groaned. "The data center itself has layers of guards. I'll need to use that bomb as a distraction."

"No," Mill said. "No more suffering for political gain."

A smile crept over Ruug's face, perhaps at the idealism on display here. "Youngling, your friend trusts me. You should, too." She gestured at the bomb's explosive material. "I'll use a fraction of that on an environmental scanner, about a kilometer from the data center. It's uninhabited and isolated. But our security is on high alert. That should pull a number of guards from the building to inspect. I'll call it in myself."

"What about Ketar?"

"I'll drop him off at the infirmary. And tell them to sedate him, that he's under arrest. If—no, when—he comes to, he'll identify me as a traitor. I don't know what will happen then. But," she said, adjusting the unconscious Neimoidian on her shoulder, "hopefully you'll be offworld by then."

CHAPTER 46

ANAKIN SKYWALKER

THIS WAS ANAKIN'S SPECIALTY.

He dashed forward, moving with stealth and speed; if Mill and R2-D2 hadn't been with him—even if Obi-Wan hadn't been with him—he'd have gotten there in half the time. Mill's hunch that the infirmary neighborhoods were lightly guarded proved to be completely accurate, and R2-D2's constant scans confirmed that patrols clearly focused on the immediate area around the governmental offices. When the data center was within reach, he paused only to check with Mill.

"I'm okay," she said, "I'm fine."

"Are you sure? Obi-Wan says that is the largest infirmary."

Mill straightened herself after a brief pause to catch her breath. "If I can handle Ketar, I can handle this. Besides," she said, marching with a confidence that may have been for show, "I'm beginning to find that it's not their suffering that slows me down. It's that I want to help them."

"Hold on to that," Anakin said. "The way you care about others will power you through adversity." From the corner of his eye, he caught Obi-Wan shooting a second glance at this, though he quickly marched forward, eyes focused on their destination.

"That's the environmental scanner Ruug mentioned," Obi-Wan said, pointing to a thin tower with equipment sticking out of a collection of buildings. "And that's the back entrance where she's supposed to meet us." They overlooked a plain domed structure with a short cylindrical stack on top, the only decorative flourishes being the statues in the front courtyard; there were equal numbers of guards at the front and back loading areas. To the side sat five massive tents, medical droids hauling the occasional cart back and forth between them.

The sky flashed before a plume of smoke went up at the scanner. They all turned to see one of its supporting legs collapse as the tower imploded, the equipment at the top falling straight down.

"That's our cue," Anakin said. Ruug's distraction worked; most of the guards surrounding the building took off, and a number streamed out of the building as well. They leapt down, staying among alleys and side streets to circumvent the infirmaries.

As they passed by the final tent, Mill took in a breath. Anakin turned to her, though they kept moving. "Are you all right, Mill?"

"I was wrong," she said. But unlike other times when her abilities seemed to take the air out of her, she remained steady on her feet. "I thought they'd left the infirmaries unguarded because they didn't care. But it's to give the patients a more restful space. Their culture cares deeply about their sick and wounded. It's not something that the outside observer would see."

"You got all that from walking by them?"

"I sensed them a little differently here," Mill said. They stopped, Obi-Wan peeking around the corner before signaling them forward. "All the other infirmaries are free of guards. This one has some close by. They seem to tense up when they're around military. And the guards are mindful. I think it's that risk calculation you told me about." She turned to Anakin, her eyes clear. "They care about their people, especially in a time of mourning. I don't know about the Trade Federation, but *Neimoidians* care about their people."

Anakin nodded, but he only had a few seconds to take in her epiphany before Obi-Wan waved them ahead. Perhaps they'd all made the mistake of lumping the population in with the government. Obi-Wan led them to the side of the dome, an area with significant tree cover, before vaulting upward on it, using Force-assisted balance to scale the curved side. Though Mill moved more slowly than the adults, she proved to be a capable climber, keeping pace with R2-D2 boosting next to her.

"Ruug says this is the area with the least cam coverage," Obi-Wan said as they made it to the top ledge. From where they knelt together, the lone guard on the back side appeared to be no more than an insect standing its ground, though the local faux emergency drew out the rest of the office workers as well. They scattered, looking like dots moving on a board from their distance, though another one emerged from the opposite side, dashing *inward* instead of away. "There she is." Obi-Wan adjusted his balance on his heels, then pointed to the top cylindrical structure. Anakin nodded, then led the way to the roof hatch where Ruug would let them in undetected.

"Welcome to the governmental data archive," Ruug said, waving them inside. She toggled the button again on the device in her hand, an orange translucent beam bursting outward; she'd done the same on their way in, to create a rolling window of disabled surveillance. "If I wasn't getting arrested for treason before, any records of me doing this will surely get me the brig."

"You're doing this for the right reason," Obi-Wan said with a nod. "Mill, can your abilities monitor the outer hallway for movement?"

"If I really concentrate, Master."

"Do it. Alert us if anyone starts coming toward us." Obi-Wan looked at Ruug, who nodded in return. "We can't be too cautious."

R2-D2 rolled in and immediately chirped about looking for an access port. "Here," Anakin said, tapping on a knee-level port built for astromech droids. The screen above came alive with lines and lines of text that at first showed what he assumed to be Pak Pak, but several seconds later all the text flipped to Aurebesh characters. Ruug stepped over, swiping at the screen and drilling down through various folders until she tapped at two sets of files.

"This is it," she said. "Bring these to the Republic. Any copies self-delete within a standard day for risk mitigation. That's why my source had to slice directly into the archive. If you're going to transmit it, you need to send it now, and the receiver will have to capture it securely."

R2-D2 beeped an affirmative and a download bar appeared on the screen, incrementally filling from empty to full.

"Do you wish to present it yourself to the Republic?" Obi-Wan asked. "We can grant you amnesty. You will be protected. Perhaps you can even lead the negotiations with the Trade Federation."

"I promise you, nothing would happen to you," Anakin said, and inside, he felt the sun-dragon roar, the way it always did in the furnace of his heart during these circumstances. When anyone showed loyalty to Anakin Skywalker, they became an ally for life. And if they ever betrayed him, that intensity would immediately invert into something much more dangerous.

Ruug looked back and forth between the two Jedi Knights, then at the youngling who suddenly seemed capable beyond her years, despite the fact that she didn't even have her own kyber crystal yet.

Anakin knew Ruug's answer simply from the look on her face.

"I love my homeworld," she said, turning to the screen above R2-D2. "I love my people. I've done so many terrible things on their behalf because I believe that they are worth it. You're right; I could go with you to Coruscant and become a negotiator. But my place is here. I've spent my life fighting on the inside for Neimoidians. Perhaps not always for the Trade Federation. But for my people. Whatever happens to me, I will continue that fight."

Anakin looked at Obi-Wan, who merely nodded. "We understand," he said, extending his gloved mechanical hand. "If you ever need us, you have friends in the Republic." Obi-Wan had been right about her. And for that, he was grateful.

For that, he would fight for her. Strange that he felt that, even for someone who was Neimoidian, who had worked for the Trade Federation. The epiphanies that only came with experience settled in, his own deeply held beliefs that formed early gradually reframing into a whole new perspective.

Ruug took his hand, and through the glove and synthetic sensors, he felt the warmth and weight of hers against his. Of the many species he'd encountered across his entire life, it dawned on him that he'd rarely stood this close to a Neimoidian before, despite how much they influenced the direction of his life. A chime came from the archive, and R2-D2 dislodged from the terminal; the droid backed up before his dome slid open, a small sensor dish elevating upward. Rapid beeps came along with an electronic groan, one that the astromech usually saved for frustrations.

"What's with the droid?" Ruug asked.

"Transmissions to Coruscant are jammed. A leftover from the rules of my stay. Artoo," Obi-Wan said, "is there anything you can do to delay the self-deleting files? Perhaps rolling copies of copies?"

Before R2-D2 could respond, Anakin put a hand up. "We may not need to do that. Artoo, can you transmit to a ship traveling to the Mid Rim?" One affirmative whistle later and suddenly Anakin felt stronger, more capable of defeating any obstacle. Thoughts about Padmé combined with a rush of adrenaline greater than any spice or drink combination could achieve. "I'm friends with a senator we can trust."

Obi-Wan's head tilted sideways.

Anakin knelt down in front of R2-D2, quickly reciting memorized details about connecting to secure comm channels, something that he held on to as tightly as the hand of his wife.

Because in some ways, those letters and numbers held their marriage up across the stars.

CHAPTER 47

OBI-WAN KENOBI

THERE WAS A BRIEF MOMENT in the relationship between Obi-Wan Kenobi and Qui-Gon Jinn when the apprentice went behind his Master's back as he searched for his true path forward. A brash young Padawan at the time, so insistent on following the Jedi Code that he bristled at Qui-Gon's hesitation regarding a treaty with the unscrupulous Czerka corporation and the planet Pijal—hesitation created by Qui-Gon's own moral compass.

In the end, years later, Obi-Wan understood his old Master's objections, something where balancing right and wrong, good and bad failed to produce a clear outcome.

He was pretty sure that Anakin's defiance of the Jedi Code right here did *not* fall into the category of "moral compass." Because Anakin didn't acknowledge it or defend it. He did, however, fail miserably at hiding it.

Obi-Wan sensed *everything,* as soon as Anakin said, "Mid Rim." In circumstances like this, he usually prefaced any conclusions with questions, internal or otherwise, and allowed things to fully play out.

But in *this* moment, he didn't need to. The surge of emotion that came with those words was enough for Obi-Wan to understand the situation. And it had little to do with the strategy for transmitting the data to the Republic or the possibilities of Ruug's decisions. Everything here connected to thoughts about Padmé Amidala, the way that Anakin managed to steer the mission over to her. Was that his intention this whole time? Or did he take advantage of the situation whenever he could?

Or perhaps it was a mere coincidence and Padmé really was the best choice here? She was accessible, and securing a trusted transmission route to Coruscant was the top priority.

R2-D2's projection lamp lit up, and the glowing figure of Padmé Amidala appeared. Despite the bright colors of the hologram, her exquisite purple dress's finely detailed copper embroidery was still distinct, but Padmé herself presented more casually, with curly hair down, no overcoat, and only a simple gold pendant with a metallic spiral design. "Ani! It's—"

Though the image stood only as tall as a lightsaber hilt, her transformation was clear. Her head tilted slightly, as if identifying the people standing around Anakin flipped a switch. "Master Skywalker," she said, her voice shifting into formality.

"Senator Amidala," Anakin said, returning the professional tone of her speech. Obi-Wan chose not to look directly at Anakin, instead judging his reactions and expression through a distorted mirror on a reflective piece of metal from the data center's console. But even though Anakin spoke in a low monotone, his mouth kept fighting a smile and his eyes failed to hide anything. "We have urgent data to send to you. We are at a secured location on Cato Neimoidia, and transmissions to Coruscant are blocked."

"Senator," Obi-Wan said, keeping up the guise of formality for the conversation, "this is self-deleting data. You will need to capture it in permanent form, then transmit it to the Jedi Council for analysis. We believe this information can be vital to de-escalating the war, and perhaps convincing either the Trade Federation or the Separatists to enter negotiations." He looked at Ruug before continuing. "Perhaps both."

C-3PO stumbled into view. "Oh! Master Anakin! And Artoo-Detoo. Among my capabilities is the ability to capture image or text data into a permanent format capable of download by any standard secured Republic system. Though I usually use this for translation of memos sent in non-Basic languages as they are streamed in transmission, it can be applied here. It may require—"

"Thank you, Threepio. Yes, Master Kenobi, we can handle this information."

Anakin began explaining the technical aspects of what they needed, which got the practical part of the job done. But his feelings were clear, so much that Obi-Wan didn't need to watch the reflection to sense them; being in the room was enough. Despite how they dressed up their words, Padmé's reactions broke enough from her usual stoic formality to inform the situation, her gift for disciplining herself in the name of diplomacy exhibiting a hairline fracture in front of them.

Up close, their bond became clear even as they tried to hide it. For the uninitiated, that deception would have worked. But he knew Anakin well enough to read his every movement; that, in turn, reflected on Padmé.

Another epiphany soon dawned on Obi-Wan: It also reflected on *himself.* For all the stubbornness, the arguments, the subtle disdain that they sometimes had for each other, a new form of Anakin was emerging, something more authentic and human coming through since his promotion. Their conversations still manifested as competition, but rather than trying to step on each other, they'd made a subtle turn to verbal one-upmanship.

All it took was leaving behind the bond of Master and apprentice. For a moment, Obi-Wan's mind drifted from the mission, a volley of relentless questions whipping through. Was Anakin like this because Obi-Wan tried *too* hard to live up to Qui-Gon's dying request? If he had been more like Qui-Gon and less like what he *thought* a Jedi mentor should be, would Anakin have such defiance in him? As Anakin and Padmé oversaw the data upload, Obi-Wan finally identified this strange feeling in him, something so rare and foreign that it took a barrage of questions and the weight of self-doubt to recognize:

Regret.

Qui-Gon had occasionally revealed his own questions and insecurities, even turning down a seat on the Jedi Council to remain Obi-Wan's teacher, yet did it ever coalesce into something quite like this?

But, as he'd been trained since he was a youngling, Obi-Wan let the feeling go, allowing it to evaporate into nothing rather than stifling it down into a scar that might fester. He faced new questions as he watched the subtle exchanges between Anakin and a holographic Padmé—the way the young Jedi Knight allowed a smile to break through over something as benign as "seventy percent uploaded," the way the former queen of Naboo held her gaze much longer than she should have, and the way Anakin's feelings radiated outward, as if his heart were a sun heating the entire data center.

What might he learn from this moment—about Anakin, about himself, about their time as Master and apprentice?

About how things needed to move forward, one way or another?

The last few days only reinforced Anakin's overwhelming willingness to simply *care*. That caring someday might make the difference between life and death, a right decision and a wrong decision stemming from a mere blink of emotion. Earlier that day, the situation with Ketar would have been vastly different in a manner of seconds.

In war, seconds might define the fate of the galaxy.

The status bar on the screen crept to full before flashing several times as confirmation. "I see it," Padmé said. "Threepio and I will begin processing it."

"We'll contact you once we're off Cato Neimoidia," Anakin said. This time, he angled himself away from watching eyes, though his reflection gave away that he'd saved a soft look for the senator.

"Understood, Master Skywalker," she said, an intentional monotone worthy of her time as queen of Naboo under all of the makeup and headdresses. Her image faded away and R2-D2 disconnected from the terminal with his usual chatter.

"That's right, Artoo," Anakin said. "Let's head out."

"Wait." Ruug held up a hand, the surveillance blocker in her palm. "There's something I need to do." She pulled the sniper rifle off her back and lodged it into her shoulder with her other hand, her thumb flipping a switch on the side. Servos and actuators whirred inside the weapon, the barrel withdrawing to a length of a standard-action rifle.

"What is this?" Anakin said, his instincts getting the better of him. The young Jedi's blue lightsaber came to life, its glow filling the dimly lit archive.

"Wait," Obi-Wan said. "Lower your weapon. Ruug, are you taking us in?"

"We are still on opposite sides. It's important to remember that." Ruug blinked, the red of the terminal screens reflecting off her green skin as much as Anakin's blade. "I am not taking you in. But I need it to look like I tried."

"What are you talking about?" Anakin said, an impatience growing in his tone.

"I'm staying here. I'm an active guard. But Ketar will identify me as a traitor. My best chance at avoiding execution so I can keep fighting for Neimoidians is to fight *you*."

"Ruug, you are my friend. I respect your crusade. I do not wish to fight you," Obi-Wan said.

"If you respect what I stand for, then I need you to face me in battle now." She lifted the surveillance disabler. "I'm going to turn the surveillance system back on. And then Cato Neimoidia will see me 'defend' the data center. You will overpower me and escape. We need to make it look good."

Obi-Wan had just lectured Anakin about impossible choices. Raising his lightsaber against Ruug was yet another one. "I understand. But if we do this, I will be the one. Anakin and the youngling should head to the ship."

"Agreed." Ruug looked up and around, presumably at security systems and surveillance cams embedded into the walls, things that only a native Neimoidian with commando training would understand and expect. "You should go," she said to Anakin.

"I'll catch up," Obi-Wan said, giving Anakin a nod. "Mill, is the way clear?"

"Yes, Master," she called out as she perched by the exit.

"Let's hurry," Anakin said. He stepped forward, the tails of his dark tunic whipping out behind him as he moved to the door, only pausing to catch Mill at a standstill.

But she wasn't petrified by fear or other people's suffering; instead, wistful eyes sat over a quiet smile on her face. "You're a good person," she said to Ruug. "I can feel it."

"Youngling, I hope you have many years knowing much more than this war."

"We will try to make that happen," Obi-Wan said, pulling out his lightsaber. Anakin took Mill's hand, the security door sliding open to let them out, followed by R2-D2 rolling as fast as possible. "If we see each other again, it may be on the battlefield."

A heavy exhale came from Ruug, something that carried enough weight to break her soldier's stance, if just for a second. "If that does happen, then at least it'll be honorable. But let's hope cooler heads are listening."

All Obi-Wan could do at this point was nod. "I am ready."

"For independence," said Ruug, her thumb flicking a side switch on her rifle's grip. A high-pitched hum came from the weapon, indicating that its firing chamber had hit maximum charge.

Obi-Wan flexed his fingers over his lightsaber hilt then whirled it into a ready position, his right hand high behind him while the blade lay parallel to the floor, the heat from it palpable against his cheeks. His weight rested on his back foot and his left arm extended fully, two fingers out for precise balance. "For the Republic."

A click sound echoed off the archive walls as Ruug reactivated the surveillance system.

CHAPTER 48

ANAKIN SKYWALKER

HALFWAY TO THE SHUTTLE, THE alarm sirens rang out across the city.

Then came the battle droids.

"I guess they saw Obi-Wan," Anakin said. Mill kept pace as they continued, alley upon alley, block after block. The path, which seemed so free of any resistance not too long ago, now filled with random sprinkles of battle droids. Which meant the use of a lightsaber as needed, deflecting blaster bolts and slicing through the opposition, and though it was all necessary, such actions seemed to wear at Mill's emotional defenses. He moved with a swift precision, at times more in tune with the currents of the Force than he was even in the arena at Geonosis. Despite the hindrance of his mechanical arm, his lightsaber swung from side to side, tilting from angle to angle, covering from forward to backward, all to protect Mill as they dashed ahead, the volume of battle droids increasing the farther they went.

R2-D2 trailed behind, but between the rockets in his legs and some well-timed electrical zaps, the astromech's history of effective movement in combat came through once again. At least until a stray blaster bolt finally caught up with his luck, frying one of his boosters so he could only roll to keep up.

"I think we're clear," Anakin said, leading Mill up and over a building before breaking hard to the side and pointing at a sewer grate. R2-D2 beeped an affirmative, rolling around the building to catch up on the other side, continuing scans for seeker remotes or battle droids. The grate proved heavy, but the combination of adrenaline and Force-assisted strength quickly pushed it aside to let Mill drop down. R2-D2 followed, floating down with wobbly single-rocket power, and finally Anakin disappeared as well.

With the Force, Anakin pulled at the grate, dragging it back into its place to cover their tracks. They moved quickly, taking advantage of the cover. R2-D2 projected a map that connected the underground passages into segments that brought them close to their ship.

"There it is," Anakin said as they turned the corner, a half circle of light awaiting them at the end of the tunnel. R2-D2 beeped some directions about what lay ahead—a small drainage waterfall that poured out over a ledge all the way down to the planet's surface. More important, their ship was parked directly above them. After a few calculated Force-assisted jumps, the only remaining hurdle would be Obi-Wan's return. Yet something strange awaited them at the end of the tunnel, and it took Anakin several seconds to realize that the low rumble he heard came from a *ship* hovering at the exit rather than anything to do with the tunnel itself. A strange ship, for sure, one with a bulbous front cockpit and a thin line for some sort of tall tail fin.

"Wait." He broke into a crouch, now reaching into the Force to heighten his senses. "Stay behind me," he said, one arm out to act as a barrier for Mill and the other holding his now-lit lightsaber. "Something's not right. I think I've seen that ship before."

As he said that, a mechanized buzz echoed from the hovering craft and Anakin squinted until he saw that the noise came from the cannon atop the tail fin—and as he adjusted his angle, it became clear that it wasn't just a tail fin, but a half-circle fan blade, the cockpit sitting in the middle. The cannon shifted slightly and Anakin draped his body over Mill when he realized what was happening.

The sound of a single cannon burst quickly became a rumble of breaking duracrete and the clang of falling metal, the bright exit disappearing in an instant. Now trapped in complete darkness, Anakin held his lightsaber in front of him, both a defensive stance and an effort to provide some light, though at this point his Jedi senses would be of greater use.

"I'm okay," Mill whispered. "I just—"

"It's you, isn't it?" That voice. It boomed out, ringing through the tunnel. Anakin knew *exactly* who was speaking:

The mystery voice from Obi-Wan's comlink.

The question was halfway between cold threat and amused mockery, and his eyes searched the darkness for its origin. "So, you're Kenobi's partner."

His instincts called at him to fly forward at the mystery figure, lightsaber swinging. Had he been alone, that might have been an acceptable strategy. But the encounter with Count Dooku on Geonosis lingered in his mind, and while he gripped his lightsaber hilt with both hands, a moment of doubt slipped in: Would his mechanical hand move with the exact blend of precision and power the moment required without any visibility to aid him?

"Go to the corner and hide," Anakin whispered. "Stay out of sight. Artoo, protect her." His voice rose to a full shout, loud enough to cover the sound of Mill sneaking off. "We're just passing through. We'll be offplanet in minutes. I suggest you step aside as we move that rubble. If"—his eyes scanned for any movement in the black—"you want to live."

"Is that a threat?" the woman said with a laugh.

It *had* to be Dooku's agent.

"Kenobi, I could deal with. He's so polite. But you. You are more . . ." As she spoke, Anakin approached, the hum of his lightsaber tracking with his forward movement. ". . . curious." His boots stepped with a measured gait, a conscious effort to slow down and stay grounded.

"I've dealt with Dooku's minions before."

"Oh, I am aware of that."

"It's never ended well for them. What makes you think you'll have a better chance than the last one?"

The woman's only response was a laugh that rang through the dark, then nothing.

Then footsteps. Pounding against the stone of the tunnel, whirring by him so fast that he couldn't get a sense of where or how. He swung his lightsaber out, a clear arc in front of him, though it failed to connect. The footsteps continued, rushing in front and behind, all around in a loop up the circular tunnel, and Anakin shut his eyes, letting the Force guide him, telling him where to angle, where to step, where to turn.

Both hands gripped his hilt, the flesh of his natural hand working with the mechanics of his gloved limb. He took a split second to think about how to internally calibrate for the difference, but that opening was enough for the steps to stop, a foot ramming him in the gut before two glowing red lines blazed to life.

Weapons of the Sith.

Anakin's lightsaber swung halfway up, sparks bursting off as the blades pushed against each other. The brilliance of the weapons painted the space, and they fought with each swing meeting another swing, the burning impact creating a storm of flashes throughout the tunnel. His hands held the hilt overhead, advancing with the bright blade ready, looking for an open area to strike. But what this woman lacked in re-fined technique, she made up for in speed, and they circled each other as they fought, the pop and snap of lightsabers loud enough to bounce off the tunnel's stone walls.

"You *are* strong. Count Dooku will be most interested in your prog-ress." She attacked, her blades crossing against his, a test of strength as they pushed against each other.

"I've already met the count. He's far less interesting than he seems to think." His mechanical wrist flexed and he tapped into its innate strength, allowing him to shove the woman back before he followed up with a quick swipe. But he'd misjudged how much power came with the extra robotics, the woman stumbling back too far for his one–two combo to be effective. The woman backed off and deactivated her light-sabers again, disappearing into the tunnel; he improvised, charging for-ward again, this time back to basics: direct high and mid slashes, moves that would overpower if they connected properly.

To his left, he heard the distinct stomp of a boot pressing off the curved wall, and red lightsabers burst out over him. Anakin turned, now on his back heel, but swung hard enough to knock the crimson beams down. His balance off, he barely had time to comprehend the sound of the woman's skirt whirling around as she switched tactics, kicking him in the gut before swooping the toes of her boot into the side of his mouth. The impact caused a grunt, though he brought his blade back up for a quick block.

But it was too late.

Because while Mill didn't call out his name or yell, her sharp inhale was enough to draw the woman's attention.

"Oh." Now her blades were back up, fully readjusted in her hands. "Look at this. You're not alone." Red shadows shifted, only faint details of cheeks and eyes moving into what turned into a smile. "Now, *this* is interesting."

Anakin pushed her back, then attacked, using straightforward swings and thrusts. He moved with aggression, a willingness to leave himself with a few vulnerable openings in exchange for an assault that blanketed his opponent. His edge returned, pure mastery of form compensating for the lingering concerns about his right arm.

With the mystery woman on her heels, Anakin seized the moment. "Mill! Run to the end of the tunnel!"

What she'd do when she got there, Anakin hadn't figured out yet. But getting her on the opposite end at least put him in a position to shield her.

The two red lightsabers whirled, and Anakin heard Mill sprinting off toward the collapsed tunnel exit. Anakin dashed backward then used the Force to grasp at the mystery assailant; she stumbled, slowing her down enough that he could close the gap between him and Mill, and he reached into the Force to throw an invisible fist at the fallen rubble.

A chunk of it popped out, creating a poking beam of light.

He did it again, further debris jostling out, and again, to the point that the small hole now gave way to an opening where he could actually see the woman's fan-shaped craft.

The assassin now walked with an even pace, one red blade in each hand. Enough light shone through that details of her features became clear, from her harsh eyes to her shaven head. Her silhouette revealed a form-fitting outfit complemented with a flowing skirt, its sash belt whipping out behind her from the breeze. But before he could fully take in her distinguishing features, she dashed forward. "Who is this youngling you're so desperate to protect?" she asked. Now he wasn't just in combat with her.

He had to guard Mill from her.

She swung at him, a back-and-forth exchange of thrusts and parries, except now *she* used the Force to knock a piece out the rubble wall and throw a chunk his way. He gripped his lightsaber, still holding it in proper technique with both hands, but his organic hand wanted to move just a hair faster than his robotic hand, despite the enhanced strength and durability of the synthetic appendage.

He glanced behind him, the rubble was now about halfway cleared, enough that if Mill and R2-D2 squeezed, they could nearly climb out.

"And you, youngling. Is he your Master? Have you not gone to Ilum yet for the Gathering?"

"Don't answer her," Anakin said, taking a step forward, another two-handed slash, but one she blocked with ease. His left palm opened, pulling at loose debris through the Force to open the hole further, but she attacked quickly, a flurry of strikes.

Yet the strangest thing happened. While his fighting style often worked with a two-handed grip, Anakin instinctively parried with his robotic hand alone. And in doing so, under attack from a mysterious combatant and with a youngling to protect, its inherent differences rose to the surface. His arm didn't need to be calibrated to his old instincts. No, it was much simpler:

His *mind* had to adapt to his arm.

With that, everything shifted.

Just like his relationship with Obi-Wan, all he had to do was accept that it had changed.

"There's conflict in you, youngling. I myself was once a lost, frightened girl who didn't understand her own potential. Just like you." The woman squinted, tilting her head. "Interesting. A Zabrak. I know them well. And what is that? Now I sense something different from you. Yes.

Of course." She nodded, her lips curling upward. "Your *fear* reveals much about you. You question this Jedi life. As you should."

Whether the words were meant as a taunt to draw him out or genuine conjecture, Anakin didn't know because they triggered an instinctive reaction, a sort of autopilot among him, his lightsaber, and the Force. But rather than his arm being just out of sync with this flow, it now lined up—not a different piece of himself, but something unique and powerful, something that *added* to his abilities now that he knew how to harness it. His *need* to defend Mill, the drive to make things right, to take responsibility for this youngling he'd brought along—all of it focused into a single outburst. His lightsaber swung with frightening speed, and suddenly all of the woman's vulnerabilities became visible to him, his perception of time slowing down to show him possibilities before they happened.

He attacked, sometimes both hands joined on his lightsaber hilt, sometimes with natural flesh, and sometimes with synthetic parts— each option being used to the fullest of its capabilities—and now *he* was the relentless onslaught, the hurricane of flashing blue pushing against the receding wave of red. With each swing, he marched forward, angling the woman toward the tunnel exit, every thrust calculated to keep her off balance, to turn her two blades from an advantage to a disadvantage, to prevent her from leaping over him or utilizing the environment as a weapon.

Despite all this, the woman laughed, and suddenly her focus tilted to Mill's direction. "But do not worry, young one. You are right to question the Jedi. Let me show you another path. I will free you from the ponderous shackles of the Jedi."

His lightsaber slashed downward at her, making her unsteady, and Anakin looked as her whole body shifted. One of her blades went dark, the hilt attached back at her belt, and with her free hand she pushed through the ether to open up a larger space in the fallen debris. Then she hurled the Force against Anakin, just enough to knock him back a step, before sprinting off.

Her other red blade withdrew, also latching onto her belt and she ran toward the opening—

No. Toward Mill.

"Mill!" Anakin yelled as he started his own sprint at her. But the woman was too far ahead, and she reached out with her arm to scoop up the youngling.

Anakin's instinct kicked in. And rather than try to catch up, he reached out through the Force to secure Mill.

With his mechanical hand.

But it was too late. The mystery woman's swift pursuit allowed her to grab Mill by the waist as she landed on top of her craft. The ship dipped slightly with the impact, sinking into the fog for a moment before stabilizing—but it was enough for her to lose her concentration. Anakin's grip extended through the Force, taking the moment to pull on the young Zabrak, shaking her loose. Mill saw the opportunity as well and slammed on the woman's arm to escape her grasp. Guided by Anakin, she floated toward solid ground when he felt a pull in the other direction.

He looked up and saw the woman standing on top of her cockpit, both arms extended, Mill caught between them, a massive drop through the mist to the planet's surface below the youngling. Mill hovered through the opening, arms outstretched, Anakin and the woman equally tapping into the Force to pull her from each side. "Master!" Mill cried out. "Help me!"

She remained in midair, halfway between the tunnel's broken opening and the cockpit of the ship belonging to Dooku's agent. Through the Force, Anakin felt *her* grip tighten, like a hand interlocking with his fingers. "Come on, Mill," he said, "you can do this."

"She's *mine*, Skywalker. Let her train with a true master."

How did this woman know his name?

"Ventress!" a voice called out from above.

Obi-Wan. Out of sight, but presumably somewhere above the tunnel.

"Obi-Wan!" Anakin yelled. "I've got Mill!"

The hum of a lightsaber came to life, then Anakin saw it: a blue blade thrown with precision, not at the assassin, but at vital parts in the hull of her ship. It pierced into its side, a puff of smoke followed by a short burst of flame, and the ship began to sink—not a full-speed nosedive, but the gradual descent of key systems failing. The hilt flew back, and Anakin heard it slap back into Obi-Wan's palm.

Mill soared to Anakin, landing in his arms. He set her immediately down, then dashed to the edge of the open tunnel to see this woman—*Ventress*—scrambling to get in the cockpit as the ship gained more and more downward momentum.

"Anakin, I suggest we leave *right now.*"

Anakin looked up to see Obi-Wan peering over the ledge, one hand extended. Without asking, Mill grabbed it. Anakin boosted her up, then climbed to meet Obi-Wan, who used the Force to help R2-D2 steady himself with just one working rocket. Mill stood with heavy breaths, but as she took Anakin's hand, her head tilted up and a small smile crossed her lips. "Are aggressive negotiations always like this?"

Anakin closed the boarding ramp while R2-D2 scanned for any signs of Ventress or her ship. The hydraulics hissed as the hardware pulled upward to seal them back up, and the *Norriker* rumbled with a start-up as rough as its external condition.

"You all right?" Anakin asked, gesturing at the burn marks on Obi-Wan's tunic.

"Ruug puts up a tough fight," he said, glancing backward. "She's a survivor. I have complete faith in her."

"I could say the same thing about Mill." He pointed at her in the back room, her legs crossed as she sat on the floor. "That woman, she is a dangerous threat, we need—"

"Yes." Obi-Wan nodded, deep lines of concern across his brow. "I understand. Dooku's agent. I have a feeling we'll see much more of her." He shook his head, his shoulder-length hair flowing from side to side. "The youngling is safe?"

"Shaken." They elevated, the cityscape below them becoming smaller and smaller. "But safe. She's brave."

"She is a Jedi," Obi-Wan said, with such belief in his words, an absolute synthesis of bravery and purpose, as if it were impossible for the two to be separate, whether Initiate, Padawan, or Jedi Knight.

Anakin turned away from Obi-Wan, thoughts pulled in so many directions as the shuttle broke atmosphere. The galaxy map appeared on the main console, and Anakin punched in coordinates to Coruscant, mapping out a zigzagging route designed to shake any suspicion the Trade Federation might have of a suddenly departed shuttle.

"What about you?" Obi-Wan asked. "You are safe as well?"

"Me?" Anakin looked at his mechanical arm, the fingers gripping the shuttle throttle in a way that started to feel more instinctive. "I may have to start training a little differently." The blanket of stars in front of them bled into starlines and the shuttle shook as they entered the tunnel of hyperspace. "But I'm fine. I always am."

CHAPTER 49

OBI-WAN KENOBI

SENATOR AMIDALA APPEARED ON THE shuttle's communications screen, a more formal version of herself compared with several hours ago when they had interrupted her journey from Coruscant to Naboo. As if her clothes were her armor, her entire demeanor changed with the shimmering dark-gray cloak draped over her shoulders and hair molded into an oval metal headpiece; the simple pendant from earlier had been swapped for more ornate jewelry. Though Anakin still carried himself differently when Padmé was involved, her subtle glances or the split-second lingers disappeared with her more formalized attire.

Was this the level of control that came with being queen at a Padawan's age?

"Threepio and I have processed the data. I've also viewed a recording of Master Kenobi's speech on Cato Neimoidia. Obi-Wan," she said, eyes turning to him, "I agree with your findings. There is a clear third party here, which puts the entire balance of the galaxy at risk. I will share it first with the chancellor, then the Senate's security committee."

"Palpatine?" Obi-Wan asked, a rare slip in his discipline.

Anakin turned with a quizzical look on his face, and even Padmé's head angled at the question. "Is there a problem with the chancellor?" she asked.

This was not the right company to question Palpatine. And while the chancellor steered the Republic through many layers of bureaucratic churn, often toward a more effective society compared with his predecessor, he still operated under a politician's mindset, allowing cultural passions and prejudices to influence his agenda. Something like this needed more objectivity.

"It is not a problem with the chancellor. Or any single individual. Given the nature of this evidence, I feel it is best served by being released independently, directly to the public. Without the filter of politics."

"Master Kenobi, I respect your opinion but this is a matter of security. It must go through Republic channels. And," Padmé said, "I have known the chancellor a long, long time. We may not agree on everything, but I know he will give it the appropriate consideration."

"I trust him," Anakin said, an almost reflexive defense. "He's a good man."

"I've already let his office know that I have an urgent communication for him. As soon as we enter orbit around Naboo, I will present this to him personally."

"Thank you, Senator," Obi-Wan said, bowing his head. "For all of your service."

"I look forward to seeing you two in person again soon."

"Me too," Anakin said. Again, his energy surged, and as it did, a small despair crept into Obi-Wan's thoughts.

Anakin just couldn't help himself.

And didn't that explain *everything*?

Anakin stood up and pointed to the back storage room where Mill rested. "I'm going to check on Mill," he said. "Maybe try to get some sleep myself. Artoo, can I trust you to fly the ship?"

From the cockpit, the droid beeped.

"Very funny, Artoo," Obi-Wan retorted. "Just because I don't like flying doesn't mean that I'm not capable of it." Then his voice dropped as he glanced back at Anakin who was checking the control panel one last time. "Though I certainly don't mind staying here for a moment. I have to contact the Jedi Council anyway."

Obi-Wan waited for Anakin to be out of hearing range to begin the discussion with Yoda, Mace Windu, Kit Fisto, Even Piell, and the rest of the Jedi Council, and while most of it focused on a chronological recap of events on Cato Neimoidia—and the emergence of Asajj Ventress—there wasn't much to say from a strategic perspective. The next step lay in the hands of the chancellor, something that both Yoda and Mace seemed to embrace on the same level as Anakin and Padmé.

There was, however, one further revelation from recent days that needed dealing with. "Master Kenobi, more to say, have you?"

Seconds. They had been mere seconds away from Ketar detonating the final bomb himself, and any sort of emotional entanglements—or simple *caring*—could easily pull someone away for those slivers of time. Had those seconds come in another situation, one where Anakin's decision making might make or break the galaxy, how would his personal feelings interfere?

The issue required a confrontation. But as Obi-Wan considered the flickering images of the Jedi Council, he asked himself: Should they be the first to know?

No. Obi-Wan should speak to Anakin about this before presenting it to the Council. At the very least, he owed that to his former apprentice.

"Nothing else. We will arrive at Coruscant shortly."

"Very well," Yoda said. "Upon your return, speak to you I will. Impressive diplomacy, Master Kenobi. Very impressive."

Obi-Wan responded with a simple nod, his mind too preoccupied with the weight of Anakin Skywalker to really consider what Master Yoda's cryptic farewell meant. The image of the Jedi Council faded as he leaned back in the rickety chair, squeaks and squeals coming from its old joints. He listened for noise from the back storage space, and Anakin's deep, muffled voice clearly registered, followed soon by Mill's similarly muffled voice. Their old ship may have been built for hauling deliveries, as privacy didn't seem to be a concern.

Obi-Wan shook his head and told himself to be productive at a time like this, at least until a quiet moment with Anakin presented itself. He considered a restful meditation, and though he'd accomplished that in many uncomfortable places before, this particular ship offered enough physical irritants to make that impossible. Instead, he turned on the comm system again, this time tuning in to the HoloNet in case Count Dooku made any sort of public statement about the events of the last day. But the fallen Jedi Master wasn't on the screen when he turned it on. Instead, he took in a quick gasp, one that he really hoped Anakin didn't hear.

Because on the screen, the words LIVE BROADCAST in the upper corner, stood Satine Kryze of Mandalore.

"This newly formed Council of Neutral Systems will stand on principles, not violence. For once we commit to violence, we have already lost." The cam hovered close to Satine's face as she spoke from the Royal Palace on Mandalore, her purple headdress and swooping neckline of her blue outfit rivaling Padmé's in elaborate design. "Extremism is rising across the galaxy. It must be extinguished before more lives are lost. There is only one solution for all of us, on all sides: de-escalation. And there is only one path to de-escalation: refusing to contribute to this war."

That line made Obi-Wan sit up. Was she quoting his speech or was this just the most incredible coincidence? He watched now, previous fatigue traded for a spike in attention, and though she argued *against* what he lobbied for, she framed it in the most compelling way, a statement delivered to urge planets and systems to reconsider their stance on the Clone Wars, no matter what side they were on.

"War is intolerable, and for those on either side that believe it is the only way, listen to me now: That is wrong. Killing will only beget more killing, and Mandalore will *not* be a part of it. I know many, many others feel the same way—and they all see how *logical* peace is. Whoever is out there, whoever is listening, know that the Council of Neutral Systems stands for peace. And we invite all of you to stand with us."

The screen flipped over to a HoloNet News reporter who promptly began chattering over images of Satine mixed in with Count Dooku,

Chancellor Palpatine, and clone battalions. "That was Satine Kryze, leader of the Council of Neutral Systems. As the duchess of Mandalore, Kryze has rejected Mandalore's history of violence for a pacifist movement, and now she is asking others to come along. Is this a reasonable path given the terrorist attacks of the Confederacy of Ind—"

Obi-Wan flipped a switch on the console and the signal faded to black, though her words repeated in his mind. "Killing will only beget more killing, and Mandalore will not be a part of it."

Even during that brief period together, when Satine's idealism intoxicated Obi-Wan's youthful enthusiasm, she talked of a peaceful Mandalore. Such an idea seemed as impossible as arguing with gravity itself, and yet, there she was, organizing entire star systems to join her pacifist movement. Had they run off together, had he left the Jedi Order and she chosen a completely different life, what impact would they have had on the galaxy? And now, because they grew past their feelings and trusted in their paths, she led Mandalore in bold new directions while he sat newly appointed in the rarefied air of the Jedi Council.

The door to the back jammed halfway across, and Anakin's fingers gripped the edge, pushing it free. "Ugh," he said, coming out of the back room, "this ship is too bumpy to get any rest. I heard you watching the HoloNet. Anything interesting happening out there?"

The opportunity for quiet conversation was here, and he knew exactly what to say, how he wanted to say it. Yet Satine's words jarred him off that path, creating a hesitancy to use the moment presented in front of him. Obi-Wan watched as his former apprentice knelt down to examine the door's sliding mechanism, likely already considering all the options he had to fix it.

It took a little bit of time and discipline for both Obi-Wan and Satine to find their way.

Could Anakin achieve that same maturity? Of all the questions impossible to answer over recent days, this proved to be perhaps the most inscrutable.

And inscrutable meant that he would be patient. For now.

"Nothing important," Obi-Wan said.

CHAPTER 50

ANAKIN SKYWALKER

CORUSCANT'S MIX OF FRESH AIR and industrial fuel burn felt like home to Anakin.

Strange for someone who grew up on a desert planet that seemed to collect most of the galaxy's discarded technology. Mill, on the other hand, didn't seem nearly as enthusiastic about the return. Her shoulders slumped and she avoided anyone's gaze, instead looking down or away the whole time.

Obi-Wan marched off without a second thought, and R2-D2 rolled behind, wheels bumping over the uneven deck plates on the loading ramp. "I see Master Yoda down there," she said as Anakin knelt down. He glanced over his shoulder to see the Grand Master ambling toward Obi-Wan, moving gingerly with his cane to meet Obi-Wan halfway up before promptly starting their discussion.

"Looks like he wanted to debrief Obi-Wan immediately. But hey," Anakin said, his cheeks lifting with a smile, "this is good timing. I can tell him about everything you've accomplished. You're close to the age for being selected as a full Padawan. I imagine once word gets out, several Jedi Knights will want—"

"Master," Mill said, looking up at him. Their eyes finally connected, and he could see the confidence she'd built up over the past few days lurking behind a sudden nervousness, something that seemed out of character for the person she'd become.

"I know you feel like you don't fit in. I feel that way, too. A questioning," he said, and though he didn't want to mention Ventress, he considered her very words in the tunnel. "But you can turn that into something stronger. Your empathy, your abilities. They set you apart. You deserve to be a Jedi. You've connected with the Force. You've learned to control it." Anakin thought back to a quiet moment with Qui-Gon, something hidden from everyone else, possibly even Obi-Wan, on the passage to Naboo. He repeated the fallen Jedi Knight's words now, in a position where they'd never felt so true. "It will be a hard life. But in the end, you will find out who you are."

"I understand," she said. Which should have come with joy, but her look gave away that further gears turned in her mind, a new consideration—if not peace, then some sort of resignation.

"I can sense the uncertainty in you. And when I feel that way, I think back to a story my mother used to tell me."

"Your mother?" Her focus changed, eyes dropping into his chest, as if she saw right into the very essence of his being.

"Yes. This story is one of my earliest memories." Anakin hesitated, the confluence of different emotions stealing his breath for a moment. "It's about a Tatooine myth: the sun-dragon. The sun-dragon is a beast that lives inside a star, guarding everything it treasures. Nothing could hurt it. Not fire, not flame. It survived through the most impossible circumstances, even life in the core of a star. Because the sun-dragon had the biggest heart in the galaxy, a burning furnace powerful enough to protect everything and everyone it loved.

"My mother used to tell me the story in different ways. A celebration for good days. A lesson for bad days. But it always returned to one thing, the most important thing: Your heart can take you where you want to go. Where you *need* to go. Because it is strong enough. That's why I'm telling you this now." Anakin put his hands on her shoulders, just as Qui-Gon had so many years ago. "*You* are strong enough.

Through everything we've faced in the past few days, you've shown me exactly who you are. You're brave. You're smart. And you have a unique gift, unlike any I've encountered within the Order. You can do anything your heart wants."

Mill's lips pursed, her eyes dropping, not in defeat but clear contemplation. "You really believe that, don't you?"

"Yes. Mill, I believe that more than anything." He moved to sit down on the rickety deck plates, his intentions turning in a way that he wished Obi-Wan had done more often. Though perhaps his own stubbornness, his constant need to one-up his mentor, ate up so much of their relationship that a moment like this proved impossible. "Sit with me. Breathe. Just breathe, and feel your place in the Force. You'll see. You'll see everything."

The floor shook slightly as Mill sat down as well, the different distribution of weight tilting the uneven deck plate. He watched as she closed her eyes, then fell into a near-motionless state, the only movement coming from her breathing and the occasional flutter under her eyelids. Seconds passed, then minutes passed, the world feeling still enough that Anakin heard Obi-Wan and Yoda's voices, but he couldn't tell how close or far they were.

"I feel the Force," she whispered. "Join me in meditation."

Anakin complied with the youngling's request, closing his eyes and reaching into the Force. Currents surrounded him like waves in an ocean, each one pushing and pulling at different pieces of him. His time with Padmé. His changing bond with Obi-Wan. His loyalty to the Republic, to Chancellor Palpatine, how the recent days both challenged each of these, and yet brought them all closer together, perhaps even bringing them toward a unification. He let himself float in this space, the pulsing currents batting him around. Within this ocean of the Force, a presence existed—no, an awareness, one that Anakin would encounter at times of extreme duress or deep meditation, something that felt like equal parts guidance, soothing, and questioning, something that despite his best intentions, he didn't listen to.

Qui-Gon Jinn.

That came and went, replaced by something much more tangible: his mother, telling the sun-dragon story as if she sat on the edge of his bed, as she did on so many nights in their small Tatooine home.

The sun-dragon. *He* was the sun-dragon, with a heart more powerful than a star. He could do anything if he just cared enough.

No.

He *would* do anything.

He would do *everything*.

His existence in the Force was not a tug-of-war between duty and love, between friendship and partnership. It was all of those things at once. He would not try to stifle himself into just one path; his heart would burn bright and commit to all of it.

He felt it now, the voice in his head whispering a simple truth: This was Anakin Skywalker, the one who would simply *find a way.*

Mill broke him out of meditation with a sharp gasp. Anakin opened his eyes to find her looking straight at him. "I understand," she said, and though she'd said those exact words just minutes ago, something about them carried a different weight, almost an inquisitiveness.

"You said that before," he said, a return to the physical realm that proved more jarring than most meditations.

"Yes, but this time, I understand so much more. *About* so much more." Mill looked like each consecutive word lifted a weight off her shoulders. She got up first, this time holding her hand out. Anakin took it, despite being older, taller, and significantly stronger than her, and yet her firm grip felt like it pulled exactly the right amount to lift him onto his feet.

"Thank you, Master Skywalker. I want you to know . . ." She clasped her other hand around his, then shot him a look, her smile content but her brow curious. "I want you to know that I appreciate everything you've done for me."

"Of course. Are you ready, youngling?"

She nodded. "I am."

They turned, only to find Yoda and Obi-Wan still standing halfway up the ramp rather than moving on. How much had they overheard? "Master Yoda," Anakin said, his voice dropping to his usual deferential monotone. "I'm sorry, I didn't—"

"Deep meditation, you were in. An important moment." Yoda tapped the ramp with the cane, its tip getting stuck for a moment in the grating. "Passing wisdom," he said, in a slow and generous tone. "Something to say, youngling?"

"I do, Master Yoda." Anakin shot her a grin and an encouraging nod as she looked up at him. "I feel the Force." She took in a breath and nodded as well, but this may have been more for herself than to acknowledge Anakin's gesture. "I feel the Force, but I have no desire to ever become a Jedi Knight."

CHAPTER 51

OBI-WAN KENOBI

MILL'S WORDS LEFT THE TRIO of Jedi quiet. Yoda let out a curious "hmmm" while Obi-Wan opted not to speak. It wasn't his place.

But he watched Anakin with interest. He'd watched the entire thing this way, both the conversation and impromptu meditation between Anakin and Mill, Yoda observing on the boarding ramp with enough presence to understand that something important was happening, that the flow of the Force was shifting—not in large, galaxy-changing ways, but something more personal. "Important, these quiet moments are," Yoda said before they took several steps up the ramp. "Echo forward, they do."

Anakin's eyes went wide, as if he couldn't comprehend the youngling's statement, or her intentions. Moments after he'd connected with Mill on such a deep level, after revealing something so personal as a story his mother told him, his expression ran a complete cycle of emotions. Obi-Wan knew what he would expect if it had been a conversation between them—arguing, of course, regardless of the topic, along with a nearly instinctive opposition leading to Obi-Wan's eventual sigh of exasperation.

And on the very rare occasion, irritation would overtake him enough to make a snide comment or scold.

This, of course, was different—and also different from the conversations he'd observed with Padmé. Obi-Wan cleared his mind of judgment, instead letting himself observe objectively. Though it seemed like minutes passed in silence, only perhaps ten or fifteen seconds ticked by, and finally Yoda answered Mill in a way surely designed to push everyone to consider further.

"Trials will determine that. Your true path, find you it does."

Mill looked up at Anakin, an uncertainty in her eyes at Yoda's noncommittal statement. "Master Yoda," Anakin said, a calm gravity to his voice that Obi-Wan rarely heard—in fact, may have never heard. "In recent days, I have learned to trust Initiate Alibeth's judgment. She is wise and brave, with a unique connection to the Force that guides her path. If there's one lesson I've passed on to her during our short time together, it's to trust in yourself. I believe we should listen without judgment to her feelings on this."

Between Anakin's short speech and the quiet moments with Mill, it dawned on Obi-Wan that the young man's actions reflected the teachings of someone else:

Qui-Gon Jinn.

Anakin stood next to the youngling, and all of the concerns about how much he was guided by *caring* instead of faith in the Force suddenly took on a new context, the typical stoic discipline of their ways always fighting with Anakin's overwhelming impulses. This was a problem, wasn't it? But it also encompassed the way Qui-Gon would have taught him.

Another question came to Obi-Wan, something that stunned him enough that his shift in demeanor even caught Anakin's attention. If he had just a drop of that willingness to think *outside* of the Jedi way, would things have been different with Satine?

Obi-Wan felt his pulse accelerate, a discomfort at such a thought before he let it drift away, accepting that it would pass. Or at least, he tried. Despite a lifelong instinct for clearing his mind, questions began rolling up on one another, all leading to a consideration about what it would be like to feel the way Qui-Gon did—and to see it to such an extreme as Anakin did.

Was it wrong? Or just *different*?

They stood in the entry of the barely functional shuttle, a constant dripping noise coming from somewhere since the vehicle docked. Yoda watched, his face neutral as he awaited something from Mill. Anakin also watched her, but an urgency colored his look—it was clear he wanted Mill to have whatever she wanted, even if he didn't fully agree.

Right then and there, Obi-Wan finally understood that he'd been wrong about what Qui-Gon meant to either of them. So wrong, in fact, that it astonished him; it took a decade, an emerging war, and the dual promotion of Anakin's Jedi Knighthood and Obi-Wan's ascension to the Jedi Council for him to realize this.

Anakin had said before that Obi-Wan was the closest thing he had to a father, but that wasn't totally true. However brief or long, Qui-Gon molded both of them, ushering them into paths based on a belief that they had greater destinies. Their lives were not intertwined by the ties of Master and apprentice, or any fatherly relationship. It was greater, longer than that, a bond that grew from the moment they shook hands on the queen's ship above Tatooine.

Obi-Wan and Anakin were forever bound by something without rules or obligations, something intangible yet powerful and fragile: the faith that Qui-Gon Jinn had in each of them.

With that epiphany, it was as if the universe tilted, colors and light and sound absorbing into his senses through a slightly different filter. Yet in a blink, it all became part of Obi-Wan Kenobi, his disciplined Jedi mind so committed to a life of flow that these monumental shifts simply integrated into his very being.

"Tell us, youngling," Obi-Wan said in a soft voice, though his eyes connected with Anakin. "We wish to hear."

"I have a *different* way of connecting to the Force," Mill started.

"She is special. I've seen it myself," Anakin said. "Go on. You can tell Master Yoda." The youngling nodded, then gulped with hesitation. "I believe in you."

Anakin's short expression of confidence opened the door for Mill, as if all she needed to speak was someone's encouragement. Yoda listened with intent while Anakin waited, letting the youngling take the lead. The gentle prodding, so different from his fierce determination on the battlefield—or in an argument with Obi-Wan—proved to be the difference. His feelings, the way they pulled at him, a potential distraction in a time of war—they also powered him to connect with Mill in ways that Obi-Wan didn't comprehend.

That insight required a certain maturity that hadn't existed in him as a Padawan. Or maybe Obi-Wan simply hadn't let himself see it before.

Yet here, on the boarding ramp of a ship that barely held together, he began to understand.

Anakin had faith in Mill. And finally, after so many years of self-doubt and petty gripes, Obi-Wan found himself starting to truly recognize Qui-Gon's faith in Anakin.

CHAPTER 52

ANAKIN SKYWALKER

PALPATINE'S SPEECH PLAYED OUT IN front of them.

Anakin and Obi-Wan stood in the alcove of the Senate, watching the mix of theatrical oration and dense political policy. Somewhere on the other side of the massive rotunda sat Padmé, probably with Bail Organa. Other Jedi lingered in the outer hallways, listening as their fate would be decided by politicians rather than the Jedi Council, though many remained in the Jedi Temple itself.

"It is profoundly disappointing that in the aftermath of the Cato Neimoidia tragedy, the Trade Federation today has reaffirmed its commitment to neutrality, despite the overwhelming—and dare I say—disturbing evidence presented by the Republic. The fact that other sinister forces are at play is clear. And the only choice is this: we must do whatever we can for this war to reach its conclusion as quickly as possible."

Anakin found Palpatine's words righteous; they came loaded with an understanding of the fragility of the situation that others lacked. Obi-Wan, on the other hand, held a grim pose, hand over his beard. "We know that there are those attempting to take advantage of this conflict.

It poses a threat to our short-term and long-term stability. The only answer is decisive strategic action." Scattered voices began murmuring from the nearest pods. "The rise of extremism necessitates a bold new initiative: the official integration of the Jedi Order into the Grand Army of the Republic. Such an action will allow Republic forces to push further, strike harder, and move more swiftly." Shouts came from various pods, with applause and cheers sprinkled between. "This initial surge may cause a strong reaction from the Separatists. They may resist. But between the strength of our clone army and—" Palpatine paused, and Anakin knew him well enough to know that the shift in tone meant the smallest smile crept onto his face. "—the *wisdom* of the Jedi, we will defeat the Separatist threat and ensure unity in the Republic. Peace is within our grasp, and now is the time to take it."

Applause roared from the Senate pods, a patriotic fervor delivering a sustained cheer for the chancellor the likes of which Anakin couldn't recall. Though, to be fair, he didn't really watch many political discussions.

Obi-Wan clearly didn't agree. "You look unhappy," Anakin whispered. "A faster end to the war is a good thing. The chancellor will be able to take more decisive action now."

"I already know what 'accelerated integration' means." Of course Obi-Wan would know. In recent days, Anakin's former Master received word that the Council found his performance on Cato Neimoidia so impressive that his seat would become permanent. If he'd had any reservations about filling Coleman Trebor's boots, though, Obi-Wan didn't show it, at least not to Anakin. Instead, the only constant on Obi-Wan's mind seemed to be the state of the war: who fought where, what intelligence was learned, how quickly the skirmishes spread—and how the Republic now had much more influence in Jedi affairs. "The Council was informed several days ago, but we were instructed to keep quiet until this formal announcement." Obi-Wan turned without even a final look as Palpatine continued on about General Grievous's recent strike on key supply chains for war munitions. Anakin followed him, a casual stroll in the Senate's near-empty hallways despite the high-alert circumstances swallowing the entire galaxy. A cleaning droid passed by, chirping about being low on charge, but the rest of the building's visitors clustered around Palpatine's speech. "We will be generals commanding troops."

"We're already 'generals commanding troops.' 'General Skywalker,'" Anakin said, doing a poor imitation of the clones' accent.

"No, I mean officially. Generals of the Grand Army of the Republic. Padawans will be commanders. The Jedi will hold true military standing in terms of strategy and resources. Our relationship with the Republic will now go far beyond peacekeeping and mediation." Obi-Wan never let his feelings show, but as he continued describing the emerging military responsibilities of the Jedi, his face turned ashen. "We will be provided additional weapons and armor."

"I don't need armor," Anakin said. They stopped in front of a screen broadcasting the HoloNet, a newscast showing recordings of the trial from Cato Neimoidia—and Anakin soaring in for the rescue. "See? Does it look like I need armor?"

Obi-Wan shook his head, Anakin's quip likely interrupting his internal risk/reward calculations of how much armor would impede his agility versus adding an extra layer of protection. "What have we gotten ourselves into?" he asked with a sigh.

"Body armor, apparently."

"The Jedi negotiator, Obi-Wan Kenobi, pled the Republic's case," said the reporter on the HoloNet as the recording switched to Obi-Wan's speech on Cato Neimoidia, though his words carried a strange cadence.

"I have seen the evidence. I have seen it, in my own investigation as well as data gathered by others—evidence pointing to the Separatists."

"That's weird. Did you see that?" Anakin asked. "Isn't that when you talked about the Republic materials?"

The recording cut again to Anakin, this time as he launched his lightsaber through two groups of battle droids. "Fortunately, Jedi Knight Anakin Skywalker was there, truly a hero with no fear as he took on the oncoming armada . . ."

A low groan came from Obi-Wan, any levity from quips about body armor seemingly erased. "The HoloNet is nothing but propaganda for politicians. It's not exactly known for its accuracy."

"I don't know," Anakin said with a laugh, "'Hero with no fear.' I thought I looked pretty dashing there."

"Anakin . . ."

"I'm serious." He pointed to the action on-screen, like something out of a holodrama rather than a news report. "You know, if we're going to be on the 'Net together, you might want to cut that hair."

"What?" Any grim hesitation from Obi-Wan disappeared, instantly switching to a surprise defensiveness.

Did Obi-Wan actually care about his appearance? Anakin reveled in this evidence of unexpected vanity from his former Master—though he chose *not* to disclose how he and Padmé mocked Obi-Wan's shoulder-length locks. "I'm just saying, people are going to be seeing a lot of us."

Us.

This was Skywalker and Kenobi as they should be: a team built on emotion and intellect, bravado and control, fire and ice.

And despite no longer having the formal bond of Master and apprentice, they would always be connected. In fact, they were *better* this way.

Qui-Gon Jinn would have agreed. Anakin was certain of it.

CHAPTER 53

MILL ALIBETH

THE HANGAR BAY LOOKED THE same as the other times Mill had seen it since Geonosis, at least at first glance. Ships came and went, Jedi walked with their Padawans, clone troopers carried supplies and weapons. But upon closer look, things had changed since the recent Jedi Military Integration Act. Around the galaxy, skirmishes intensified, the shift in Republic policy provoking an increase in Separatist activity, leaving scattered battle damage across gunships.

And some of the Jedi had adopted plated armor covering their chests, shoulders, and forearms, subtle changes to their tunics to accommodate the change.

Including Anakin and Obi-Wan, who currently stood over a supply crate examining armor pieces.

"This is purely a trial period." Anakin lifted his arms and twisted his body. "No long-term commitment." He pointed to Obi-Wan's left arm, which now carried a white armored vambrace. "I *just* got used to my arm, now this?"

"I think it's quite practical," Obi-Wan said, turning to examine the Republic crest painted on his shoulder pad. Something else about Obi-

Wan looked different, and it took Mill several seconds to put it together.

Obi-Wan's once-long hair now sat neatly trimmed with a simple part to one side.

"It's so bulky. I just can't—" Anakin paused, then turned. "Mill."

"Master Skywalker." Obi-Wan gave a polite bow as she turned to him. "Master Kenobi."

"You look happy," Anakin said, relief coloring his tone.

Happy may not have been the right word. *Content* felt more fitting. A long journey into deep space as war broke out across the galaxy—would anyone be happy about that? But Yoda's suggestion that she use her innate abilities to assist Rig Nema in providing specialized medical and spiritual assistance for war-wounded Jedi, such a task felt far more important than building a lightsaber.

"We're leaving soon." She pointed far across the bay at the red *Consular*-class cruiser separated from the rows of warships, something designed only for a handful of passengers and medical supplies. "Master Nema says our first stop is Valo."

"You have found your path, youngling," Obi-Wan said. "I wish you great success in it."

"I wouldn't have without Anakin. Before we set out, I wanted to say thank you." Anakin knelt down and took her hands, and though he probably didn't realize it, such an act connected them in the Force the same way it did when they were in deep meditation together above the boarding ramp.

She saw it again, as if the Force put Anakin's inner storm directly into her mind:

A blanket of deep black, and in the center of it, a bright, burning sphere.

No. Tiny white dots littered the blanket, a canvas of space. And in the middle of it all sat the molten intensity of a star.

During meditation, she saw this, a peek into what must have always been going on inside Anakin's soul. But here, with Master Nema training her abilities for greater control, greater insight, the vision took her *into* the star, beyond layers of whipping flares and surface fire.

Deep within the star swirled the form of a dragon, its long body twisting and twirling. And between the flaming claws, the dragon clutched something . . . inscrutable. A brilliant, fragile light, something that *felt* like it could either explode or extinguish if the dragon let go for just a second.

"I believe in you, Mill. Always remember that."

"Thank you, Master Skywalker. I will." She let go and turned tentative steps toward Master Nema's craft. Her pulse quickened, two paths emerging before her: one where she said something now and one where she remained quiet.

"I think you made an impression on her," Obi-Wan said, probably with the assumption that she was out of earshot. "Perhaps you're ready for a Padawan."

Speak or silence; the choices weighed on her with each step.

"What? Absolutely not. That sounds like the worst idea in the galaxy." Mill stopped.

She had to. She owed Anakin that much.

Mill turned around, then began to walk back.

Her movement caught both men's attention, and without any further word, she took Anakin's hands again and looked at the deep-blue eyes that suddenly reflected everything she'd witnessed through the Force. "There's something I want you to know."

"What's that?"

Master Nema explained Mill's gift as a connection to the way emotions pushed and pulled at the Force. And now she saw into his very essence—a smoldering furnace of a heart, a passion so furious that the intensity of his feelings might be the very thing to incinerate himself into his worst nightmare: a cold, withered dragon's final grasp for control, its brilliant home burned away into a lifeless lump of minerals.

The life of a Jedi, in all of the Order's forms, meant a life of sacrifice. But not to the point of self-destruction.

He could choose differently. If someone just gave him permission.

If Mill never crossed paths with Anakin Skywalker again, she hoped that she might offer a single truth, a drop in the ocean that might ripple out with unseen possibilities. "You don't always have to be the sun-dragon."

All around them, clones moved quickly, sometimes sprinting to a transport. Droids pulled supplies and weapons on repulsorlifts. Jedi Knights and Padawans walked in pairs, talking and pointing. Ships lifted and zoomed out, or stumbled inside, damaged wings or tails or thrusters bringing them to a shaky return home.

In between all of that, Anakin's face froze. Mill blocked it all out, even Obi-Wan's reaction, whatever it was, and focused only on Anakin as he slowly closed his eyes, silent.

She let go of his hands and walked toward her future with Master Nema.

CHAPTER 54

OBI-WAN KENOBI

HAD OBI-WAN EVER SEEN ANAKIN *stunned* like that? Not speech-less, like when Obi-Wan expressed his gratitude on the rooftop during their escape, and not shock, like when the Republic swooped in over the Geonosian arena, but the eyes-closed silence resulting from a single sentence carrying the weight of the galaxy.

He'd overheard Anakin tell Mill part of the sun-dragon story right after they landed on Coruscant, but he'd simply assumed that it was a tale parents told their children, a fable to steer them in the right direction. This clearly struck Anakin in a much deeper way—was it because of whatever happened on Tatooine with his mother? Or because of his bond with Mill? Or something to do with Padmé?

Or *all* of it?

"Anakin," he said softly, putting one hand on the armored shoulder of his former Padawan, "I have known you since you were a little boy, and not once did you tell me about the sun-dragon."

Anakin opened his eyes and turned to Obi-Wan, a rare wistfulness to the light in his pupils. "My mother . . ." he started, his voice trailing off, and Obi-Wan realized that Anakin might be revealing much more than a childhood fable.

Perhaps he was finally ready to discuss the recent events on Tatooine, the thing he'd been so cryptically avoiding.

"My mother," Anakin said again.

Obi-Wan gave him space, an invitation for Anakin to finally disclose what had really happened, why it so clearly troubled him. For a moment, Obi-Wan chastised himself for not asking earlier, for not simply acknowledging out loud that he'd be available whenever the truth was ready to surface.

"On Tatooine," Anakin continued.

But such coercion felt against the Jedi way. They lived a life guided by flow, not emotion. Anakin still had to master that fact. Obi-Wan told himself to be patient, and when Anakin was ready, then he would be ready in return, whether that was now or later. If a war slowed that down, then they would figure it out at the right time. The galaxy, after all, needed them at this moment.

"My mother," he said one more time before taking in a large gulp of air, and the light shifted in his eyes. "She would tell me that story. On hard nights." Obi-Wan smiled, then tucked away his own feelings on the matter for a later, more appropriate time. "It's something I kept close. I only seek it when I need to remember what should guide me." His eyes dropped, then his hands adjusted the armor over his chest. "I've only told a few people about that." His lips pursed, and Obi-Wan let him be wherever he was until Anakin's focus returned to the hangar bay, surrounded by machines of war.

A few people? Did he tell Padmé that story?

Anakin glanced up, then reached down to the supply crate at their feet for a white armored sleeve before handing it to Obi-Wan. "Maybe I'll tell you the full story soon. Over lunch," he said, his mood resetting. "It's been a while since I've been to Dex's."

This tale clearly meant something to Anakin beyond the usual importance of a child's favorite parable—and if he'd told Padmé about it, if he'd let her behind his defenses, then perhaps she also knew much more and—

Obi-Wan stopped himself there, letting the thought pass, along with the urge to either confront Anakin about his infatuations or tell the Jedi Council his concerns. Instead, he asked himself a simple question, one that crystallized the truth of Anakin's past, present, and future:

Did he believe that Anakin would make the right choice when called upon?

Obi-Wan watched as Anakin looked at Mill, tracking the youngling with pride across the hangar bay as she strode with confidence. That single look presented the answer, plain as day. Because Anakin had given that to Mill, not with Force training or lightsaber techniques, but simply by caring.

By *being* Anakin Skywalker, the Chosen One.

Without hesitation, without questioning or searching for justification, Obi-Wan found himself saying yes.

Qui-Gon Jinn had a pure and unwavering faith in Anakin. Obi-Wan was merely the conduit for that.

And that was all he needed to know.

Obi-Wan attached the armor to his forearm, then moved in precise defensive motions, seeing if the molded piece of plastoid alloy inhibited him in any way. "Just say the word and I'll have Dex reserve our table."

Footsteps approached, a clone trooper with yellow trim across his helmet trotting up to break their conversation. "General," he said, "the report you requested." Obi-Wan took the datapad from the clone's outstretched hand before giving a quick nod of acknowledgment. Anakin angled for a look, and Obi-Wan turned the datapad to show him the latest findings.

"Thank you, Commander Cody. I look forward to working with you more."

"From Cato Neimoidia?" Anakin asked, his brow narrowing as he squinted at the screen, any pull toward personal history now reset to the context of war.

"Indeed. But not quite the business we were involved in. A prisoner transport crashed several days ago on the surface. The official story is that all five prisoners aboard died." Obi-Wan ran his hand through his now-trim hair. He scanned through the details on the screen, searching for something concrete, then held it up for Anakin to see. "There it is."

Anakin pointed at a single line on the datapad's screen. "Only four bodies were found."

File upon file swiped by, a comprehensive list of prisoner histories, transport schematics, crash site investigations, and other key details put together by Republic intelligence. "And one *unidentified* prisoner is simply presumed dead." Obi-Wan locked eyes with Anakin, a galaxy of possibilities now between them. "Shall we go to Dex's now? He does cook well, but I really go more for the conversation."

Anakin set his armor pieces back into the supply crate, then gestured at the exit. "It's like you said. Whenever it's us, things get complicated."

Which was true. But recent weeks had also shown the other side of that: As long as they were together, complications were no challenge. Not for Kenobi and Skywalker.

Though they strode forward together with purpose, Obi-Wan caught Anakin looking back over his shoulder. He tracked his gaze across the bay to Master Nema's ship as it elevated off the floor, taking Mill Alibeth to her destiny while the two of them walked off toward their own.

RUUG QUARNOM

RUUG HAD PLEDGED HER LIFE to the Neimoidian people. So it seemed fitting that she stared down her end somewhere on the surface of Cato Neimoidia.

Since escaping from the disabled prisoner transport, she'd landed somewhere far beneath the city of Kyr Uneris, ankle possibly shattered, but a splint and cane crafted from vines and branches got her at least to a place free of wildlife dangers—enough shelter of wood and rocks and mist to think of some possible plan. And though her options were few, she thought she had a chance.

After all, she was a mere political prisoner. Why would she be worth the hunt?

Then she saw the platoon attack craft land. Quickly followed by the familiar sound of battle droids unfurling in unison, a *clack-clack-clack* of activation. So many came into sight through the thick mist, in fact, it demonstrated just how many the Trade Federation factories pumped out, as if these war machines were mere datapads for students across the galaxy. Ruug estimated nearly a hundred fanned out, marching forward with their clanking rhythm, the occasional mechanized voice reporting scans.

But in the distance, something appeared.

A glow.

No, two glows.

And despite being cornered between rocks and trees, half buried under leaves and sticks for stealth, Ruug found herself leaning forward, watching in amazement as the back row of battle droids simply . . . disappeared.

Then it happened to another row.

And another. And another.

A systematic erasure, and Ruug blinked to see if perhaps the mist simply got thicker and masked the droids.

But no. Those two little blue lights buzzed through the droids from behind, cutting through them like a knife through nerf butter. The battle droids finally noticed that their numbers were rapidly diminishing and, nearly in sync, they all turned and began a hail of outward blasterfire. And the red blaster bolts spiraled off in every direction, the blue glows deflecting them as easily as rain bouncing off a speeder's windshield.

The blue beams moved in complete harmony, two ends of an infinite tether, one a blunt instrument attacking with frightening speed and power and the other a graceful dance of precise violence. Where one moved, the other complemented. Where one attacked, the other defended. Where one swept, the other struck. They charged through the battalion, brilliant laser swords in a controlled hurricane that whipped apart row upon row of battle droids until the last one fell with a mechanized groan.

They moved forward in determined silence toward Ruug. Her hand gripped beneath her, dirt and shed korgee fur between her fingers, and eyes blinking through the thick Cato Neimoidian air, pulse quickening as she saw her future in front of her.

Through the mist, two silhouettes emerged, the glow of their blades giving off enough light to eliminate any doubt of who approached, of who could pull off something as impossible as this rescue.

There stood Obi-Wan Kenobi and Anakin Skywalker, brothers-in-arms of the Jedi Order.

And together, they were unstoppable.

ACKNOWLEDGMENTS

When I first signed with my agent, Eric Smith, he asked about my pie-in-the-sky writing dreams. I immediately said, "*Star Wars.*" Not just any *Star Wars,* but specifically the prequel era. So it is not hyperbole to say that this is a dream project. And getting here meant a lot of help, from my agent letting the Del Rey team know that I was very interested to Tom Hoeler taking a chance on me in the *From a Certain Point of View: The Empire Strikes Back* anthology with my Palpatine/Anakin story "Disturbance."

Along the way, I owe a huge debt to Delilah S. Dawson, Michael Moreci, and Rebecca Roanhorse for helping me get on the Lucasfilm radar. And an extra shout-out to Delilah for being the best Spacy Auntie as she guided me through the practicalities of extreme *Star Wars* deadlines.

I'm also extremely thankful to work with Alex Davis on this project. In our first phone call, I gave a short pitch that invoked the imagery of the sun-dragon from Matthew Stover's epic *Revenge of the Sith* novelization, and Alex picked up on it instantly. I knew right away we were both made for this project.

Still, writing this came with challenges that needed prompt and thorough assistance. Amy Ratcliffe provided feedback on the initial synopsis. Fellow 2022 *Star Wars* authors Kiersten White and Adam Christopher kept me sane with our ongoing chat/panic thread about process and deadlines. EK Johnston sent me an early copy of *Queen's Hope* to help me sync up our timelines and discuss all things Padmé (including selecting her wardrobe for this book). Rowenna Miller and Peng Shepherd helped with some world-building ideas, and Catrina Dennis nailed down obscure details about Ventress's outfit.

A huge thanks to Kelly Knox for quickly answering my many, many obscure canon questions. Kelly is truly worthy of overseeing the Jedi Archives, or at least a massive library of DK *Star Wars* books.

My HarperCollins editor, Margot Mallinson, also deserves a hat-tip for letting me move my deadline by two months to accommodate this dream project.

With original characters, I always imagine actors for voice and rhythm when I start writing. In this case, I should note that Ruug came from Nana Visitor's Kira Nerys and Ketar came from Josh Keaton's Ocelot, while Mill was highly inspired by Nausicaa, the titular character from Hayao Miyazaki's brilliant film.

This book is an extension of the work done by Hayden Christensen, Matt Lanter, Ewan McGregor, and James Arnold Taylor, along with the cast and crew of the prequel trilogy/*Clone Wars* TV series and, of course, George Lucas and Dave Filoni. Thank you for bringing Anakin and Obi-Wan to life. I'm forever grateful to help tell a little part of their story.

Finally, when my agent called with this offer, I hesitated because I was already under contract while dealing with my day job and our pandemic parenting difficulties. My wife, Mandy, pulled me aside and said, "Do it. We'll find a way to make it work."

I love you. You know.

ABOUT THE AUTHOR

MIKE CHEN is a critically acclaimed science fiction author based out of the San Francisco Bay Area. His debut novel, *Here and Now and Then,* was a finalist for the Goodreads Choice, CALIBA Golden Poppy, and Compton Crook awards. His other novels include *A Beginning at the End, We Could Be Heroes,* and *Light Years from Home.* He has also contributed to the *Star Wars: From a Certain Point of View: The Empire Strikes Back* anthology and covers geek culture for sites like Nerdist, StarTrek.com, and The Mary Sue. In previous lives, Mike worked as a sports journalist covering the NHL, a DJ, a musician, and an aerospace engineer. He lives with his wife, daughter, and many rescue animals.

mikechenbooks.com
Twitter: @mikechenwriter

ABOUT THE TYPE

This book was set in Minion, a 1990 Adobe Originals typeface by Robert Slimbach (b. 1956). Minion is inspired by classical, old-style typefaces of the late Renaissance, a period of elegant, beautiful, and highly readable type designs. Created primarily for text setting, Minion combines the aesthetic and functional qualities that make text type highly readable with the versatility of digital technology.